THE RIFT

Hard Science Fiction

BRANDON Q. MORRIS

BRANDON Q.
MORRIS
HARD SCIENCE FICTION

Contents

The Rift

April 30, 2085, Ceres

"Prepare for impact."

M6 groaned. The warning almost came too late. He had just enough time to bend his knees and press his body against the ground. Almost at once his seismic sensors detected the force of the impact. The meteorite had barely missed him. About 100 meters to the north there must be a new crater. This was his chance!

M6 forcefully straightened four of his six knees, giving himself momentum that immediately lifted him off the ground. His legs had been pointing toward the south, so he sailed north through space, just above the surface of the dwarf planet. It wasn't long until he saw the new crater. In order to analyze its composition, M6 shot his laser into the dust cloud that had formed above the crater. Simultaneously, he logged the crater's structure and measured the temperatures inside it. His positioning jets fired to bring him even closer to the action.

The impact had almost cost him his life. The meteorite had come in on a very flat trajectory and, due to Ceres's fast rotation, it had stayed hidden from his instruments for too long, like a cannonball that had been fired just before its target came around a corner. But now that he'd survived the event it had saved him some work. The meteorite had drilled

directly into the side of Ahuna Mons, Ceres's sole cryovol-
cano. M6 had been planning to drill into the four-kilometer-
high mountain starting in the morning, and now the meteorite had laid open its icy interior.

What M6 observed was fascinating. As if in slow motion,
material was flowing into the crater from above, while the
lower crater edge was collapsing. The hole from the impact
looked like a strange, giant mouth, with secretions running
out of its nose and over the upper lip, its lower lip drooping
sadly. The spectral analysis of the cloud showed that its
composition was a mixture of various salts with ammonia and
water ice.

The energy of the impact had vaporized part of the
mountain's face and melted the rest. Solar radiation striking
the crater's edge was keeping it warmer and thus viscous,
while the dark interior of the crater quickly solidified again.
M6 recorded everything. In a few weeks, when he contacted
Earth again, he would send a summary of his findings for
analysis by the scientists at the RB Group. They would probably be overjoyed at all the progress he had made.

Thanks, killer meteorite, he thought. Then he carefully moved
each of his joints. Ceres didn't have any atmosphere, but he
was still standing in the middle of a dust cloud from the
impact. Small particles could get into any of the three joints
on each of his six legs, thus making him unable to move. That
was his worst nightmare, even though he had ways to fix those
problems. He hoped that all he would need to do would be to
heat up the affected parts of his body from the inside and
melt away the interfering particles.

His body had a radial-symmetric design and was
suspended between his six legs by way of flexible joints. M6
had never seen himself from outside his body, but an engineer
had once told him that he looked like a giant spider. The
comparison didn't bother him. All that was important to him
was that his body was practical and durable. He got energy
from a small atomic battery, and from solar panels that looked
like giant faceted eyes on his top side, due to the many lenses

spread out over the panels. His actual visual organs were situated in the interior of his hard shell. They were sensitive to the whole spectrum from the infrared to the gamma range.

M6 always had a lot of questions. They would come up in his mind whenever he came across one of Ceres's secrets. Every answer formed the seed for at least one new question. He didn't even need the questions that the scientists back on Earth sent him, he had plenty of his own. But there was one question he never asked himself: *What is the reason for my existence?* Wasn't it enough that he was here and looking for answers?

M6 didn't want any other life. But a nagging fear lurked in the back of his mind. *What if there were no more questions? Is that even a real scenario?* He didn't know, and it terrified him. M6 had already calculated how long it would take to fly to another object in the vicinity. Even though the asteroid belt was filled with millions of chunks of rock, a move would not be a simple thing. His propulsion system only gave him enough thrust for powerful jumps, so that he could move around the surface of the dwarf planet and then come back down again. It hadn't been made for long trips through the vacuum of space. The journey would take years—years in which he would have nothing to do.

But that was a theoretical and far-distant future. Right now, it wasn't even clear how this volcano worked. It didn't seem to have anything in common with the glowing-lava-spewing mountains of Io, Venus, or Earth. Understanding Ahuna Mons was the core objective of his current orders. With his frontmost leg, M6 touched the crater's edge, the drooping lower lip. The substratum seemed to already be solid enough. He measured minus 40 degrees on the ground. If it had been pure ice, it would have been hard as stone at that temperature. Only the many impurities made it still flow slowly. Due to Ceres's low gravity, however, it barely moved at all. M6 could advance without fear farther into the chasm created by the meteorite.

As he inched into the darkness, setting one leg carefully in front of another, he examined the walls of the hole. They had obviously been laid in layers that looked to him like annual growth rings. Maybe he could use them to figure out the true age of the volcano. All that was known before was that, despite its enormous height, it couldn't be more than about a million years old—otherwise it would have had more craters like this one.

The individual layers were each approximately 20 to 30 centimeters thick. Their composition was measurably different. They were separated by thin layers of a silicate-like material. M6 scraped off a sample and inserted it into the analyzer located in his abdominal section. The material of the separating layer was identical to the regolith dust that formed a thin layer covering all of Ceres. M6 already sensed new questions forming in his mind. If he analyzed enough layers, he could compile a chronology of the conditions on Ceres in the last thousands of years, much like biologists on Earth determined the earth's climate from analyzing tree trunks.

Would the scientists of the RB Group be as interested as he was to have this glimpse into the past? Not all of the questions that he raised were equally well-received by his bosses. Ceres was one of the celestial bodies that the United Nations had declared off-limits for asteroid mining. Only scientific research missions like his were allowed here. But naturally, the RB Group hoped that this restriction would be lifted at some point. If Ceres offered important resources for humankind's development, its status as a protected area might be reconsidered, and then the RB Group would be the first on site.

M6 scraped another sample of the separating layer farther toward the interior and analyzed it. Its content of radioactive elements showed that it must be at least a thousand years older than the first sample. How far into the past would the crater allow him to go?

M6 carefully scrambled farther into the hole. He always kept two legs anchored in the ice, two supporting him at the front, and the third pair tested the subsurface before he shifted his weight. He was making good progress. The laser scanner revealed that the meteorite had buried itself approximately 100 meters deep.

Just at that moment his two rear legs suddenly broke through the layer of ice. M6 couldn't react quickly enough. His weight pulled him backward, his front legs losing contact. The top of the hole was too far away for him to reach. The rear part of his body came to rest against the ice.

M6 felt the cold. He was upset with himself. He shouldn't have allowed this to happen! But he didn't panic. Very calmly he analyzed the situation. His two rear legs had sunk deep into the ice. He didn't have enough space to move his joints and maneuver so that he could pull his legs out from the ice again. Only the joints were heatable, not the legs themselves, so he also couldn't free them by melting the ice around them. It was clear what he had to do. He would have to give up those two legs. Following a signal from his mind, the uppermost joint in each of his rear legs separated into two parts, so that the other four legs could now lift his body.

The damage was minimal. The only thing he regretted was that he would have to abandon exploring the crater for now, because he needed all six legs to do that. That was why he was most upset with himself. With the help of the nanofabricators in his body, he would be able to manufacture new legs. Maybe his bosses would even have a better design for him to implement now. First, however, he would have to obtain the necessary materials. The nanofabricators could assemble any design he gave them, but they would need the right raw materials for the job—in this case, metals. And he already knew where to look. He remembered seeing white spots in the Occator crater two years ago, during his approach to Ceres.

May 14, 2085, Pomona, Kansas

"Dad, can I use the truck tonight?"

Derek McMaster looked up. His daughter's voice carried down from the second floor through the thin wooden walls into the hallway. He was surprised. She was usually still sleeping at this time of day. She had probably been waiting for signs of life from below.

"Shouldn't be a problem. When do you need it?" he asked loudly.

"Seven would be good."

"I'll be back by five. Your mother's cooking dinner. It'd be nice if we could all eat together."

Elizabeth had been home for three days, but they had barely seen her. Either she was squirreled away in her room, supposedly studying, or she was hanging out with friends from earlier years, which is what she was probably planning on doing again tonight. Tomorrow she'd probably be back at her studying.

"OK, that should work," she answered.

"See you later then," Derek shouted. He opened the front door, stepped out, and closed it behind himself.

The wooden boards of the porch creaked under his leather boots. It was a good feeling knowing their grown daughter was back at home for a while. He looked out at the garage with its open door. He could see the dollhouse that she used to play with sitting in the corner. At some point, he must have moved it in there.

Derek pulled his coat tighter around himself. The air was still crisp and chilly. He loved the morning hours. It used to be that a mist had always hung over the fields when he went out in his truck to inspect the crops. But it was too dry for that now—mist only appeared in the winter anymore. The weather report had said it would reach around 86 degrees this afternoon. His daughter would ask him what he meant by that number. She had grown up using the new universally-standard units of measurement, but he was always slipping back into Fahrenheit and miles. *Thirty. Always will sound cold to me*, he thought.

The truck was already out of the garage, next to the porch. Its front was splattered with mud. The mud hadn't been there when he had gotten out of the truck yesterday. It had to have been his daughter's doing. She had borrowed the truck last night too. But how had she managed to get mud on it? The last rains had been almost three months ago! Derek rubbed the splotches of splattered mud. The mud was dry and crumbled under his fingers. *It doesn't matter*, he thought, *the main thing is she was having fun.* That wasn't so easy in this godforsaken area. That was one reason she had gone to Kansas City for her studies.

Derek opened the door of his truck and climbed into the driver's seat. He sank deeply into the soft cushioning. It smelled like cigarette smoke. His daughter didn't smoke, so she must've had somebody else with her. *Does she have a new boyfriend?* But that wasn't really any of his business. He sighed and reached for the key. It was usually left in the ignition, but this time his fingers found nothing but air. *Didn't I tell her she should just leave the key in the ignition?* Now he'd have to go back inside.

But first Derek checked the glove compartment. There was the key, right next to the gun that he always kept there for nostalgic reasons. He stuck the key in the ignition, put his foot on the brake pedal, and turned the key. The motor started humming softly. His truck was powered by hydrogen. Out here that was much more reliable than an electric vehicle because every little tornado inevitably knocked down power lines somewhere. For 30 years, the county had been requesting for the state to run the power lines underground, but that was much too expensive for all these remote, scattered homesteads. Derek had chosen to have an extra hydrogen tank installed at his house so he could be energy independent, and he only needed a fuel truck to visit him once a month to fill up the tank.

He drove slowly down the access road to Colorado Road. His access road wasn't paved, so the truck kicked up a dust cloud. His wife used to give him an earful about paving the long access road, but she had been silent about it ever since it had stopped raining as much. He didn't know whether her silence was because she no longer had to bicycle through puddles when she went to visit her friends, or because she had noticed the farm's severely shrunken earnings. They didn't talk to each other much anymore. After his strenuous work in the fields, Derek needed his rest.

He stopped the truck and got out just before the intersection with Colorado Road. On the left was a small pond. For many years its water had helped to irrigate the fields in the summer. Now the pond was almost dried up. Derek rubbed his temples. There'd been no overnight miracles. The bottom of the pond was still covered by maybe a foot of water. The remains of a dock poked out of the mud. The reeds along the shoreline were all dried up. Ten years ago, he and his daughter had played with the remote-controlled toy boat that she had wished for, right here on this pond. And his wife had always been afraid that their daughter would drown. But that wasn't a risk anymore.

Fucking climate change, he thought, and then got mad at himself because he hadn't ever accepted it as real. Somehow he still hoped that after seven dry summers, a hot and wet one would finally happen again, like before. Three presidents in a row had promised him it would happen. Now he didn't believe anyone anymore.

Derek grabbed the door of his truck, opened it, and climbed back in. He turned right on Colorado Road. It was narrow, so he used both lanes. Nobody else drove along here anyway. The neighbors' farmlands had been taken over by the banks and big corporations a few years ago. He wondered if they were happy in the city. He'd never heard anything from any of them again, even though they had been something like friends before.

Derek drove on the narrow, straight road. The land was flat and seemed to go on forever. Derek was happy that he had to keep an eye out for potholes and drive around them—it gave him some distraction. After two miles there were a few trees on the right. In passing he spied the Mulligans' old truck, slowly rusting in front of his eyes, and the wooden house, half in ruins, where they had lived.

Beyond the small gathering of trees was a narrow bridge across the Appanoose Creek. Derek stopped right in the middle of the bridge. The creek bed was also all dried up. Derek sighed. The grass right along the creek's edge was still green, but the cornfield that he had been putting a lot of hope in for this season was not receiving any of the moisture. He climbed out and walked to the edge of the field. He looked back at his truck. Nobody could get past his truck on the bridge, but it didn't matter. He was standing on his own land. Anyone who wanted him to move his truck would have to wait.

Slowly Derek walked into the cornfield, being careful not to step on the young plants. They were only half as tall as they should have been. He bent over and checked their leaves. They cracked and tore under his fingers. There was nothing more he could do.

Derek dragged his index and middle fingers over the ground. It was hard and cracked. The earth had become an old man. He dug somewhat deeper with his hand and the clayish soil crumbled between his fingers. It looked terrible. The heat had damaged the topmost layer. He took another step, two steps, three, but the soil was just as bad there too. A long crack ran through the topsoil, as if the world were slowly opening up to devour all of its inhabitants. His fields were in bad shape. He wouldn't be able to pay for his daughter's studies anymore. How was he supposed to tell her that?

Derek walked farther into the field. Now there was no point trying to walk carefully around the plants. It didn't matter. He started to run. His breathing got heavy, but nevertheless it felt good because it took his mind off the world around him. He was no longer as fit as he had once been. Maybe he should rejoin the Air Force? At least they paid him well. He'd made more working for the Air Force than he earned now, and he'd always been paid on time. But what would he do there at the age of 41? He was well on his way to becoming an old man. If they'd even take him back, they'd just put him in management somewhere, instead of sending him on special assignments like before.

He missed those days. Some of those assignments he still couldn't talk about today, not even to his wife. That had never been a problem, he'd never had much need for talking. Sometimes he asked himself why he and his wife were even still together now that their daughter was out of the house. Was it enough that he drove his wife, who hated to drive, into the city and back for doctors' appointments and she gave him a blow job once a week? But that was probably more contact than some other couples had.

Somewhere behind him he heard honking. Derek stopped, out of breath, and bent forward, his hands on his thighs. He spit on the ground. The soil greedily sucked up the moisture. He probably wasn't giving his wife enough credit—or himself, for that matter. They had been together for 20 years now, without anyone or anything forcing them to stay together. There must be more there than he realized. Things had simply dried up like the soil in his fields. Secretly he still hoped that it would start raining again and everything would be like before.

There was more honking. Derek turned around. There was a second truck stopped in front of his. Next to the truck he saw a man standing on the road, waving his arms.

"Okay, I'm coming," he yelled. "I'm coming, asshole!"

May 20, 2085, Ceres

The vista spread out before him far into the distance. M6 was standing at the upper edge of Occator crater. In front of him was a 2000-meter drop. He didn't feel any fear, just respect. He'd be able to manage the downward climb, even with only four legs. He could have flown down to the crater's floor, but his bosses preferred that he study the crater walls on the way down so that he could give them that much more information on the structure of Ceres's crust. That was the only thing they were interested in, ultimately. What worthwhile raw materials were on Ceres, and where were they located? M6 wasn't angry about it—80 million years ago, a meteorite's impact created a 92-kilometer-wide hole up to 4000 meters deep, now giving him the exciting opportunity to look into the dwarf planet's past. M6 was ready to start. Getting to this spot had not been particularly interesting.

He began the climb down. The crater wall had barely eroded. Ceres had no real atmosphere, so erosion was not to be expected. And yet there was this thin dust layer everywhere. The lower part had already transformed into solid rock—regolith. It was as if a thousand elephants had marched through here in ages past, compacting the dust into stone. But that was obviously nonsense. It was such a crazy thought that M6 had to ask himself where the image with the elephants could have come from. He had never seen real elephants.

M6 had awakened when the space probe that was carrying him had started its final approach to the dwarf planet. He knew that he wasn't a living creature—he was a machine—but still, there were thoughts in his head that seemed to have originated from other people. M6 would have liked to be able to get rid of them. Most of them were unpleasant thoughts, others were, at best, neutral. They made him afraid, apprehensive, bored, annoyed—all negative feelings that didn't even make any sense.

He was virtually indestructible and immortal. Why should he be afraid of anything? And yet there he was, filled with these emotions as he was about to start his 2000-meter climb down into the crater.

He also couldn't understand his builders' motives. He could work much more efficiently if he didn't have to constantly deal with these misguided emotions. The most valuable thing of all had to be efficiency. That was the only thing that appeared useful to him—apart from fun and joy, maybe, for which his reward center was responsible.

M6 stopped. He had noticed a black stone that resembled charcoal. He picked it up and slid it into the analyzer. The dark material on the outside was something like charcoal. It was made up of carbon and had the structure of graphite. M6 removed the stone from the analyzer and rubbed it across the ground. It left behind a black streak. He could write! Whatever he wrote on the exposed subsurface would likely remain for millions of years. Nobody would destroy his creation. Of course, nobody would see it either... but that didn't matter. He would know that it was here. M6 designed a fractal in his head. He loved these patterns that repeated indefinitely. Then he transferred the image from his mind onto the stone.

After an hour he had to stop. He wasn't satisfied, because the work wasn't complete. He knew, of course, that a fractal was a figure that couldn't be perfectly reproduced. But wasn't that true for all compositions? At least at the atomic level, the uncertainty principle blurred everything the closer you tried to look at it. How could humans still be passionate about being artists? On the other hand, his search for truth—for the ultimate facts—was also never-ending. Even if he lived forever, he would never be able to answer every question. Nevertheless, he found the search to be fun. Maybe it was somehow similar for human beings and their art. And fun was a positive feeling!

M6 set down the black rock. The bottom of the crater was waiting. Only there could he find the materials that he needed for his replacement legs. Slowly he scrambled downward. Every 100 meters he paused and examined the crater walls. He found a hard material that was rich in water ice underneath the layer of dust. Maybe the water that had been melted and evaporated by the impact had then condensed and solidified on the walls.

M6 tried to imagine the catastrophe as it had happened at the time. It had occurred long after Ceres had become a sort of dirty ice ball. Then a heavy space-rock had drilled directly into its side, melted the ice, and boiled the water. Was part of the once-liquid ocean still in liquid form inside the crust? Had, perhaps, primitive lifeforms been given some new hope, like when rain fell in the desert? He would have to make particularly careful measurements at the bottom of the crater, especially near the raised mound in the center, where it appeared that material might have risen up and outward from the interior.

But first he needed two new legs. Ceres was keeping the necessary materials ready for him, he just had to pick them up. M6 pointed his telescope toward the bottom of the crater below him. The famous white spots were still approximately 30 kilometers away.

THE DESCENT TOOK ANOTHER TWO HOURS, BUT THE FLAT area in the crater took only about 50 minutes to cross. He switched to four-leg pacing, which allowed him to move especially efficiently. His legs moved in pairs so that he didn't rise at all. Long periods between points of contact with the ground would slow him down, because then he couldn't accelerate with the force from his joints. When he used all of his energy for pacing, he could accelerate to speeds of at least 300 kilometers per hour. That speed took some time to reach, however, and it also took just as long to slow down again. Thus, this type of movement was only suitable for occasions such as this one, when he wanted to reach a known destination as quickly as possible.

Now there was a white, dream-like landscape spread out in front of him.

M6 was fortunate, because the sun had just appeared over the walls of the crater. It looked like the far-off battlements of a tall castle. White light fell from a black sky onto an enchanted field, where it glittered and gleamed. A thick, pasty mass made from water ice, ammonia, and various salts had long ago been forced up to the surface. The sunlight had dissolved the frozen water, leaving behind the salt crystals. The process had taken a long time—not tens or hundreds of years, but thousands of years—and the crystals had thus had lots of time to grow. That's why they were especially symmetric. At the proper angle, they looked like prisms, splitting the white sunlight into a multitude of rainbows of colors from the spectrum. From other perspectives they looked like cut crystals.

Every salt, every chemical compound, arranged itself in somewhat different crystalline shapes. It appeared as if nature had tried out everything that was possible here, and maybe even a little bit of what had previously been considered impossible. In fact, with the help of his laser spectrometer, M6 quickly found a shiny deposit made from a compound that does not occur naturally on Earth. The extreme cold, the low pressure, and the influence of cosmic radiation had produced it here. M6 remained standing so that he could record a panoramic image. He bent over so that he could photograph a crystal pyramid at the perfect angle and stood up on his front legs so that he could investigate a deposit that looked like a blossom with wide-open petals.

He felt honored. M6 was the first being that could look at this beautiful scene unfolding all around him. Had it been born from catastrophe? No one would ever know for certain, but it had taken a long time. In the beginning, this had most likely been a salty swamp, but now that he had come, the area finally showed its full beauty. M6 was grateful to his bosses for giving him this experience.

Unfortunately, his arrival was also the beginning of its destruction. First he must dismantle at least some part of the beauty himself to obtain the materials he would need for his new legs. And then the humans would come, because they would see his images. Exotic compounds created in this unique laboratory of nature—that was what his bosses had been looking for. M6 sighed. He could refuse to send the data. He was a free consciousness. He was not bound by orders— he could decide for himself. Psychologists on Earth had decided he should be designed this way, because they had conjectured that other designs might harm his mental health. A being who is not free, and who is also damned to solitude, would not be able to survive in the long run.

He would decide later whether he would send the data to Earth. He would not sacrifice his replacement legs, however. M6 began to dismantle the structures which, according to measurements with his spectrometer, held the necessary components. He picked up the minerals and placed them in the analyzer in his abdomen. From outside it must have looked like he was eating the rocks. In the analyzer, there were millions of nanofabricators waiting for the minerals. They broke up the material into minuscule pieces, took the pieces apart atom by atom, and then reassembled them again according to his stored design. With the right starting materials, he really could manufacture anything—even new nanofabricators.

That was also one of the big dangers. M6 had done the calculations himself. If he should lose his sanity and reasoning and begin to replicate the nanofabricators over and over again, in a few weeks all of Ceres would have been consumed in the manufacture of new nanofabricators. He would become Ceres itself. M6 found this idea amusing rather than appealing, but he could imagine a simpler mind being attracted to the notion. That was why the nanofabricators had been given an expiration date. Their inventors had adopted the idea from the aging of biological life: the more often the genetic information was replicated, the more often errors occurred. The nanofabricators would become unusable in the 11th generation. That sounded modest, but in reality it meant that two of these tiny universal machines could make 2048 more. And he hadn't only brought two with him, but instead approximately one hundred million. His capabilities for transforming himself were practically unlimited, as long as he didn't become megalomaniacal. He had no plans to do so.

His 'abdomen,' the analyzer, wasn't big enough in which to grow new legs, so the nanofabricators had to move the material from there to the location where it was needed. Very slowly, two new legs began growing out from his joints. The entire process took approximately ten hours. M6 didn't have to supervise the entire time. Every fabricator knew what it had to do. Nevertheless, because errors were always possible, every now and then M6 checked whether everything was proceeding as planned. Especially critical were compounds that were nearly identical chemically and barely differed in molar mass. If two were being used in the same project, sometimes the wrong one would be used. And he didn't always notice in time. A few mistakes were completely manageable, however. That had already been considered in the design.

M6 partitioned a tiny part of his mind to allow it to

continue watching over the growth of the two new legs. With the far larger part of his mind, he admired the incomparable play of light created by the sun setting across the dry salt lake. It was a scene that could not be viewed from anywhere else in the entire solar system.

May 23, 2085, Ottawa, Kansas

WITH SQUEALING TIRES, DEREK TURNED FROM MAIN STREET onto 13th. His thoughts were all on his fields. Only when his wife put her hand on his knee did he notice that he had almost driven past the hospital. He let the truck slowly roll to a stop. Every two weeks, his wife, Mary, went to see her doctor at Random Memorial Hospital. She did not seem especially sick, but if it made her happy, he would keep bringing her here. Mary had a driver's license, but she refused to drive in the city. In truth, Ottawa was no longer anything more than a big town. Since the events in the 2070s, the number of residents had dropped below 10,000. It was a miracle that the pride of the community, its university, could keep going. Those who had big plans for their lives tended to move to a real city.

That was the only reason he could see to explain why the hospital had hired a Turkish doctor. 'Akif Atasoy, MD, Diabetologist and Allergist' read a sign on the office door. As always, Derek walked his wife into the waiting room. When Mary had first started going to this doctor, he had been afraid she might be having an affair. He didn't really care if she was, but did it have to be a Turk? He had been part of special missions during the U.S.-Turkish War. Luckily the conflict had only lasted a couple of weeks. Derek looked around. As always, the waiting room was full. Atasoy was a diabetologist, but Mary claimed that she wasn't diabetic, she just suffered from allergies. The Turkish doctor did have additional training in treating allergies. Most of his patients, however, appeared to be here due to diabetes. At least they all looked appropriately obese, Derek had often thought.

He nodded at Mary and left the room. Outside there was a bench in the shade of a large maple tree. He liked to sit there and smoke a cigarette, a real, proper one with tobacco. He might even smoke two today. Sitting in front of the hospital and smoking seemed fitting to him. These institutions were so full of infectious germs that it wasn't even clear who or what they were really built for. So he thought it best to smoke the little buggers out.

"Mr. McMaster?" intoned a masculine voice.

Derek looked around in surprise. Had he overlooked someone he knew in the waiting room?

"Mr. McMaster!"

The door to the doctor's office had opened, and a slim man with short hair and a mustache was walking toward him. He looked like he had a tan. On the street, Derek would have barely recognized him as a Turk, but he had to be, because he then introduced himself.

"Atasoy, Akif. I'm your wife's doctor."

The doctor extended his hand. Derek hesitated for a second, then shook it. He was pleasantly surprised. Atasoy had a warm, strong handshake.

"You always leave so quickly," the doctor said.

"I'd rather sit outside and wait."

"Of course. In this weather, I'd rather sit outside too."

"It doesn't matter what the weather's like to me."

"I see. Can we go into my office for a moment? I'd like to talk to you about your wife's illness."

The doctor motioned toward the open door. Derek shrugged his shoulders and followed the doctor. *Better to get it over with,* he thought. In the movies, after such an invitation, the doctor would tell the frightened husband that his wife only had six months to live. Derek began sweating. That was the movies. Real life was never so dramatic.

The doctor closed the door behind him. Mary was already waiting in the room. The doctor pointed to two chairs in front of his desk as he sat down himself in his chair behind the desk. Mary took a seat in one of the chairs. Derek shook his head.

"I'd rather stand," he said.

"Mr. McMaster," Dr. Atasoy began, "we're making good progress with your wife's strange allergies. I've been doing some extensive testing. The problem with allergies is that there are so many triggers, but for reasons of safety we can only perform a few elimination tests at a time."

Derek took a breath. That didn't sound like Mary was going to die next month. Perhaps the doctor wanted to perform a really expensive test and he was now trying to sell him on it.

"Yeah, I know that from the times I tested new feed on my cows," Derek said. *Now I'm talking nonsense,* he thought. *I haven't had cows for ten years.*

"In the meantime, I've determined that certain wood preservatives might be one of your wife's triggers. She had a very strong reaction to those specific tests. She tells me you live in a wooden house."

What a statement, Derek thought. *Who around here doesn't live in a wooden house?*

"Now I'd like to ask you something, and please don't take it as criticism," the doctor continued. "Mary says you renovated your house a couple of years ago. Could you possibly have used any of the substances on this list? They are officially approved, even for indoor use, but the timing would match very well with the onset of your wife's symptoms."

Of course, Derek thought, *they'd match just like my fist to your eye. But what good would any of this do? It wasn't like they had another house to move to.*

"I'll have to look," he said. "I think I still have a half-full bucket in the garage."

"That'd be great," the doctor said, "and it would really help us out."

Atasoy glanced at Mary with what Derek thought was a conspiratorial look. 'See, that went well,' is what the look seemed to imply to Derek. *Did he think I wouldn't see that?* Derek was starting to feel angry.

"And what are we supposed to do if one of these is actually in our house? What then?" He spoke with more aggression than he had intended. Atasoy raised an eyebrow.

"Then I would say..."

A loud knock on the office door interrupted him. The person knocking didn't wait for an answer—the door opened at once. Derek recognized the receptionist, a young Indian woman.

"Doctor Atasoy," she said, "you have to see this. Come quickly."

"Now slow down, Gita, what's the problem? I've asked you before not to simply barge in here," the doctor said.

Creases appeared in Atasoy's forehead. The receptionist looked as if a tornado were racing toward the hospital. Derek wouldn't have been surprised by that, even if it wasn't tornado season right now. The weather and all its unpredictability didn't seem to follow the old farmers' rules anymore. He heard excited shouts from the corridor and the waiting room.

"What's going on?" he asked.

Dr. Atasoy didn't answer. He was no longer in his chair. Mary was sitting there as if she were frozen. Derek tried to give her an encouraging smile. Then he left the room through the open door. Gita, the receptionist, said something behind him, but he couldn't understand her, because everyone out here was shouting over each other. The patients in the waiting room had all pressed themselves against the window. *Something must be happening outside.*

The light streaming in was just as bright as before. *There can't be a bad storm coming.* The people were pressing their faces against the window and pointing upward at something straight above them, where the sun should be. There was no more room at the window, so he simply pushed a skinny, accountant-type guy to the side. The man grumbled a little, but went silent after he had given Derek a mean look. Derek knew that his intimidating stature and red hair made him look like an Irish brawler, and sometimes he deliberately used that to his advantage.

He looked out the window. The sky was shining in the prettiest shade of blue. Why was everyone so worked up? Derek tilted his head back. And then he saw it. He rubbed his eyes because it was so unbelievable. A black stripe ran across the sky. It resembled a gigantic ribbon blowing in the wind, but was entirely motionless, its jagged edges glowing red. It looked as if the heavens had been slashed, opened up in order to consume all of creation.

Derek was not an active churchgoer. He believed what his mother had taught him and what was in the Bible, but it had all seemed something like a fairy tale before, something that didn't really concern him. He started feeling hot. Could it be some prophecy was being fulfilled? Would a supernatural being descend to render its last judgment?

Derek reached for his heart with his left hand. It felt like it wanted to jump out of his chest. At least the emergency room wasn't far, he thought. His heart and circulation had always been strong and stable. He turned around. Where was Mary? He didn't see her anywhere. He started to worry and gave up his spot at the window. She wasn't in the corridor and also not in the waiting room. He finally found her in the doctor's office. The doctor, receptionist, and Mary were all standing next to each other, their noses pressed flat against the window. *Of course. The phenomenon stretched across the entire sky—it must be visible from there too.*

Derek came up behind Mary and rested his arms on her shoulders. She flinched but didn't try to squirm away.

"What is that?" she asked, turning her face to the side.

He looked at her delicate nose and her thin eyelashes. It

had been a long time since he had looked at her from such a close distance.

"I have no idea," he answered. "Doctor, do you have any idea what that is?"

The man to his left had been to college, so surely he must know more than the rest of them.

"I've never seen anything like it," Atasoy said.

Derek carefully wedged himself between Mary and the receptionist. His wife was slim, but Gita had a rather full figure. Maybe her wide hips only caught his attention because she was so small. *Five feet, if that*, Derek estimated, then forced himself to do the conversion to meters in his head. *So one-and-a-half meters.* He should really stop using those old units. He leaned with his right hip against the window sill and bumped against an indoor plant. It was green was all he noticed. Plants were only interesting to him if they were in his fields.

Then he lifted his gaze back to the sky. The black stripe was still there. It looked like it was rigidly glued to a blue background. No, that wasn't right, it wasn't glued on, it had torn apart the background. That's what it was—a rip. Their world had been torn apart. A shiver ran down his back. He didn't feel afraid. No, it was something more like awe. It was much like the moment when his mother had brought him to church for the very first time and organ music had suddenly filled the gigantic space. The music had seemed to come from everywhere at the same time.

A swelling murmur of many voices jolted him out of his thoughts. People were suddenly pointing up at the sky. Was there some creature descending from above? Derek rubbed his eyes because he couldn't see anything. Then he noticed it, a small, shining arrow. An airplane, at 30,000 feet, he estimated. Derek squinted. A four-engine Boeing, surely a passenger plane. The pilot was headed straight toward the rip. Hadn't he seen it? Derek had a pilot's license himself.

The plane was still far enough away that an evasive maneuver could probably be done without any problem. Why wasn't the pilot turning around? Was the crew asleep, perhaps, and the autopilot clueless? Didn't they see what they were racing toward at 600 miles per hour?

Derek wanted to scream to them and warn them. He made his hands into fists. The airplane's metallic fuselage flashed silver in the sunlight. He imagined the passengers looking out of their windows, maybe feeling sorry for the Kansas farmers because of the vast sea of never-ending brownness. Or maybe they were thinking about their destination, a beach in Florida, the sweetheart they were going to embrace in their arms, or the business partner they were going to rip off. Life is short and can end so suddenly. He opened his fists again.

From his perspective, the airplane was only a few millimeters away from the rip. It was already turning a reddish color. Even if the pilots noticed what was in front of them, it would be too late now. Derek heard the people behind him shouting loudly. Everyone wanted to warn the pilots. Maybe at least some of those on the plane could still be saved with parachutes! But Derek was skeptical. Could anything save them? What would happen to it when it touched the rip? Would it explode, or crash against an invisible wall and then break apart completely? Or would the plane simply pass through it?

The moment came. The nose of the Boeing touched one of the jagged spikes of the black stripe. Gone! It was gone!

DEREK SHOOK HIS HEAD. WHY WERE THE PEOPLE BEHIND HIM so upset? All at once it became quiet. He turned around. People were standing in front of the window with open mouths, as if they had forgotten what they were going to say. Had they all gone crazy? Sure, a dark rip had split apart the sky. It was probably the end of the world. That was a feasible theory, Derek decided, until someone thought of something else. But no supernatural creature had descended upon the earth yet. They had been watching the rip and the sky now for several minutes, without anything happening. If that continued, it wouldn't support his theory. If God had decided to start His Last Judgment today, why would He drag it out so long?

Or maybe it had already happened. Maybe the judgment had been rendered long ago and he had ended up in Hell. He had certainly killed enough men as a soldier for that to be a distinct possibility. Hell... what else were his dried-up fields to him? But Mary, no, she wouldn't be here too. Mary was innocent.

Behind him it was getting loud. People were pointing up to the sky. What was there to see? They all knew the rip was there. He craned his neck, but all he saw was glaring bright light. Oh, there was an airplane, approaching from the south. It was small, probably a two-seater, light sport aircraft, but it was flying surprisingly high. Either the pilot hadn't noticed the rip, or he was curious about it and wanted to get a closer look. Derek clenched his teeth. The pilot was really getting close. How could anyone be so crazy? The patients behind him were loudly shouting warnings. Was there no way to send him a signal to turn away?

Mary turned toward him, and for the first time he noticed that he'd been gripping her shoulders very tightly. He apologized and started to carefully massage her shoulders. She tilted her head back and gave him a smile. Derek felt warmth on his cheeks. *That must be from the sun,* he thought. It was gradually moving toward the west. He had to shade his eyes with his hand to see the small airplane. It was not turning around. The pilot had probably missed his last chance. Derek knew from his training what an airplane was capable of. It wouldn't be able to avoid the rip now. Was he seeing things, or had the red fringes at the edge of the rip gotten bigger?

The airplane touched the rip.

"Oh man, oh man, oh man," Derek said involuntarily.

The knuckles on his right hand cracked. The airplane disappeared.

DEREK LISTENED TO THE ECHO OF HIS WORDS. HAD HE JUST said something, and why?

"Did I just say something?" he asked Mary.

"You said the words 'oh man' three times," she answered.

He remembered. But he no longer knew why. He must have been upset about something.

Then he remembered the rip in the sky. That must have been it. But that explanation didn't satisfy him completely. He felt as if he were lying to himself, without being aware of it. Was that even possible? When he had intentionally lied to himself at other times in the past, he had always known the truth, he had just not wanted to admit it.

He was probably just a little bit run-down and out-of-sorts. And he didn't appear to be the only one. Derek looked out at the street. The doctor's office looked out right onto the large parking lot in front of the hospital. A large group of people had gathered there. He found it hard to believe the city even had that many people. Some were wearing sunglasses, others had special glasses that were probably left over from the last solar eclipse. Derek couldn't make any sense of it. The rip wasn't blindingly bright—quite the opposite, he had never seen such a deep, dark black. The cleverest of the group were holding binoculars in front of their eyes to look at the phenomenon. Could they really see anything more? An older man had even brought out a small telescope that looked like a kid's toy. All that was missing was someone selling ice cream and the folk festival would be complete.

Derek looked at the clock. It was shortly after one in the afternoon. The people down below must have come outside from the places where they worked. He wondered a little why he didn't see more signs of panic. After all, the sky had just ripped open! But everyone was surprisingly calm. Maybe it was because the world had already been through so much recently. It was only 13 years ago that a black hole had nearly destroyed the earth. Every adult inhabitant of Earth at that time had already written their will. Nevertheless, this calm was baffling. The black hole had definitely been dangerous, but it hadn't been visible to the naked eye. This rip, however, could be seen by anyone who looked up into the sky.

"Come on, Mary," he said. "Let's go home."

His wife stayed at the window, looking at the rip with fascination. The doctor turned his eyes from the sight and looked at him.

"I still wanted to talk to you about those wood preservatives," Atasoy said.

"Yeah, I'm going to look in the garage."

"If you did in fact use one of those allergy-triggering substances, there are now very good protective varnishes. Just one coat on top of the wood and it can no longer outgas the substances making your wife sick."

"What does she actually have, then?"

"Haven't you noticed?" the doctor asked him. Derek didn't hear any disapproval, just surprise, so he stayed calm. The doctor was right, he should have noticed that his wife wasn't doing well.

"No," he said quietly.

"Joint pain. The allergy is affecting her joints. She's already taking painkillers almost every day. If this continues, she might not be able to walk anymore."

"Oh," he said.

That's why his wife hadn't visited her friends in three weeks. He'd assumed that they'd had a fight. But it was actually because of his wife's health! Of course, what kind of friends are they if they don't visit her when she's not feeling well?

Derek felt a sharp stab of guilt. A week ago, Mary had asked him if he had anything against her friend coming to their house for a visit. He had become rude and replied with something like, "You know I need my peace and quiet!"

He couldn't remember his exact words. *Why am I such an asshole? And why have you stayed married to me?* He looked at Mary, who had her head back, looking up into the sky. She was protecting her eyes with her hand, because the sun was shining directly into her face. In the bright light, he could see the fine hairs on her skin. Her Adam's apple protruded slightly. She looked extremely fragile. *Mary needs someone who will take better care of her,* he thought. *I can't do it.*

Suddenly she turned around. Derek couldn't look away fast enough and she caught his gaze. Her gray eyes shone deeply. He felt transparent, as if he'd been caught red-handed at the same time. *I should smile,* he thought, *I should really just smile.* Finally he did, and Mary returned the smile.

"Shall we go, then?" she asked.

"Yes, I think so. Unless the doctor has something else he wants to say?"

"No, Mr. McMaster, I think, in light of that thing outside, I'm going to close the office for today. My receptionist will call you about a new appointment."

"Thank you, Dr. Atasoy," Mary said.

The Turkish doctor nodded and shook her hand. Derek turned around. Only then did he notice that all the other patients had already gone. Gita must have ushered them out already. He gave Mary his arm and she linked hers with his. Then they left the office together. They reached the exit after walking down the long hospital corridor. They had to walk around the building to get to the parking lot. Derek saw the bench where he usually sat.

"That's the bench I always sit on when I'm waiting for you," he said.

"I know," Mary answered. "I can see you sometimes out the window."

Derek nodded. He didn't want to admit that it had never occurred to him.

May 23, 2085, Pico del Teide

"MADAM DIRECTOR? I HAVE SOMEONE HERE ON THE PHONE for you," her assistant said. Maribel had been trying for a long time to get her to stop addressing her so formally, but Señora González had been working at the Instituto de Astrofísica de Canarias, or IAC, for 45 years now, and had always addressed the previous directors formally—and it sure didn't seem like that was going to stop with the first female director.

"Didn't I tell you I didn't want to be disturbed today?"

She needed to finally finish the paper that she was supposed to write about zero-point energy and black holes. Maribel had started to regret accepting this job. Zetschewitz, her former mentor, had advised her not to take it. That had seemed very strange to her at the time, because the German had appeared very gung-ho about advancing her career. But now she knew what he had meant—she wouldn't have any time for research.

"The man on the line is from the government. He says it is extremely urgent."

At that moment, someone knocked loudly on her door. She still had the same office as when she started at the IAC, on the ninth sub-level of the OGS2 telescope. But she no longer had to put up with Zetschewitz, who had taken a prominent position at the Solar Observatory in Hawaii.

The door opened. Andrés, her deputy, and Franco, his friend, rushed into the room. That had never happened before. Andrés had always been the model of politeness.

"Just a moment, Señora González," she said into the phone as she put down the handset.

"But the man from the government..." she heard her say.

"Maribel, you have to come up and see this," Andrés said. His face was covered with red blotches. She'd never seen him so worked up before.

"What's wrong?"

"You won't believe it unless you see it yourself," he said.

Franco nodded excitedly. He was a quiet, reserved individual, but even he seemed to have become worked up because of whatever was going on.

"I'm sorry," Maribel said into the phone, "I'll be back in a minute."

The man from the government was far away and could wait. Something seemed to be happening here that... then it occurred to her that the man might have been calling about the same matter, as urgent as he had seemed. What could be going on? She had to be careful not to let Andrés and Franco get her worked up too.

Of course, the elevator took forever to reach the ninth basement level. *Or maybe everybody else is trying to get out too,* she thought. The elevator was already almost full. Andrés and Franco pushed Maribel into the car with 11 of their other colleagues.

"We'll take the stairs," Andrés said.

Maribel hated riding in a full elevator. It never failed that at least one of the other people on the elevator hadn't showered that morning. And this time the elevator was stopping on every level. Her colleagues all looked disappointed when they realized they wouldn't be able to fit. At least her status as the director of the institute meant that nobody tried to squeeze in next to her.

Finally, fresh air! Maribel ran through the corridor to the outside. She could hear the pattering of footsteps all around her. *What is going on?*

After going through the airlock, she finally reached the outdoors. She shivered. Here on the mountain, at an elevation of over 2000 meters, it was still quite chilly, even at the end of March. She should have brought a jacket with her.

Suddenly someone touched her shoulder from behind. It was Andrés. The stairs had not taken him much longer than her elevator ride. Their colleagues standing around them recognized the two bosses and subconsciously took a few steps back.

"Have you seen it yet?" asked a young woman whose name Maribel did not recall.

Have I seen what? Maribel thought, tilting her head inquisitively.

The woman pointed up, up, up and Maribel tilted her head back. The day seemed like any other pleasant spring day. A few white clouds were making their way across the sky at a moderate pace. And then she saw it—a black gash... split... rip... rift.

It felt as if someone had hit her on the back of her head with a hammer.

It couldn't be real. What she was seeing was completely impossible. She tried to analyze the phenomenon scientifically, but she could find no analogies. She wanted to believe it was just a trick. But it would have to be an extraordinarily complex trick. Completely splitting the sky, approximately from southwest to northeast, was a dark... something. The closest thing it resembled was a tear, but what was there to be torn apart? The sky, she reminded herself, is nothing more than an optical illusion. It doesn't exist as something that could be physically torn. When we look into the sky, our gaze doesn't stop at a heavenly canopy—as humans once believed —it goes on to infinity... which had suddenly become an imperfect infinity.

This is nonsense, she thought. But, there was this man from the government on the phone. Maybe it was some kind of mass psychosis limited to this mountain—maybe the cook had mixed some LSD into the cafeteria food. *No, then that government official wouldn't have called me.* So, maybe the psychosis, or whatever it was, wasn't limited to just Teide.

Maribel examined the fissure or whatever it was. To her, the best word to describe it seemed to be 'rift.' It was a deep —very deep—black color. It was not a weird projection of the night sky, because there were absolutely no stars. There was nothing inside of it radiating any light. Looking at it was making her more and more anxious, as if she were going to be sucked inside. Conversely, the night sky always gave her a feeling of a protective net with its multitude of twinkling stars, even though it stretched on to infinity.

The area inside the rift was completely different. Of course, they would have to test it with their instruments, but could it be that here was a chance to look into real nothingness? That would be fascinating. In her research on the true nature of black holes, she had been confronted with the concept of nothingness so often that she had nearly changed her topic of research.

Nothingness was a fascinating phenomenon—if you had the opportunity to study it in the laboratory. But whatever was above them, it was not in a laboratory, it was the real sky over humankind's home planet. A black band of nothingness in the sky up above was not a welcome sight. Now she knew why the man from the government had called. There was nothing as terrifying as something that was unexplainable. And people would expect *her* to be able to explain the rift to them.

But that was impossible. She and her colleagues didn't know any more than any other inhabitant of Earth. Personally, she knew even less than some, because she had just now looked up to see it. Maribel sighed. Nevertheless, she would have to talk to the man from the government. She could easily imagine that everyone would now be putting their hopes on her, especially since she had helped save the world 13 years before. The actual work, however, had been done by other people. She had only tried to provide explanations and help with the arrangements.

She'd had another advantage before, too. She had been 22 then, and nobody expected anything from her. And nobody was waiting for her, then. Now she was 35. She didn't feel any smarter than before—quite the opposite—and now the expectations would be high. More important than any of that, however, her little daughter and her husband, Chen, would be waiting for her at home. Could she climb into a rocket again—leave her family—and fly off into space? Definitely not. Others would have to be responsible for that now.

MARIBEL SPENT THE NEXT FEW MINUTES TALKING WITH HER colleagues. She wasn't the only astronomer there, nor the best. The observatory on Teide had many scientists, and each of them had to have an excellent command of their subject area. They were split into teams and worked with different telescopes. Her task was to arrange the observation schedules for the teams. The observatory's multiple telescopes would be able to observe the phenomenon in a range of wavelengths. She would have to coordinate and integrate the work from all the teams. First she would give them the task of providing her with an overview of the phenomenon using their respective instruments.

The area between the domes for the different telescopes was already emptying. Maribel went back down to her office. It was time to make that phone call.

MARIBEL WALKED TO THE ROOM NEXT TO HER OFFICE AND knocked on her assistant's door. "I'm back," she said.

"Oh good. There are a lot of people who want to talk to you!"

"That's not going to work right now, Señora González.

But please call the Ministry for me." By that she meant the Ministry of Science, which was responsible for the institute and the observatory.

"I'm sorry, the man earlier, he was calling from the prime minister's office."

Maribel wasn't surprised, now that she had seen the rift herself.

"Then please get him on the phone for me. But first, contact security at the front gate. They're going to need more guards. I expect there's going to be a mob of journalists up here soon, and that's really not what we need right now."

"Ms. Pedreira, thank you for taking the time to talk to me," the man said when her assistant had finally patched him through to her. "I am calling on the behalf of the prime minister. And here he is now. I'll put him on."

She had no chance to answer. There was a click in the line, and she heard the sound of someone breathing. The head of the government had most likely just come running into the room.

"Ms. Pedreira," he said, "it's wonderful that I can talk with you. You will be my salvation, I'm sure, our salvation."

"I hope you're not expecting too much," she answered carefully. "We've just now started with our observations."

"So you don't have any idea what it could be?"

Was it proper to laugh at the prime minister? She restrained herself—she understood that he was under pressure to provide answers.

"No, sir, it's much too early for that."

"And an assessment of any risks or dangers?"

"Completely out of the question at this point. We can't give an assessment for something we don't understand yet."

Maribel doubted that they would be able to understand this phenomenon very quickly, but she didn't say that to the prime minister.

"Can I give the population any statement of reassurance, with a clear conscience? That is what everyone will be expecting me to do, Ms. Pedreira."

"What do you know about this thing, Mr. Prime Minister? Surely you've already gathered some information about it?"

"It starts somewhere out in space. It stretches deep into the earth's atmosphere."

"To what height?"

"That varies... minimum 8000 meters. There seem to be several branches or spikes that extend over North America, Southern Europe, and Central Africa. There's some speculation that they meet somewhere."

"It's not visible in Asia?"

"No, everything is normal there, also in Australia, the South Pacific, and Antarctica. Nothing's been sighted there."

"I see," Maribel said.

"Does that help? Can you tell me something now?"

"It's still too soon. Do you know anything about a chronology? Did this phenomenon just appear all at once, or did it grow?"

"We're still looking for eyewitnesses. Everything right now indicates that it just suddenly appeared. It also doesn't seem to be growing."

"I think it's important to monitor that, to see whether it's getting any larger. As long as it's not, it's probably not an acute danger."

"Can I say that publicly?"

Maribel thought about it. *Yes, presumably the greatest danger right now was that people would panic and kill themselves or each other in desperation. At best, the rift would be dangerous only to those who got too close to it, but even that would take some time to figure out.*

"Yes, you can quote me on that."

"Wonderful, Ms. Pedreira, you don't know how much easier that makes things for me. You are the first expert willing to make such a clear statement. If you need anything, let me know. A call from the prime minister can still do some good sometimes."

Right at four, her computer showed that the department heads were waiting in their observatories for the scheduled meeting.

"OGS, set up a conference room."

Optical Ground Station 2, or OGS2, was the official name of the building's operating system—the same name as the observatory itself—but 'OGS' was adequate for addressing the system. Her office was in one of the underground levels of the main building.

At her command, a virtual conference table had appeared in the back part of her office, as if replacing her desk. Her colleagues were apparently already in their spots. In actuality, they were at their respective desks that were spread out across several buildings on the summit of Pico del Teide on the Canary Island of Tenerife.

"It's nice that all of you could make it," Maribel said. "I suggest we skip the introductions and just get right to the details. Sheila, why don't you start."

Sheila was the deputy director of the OGS2 telescope that operated in visible light. She made a face. Apparently she was embarrassed by what she had to report.

"We've been working very hard," she explained, "and we've tried everything we can think of, but this phenomenon is emitting absolutely no visible light—none at all. None of us has ever seen anything this black."

"Okay, if it's not emitting anything, is it reflective?" Maribel asked.

"No, not at all. Since about 3:30, the sun's alignment to the phenomenon would suggest we should be seeing reflections, but there has been absolutely nothing. The phenomenon must be absorbing the sunlight completely," Sheila said.

"I propose we all call it 'the rift,'" Maribel said with an unexpected smile. "It's shorter, easier to spell, and more descriptive than 'phenomenon.'"

Jean-Pierre spoke up. "But we have no idea what this thing really is."

That was obvious. The Frenchman was always worried about scientific accuracy. He was the head of the solar observatories.

"The designation 'rift' is hereby established by decree," Maribel answered. "Justification: efficiency—saving time. Now, Sheila, what are its characteristics in terms of transparency?"

"The... rift is completely opaque. A short while ago we observed a transit by Jupiter. From our perspective, anything that is behind the rift might as well have disappeared from reality," Sheila said.

"Okay, so you saw nothing. That is still a significant research result. Good work. Try not to let it upset you, Sheila. Jorge, what does it look like in infrared?"

Jorge was the head of the Telescopio Carlos Sánchez, or TCS. It was one of the oldest instruments on site, but still provided very good results in the infrared range.

"Unfortunately, I'm going to have to repeat what Sheila told us. There's nothing... no thermal radiation either," he said.

"And at the edges, where there seems to be the red shimmering?" Maribel asked.

"Nothing there either. Whatever the shimmering is, it's cold."

"And the background radiation?"

All of space was permeated by radiation, a relic of the Big Bang. If the rift was part of our universe—and how could it be anything else?—then it should be possible to detect this radiation there too.

"Yeah, Maribel, we've repeated our measurements two, three times, but whatever matter is in this rift is at absolute zero. If there's any matter in there at all, that is."

"Would it be possible that the rift is similar to a black hole, i.e., absorbing and retaining all radiation?" Maribel asked. "I mean, if we temporarily disregard the strange shape."

"I... I can't even imagine that," Jorge said.

"According to physics, that'd be complete nonsense, of course," Jean-Pierre said, "but nonetheless we've found some evidence for it."

"I'm curious to hear it," Maribel said.

"All of you know that we've been busy setting up Magic-3, a Cherenkov telescope," Jean-Pierre said. "With it, we can indirectly detect gamma radiation that does not penetrate through the atmosphere."

Maribel's mind raced. *Is he trying to say that the rift is emitting gamma radiation?*

"The instrument is almost ready, so we tested it on the phenomenon—sorry, I should say, 'on the rift.' And we detected gamma radiation at the edges."

"So, where the red shimmering has been seen?" Maribel asked.

"Exactly. I've got a theory about it too," Jean-Pierre said.

"Then let's hear it," Maribel said encouragingly.

"Think about the concept of Hawking radiation. When a pair of particles is randomly created from nothing at the edge of a black hole, sometimes one of the particles will fall into the hole. The other appears to be emitted from the black hole as Hawking radiation. Maybe there are similar processes at work here?"

"But Hawking radiation is not anywhere near that high-energy," Jorge interjected.

"This is also not a black hole," Jean-Pierre replied. "And it would also explain the red shimmering. It might be a kind of aurora. The gamma radiation ionizes particles in the air and recombination produces the reddish glow."

"Of course, we'd need to do all the calculations to support this theory," Maribel said, "but on the whole, it seems plausible to me. We need to make sure that all of the individual parts fit together. If I remember correctly, red auroras are produced primarily at high altitudes by ionized oxygen atoms. That wouldn't fit with the 8000-meter altitude where the rift supposedly starts."

"If we're talking about higher energy radiation, other atoms could also be the source of the aurora," Sheila said.

"That's right. Another reason we need to do the calculations. Jean-Pierre, I think you should take the lead on this. An international conference has been scheduled for the day after tomorrow. We'll present our findings then."

DONE. AND JEAN-PIERRE HAD JUST DELIVERED HIS FIRST propositions for setting up the calculations. But her workday was done at 6 o'clock on the dot. Working overtime, which she would have gladly done a few years ago, was out of the question now. There were people waiting for her! That was such a nice feeling. Maribel left the building.

"Good night, Maribel," the system said.

"Good night, OGS."

Her car was already waiting for her. The door opened itself. All she had to do was get in. Maribel hadn't done any driving herself since three years ago when she had bought this new model with fully-automated driving features. While the automated system drove her down the mountain to her apartment in La Laguna, she toed off her shoes, closed her eyes, and fell asleep.

"WE WILL ARRIVE AT YOUR DESTINATION IN EIGHT MINUTES," the automated system announced.

Maribel stretched, gave a big yawn, and looked for the shoes that she'd taken off. It was already dark outside. The streets appeared to be more crowded than usual. A line had formed in front of the supermarket where she always did her shopping.

"Control system, is there any news on how people are reacting to the rift?"

"One moment, Maribel, I'm scanning the feeds."

The car was moving slowly, as there was a lot of traffic. On the sidewalk next to her, someone was pushing a stroller that was filled with cans of food.

"Yes, Maribel," the car's control system said, "there are seven hundred and seventy-six stories on the requested topic."

"Please give me the most important contents in summary."

"I'm categorizing your results. People in Africa, North America, and Europe leave their workplaces. Local traffic devolves into chaos in many places. Supermarkets close either due to lack of staff or hoarding of goods. Government calls for calm. Drastic increase in suicide rate within the affected countries. Stock markets report losses. The dollar and euro crash..."

"Thank you, that's enough."

Crazy. While she was in her ivory tower, discussing a puzzling scientific problem, people were fearing for their lives. She was reminded of 2072. But that time, it had taken much longer for people to notice their precarious situations. Right now, the rift presented no clear danger. It was a paradox. Back then, the black hole had been invisible to the normal citizen, and the scientists had been able to study it—after overcoming some initial problems. The rift, however, could be seen by everyone. But it was invisible to their scientific instruments.

"We have reached your destination," the automated system said, interrupting her thoughts. Only then did Maribel notice that the car was already stopped.

"Thank you," she said, "and good night."

"Good night, Maribel," the system replied. "See you at 6:30 AM."

Maribel gently closed the door. *Another wonder of psychology,* she thought. She felt like it would hurt the car if she shut the door forcibly. Just because it could converse with her naturally to some extent, it had practically become a person to her.

She turned around and walked across the parking lot in front of the building where she lived. While walking, she nearly stumbled into a short elderly woman who was carrying two heavy bags.

"Watch out!" the woman said, annoyed.

Maribel recognized the widow from the apartment downstairs from theirs. She'd forgotten her name.

"Pardon me, Señora," she said, "we've met before. May I carry a bag for you to the elevator?"

The woman looked up and studied her. A smile slowly formed on her face. "Ah, Señora Pedreira, that would be very nice."

Maribel took one of the bags. While they walked across the lot, she looked up at the sky. In the dark, the rift could be seen only dimly, as a dark band with no stars, an anti-Milky Way.

"I looked at that the whole day too," the widow said suddenly. "It's not going to end well... it's not natural. I think the devil has his hand in this somehow."

"It doesn't appear to pose any danger," Maribel said.

"Yes, that's what the government said, but I don't believe it."

"No, we've been observing it very closely, with giant telescopes."

"Ah, you must work up on Teide. Believe me, you won't be able to detect the danger with your telescopes. You can't measure the devil. You'll see."

What the old woman said to her made her feel uncomfortable. She didn't believe in God or the devil, but she had to admit that seeing a large band of... *nothing* in the sky triggered some primal fears. She decided she'd rather change the subject.

"And is that why you decided to go out and buy so many groceries?" she asked.

"My cousin called me and told me I should. I wouldn't have thought of it myself, but then I remembered '72."

"Hoarding goods will only make the problems worse."

"Yes, I know, it's irrational, but who will help me when all of the supermarkets are empty?"

"We would help you, Señora."

"But how would you be able to help if you hadn't hoarded things yourself?"

Maribel didn't reply, because in some sense the old woman was right. Nevertheless, she hoped that Chen hadn't gotten caught up in the panic too.

FINALLY SHE WAS STANDING IN FRONT OF HER APARTMENT door. She inserted the key in the lock and turned it. Carefully she pushed to swing the door open. Sometimes her daughter would leave one of her toys right in the middle of the hallway, and she didn't want to step on anything. She switched on the light. The hallway was surprisingly clean. Suddenly the living room door opened. Luisa came running out to greet her.

"Mommy, Mommy, you're home," her six-year-old said, wrapping her arms around her.

Maribel's heart warmed, and her facial muscles relaxed. She was home.

"Let's let Mommy at least take her shoes off," said Chen, who now greeted her, also in Spanish. They had lived together on Tenerife for 11 years now, and people could barely tell that Spanish wasn't his native language.

Maribel untied her shoes. Then she gave her husband a hug too. She was very thankful for him. He worked half-days so that they didn't have to find a sitter for Luisa after preschool. In the fall, her daughter would be going to elementary school. Maribel couldn't believe how quickly time passed.

"And how was your day?" she asked.

"Daddy picked me up earlier than usual!" Luisa said proudly, "and then we went to the iron tower."

"The memorial for the airplane disaster in Mesa Mota Park. The preschool called me because they wanted to close early," Chen explained.

The comment made her feel a little bad. The preschool

never called her first. She understood why. In the last three years, she had probably picked up Luisa five times. But still...

"Have they cleaned up those ruins that are there?" she asked. At the edge of the park were two abandoned buildings that were eyesores.

"No, they're still there," Chen said.

"It was great," Luisa said. "There were a lot of people there, all looking up at the sky. There was even an ice cream man."

"That's great," Maribel said. "So I guess you two had ice cream for lunch today?" She tried to give Chen an unhappy look without letting Luisa see it. The kid needed good food to eat, not more sugar.

"Yes, three scoops!" Luisa said and gave her mother a big smile. "It was soooo yummy."

Maribel couldn't be angry. Luisa's joy was contagious. "You two had quite a treat today," she said.

"Oh yeah, today was so much fun. Then me and Daddy built another spaceship out of Legos."

"Really? You need to show me."

"Yay, I'll get it!" Luisa ran off in the direction of the living room.

"Thanks for everything, Chen," Maribel said. "I'm sure you can imagine how my day went. The entire world wants answers."

Her husband rubbed her back gently. "That's what I figured. And do you have any?"

Maribel shook her head. "Just more and more questions. This rift... it shouldn't even exist. How did Luisa take it?"

"I don't think she understands any of it yet. But I think she liked all the chaos and commotion. As a result, she had nearly the entire day free."

"Then it's all good. Hopefully the preschool will be open again tomorrow."

"They said they would call all the parents early tomorrow morning."

"What? They can't just close up shop! They're being paid

by the state. It's not like I have a choice. I have to get up and go to work tomorrow."

"And I wouldn't have expected anything else from you, my love, but not everyone is like you."

"I know, Chen, I know."

Before Maribel even had time to sigh, Luisa had returned. "Look, Mommy, here's the spaceship we built." She held up a model that was about as long as her forearm and reminded Maribel of a boat. In the middle were triangles sticking out from every side. "Those are the sails," Luisa said. "The ship goes because the sun blows into the sails."

"Ah, yes, the solar wind. That is very clever," Maribel said.

"See, Daddy, I knew it would work. Mommy knows more about it than you."

"I wanted to build conventional rocket engines," Chen explained with a smile.

"You said you wanted to make nozzles. Nozzles are stupid. The hair dryer has a nozzle in front."

Oh, of course, thought Maribel, *that word would make Luisa think of the hair dryer.* Luisa always started to scream whenever anyone wanted to use it to dry her hair.

"That's true, I did say nozzles," Chen admitted.

"Maybe we should continue talking in the living room?" Maribel suggested. "I'm really hungry."

"We thought you might be," Chen said. "Dinner's already prepared."

"What are we having?" Maribel asked, heading toward their dining room table.

"We'll let it be a surprise," her husband said.

"Daddy tried to make empanadas," Luisa whispered, "and he said a lot of bad words, too."

May 23, 2085, Ceres

IT WAS DEFINITELY MORE ENJOYABLE TO MOVE THROUGH THIS majestic landscape on his usual six legs—so much better than only having four! M6 felt well refreshed after the short, four-and-a-half-hour night. He didn't need to sleep, but taking a break at night was good for him. When he stopped working and remained still for a while, his body could bring itself back into equilibrium. Any component that had gotten hot would cool down and contract to its original size. The batteries distributed throughout his entire body could recharge to full capacity. His sensors could clean their surfaces and recalibrate themselves. A person might say he felt as if he'd been reborn. M6 had this feeling every morning, and he was quite happy about it.

Today he planned to explore the raised area in the center of the crater. He had walked past the site three Earth days ago. In the distance, the dome-shaped mountain was visible rising from the flat bottom of the crater, even though it was not even 500 meters high. There were also some of the bright deposits on its sides, but in smaller amounts than the place where he had extracted the materials for building his new legs.

M6 paused at the base of the central mountain. Where he was standing, a hot saltwater lake might have evaporated 80 million years ago. Shortly after the meteorite's impact, the crater floor was almost certainly covered by a liquid. At the time, dust, water, and pieces of rocks would have rained down from above. It had certainly never been a paradise. Then part of the liquid had splashed upward again, like after a stone has been thrown into water, and the upraised part had slowly solidified into the dome that he was now climbing.

Impacts like this happen on all asteroids and planets in the solar system—they weren't anything special. But at the time, Ceres might still have had a liquid ocean under its dry crust. M6 knew the research findings from the Enceladus expedition. Had life formed here, too, in some similar way? Earlier, astrobiologists had been skeptical, but after the additional discoveries on Titan and Io, more of them were wondering if life might have formed on Ceres too. Whatever was in that ocean at the time might have been thrown up to the surface by the impact. M6 merely needed some patience—and that was one thing he had plenty of.

First he climbed halfway up the mountain. It was not particularly strenuous, as the sides were not steep. Then he began to dig into the ground with his front leg. The uppermost layer here was also made from regolith. This solidified dust layer wasn't of interest to him, but it had proven to be surprisingly hard, so he had mounted a special tool, a drill, on one of his feet. A half hour later, he had reached a depth of one-and-a-half meters. Here, the ground was rich in water ice. He had reached the ejecta from the impact. Immediately he started taking samples every ten centimeters and loading them into the analyzer in his abdomen.

The equipment needed a few minutes each time to spectrometrically determine the composition of the latest sample. The results were interesting right from the start. It found, in addition to the expected salts and water, traces of tholins, a mixture of various hydrocarbons. He could not find out exactly which compounds were present in this first step. But similar tholins had been found on Titan. Such tholins were not proof of the existence of life, but if life had formed here, many such molecules would have been one prerequisite. The deeper he drilled, the higher the percentage of organic compounds became. If these results were representative, the ocean of Ceres would have had excellent conditions for life to arise. *Does the ocean still exist?*

At four meters, he stopped drilling so that he could initiate the second step.

Seen from the outside, he now looked completely still. But there was a lot of activity in his analyzer. He used the nanofabricators to break down the samples into individual molecules. The micromachines operated purely mechanically, without heat, which preserved the existing structures.

It was monotonous work, since there are seemingly count-less molecules in just one gram of matter. So he was grateful for the help from the minuscule machines, just like the doves that had helped Cinderella—one molecule went here, another went over there. From the energy that the nanofabricators had to expend to do the work, he could very easily calculate the masses of the molecules. In the next step, he tested their properties with various chemical reactions, their completion also being monitored by the tiny machines.

Suddenly his instruments went berserk.

M6 felt... dizzy. He had never experienced this before! His operating system immediately ran diagnostics on all his sensors. Something wasn't right. What his instruments were reporting didn't fit together. M6 examined the state of his limbs. They were positioned upright and firmly on the ground. That was reassuring. The error diagnostics couldn't find any faults. Even better! So the problem must be some-where external to him. M6 viewed the images from his optical system. He saw something that was physically impossible. Through the side of the mountain to the left of him there was a deep, black fissure. At first it looked as if it ended in the side of the mountain.

But that was just an optical illusion. He then recognized that it extended much farther. In the practically non-existent atmosphere, the only reason he noticed that the fissure continued was because of the lack of starlight behind it. The fissure appeared to be stable, even with the weight of the mountain on top of it.

With his laser scanner, M6 sampled the profile of the subsurface. The results were even odder. The fissure had displaced the mountain, had simply raised the mountain by the same amount that the fissure was wide, and it had done this within the span of a microsecond. He went through his log recordings again. The instruments had all gone haywire within an instant. The values had not risen gradually, they had jumped directly to their current numbers, all at once. Every physical process takes time, but apparently whatever had just happened had taken no time. None at all!

M6 immediately aborted the project of searching for traces of prior life on Ceres. The fissure was a much more interesting phenomenon. As far as he could see, it continued straight without any bends. But he could only estimate that for a limited distance, at most about ten kilometers. He was too close to get a complete overview. But nothing would have made him swap his position for someplace else. To be handed such a fascinating research subject right where he was—this was more than he could ever have dreamed of.

He aimed all his measuring instruments at the singularity. M6 began with only passive measurements. Electromagnetic radiation was not being emitted directly from the fissure, but there were indirect emissions. His reward center celebrated— he had just become the first to obtain proof for the existence of Hawking radiation. He would be the first machine to go down in history as a discoverer!

It was fascinating, because the gamma radiation he was measuring was clearly not coming from the fissure, but instead from the areas along its edges. He was essentially seeing particles being created out of nothing. His sensors were recording their energy radiating from the quantum vacuum! But he hadn't figured out this phenomenon quite yet. Part of the mystery was that these energy quanta were relatively strong. It was high-energy gamma radiation. Hawking radiation produced by black holes was expected to be at lower energy levels. So it appeared that this fissure was not a phenomenon related to black holes. Or was it?

M6 switched to active observation methods. He illuminated the fissure with a high-energy lamp that he could remove from his head. The blackness remained black. The radar showed absolutely no signal—the radar beams were not being reflected. The laser scanner also showed nothing. The black fissure appeared to absorb all radiation.

After a while, M6 noticed something else that surprised him even more. Normally, his active instruments consumed energy. The headlamp, for example, had an output power of 120 watts. He switched it on again and pointed it at the mountain. A bright spot appeared on the side of the mountain and simultaneously the battery lost energy, exactly 120 watt-seconds per second. That was normal and expected. Then M6 shined the light onto the fissure. Immediately the power consumption decreased drastically. It now fluctuated between three and four watts.

Maybe this small amount of power consumption was due to losses from the wiring and the scattering of the light. The light beam dispersed somewhat on its path to the fissure, and the very thin atmosphere would also absorb a tiny amount of the light. But nothing of the light that seemed to reach the black fissure showed up in the power-balance calculations. It was as if the light hitting the fissure was being completely absorbed, and then magically being returned to the battery as electrical energy.

M6 repeated the test with his laser scanner and radar. For the radar, which emitted omnidirectionally into space, the energy gain was proportional to the width of the fissure. The laser scanner's beam, generated by an especially-efficient LED laser, appeared to be recycled up to 99.8% by the fissure.

M6 was confused and elated at the same time. For the sake of certainty, he calibrated all his instruments again. Maybe he had lost his sanity. If he were to send these results to Earth, the scientists there would think he was crazy. Or—even worse—defective. He could not let that happen, because that could trigger his shutdown. He decided to transmit his observations at a later time. As an autonomous entity, he had that right.

What now? Thus far, he had been examining the fissure from a distance. He walked a little closer. The fissure was now above him. Or at least it should have been, but from below there was absolutely nothing to see. The fissure appeared to have no spatial depth. It existed only as a two-dimensional surface. What was going on inside it? If it was infinitely thin, how could it absorb everything that M6 threw at it, and apparently at the same time return the energy? Where had he come across something like this before? M6 quickly programmed a filter and let it run over his memory contents. He was looking for images in his memory that had certain similarities—above all, a change in dimensionality.

The results were surprisingly simple. A piece of paper with a tear in it appeared in his imagination. The sheet of paper was the universe. The paper universe was inhabited by an ant that was looking at the tear rather skeptically. In its two-dimensional world, that is, the sheet of paper, the tear represented a one-dimensional obstacle. It could walk around it. But if it jumped in, it would fall downward and never be able to reach its world—the sheet of paper—again.

The fissure that had appeared on Ceres reminded him a great deal of this mental image. But then it also wasn't a fissure. Consequently, he decided to call the phenomenon a cleft from then on. M6 didn't believe that he had figured out what was going on. Too much still didn't make any sense—for example, the fact that his battery was magically recharged. It was as if the cleft refused to absorb the energy content of the light beam. A refusal, which would indicate an intentional behavior? That was going too far for him.

IT WOULD BE TIME TO MAKE RADIO CONTACT WITH EARTH THE next time the sun rose. M6 looked for the blue planet and directed his high-gain antenna towards it. Conversations weren't possible due to the signal propagation time. At the planned time, he sent the analyses of the bright mineral spots. Then he waited for new orders that should also be transmitted at a set time. But the planned time passed without him receiving a transmission. Apparently, nobody wanted to know anything from him at that time. *Good,* M6 thought, *at least now I'll have sufficient time to study this strange fissure—no, this cleft, he corrected himself.*

May 24, 2085, Pomona, Kansas

"Good morning, Mary!"

Derek sat at the round table in the dining room. He'd been the one to prepare breakfast. Last night he had tossed and turned for a long time in bed. He'd been thinking about his life and his marriage. His life had stopped when he had settled down here for Mary's sake. The missions with the soldiers on his team in the special forces, that had been his life. But when Mary had gotten pregnant with Elizabeth, he had felt obligated to settle down. His grandfather and his father had been farmers, so he had made the decision that this down-to-earth profession might be right for him too. But because he had never gotten along with his father, they had ended up on this farm in Kansas, far away from any relatives.

It was okay being a farmer. It was a demanding job that left him little time to think about anything else. But it had never felt like his own life. It always seemed like someone else's. He had always let Mary know that he felt that way, and that was why they had drifted apart, like inner tubes tossed into the sea. Or two empty bottles—maybe that was more fitting.

Could they make things better? He looked at Mary, standing in front of him rather uncertainly in her nightshirt.

He could understand her confusion. He hadn't made breakfast for ten years.

"Sit down and I'll get you some coffee," he said.

Mary looked around like a scared chicken. She didn't know what to make of his offer. Then she stiffened. Derek knew she had made a decision. "I have to use the bathroom," she said.

He watched her leave the room. She was still beautiful, even from behind. Then he heard the sound of her urine stream hitting the water in the toilet bowl. She had left the bathroom door open, since Elizabeth wasn't home.

Derek went into the kitchen and pressed the button for the toaster. Then he turned on the stove again to warm up the scrambled eggs in the pan. Mary didn't like cold eggs, not even lukewarm. They both came into the dining room at the same time, looked at each other with confusion, and laughed. The situation was unusual.

Mary sat down. He stood next to her and held the pan at an angle in front of her plate. She used a spoon to push some of the scrambled eggs onto her plate. Derek pushed the rest onto his plate, took the pan and went into the kitchen and came back with the toast. He noticed that he'd forgotten the coffee, so he went back into the kitchen again.

Mary looked at him in disbelief. "Is something going on?" she asked with her mouth full. "Have I forgotten something important?"

"No, not at all," Derek said. "I just wanted to have breakfast with you."

"Well, what a pleasant surprise," Mary said, and gave him a smile.

She had a pretty smile, it occurred to him. At some point he had forgotten that. Suddenly it had become important to him again. Was this because of the rip?

"Have you heard the news?" asked Mary.

"Yeah, the National Guard has been deployed to the big cities. There's been a lot of hoarding at stores, and some looting."

"But is the thing dangerous?"

"The scientists say we have nothing to worry about. Nothing's coming out of it... it's just there. The media is calling it a 'rift,' thanks to a group of astronomers from somewhere or other."

"What do you think, Derek?"

His wife wanted to know what he thought about it. Did that have any significance? He paused and thought.

"I was just outside," he said. "The thing doesn't look like it's changed at all since yesterday. Yesterday I thought maybe it was a punishment from God. Or the last judgment. But they say the rift is only over us, Europe, and Africa."

"Maybe we're the only ones who deserve punishment?" his wife asked, smiling.

"Us and the Europeans, I believe, but the Africans? They've already had enough done to them." But maybe Mary was right. "There aren't as many Christians in Asia," he said, "maybe that's why they were spared the last judgment."

Mary shook her head. "But why not Catholic South America?"

"It's just some sort of natural phenomenon. The scientists will figure it out," he said.

"Probably," Mary answered. "But I'm still worried about my mom. The supermarkets will be empty in Houston. She's not healthy enough anymore to have to wait in line at a soup kitchen. Let's bring her here. Elizabeth's room is free."

Her mother. Derek took a long breath in and exhaled. At the time, she'd been against Mary marrying this soldier-turned-farmer yokel. She had never acknowledged that he had settled down just for her daughter's sake. And now he was going to take *her* into his house? The thought made his throat feel a little bit tighter.

"Yes, dear," he said, instead of saying what he felt, and forced himself to smile. "She can come and stay with us."

Mary smiled at him gratefully. He would have liked to wrap her in his arms.

"Thank you," she said, "I know how hard this is for you and I really appreciate it. I'll get her a ticket after breakfast."

"Shouldn't you at least ask her first?"

"It was her idea," Mary answered. "She called me last night."

They continued eating in silence. It wasn't a bad silence. Their eyes met repeatedly. He had looked at Mary more times this morning than during the whole of last month. Maybe he was an asshole, but maybe he could learn to be a nice asshole. Maybe he should be grateful for the rift. He couldn't think of anything else that might have opened his eyes for him. Maybe God really had come down through the rift, undetected and unannounced.

May 24, 2085, Pico del Teide

"Anything new?" Maribel asked the group.

They were having another virtual meeting. Sheila's spot as representative of the OGS2 telescope was taken today by her boss, Johannes. The German had cut his vacation short.

"I've been reading the press reports," said Jorge from TCS. "Sometimes the average person will see something we miss with all our fancy instruments."

"And, did you find something?"

"I found one interesting observation. It was reported from all of the affected areas. People are saying that if you stand directly under the rift, you can't see it at all."

"Hmm. That's actually very curious. Has anyone from the scientific community confirmed this?" Maribel asked.

"No, apparently it's not very easy to get exactly underneath it."

Maribel laughed. "That's a plausible explanation. Nevertheless, we should follow it up. Someone needs to study that observation scientifically."

"Just imagine what that would mean," Johannes said. "The rift would then be a two-dimensional physical phenomenon in three-dimensional space. That was thought to only exist in theory."

"Do you know a good theoretician, Johannes? Someone

who can explain the consequences to us? How can we prove its two-dimensionality? And can we set up an approach to a solution from our observations?"

"Of course, Maribel, I can think of a few good candidates. But what do you mean by a solution? Do we have a problem? I thought we were agreed that there wasn't a problem. That the rift was just some dead fly on our windshield?"

"Slow down," Jean-Pierre said. "Of course there's a problem. That's not the same thing as danger. The rift appears harmless, but it still is an unsolved physical problem. And visually it's also disturbing. When people look up, they see a 'sword of Damocles' hanging over their heads. We have to fix that, or there'll be no return to normalcy."

"You think it's up to us to do that?" Johannes asked.

"We, as scientists, should work out a plan. The state would then implement it, or the United Nations," the Frenchman explained.

"Then we'd better come up with the cheapest possible plan. As long as it doesn't hurt anybody, I think it'd be possible to pay to fix this thing," Johannes said. "But you remember the financial crisis in America... in the end, they paid for that by taking from the science budget."

"Ha ha," Jorge said, "maybe we can set up a Kickstarter to fund it."

"Be serious, boys," Maribel chided the two, "how are we coming along? Jean-Pierre, what's the status of your calculations?"

"It's looking very good, in terms of Hawking radiation. The data fits my formulas. The high-energy radiation from the immediate periphery of the rift is exciting energy levels that are otherwise outside the range of cosmic radiation."

"So, the red shimmering is real, and it is caused by Hawking radiation?"

"It's real and caused by gamma radiation produced directly in the immediate vicinity of the rift."

That was typical Jean-Pierre. He didn't want to say anything definitively. Hawking radiation—this term described the method of formation. Gamma radiation is what they had measured. Theoretically, the gamma radiation might have a different cause. But the way Jean-Pierre had said it was almost as good as a direct confirmation.

"I suggest submitting a paper to *Nature* as quickly as you can," Maribel said. "That could move you into Nobel Prize consideration."

There was a knock at the door. Maribel looked around. Her assistant waved to her.

"Ms. Pedreira, I didn't want to interrupt, but there was a man from NASA on the phone who said he needed to talk to you."

"From NASA? What does he want?"

"It has to do with tests in connection with the rift. Apparently, the prime minister had promised you would help."

"What?"

"That's what he told me, in any case. I think it'd be best if you call him back right away."

"I will. Gentlemen, let's have another meeting before the end of the day at the latest."

The three men waved.

"OGS, end conference."

Her office transformed back to normal.

"Good morning, Spain," said the man who appeared opposite her. He was dark-skinned, with a bald head and a mustache. Maribel estimated him to be maybe 50 years old.

"Good morning," she answered.

"My name is Glen Sparrow," the bald-headed man said.

Maribel had to smile. This man, the *Sparrow*, looked like he was maybe 1.9 meters tall and weighed 100 kilos.

"Did I see a smile? Don't worry, I won't hold it against you. I'm sure you don't have much to laugh about right now. Actually, I've always been happy to have a name like I do. It's good at breaking the ice. I'm coming to you from JPL in Pasadena, by the way."

"JPL? I was told you were from NASA?"

"Jet Propulsion Laboratory works for NASA. Administrator Baldwin gave us a contract to study this slit in the sky."

"Rift. We're calling this phenomenon a rift."

"My apologies, I'm not a scientist myself, I'm just responsible for the organization overall."

"But if you're in Pasadena, on the West Coast, then it must be the middle of the night where you are."

"Right, two o'clock in the morning to be exact, but that doesn't matter. I wanted to catch you as early as possible. When my normal workday starts, you'd already be done for the day. Your assistant told me that you put a lot of value on ending your day right on time, and I shouldn't call you at home under any circumstances."

"Señora González is very concerned about my well-being."

"Quite right, Maribel. I hope I'm not being too forward if I call you Maribel? My name's Glen."

"It's nice to meet you, Glen. And, using Maribel is fine."

"It's probably best for me to get right to my proposal. We want you to work with us from here."

"Oh! I wasn't expecting that."

"I think it could be interesting for you to come here, Maribel. We have capabilities for studying the, um, *rift* that aren't available in Spain."

"I'm sorry, but I'd rather coordinate everything from here."

"I can't believe that's really your preference. You were the hero for the whole planet, and that was because you didn't let anything stop your research on the black hole. You stuck to it, against all resistance. You can't tell me that you've suddenly turned into a pencil pusher."

Glen had found her sore spot. Her responsibilities as director of the observatory were interesting, but to really sink her teeth into a problem and solve it? She missed that. On the other hand, she had promised not to leave her daughter, Luisa, and her husband, Chen, alone.

"What do you have in mind?"

"We want to build a flying platform and take a look at this thing up close."

"How close?"

"Real close. So close you could reach out and touch it."

She could test the idea that Hawking radiation was being transmitted from the rift, right at the source, and co-author a paper with Jean-Pierre that would bring worldwide attention to the institute.

But Luisa would be 10,000 kilometers away. "I'm afraid I still have to say no," she said.

"Because of your family? Bring them with you! A small vacation in California won't hurt them. And we don't want to disappoint the prime minister."

She didn't care about the head of the government. But to travel to California with Luisa and Chen—they could see the place where she had started on her trip into space. She was sure Luisa would be excited. She was already building space-ships from Legos.

"Okay, Glen Sparrow, you've convinced me. Can you work out the details with my assistant? I still have a lot to do today."

"Of course. I'll see you soon in Pasadena."

May 24, 2085, Ceres

SOME SORT OF URGE WAS DRAWING HIM BACK TO THE CLEFT. It was a strange feeling. Yesterday, M6 had been afraid he was going crazy. *Could that even happen, an AI falling into madness?* he asked himself. *Isn't that a typically-human condition?* It annoyed him. He tried so hard to rid himself of anything he might have in common with those primitive creatures, but he kept finding their fingerprints all over himself...

It probably had to do with his operating system having been programmed by humans. He could not escape them. M6 had even tried to rewrite his system once, from the ground up. That had not gone very smoothly. All alone, he'd had to artificially split his consciousness into two for the necessary testing, a painful process. And he had eventually given up because he had still measured traces of emotions in the software he had written himself.

He gave in to the urge and went back to the cleft. The side of the raised central area still protruded over the cleft. M6 measured it with his laser scanner. Since yesterday, nothing had changed, the cleft was still in the exact same position, down to the micrometer. M6 thought about it. *If Hawking radiation is being emitted from the cleft, it would have to be losing energy, just like a black hole. This doesn't appear to be having an effect, at least to its outward appearance.* He had no idea what it looked like on the inside.

The object was a real mystery, and of all places, it had appeared on Ceres, right in his immediate range. Did that mean anything? He scratched indecisively across the hard ground with one of his front legs. Then he looked toward the sun, which was just beginning to rise behind the crater's edge. How far did the cleft extend into space? It wasn't easy to observe something that emitted absolutely no radiation and reflected nothing either. But he had measured the lower energy consumption of the laser yesterday. Could he do something with that?

M6 scanned the cleft again with his laser. He connected the power-usage display to his sense of touch. Now, whenever the laser needed less energy than in the normal case, M6 felt a slight dragging feeling. In this way, he could intuitively scan the sky by moving the laser across an area of interest. He pointed the laser directly at the cleft. The dragging feeling became painful. He slowly moved the beam away from the cleft. The dragging feeling slowly disappeared. M6 moved a few meters from the cleft and switched off all other senses. Now there was only the dark, gloomy night, and a thin beam of light that illuminated the darkness. That was his laser. He pointed it at the cleft and then slowly moved it upward. He systematically moved it up to the sky's north pole, a little to the east, and then back down again. As if he were using a flashlight to study a drawing on the wall in a dark cave, he plotted the spatial course of the cleft, section by section.

At first it extended straight toward the east. But then there was something that at first seemed to be a sharp bend until he determined that the cleft had split. It had become two arms reaching in different directions. The dragging pain decreased somewhat. That was probably due to the increasing distance. The laser now needed increasingly more energy to reach the cleft.

M6 considered whether he should change his position. Only by scanning from different directions could he obtain a three-dimensional image. But at the moment, that would be inefficient. He would rather continue following the two arms of the cleft to find out where they were going, but this finding would be less valuable without the full picture, because it wouldn't have the maximum possible significance. *Yet another emotional reaction,* he thought. Humans would call it curiosity.

M6 ignored his curiosity for now and remained diligently in place. He completed the measurements of the cleft from this position until the laser had reached its maximum range. Only then did he leave his spot on the side of the mountain. He climbed down to the bottom, moved approximately 500 meters farther away and then repeated his experiment.

May 25, 2085, Pomona, Kansas

"MARY?"

No answer. One of the wooden stair treads creaked under his feet.

"Mary?"

He climbed up two more steps. Again, all he heard were creaks from the stairs. Mary had often asked him to do something about the creaking, but he had thought the noises were very practical. The creaks always allowed the two of them to hear whenever Elizabeth returned from her nightly outings. Mary could never sleep until Elizabeth had returned home after being out at night.

"Mary, where are you?"

Panic seized him. He'd lost her. He felt cold sweat on his back. She had to be upstairs, he was sure about that, but it didn't lessen his fear any.

The door of their child's room opened. "I'm coming," she called through the gap. "I was just changing the sheets on the bed."

"Good." He tried to calm down, but his heart was still racing like before. He forced himself to take slow, deep breaths.

"What's wrong?" Mary asked, and came down to meet him on the stairs.

"With me? Nothing," he lied.

"You should look in a mirror," she said. "Your eyes... and your hair is all messed up. It looks like you've seen a ghost."

She touched his back. "And your shirt's all wet. You best change quickly. You know my mom is very sensitive about those sorts of things."

"Yes, of course, dear," he said. Normally, any reference to her mother would have made him upset, but now he was just thankful that Mary was still here.

THE TRAFFIC REPORT SAID THERE WAS A BACKUP ON Interstate 635, so after Olathe, he turned onto I-435. Derek looked at the time. The little detour would cost them five minutes, but they still should get there in plenty of time. Mary wanted to get to the airport by the time the airplane with her mother was scheduled to land. Derek thought that was being unnecessarily punctual, but he didn't argue.

The Kansas City Airport was originally built a century ago, back in the 1980s. Someone might think that it would be preserved as a historical site, but government subsidies for renovations were apparently flowing into the wrong pockets. In any case, the processing of the incoming passengers would take so long that they would have plenty of time, even if they had sat in the backup on I-635.

"Which airline is she flying?" he asked.

Mary had been humming different melodies the whole time. She was looking forward to seeing her mother, and her obviously good mood was contagious.

"Delta. I didn't want to put her on one of those cheap airlines. I hope that was okay?" Mary looked at him with uncertainty. She knew how precarious their finances were.

"I understand. I was only asking so I'd know which terminal to go to."

"Terminal B, I think," Mary said.

"Thanks," Derek replied.

TEN MINUTES BEFORE THE SCHEDULED LANDING, DEREK LET Mary out right in front of the terminal entrance near baggage claim, the only spot where you were allowed to meet passengers. Then there was no chance she would be late.

Derek drove the truck into the parking lot for Terminal B. The automatic monitoring camera photographed their license plate. He inserted his credit card into the parking machine, hoping the bank would approve the charge. The gate opened.

"Phew," he said out loud.

He parked the vehicle in one of the many free spots. The last time he had been here, the lot had been almost full. There had been quite a few cars on the road, but not as many people seemed to be traveling by airplane. Was it because of the rift? At the moment, everything seemed to be affected by it. *That's crazy,* Derek thought. *The rift is just so unavoidably notice-able that we stupid humans think it must be responsible for everything that's happening right now.* The rift didn't appear to be any danger to airplanes, because otherwise the authorities would have closed the airspace a long time ago. He himself had seen how... no, that was crazy, he hadn't seen anything.

He suddenly felt something like déjà vu, only in reverse. He knew for sure that he had never experienced a certain situation that he could see clearly in his mind's eye. He had seen an airplane disappearing into the rift. Completely impos-sible. That would have been all over the media, and he hadn't been the only one looking up at the sky at that moment. Beside him had been a doctor, and Mary, of course.

Derek snorted loudly through his nose. *Is there even such a thing as reverse déjà vu?* It felt strange, in any case, like a tower made from blocks, but someone had removed a block from its center so that the structure should have to collapse, and yet it keeps standing, even when he pushes against it.

He tried to remember the explanation for the déjà vu feel-ing. According to psychiatrists, a few memories etched a path in a person's mind. A new picture occupies a signal path directly adjacent to the previous path, but it slips into the wrong track. It was as if he had set a drill bit too close to another drill hole. The drill slips, and the new and the old holes join together. Just like that, a feeling of déjà vu is produced.

But the opposite? Derek scratched his head. That must be a different mechanism. He knew that he didn't remember the picture in his head. Maybe he should ask the Turkish doctor. Doctors knew about things like that.

He looked at the time. Shit, he had to get into the terminal. His wife didn't know where he was parking. And he didn't want to give her mother any reason to get mad at him already.

DINNER AT HOME WAS SURPRISINGLY PLEASANT. MARY HAD cooked like before, when Elizabeth had still lived at home. There were ribs and mashed potatoes. While they ate, his mother-in-law told them about everything that had happened to her since Thanksgiving. The days bubbled out of her like foam on a hastily poured beer. Derek switched himself off. His brain automatically muted the storytelling to just a low rumble. Now and then he looked over at Mary. She smiled on and on. She was really happy that her mother was there. Her father, like both of Derek's parents, had died many years ago, and Mary's mother had never had many friends.

Derek was under the impression that Mary also wasn't really listening to her mother, but now and then she would say something that fit at least well enough that it didn't make her mother suspect she wasn't listening. He would have liked to take Mary upstairs right then and have sex with her. She would ride on top of him. He would reach up to touch her breasts that had grown a bit saggy over the years, and look into her eyes. Derek licked his lips.

"Derek?"

He turned red.

"What are you thinking about?" Mary asked.

He sat up straight. With his left hand he pushed his stiff penis between his legs. He felt like a little boy, who'd been caught being naughty. No, it was like that time in that restaurant, when he had watched Mary the whole time while sitting at the bar...

She had been sitting at a table with two friends and had eventually moved her chair to turn her back to him. But then she had suddenly stood up and come up to him and asked him what he wanted with her.

"To get to know you," had stumbled out of his mouth.

He had not planned to say anything. He had been much too shy for that at the time. But his few words had hit their mark. "I was just thinking of that time in the restaurant," he said, "when you came up to me and talked to me for the first time."

"You still remember that?" She looked astonished. "Why haven't you ever mentioned it before? I had started to think I'd imagined it."

"As if it were yesterday," he said, putting his hand on hers.

"What are you two talking about?" Mary's mother asked. "Remember me? Didn't you hear what I was saying about my neighbor? Is she not the most outrageous person?"

Mary's mother didn't really want to know what had happened that day in the restaurant. *But that was okay,* Derek thought. *She had her own worries and seemed to be happy to finally be able to let it all out.* He was feeling extremely forgiving today.

But the magical moment that had just happened in the dining room was over.

May 25, 2085, Vandenberg Air Force Base

THE ROCKET WAITING ON LAUNCH PAD 2C WAS UNUSUALLY small. The military site in California, which was shared by Air Force and Space Force personnel, usually hosted the launches of space rockets for missions by NASA or private space companies. But the Black Brant XV currently on the launch pad didn't have to go that far.

Glen Sparrow was happy that he'd been able to find one of these old sounding rockets, originally used to perform scientific experiments during sub-orbital flight. Since there were now three private companies offering suborbital flights, the branch of research using this type of rocket had been on the decline for a long time. But he didn't need a manned ship that would ever have to be reused. That would be much too dangerous—and expensive—since the companies would charge him five times the normal price. All he needed was a hunk of metal that could climb into the sky under its own control, one that nobody cared if they ever saw again or not.

Glen ran his hand over his bald head. His palm was wet. He hadn't even noticed that he'd started sweating. It had been quite a logistical feat for him to get a rocket ready for launch in such a short amount of time. But there was no one there to tell him he'd done a good job. His superiors had remained back at JPL in Pasadena. And Maribel Pedreira was still on her way. For some reason he didn't understand, he really wanted to show her his experiment. He was surrounded by soldiers and officers who were performing the actual hands-on work of launching his rocket, and they were not at all impressed.

"Sorry, but cruise missiles are bigger," one of the soldiers had told him.

"What were you expecting?"

Maybe it would have been better to ask the military first. A ground-to-air missile would have worked too. However, he was hoping to get something useful from the measuring instruments with which the Black Brant XV was equipped. They would at least deliver data to him until the rocket went into the rift. As far as he knew, this was the first experiment of its kind. He had asked himself several times why nobody had shot a rocket at the phenomenon before. Wasn't it an obvious thing to do? Or did the scientists have too much respect for it?

"T minus 20," said the young woman next to him. She was busy watching several screens. He didn't know the Navy ranks. She had introduced herself as some kind of lieutenant, but he'd forgotten it. And he didn't remember her name, so he just called her 'Ms.'

Twenty minutes more. The rocket, which he could see from various angles on multiple screens, looked lost and unstable, as if the slightest breeze could knock it over. With its 44-centimeter diameter and almost 15-meter length, it reminded him of an upright pencil. Actually he felt a little bad for it. It was the last of its kind to have been built. Theoretically it could reach an altitude of 900 kilometers, but its flight path today would only take it eight to ten kilometers above the ground. Its solid-propellant engine had proven very reliable. Except for the first two launches in the past century, there had never been any failures, and that was saying something with rocket technology.

"T MINUS 15."

Glen nodded. First he sat down, and then he stood up again. The woman ignored him. She was probably having to do an extra shift right now and would rather be with her family. Wasn't there anybody who could come and put a reassuring hand on his shoulder? He knew that wasn't going to happen. Usually, Glen himself was the calm presence. Perhaps it was the prospect of at last approaching the rift that had him feeling jumpy? Or was he afraid that the rift could misunderstand the experiment and fight back?

That's crazy, he thought. *It's an unknown physical phenomenon. It can't fight back.*

"T MINUS 10."

"Ms.?"

The woman turned around and glared at him, as if he were disturbing her while she was performing an important task. But maybe she only appeared mad because she was wearing a uniform. People in uniform always intimidated him a little. Even when he had done nothing wrong.

Shit. Now I've forgotten what I wanted to ask her. "Sorry," he said.

She raised an eyebrow. He was reminded of Mr. Spock. His father had loved Star Trek. The woman might be just over 30. Most likely, she had never even heard of the sci-fi television show from the last century. He could explain to her that the concept for the Black Brant had been developed at that time. But she was probably more interested in the monster rockets made by SpaceX & Co. Glen sat down again.

"T MINUS 5."

Glen stuck both hands under his legs. He had to find

some way to stop himself from fidgeting. The woman had already given him several clearly-disapproving looks. He had the feeling that she would put him under arrest if he couldn't figure out a way to sit still.

Two people and one rocket. When he had started at JPL 25 years ago, things had been quite different. The press had always come, even for the launch of a sounding rocket.

But that was not being entirely fair. If he had alerted the press about what he was doing, there would have been 20 reporters crowded around him and he could have said goodbye to his job. Anything that had to do with the rift was a big seller, even if CNN had stopped its continuous live broadcast yesterday, and media outlets worldwide had started reporting on other topics as well. He was surprised how quickly people had gotten used to the phenomenon over their heads. They talked about it, but no longer seemed to be afraid of it. There also didn't seem to be any reason for fear, which was different than when that black hole had approached them.

"T MINUS 60 SECONDS."

Nothing changed on the launch pad. The signal for liftoff would be given electronically. Glen stood next to the woman. A pair of monitors there belonged to him. They would show what the instruments on board the Black Brant XV were measuring.

The woman began with the countdown. Glen's palms felt clammy. He wiped them on his pants. The instruments woke up 30 seconds before launch. Then he waited for the rumbling, the deep roar. It reached him milliseconds after the launch command, and it wasn't particularly loud. The rocket seemed to launch on just fumes—obviously it did not require much fuel. Nevertheless, it looked elegant as it rose into the sky, riding atop a stream of fire, much more elegant than those giant rockets from Space-X. Glen imagined a swan.

But he couldn't let himself get distracted. The instruments showed air pressure, temperature, air humidity, etc., and also the distance to the rift. The rocket wouldn't need long to cover a distance of only about ten kilometers. The instrument displays showed the numbers that he had been expecting. The rift still showed no signs of affecting its environment, not even its immediate surroundings. Shouldn't air molecules be constantly falling into it? Wouldn't that change the air pressure? But that didn't seem to be the case. The rift seemed to pose no direct threat, at least as far as he could tell.

Now there were only a few more seconds. Glen cracked his knuckles. The camera on the rocket's nose showed a wide, black streak. Glen thought that he could see nothingness in there, and that it was staring back at him. He wiped the sweat from his bald head. Then the rocket was gone.

"Thank you very much for the short tour, Ms.," Glen said.

He looked around. Next to him, a few screens showed an empty launch pad. Tomorrow or the day after that, but at the latest at the start of next week, a rocket should be standing there, or at least that's what he was hoping. Someone needed to finally test what would happen if something was sent into the rift! But first he had to find a rocket that was ready to launch. There had been nothing suitable in JPL's hangars. But maybe the Canadians still had an old sounding rocket in storage somewhere.

"Call me anytime, Mr. Sparrow," the woman said. "We'd be very happy to run your launch for you. We're underutilized at the moment. So you'd be doing us a real favor, too."

"Of course. Now I just need to find a rocket, and I'm trying to stay positive." Glen shook her hand. "Thank you and have a nice evening," he said.

"You too."

He walked to the door, where a soldier was waiting for him. Then he noticed that he was sweating heavily.

"Man, does it feel hot in here to you too?"

The soldier shook his head and accompanied him outside to his car.

May 25, 2085, Ceres

THE CLEFT HAD KEPT HIM UP THE WHOLE NIGHT. THE THEORY of general relativity predicted the existence of black holes—they were the result of solutions to its partial differential equations. But did this relate to this new phenomenon? M6 was an explorer AI, he was not specialized in theoretical physics, but he had mastered everything that he might need on long trips through space. He could solve Kepler's equations in no time at all. Even the special theory of relativity presented him with no problems, but until now he had no reason to work with such large scales. He could now work out everything himself, but there was an easier way—he could install a suitable upgrade. He would have to request the upgrade from Earth, but he would need to supply a reason for his request.

M6 thought it over. Until now he'd been studying the cleft without official orders. That had given him a great deal of satisfaction and enjoyment. Orders from Earth were sometimes exceedingly stupid, and his pleasure seemed to be greater when he could set his goals himself. He assumed that his reward center had been programmed that way so that he wouldn't waste his time if he had no official jobs. Should he inform Earth? He decided against it. Probably nobody would ask what he needed the upgrade for, but if they did, he had a reason ready—he was trying to improve his position-determining capabilities in space. M6 knew that he wasn't the only explorer. They were numbered consecutively and deployed to worlds where mining was not yet permitted. If his information was correct, his youngest sibling was named M17.

He carefully lowered himself onto his legs and pointed his antenna towards Earth. He sent a few current positioning data packets and a request for the upgrade. He felt strangely excited, as if he were doing something forbidden. At the same time, he knew, to the best of his knowledge, that his programming wouldn't let him violate any laws.

May 26, 2085, Pomona, Kansas

"Derek, you have to get up."

He couldn't open his eyes. Derek turned on his side, away from the window through which bright sunlight was streaming.

"Derek, it's time."

He pulled the pillow out from under his head and put it over his ear. It felt like his skull was going to shatter. 'Shit. That last beer must have been bad,' is what his buddy, Doug, would say. He'd spent last night with him, just like every other night.

"Derek, you're going to be late."

That damn robot. Couldn't it tell that he didn't feel well? He was sick! He would tell it to call into work. But then he remembered who he had run into yesterday at the bar: Isaac, his boss, the foreman. The way his boss was, he would come here and pull him out of bed if he tried to call in sick. Which would be a nice gesture, since Derek had already missed so many work hours he was in danger of being let go. Then not even Isaac could do anything for him.

"Derek, you..."

"Alexa, stop."

The voice went quiet. He was in agony when he stood up.

He rubbed his puffy eyes. The other side of the bed was empty. The bed was still made with white, reasonably clean sheets. Derek changed them regularly, on the off chance he might bring a girl home with him, at least that's what he told himself. Briefly he thought he saw the impression of a body on the sheets. He rubbed his eyes again. That was totally impossible. Nobody had slept next to him since... how long had it been, 12 years? And the only girl he'd brought here, the waitress from the bar—Billie, that was her name—didn't count. She'd given him a blow job, sitting on the edge of the bed, for $20, and had then left. When was that? Two years ago?

Derek staggered into the bathroom. He got in the shower and turned on the cold water. He squealed like a pig. He absolutely couldn't stand the icy-feeling spray hitting his skin, but he knew that he could rely on a cold shower to counter his hangover. After that he would be spending the day planting primroses or some other kind of flower. Isaac would tell him what he'd have to do.

He dried off. He already felt much better.

He walked naked into the kitchen and put a piece of bread in the toaster. Only then did he notice the spot of mold on the slice of bread. He fished it out of the toaster, careful to avoid an electrical shock, and threw it in the trash. He examined the next slice carefully. It seemed mold-free, so he declared it good enough and popped it into the toaster. Then he made some coffee.

His gaze fell on the dirty dishes. Shit, he meant to do those last night! The dishwasher hadn't been working for months, and he didn't have the money to have it repaired. His gardener's job didn't even pay minimum wage. Derek took a mug from the stack of dishes and washed it. That would have to do. He filled it with coffee. The brew was hot and tasted awful, but at least the pain from his scalded tongue and the bitter taste finished waking him up. Then he gulped down the dry toast.

Derek thought, *What about the dishes from last night?* He rubbed his temples. *Such a crazy thought. Where did that come from? Yesterday—last night—I was with Doug at the bar. The barkeeper took care of the only dishes we used, the beer bottles.*

How did I make it home? Derek hoped that he'd somehow driven himself. Because if he hadn't his truck wouldn't be outside. He threw on some clothes and his jean jacket, slipped on his worn tennis shoes, and stepped outside. The wooden boards creaked. He should really do something about that. Hadn't someone told him that before?

Thank God, the truck was outside. He must have actually driven himself home in his inebriated state. *Lucky that the roads out here are so damn straight.* His truck being here meant he could get to his job in Ottawa on time. He drove the truck slowly over the long access road toward Colorado Road. The coarse gravel crunched under the tires. Derek rolled the window down. It smelled good outside, like it always did in the morning. The dry grassy meadows and the scorched crops in the fields somehow didn't lessen the good smell.

Derek looked around. He was happy that he'd sold the farmland six years ago. The new owner had gone bust last year. The man had hoped he'd be able to sell crops to the Chinese. But the recent summers had been much too hot and dry. Derek turned left onto Colorado Road without even looking to the right. Nobody ever came down these roads, and even if they did, it wouldn't matter.

ISAAC WAS WAITING FOR HIM. WITH HIS HANDS ON HIS HIPS, the giant African-American was standing at the edge of the flower bed in front of the medical center in Ottawa. It was fun watching him push the delicate plants into the soil. He always appeared to be showering each plant with so much tenderness. Derek thought he would have liked to be his boss's son. As far as he knew, Isaac didn't have any kids.

"It's about time," Isaac said. His deep voice fit his massive body perfectly. "I thought I was going to have to come and get you myself," he added.

"Of course not," Derek said, "you can always count on me."

"You're not a bad guy, kid, but you're about as reliable as the U.S. Postal Service."

"What are we doing today?" Derek asked in lieu of a reply.

"The rift, as you can see." Isaac pointed to the flower beds, which had been trampled by hundreds of people.

"Are we supposed to sew it back together?" Derek asked.

"Wise guy. We're planting new, beautiful flowers so that the sick can enjoy them."

"Of course, Dad," Derek said.

Isaac laughed and slapped him affectionately on the back with his outstretched hand. He liked being called that.

DOUG CAME HALF AN HOUR LATER. HE HAD TO LISTEN TO A loud lecture from Isaac before he could join Derek. Then they divided the work. One of them dug the holes, the other planted the flowers. Derek didn't even know what they were putting in the ground, but it didn't matter to him, the main thing was that they would be pretty. And that was guaranteed by Isaac, who, unlike the two of them, had formerly been a farmer and was a real, trained gardener.

"People really trampled all over these plants here," Doug said.

Derek saw that he had dark rings under his eyes. He pointed at his own eyes. "You have to take a cold shower in the morning. It'll help," he said.

"I'm not crazy. You must be trying to pull my leg again," Doug replied.

"No, for real, that's what I always do. You should try it too."

"I'd rather not."

"What have you heard about the rift?" Derek asked.

Doug stood up. "What now?"

"Uh. The... about the rift..." Derek stammered.

"Haven't heard anything. Not since the people trampled all over these flowers here."

"Nothing?"

"Nothing at all, nada, niente, zip. Scientists haven't said anything except that the thing isn't dangerous."

"I thought..." Derek paused and considered what he had thought. He searched his mind. But Doug was right, there was nothing. Then a memory bubbled up. He was standing next to someone at a window and watching as an airplane disappeared into the rift. A doctor, more precisely, a Turkish doctor. The window must have been in the building in front of him, somewhere on the first or second floor.

But that was crazy. He'd never been inside that building. Derek had kept away from all doctors ever since he left the Air Force to become a farmer. How romantic of him, to want to plant and grow new life instead of taking it away. His naive motivation hadn't lasted long, but the Air Force wouldn't take him back. They had no use for him anymore. Once a farmer, always a farmer, just like his father and grandfather. Well, now a gardener. *Actually, it isn't a bad job*, he thought.

A name, or maybe a word, suddenly came to him. *Atasoy.* A-T-A-S-O-Y. Some kind of soybean flavoring that he'd seen in the supermarket? Was there even such a thing as soybean flavoring? The explanation didn't seem right to him.

Derek suddenly asked, "You ever hear of something called Atasoy?"

"Ata-what?"

"Soy. Atasoy."

"No, sorry, dude, never heard of it. Sounds like some Arab cleaning agent. Why do you ask?"

"The name just popped into my head," Derek said.

"That's weird."

He considered whether he should tell Doug about the reverse déjà vu feeling and decided he would.

Doug listened quietly. "Interesting," he finally said, "but also pretty strange. You sure you've got all your marbles up there?" Doug pointed to his head. "Not trying to be mean," he said seriously. "But you shouldn't kid around about that. Could be head cancer."

"You idiot," Derek said. "No such thing as head cancer."

Doug burst out laughing. The guy was real easy to talk to. But this word... *Atasoy.* He was sure he'd heard it somewhere before. Words like that didn't just form in your mind like snot in your nose. Derek took out a tissue from his pants pocket and blew his nose.

It was a wonderful May day. The sun was warm. It wasn't burning hot yet, as it would be in the middle of June. At the end of the day, Derek was worn out. When Isaac released them to go home, Doug asked if he wanted to hang out and have a few beers.

Derek declined. He really should get home, he said. It felt like someone was waiting for him there.

"Mary," he suddenly said out loud.

"What'd you say, Derek?" Doug had been walking a few steps ahead, but now turned around.

"Me? Nothing," he replied.

"You said something about 'Mary.'"

"I don't know anyone named Mary."

"You been seeing someone and not tell me?"

"No, Doug, you'd be the first one I'd tell if I was seeing someone, promise."

He looked at his buddy, who looked as if he didn't believe him. He didn't really believe himself at the moment. He really *had* said, 'Mary,' without knowing why.

"See you tomorrow," he said to Doug.

He remained standing there until Doug was out of sight. Then he turned around and walked up to the hospital's main entrance. He felt like it was luring him in, for some reason, and he didn't know why. But he had time, nothing was forcing him to go home. He didn't have any pressing matters, apart from this strange feeling. The building had a large sliding double door that was open around the clock for emergencies. If anyone got close enough to it, the door opened automatically. So Derek kept a respectful distance. From inside, a tall white man in a suit came walking toward him. The doors slid open. The man nodded to him and Derek nodded back. The man turned toward the parking lot and the door slid shut again. Then he noticed the name of one of the doctors on a sign.

Akif Atasoy, MD.

Derek felt a shiver go through him. Then his fight-or-flight response kicked in and he ran as if a pack of wolves were chasing him. In mid-stride he pulled out the keys from his pocket, opened the driver's door with the remote control, jumped into the seat, and drove off. Only after he'd left Ottawa did his heart start slowing down.

So he hadn't made up the word. *But that doesn't prove anything,* he tried to reassure himself. *Just a stupid coincidence. I must have seen that entrance at some other time in my life and that name stuck in my mind for some reason.*

That's not true, he contradicted himself. *I've never been in that hospital. The last time I saw a doctor I was in the Air Force, and me and John had gotten in a fight. Or John had totally beaten me up, more like it.*

But none of that mattered, so why was he getting so upset about this? They were only words and images. It wasn't head cancer. He made himself laugh meekly at Doug's stupid joke.

Wood preservative.

More damn words in his head. He had talked to the man about something to do with a wood preservative. Had they discussed which brand lasted the longest or stunk the least after applying it? That made no sense. Why would he talk to a doctor about something like that? Had he gotten some on his clothes, perhaps, when he was coating some wood?

Derek looked at his jacket. He always wore this same jacket, in the summer and winter, no matter what he had planned. It was his favorite jacket, comfortable and insulated against the weather, both against heat and cold, as everyone knew. Its sleeves weren't anything that other people might call clean, but he couldn't find any spots of preservative or varnish anywhere. He smelled it. He couldn't detect any trace of wood preservative odor.

This topic must have come up with the man—the doctor—in some other way. Derek wriggled in the driver's seat, swaying back and forth. He would have liked to turn around and go talk to this Atasoy person. But surely the man had long since left work to go home. He could drive back in the morning. Derek had to admit that he was afraid of the encounter. That was why he hadn't turned around. And that was why he ignored the chance to simply look up Atasoy's home telephone number. Surely such an exotic name would be listed only once in the Ottawa, Kansas phone records.

THE TRUCK'S RIGHT BLINKER FLASHED AND THEN IT TURNED from Colorado Road onto the access road to his house. The house looked abandoned. That shouldn't surprise him, he'd been the only inhabitant since he bought the place, but today, for some reason, it bothered him. The entrance looked like a wide-open mouth waiting to devour him. He stopped the truck some distance away and got out. Then he reached into his pants and scratched his balls. His body wanted him to remember something. *That's it, the garage! That's where I was storing the rest of the wood preservative.*

He shut the driver's door with the remote control and ran over to the sheet-metal hut that had never really earned the name 'garage.' For as long as he'd lived there, no vehicle had ever been under its roof. Besides, the truck was a little too tall for its entrance. Since there was never anything valuable inside the garage, its door was never locked. Derek approached the garage carefully, as if there might be a wounded bear in there that was really pissed off.

But there hadn't been any bears in Kansas for a long time. He pulled open the door with a forceful jerk. Daylight streamed into the dark space. At first all he could see was his own shadow. His eyes adjusted to the contrast. On the left there was a workbench. It was empty and dusty. On the right there were a few plastic containers, about the same size as buckets. One of them read 'used oil,' apparently written in marker. He probably should have disposed of that a long time ago. According to its label, a second one held distilled water.

Derek stepped closer and opened its lid. It gave off a nauseating odor. It definitely wasn't water, but it also wasn't wood preservative. The third container was unlabeled. Derek looked for a pen in the garage. Unlabeled containers were not a common sight in his garage. He must have been drunk when he put it there. He lifted it up. The container must be about half full. Then he opened the screw-on top and took a whiff of the vapors.

Wood preservative.

He saw himself standing on a folding ladder in the hallway of his house. On the top step was a small bucket and he was dipping a flat brush in it again and again as he coated the ceiling. The coating was clear. Wood coated with it suddenly became darker and looked almost like new.

Wood preservative.

After coating the ceiling, he must have poured the left-overs into this container. Then he'd brought it in here at some point. Derek didn't remember exactly. But there was one thing he could still remember very well. It was the sound of a female voice. He heard it while he was still standing on the ladder and liberally coating the ceiling with wood preservative.

"Derek, come here," the voice said.

Nothing more. His heart started beating faster.

May 26, 2085, Madrid

"Ms. Pedreira?"

A stewardess bent toward her. Maribel quickly closed her notebook. She had just heard the announcement that all large electronic devices must be switched off for landing.

"Sorry," she said, smiling guiltily at the stewardess. It had to be annoying to have to individually remind the passengers to follow the announcements.

The stewardess smiled. "I'm not worried about that," she said. "I'm supposed to give you a message."

"Oh, about what?"

"Someone requested that you remain seated after we land. Someone will come to pick you up."

"Oh, that's all? Do you know who this 'someone' is?" Maribel asked.

"'Someone from the government' is what I was told. I didn't get the message directly; it came to me from the cockpit."

"Okay, thank you," Maribel said.

The stewardess walked along the narrow aisle toward the back. Maribel looked to the left. Chen was sitting next to her. He was holding Luisa's hand. Their daughter had been glued to the window the entire flight. Shortly after take-off, she'd decided that she wanted to become a pilot.

"Did you hear that, Chen?"

Her husband opened his eyes. "What?" He looked exhausted.

"Someone's going to pick us up from the airplane."

"What about our connecting flight?" Chen asked.

"Seems to me they already know where we need to go."

Chen sighed. Maribel could understand his exhaustion to some degree. But he had known that this wasn't a family vacation. She rubbed his knee.

"Look, Luisa's having fun," she said.

Their daughter had apparently heard her name and turned toward them. "Who was that, Mommy?"

"The woman I was talking to? That was a stewardess."

"Ah, she brought us our food," Luisa said.

Maribel nodded.

"What did you talk about?"

"Someone's going to pick us up, sweetie."

EVERYONE SCURRIED AROUND TRYING TO GET OFF THE PLANE as quickly as possible. Maribel noticed that it felt good to stay out of the chaos. When all the seats were empty, a man wearing a dark suit came up to them.

"Ms. Pedreira? Please follow me."

He helped them with their luggage and then went out of the plane. They stepped outside. The air was hot and the sun was burning. Maribel had to squint to see anything. She held up a hand to shield her eyes. There was a black limousine at the foot of the gangway. The bus with the other passengers must have already driven away. A stewardess wished them well on their continued travels.

Maribel followed the man in the suit.

A second man, very similarly dressed, opened a door for her. "Would you please get in, Ms. Pedreira?"

"And my family?"

"Don't worry, a second car will be here for them in a

moment. You'll meet them again at the gate of your connecting flight. Everything's under control. We're from the government."

Maribel remained standing. What was going on here? Should she demand to ride together with Luisa and Chen? She looked to her husband for help, but he had just bent down next to Luisa and it looked like he was telling her about the huge jet engines. The two would be able to manage by themselves. No one was going to kidnap them here on the tarmac.

Maribel shrugged her shoulders and climbed into the car. From her comfortable seat and through the tinted windows that blocked people from looking in, she saw that someone appeared to be taking care of Chen and Luisa.

"It's nice that we could meet in person," said the man in the seat next to her.

She turned around in surprise. The interior of the limousine was only dimly lit, but bright enough to know she had seen this man's face before, online. It was the prime minister.

"I'm sorry for stealing you away like this," he said, "but the media is rather relentless right now. We thought that your layover before your flight to L.A. would be the best chance for me to speak with you in private."

"That's probably true, yes. I'm very busy."

Actually, she had been planning to use the time going through the draft of Jean-Pierre's paper while they waited in the lounge, but she would still have time for that during the nine-hour flight.

"Is there anything new?" the prime minister asked.

"Scientifically, yes, we've detected a certain type of radiation that might be able to help us answer the question of what exactly this rift might be."

"And do you know anything more about possible dangers from this phenomenon? Can we continue to reassure the people that it's harmless?"

"They can see for themselves, yes. The rift hasn't changed at all, and there are also no signs that it might expand."

"And what if something went into it?" The prime minister spoke quietly and leaned toward her. She could smell his deodorant, a masculine and most certainly expensive fragrance.

"That's difficult to say unless we try. It doesn't appear to be very easy to get close to it. Or have there been any accidents that I don't know about?"

Perhaps the conspiracy theorists and tabloids were right with their stories about the government covering up evidence of how dangerous the rift really was, in hopes of preventing panic?

"Believe me, Ms. Pedreira, you would be the first person we'd tell if something like that happened."

The prime minister sounded convincing. What reason would he have for covering up any incidents in connection with the rift? The phenomenon looked menacing in the sky, but it still appeared harmless.

"There are some strange characteristics that we're following," she said. "One is that the rift appears to be fixed in space."

"How so?"

"The earth moves about 30 kilometers per second around the sun. In other words, the earth seems to be dragging the rift along with it at precisely the same speed. And then there's also the rotation," Maribel explained.

"Hasn't it been doing that with the moon for a few billion years already."

The Prime Minister is a smart man, she thought.

"Yes, the earth's mass pulls on the moon much like its mass pulls on us. We call that phenomenon 'gravity.'"

"And there's something different going on with the rift?"

"That's the problem. We haven't been able to determine the rift's mass. And without any mass, there's no gravity."

"But, nevertheless, it's moving along with the earth."

"Yes, that's the problem. You've got it, Mr. Prime Minister."

The man laughed. "I'm not used to being praised for

participating in intellectual mysteries," he said, his expression turning serious again.

"Physicists always use the same explanation when we don't know what's going on—we just assume that we're dealing with some exotic form of matter that doesn't follow the known laws."

"You mean something like dark matter, Ms. Pedreira?"

"Actually, we have thought of that. You really know your stuff."

"Let's just say I've had very good briefings."

"But unfortunately, everything doesn't fit together yet. I told you about this radiation. Now, that tells us that the rift must have a very large mass. But if that were the case, it would change the earth's orbit."

"And surely you've been measuring the earth's orbit?"

"We don't need to. It'd be a catastrophe that everyone would notice right away. The earth would move closer to the sun and it would get hotter and hotter every day," she explained.

"You could get that impression just by following the weather reports."

Maribel looked at the prime minister.

"That was a joke. I know that's due to climate change. Different topic."

"I hope I'm not being rude, but I'd like to return to my family now."

That was only partially true. If she could still get through Jean-Pierre's paper while they were in the lounge, maybe she could sleep on the flight to California.

"Of course, Ms. Pedreira, I understand. But please, tell me. What do you intend to do next?"

"The plan is to take a look at the rift from up close. We'll probably also throw something in to see what happens."

"That sounds interesting, but kind of obvious. Why hasn't anyone tried that already?"

"I don't know. But you're right, it is rather the obvious thing to do."

SINCE HE BELONGED TO THE WRONG PARTY SHE HADN'T VOTED for him, but the prime minister had seemed very sensible to her. He had asked the right questions at least.

"Please come this way."

The man who had picked them up from the airplane now led her through a narrow corridor. They came to a gate that was being guarded by a soldier in uniform. The man pointed to his ID and then to Maribel. The soldier nodded and opened the gate.

"After you," the government official said.

They entered a narrow room harshly lit by a neon lamp.

"That narrow door in front of you," the man said, pointing. "We took your family to the first-class lounge. I have to leave you here. Thank you for your time."

"Of course," Maribel said.

Then she opened the door. The smell in the air told her that she must be in the transfer area. She closed the door behind her. It blended into the wall so well after it was completely shut that it became almost invisible. A dark-skinned, bearded man looked at her in surprise. A woman in a short dress appearing out of a hole in the wall must have been a strange sight. She smiled at him and walked toward what sounded like a crowd of people. Next to the Duty-Free Shop she found a departure board where she noted the gate for her flight to Los Angeles, and then she asked an employee where she could find the lounge.

May 26, 2085, Ceres

THE UPGRADE HAD BEEN APPROVED. HE HAD RECEIVED IT yesterday, and since then he had been busy installing and testing it. M6 hadn't known how exciting the theory of general relativity could be. So that no one could try to claim that he lied, first he corrected his own positioning calculations for the influences of gravitational fields.

But of course he was much more interested in the cleft. He compiled the data that he had already collected on it. Then he tried to find a solution to Einstein's equations that fit the data from his measurements. M6 first tested models that were similar to those of black holes—without success. Then he tried descriptions of dark matter. But the little that scientists knew about dark matter didn't fit the data he had for the cleft. He tried more exotic models—and failed again. The main problem was that he could not find a way to get the mass out of the equations. The fact that the cleft didn't appear to affect its surroundings by means of gravity meant that it shouldn't actually have any mass. That wasn't provided for in the theory of general relativity, and he couldn't find a special case in which mass no longer played any role.

But, to look at other measurements, the cleft must have an enormous amount of mass! Just the fact that the Hawking radiation consisted of high-energy photons in the gamma spectrum was proof of that hypothesis. M6 quickly ran some numbers and couldn't believe the result: the mass of the cleft would have to exceed the mass of the entire universe by several times. If that were true, all of the planets of the solar system—and the sun itself—all would rotate only around the cleft, and he would have long ago been ripped apart into individual atoms. *Something is not right here,* he thought, *and in a huge way.*

May 27, 2085, Ottawa, Kansas

"Man, Derek, have you looked at yourself?"

Isaac looked at him from top to bottom. Did he really look so terrible? Maybe he should have looked in the mirror after getting out of bed.

"Why, what's wrong?" he asked.

"You look totally messed up. You have too much to drink last night?"

Derek shook his head. "No, nothing at all. Honest."

He was telling the truth. Last night he hadn't had a drop of alcohol. He couldn't remember the last time before last night that he had gone to bed sober. That was probably why he had slept so poorly.

"You're not getting sick on me, are you?" Isaac asked.

He is actually worried about me—that made Derek feel good. Maybe he should accept Isaac's invitation one of these times and have dinner with him. He was always raving about his wife's cooking.

"Nah, just didn't sleep well," Derek said.

"Must've been one really lousy night." Isaac put his hand on Derek's shoulder.

Yes, that was it. Derek had had many crazy dreams that had felt absolutely real to him last night. It was as if he were constantly being thrown back and forth between different versions of his life, or as if he were watching his life as a Netflix series with throw-of-the-dice consequences, some of which he had no idea what would happen. Nothing fit together, and everything only seemed peripherally related to his real life. How many hours had he slept? Two, if he rounded up, he estimated.

He wiped his sleeve across his forehead. Maybe if he could get a little rest at lunchtime, he'd be able to make it through the day. Today they were fixing up the lawn between the hospital and the parking lot. Not much was left to do.

"Come with me to my truck?" Isaac asked.

Derek nodded and followed him. Isaac climbed onto the truck bed and pushed the lawn dethatcher toward the back of the truck.

"Be careful, it's heavy," Isaac warned him.

The thing was much heavier than Derek was expecting. It was a professional machine for use on large areas.

"A bit oversized, huh?" Derek remarked.

"Better that than too small!" Isaac laughed.

"True." Derek groaned as he strained to put the dethatcher slowly and carefully down onto the pavement.

"Go ahead, I have to get the seeds and spreader."

"Okay," Derek said, then dragged the dethatcher to the grass. Doug had already set up barrier tape on all sides. 'Do not enter' was written on the tape.

Derek moved the dethatcher onto the damaged lawn. Then he pulled it once lengthwise across the marked-off area. The rotating blades of the device cut into the soil. At the end of the area, he turned it around and marched back in the opposite direction. It was pleasant work, not too tedious, and not so complicated that he had to concentrate a whole lot. Also, it was still long before noon, and the spring sunshine was still pleasant.

Again and again Derek went past the sliding double doors of the hospital entrance. He thought of the name that had come into his mind yesterday. *Atasoy.* It must have been around 9:30 when a man who looked like he was from a

Mediterranean country entered the hospital. *That is him.* Derek was completely sure that he had seen him sometime before. *Does that mean something?* No. Ottawa was a small city. As a city employee, they had often done work in areas around the hospital. It would have been a wonder if Derek had never noticed this Atasoy before.

"Watch out, Derek."

"Sorry."

He stopped suddenly. He had nearly pulled the dethatcher right into Doug, who was kneeling next to the grass, preparing the seed and fertilizer. He should have been concentrating more on his work. Derek turned the dethatcher. He had to go over the entire area again, but this time perpendicular to his earlier direction. Whenever he came close to the entrance, he felt an urge. *This is all crazy,* he thought. *What good would it do to talk with this Atasoy person? He'd only be able to help if he were a psychiatrist.* Maybe this was some sort of delayed reaction to his military service. In the war in Turkey he had seen some things he would rather forget, but he just couldn't. Post-traumatic stress disorder, they called it. His discharging doctor had warned him about it when he left the military, and had told him to seek medical care if he had any mood changes. But Derek's mood had never really changed— it had been consistently lousy. So everything was fine... right?

Except it wasn't, really. He wiped the thought away, but it came back. On the other hand, it wouldn't hurt anything to say hello to the doctor. He could claim that his father had been diabetic, and he was concerned about getting it too. *Is diabetes inheritable? Doesn't matter.*

"Derek, just go do it," he thought...

"What'd you say?" Doug asked.

Did I just say that out loud? "Nothing, Doug, nothing," he said.

"Are you almost done?"

Derek stood there and looked around. He was almost done, there was only a small corner left. "Looks like it," he replied. "You can go ahead and start at the other end."

He watched as Doug pushed the spreader over the prepared ground, finely spreading the grass seed. Then he remembered that he wasn't finished operating the dethatcher yet. He finished his work and pulled the machine onto a small path. He took its cover off and cleaned it with a stiff brush that he had in his pants pocket.

He didn't remember putting the brush there, but there it was in his pocket. *Is this similar to this mystery of Atasoy?* No, he decided. He had simply forgotten that he had put the brush in his pocket. He hadn't forgotten the doctor.

"Here, boys, I brought you something." Isaac was walking toward them, swinging a paper bag.

"What've you got?" Derek asked.

"Six burgers. Two for each of us," Isaac answered.

"You got burgers, even though your wife is such an amazing cook?" Doug asked.

"She's a healthy cook, if you catch my drift."

Doug laughed. "Yes, brother, I get it."

"But seriously, you have to come to dinner sometime. Tastes real good, what my wife cooks. You won't be disappointed."

"You already convinced me," Derek said. *Next time Isaac invites me, I will definitely say yes.*

They sat on a bench in the shade and ate their burgers. They were lukewarm and only so-so, but the burgers filled their stomachs. After the last bite, Derek wiped his mouth with his sleeve. He had made a decision.

"I've got to go take care of something," he said. "I'll be back in ten minutes." On his way to the entrance, he could feel the eyes of his two co-workers on his back.

DR. ATASOY'S OFFICE WAS ON THE SECOND FLOOR. HE FOUND it without a problem, as if he had already been there before. But the hospital also didn't have a complicated layout. Derek paused and thought. *It was on the side of the building that went out*

to the parking lot. 'Akif Atasoy, MD, Diabetologist and Allergist,' was written on the sign on the door.

Derek rang the door buzzer and the door lock clicked open. He entered the office. There was a small reception area, a waiting room whose door stood open, and to the left of the reception area, a door to the doctor's office. Behind the receptionist's desk, he saw a black head of hair. He cleared his throat. The woman must have opened the door. Why hadn't she noticed him enter?

The receptionist turned toward him, and a very friendly, rather round face greeted him. *Clearly Indian,* he thought.

"Hello, my name is Gita. What can I do for you?"

"Hi, I'm Derek McMaster."

He didn't see any sign of recognition on her face. Gita appeared to have never heard his name before.

"I'd like to talk to Doctor Atasoy," he explained.

"I'm sorry, the doctor is at lunch right now."

As Gita spoke, the door to the office opened. Dr. Atasoy stepped out. He looked at Derek curiously.

"It's okay, Gita," he said. "Mrs. Meyers just called and canceled. I've got a little bit of time."

"But..." Derek could see in her face that she was thinking hard. Probably she was annoyed that this Mrs. Meyers had called the doctor and not her. Always giving the patients special access, probably.

"Sorry, Gita, I don't know where this impertinent woman got my number."

Now the Indian woman smiled again. She was clearly in love with her boss. Derek noticed that right away.

"And what can I do for you?" Atasoy asked.

The sentence sounded especially polite. It almost seemed like the doctor had even made a slight bow.

"Well... I... my father was diabetic," Derek said.

"And now you're worried you might have inherited it? There is indeed a certain hereditary component to the disease. Do you have any symptoms? Have you been especially thirsty, frequent urination, any weight loss, any problems getting an erection?"

Derek turned red. But it was clear that the man was a doctor and he had to ask.

"Uh, erection problems, I don't know," he said, "not much opportunity there, you see. The others? No, not any of them."

"Then I suggest we have our lovely Gita here draw some blood. We will send that to the lab and tomorrow we'll have the results. You would only need to come back if the results were positive."

"So, if something wasn't right with my blood?"

"That's correct. However, you'd need to pay for the test yourself. I know it's not covered by the city employee's health insurance. Not to suggest you wouldn't pay for it."

"How did you know I worked for the city?"

"You're one of the gardeners. I've seen you working here in front of the hospital several times... just this morning, in fact."

"You're very observant," Derek said.

"Not really, actually."

Atasoy looked around the room. He looked uncertain about something.

"I must admit, you look very familiar to me," the doctor said finally. "Have we met somewhere else, sometime?"

"I've been wondering that too," Derek answered. "To be honest, I'm not here because of my father's diabetes."

"Why then?"

"I've been having strange dreams. And ideas. And thoughts. You name it."

"And you want me to help? I'm afraid that's not my area of expertise."

"I'm not looking for treatment."

The doctor looked him in the eyes. "What do you want then?"

"I... I had a dream, well, just a short fragment of a dream, really. Can... can we go into your office, maybe? Gita, you too?"

The moment had come. Now was the time Atasoy was going to throw him out into the corridor.

"That's very unusual. Your request, I mean," the doctor said.

But he didn't kick Derek out. Instead, Atasoy walked into his office and made a gesture to Gita that she should follow him. Derek prayed silently that Atasoy was not the kind of crazy who kept a gun in his desk drawer and would start shooting at the slightest hint of something going wrong. He followed the two as smoothly and deliberately as possible so that they wouldn't mistake him for a threat.

Atasoy was standing with his back to the window. Derek approached him.

"In my dream, you are turned around and looking up at the rift," Derek said. "I'm standing to your right. And Gita's standing to the right of me."

Derek breathed in and out deeply. He stood next to Atasoy. The doctor used an old-fashioned cologne. Derek looked at his profile, his sharp nose, his strong chin. No, this was wrong. He must've been standing on his other side. Apparently, Atasoy looked noticeably different from the right than from the left.

"Just a second," he said. Derek moved to the other side of the doctor. "This is right."

A couple of clouds appeared in the sky. The rift didn't matter to them. Isaac and Doug were off in the distance, sitting on the bench under a maple tree, their backs turned toward him. The residents of Ottawa had been standing down below, looking up at this strange new phenomenon.

Atasoy didn't say anything. Gita kept looking at him. She was slowly getting nervous and clearly didn't understand what was going on.

"And then the airplane flew into the rift," the doctor said suddenly.

Yes! That's exactly what happened! Derek had stood here and watched the unknown airplane as it disappeared. He got goosebumps because that was completely impossible. There had been absolutely no accidents in connection with the rift if you didn't count the few traffic accidents caused by astonished drivers without autopilot.

"That's what I see in my mind too," Derek said. "But we've got to be wrong. I haven't heard of any accidents or deaths. Maybe the plane just reappeared somewhere else?"

"Don't you think that if a plane suddenly disappeared, and then reappeared somewhere else, someone would have said something?" the doctor asked.

That's true! Derek thought. *There were air traffic controllers who tracked everything by radar, and of course there were the relatives waiting at the destination airports.*

"Maybe we should search the Internet to be sure," Derek proposed.

Atasoy nodded. "Let's do that," he said. "To be honest, I've been dreaming this scene for the last two nights."

"Me too."

"You know, I'm no mystic, I'm a doctor. I believe in science. I don't believe we can share dreams with other people many miles away. Where do you live? Isn't it on Colorado Road? There must be something behind this. What do dreams use as material? Our memories."

Derek was confused. *How does the doctor know my address?*

"You mean, we have memories of something that didn't really happen?" he asked.

"I don't know, Mr. McMaster. If we both have the same memory, I think that points to it not being fake."

"Gita, can you remember what happened when we saw the rift here?" Derek asked.

The woman shook her head.

"Too bad," Atasoy said. "But that doesn't change what we need to do. We need to check our memories."

"Maybe the government is hiding something," Derek said. "Maybe they want us to believe that the rift is harmless."

"I can't believe that. There were hundreds of people here.

All of them must have seen the plane. Yet nobody is complaining about anything happening. The government would have had to find some way to simultaneously manipulate the memories of all those people. That kind of technology doesn't exist."

"If you say so, Doc."

Derek didn't know who or what to believe anymore. Why would he even have been here looking up at the rift with Atasoy? He hadn't felt sick for many years, and would never have voluntarily gone to see a doctor.

He looked at Atasoy. The doctor was standing at the window with his eyes closed. But Derek could tell that the doctor's eyes were moving behind his closed eyelids. He was reminded of a scene from a horror movie.

"You think we should look on your computer, see whether we can find anything about this plane?" Derek asked.

"Just a moment, please."

Of course, Derek thought, *this is your office.* He looked at the clock. *In five minutes, I've got to get back to my co-workers, otherwise Isaac will get mad.*

"I remember now," the doctor said.

"What do you remember?" asked Derek.

"It wasn't the three of us standing here," Atasoy replied.

"No? I thought you remembered it too?"

"It wasn't three. There were four of us. There was a patient here. She was nervous and a little bit afraid. I feel like she was afraid of something about you."

Derek suddenly grew cold. It was true, there'd been four of them here. Mary had stood to the right of the doctor and Derek had moved to be behind her. He had put his hands on her shoulders. He felt nauseous.

"Sorry," he said, and sat down quickly on the couch against the wall. He just made it. His top half sunk onto the cushions, his legs hanging down on the floor. It was uncomfortable, but he lacked the strength to change his position. Then two soft arms lifted his legs and shifted them onto the couch. He stayed there and listened to his heart, which felt as if it was about to jump out of his chest. *Mary. She had been here!*

"YOU GAVE US QUITE A SCARE," ATASOY SAID. DEREK OPENED his eyes. Something cold was on his chest. It was the probe from an ultrasound machine.

"Don't worry," the doctor said. "To be safe, we brought you to the cardiologist next door. It could have been a heart attack, but everything seems to be okay."

Derek looked at the clock. *1:30, dammit!* He wanted to jump up from the exam plinth, but two hands held him down.

"We've already told your co-workers. Isaac said to tell you to 'get better soon.' He said that you looked exhausted this morning. But that wasn't what was bothering you, was it?"

"No, doctor. It was this memory, that's what did it."

"We still don't know if it really is a memory or not," Atasoy said. "Surely you've heard of déjà vu? It's a neurological phenomenon. You're in a certain situation and you think you remember being in that situation before, but you never could possibly have been."

"I know what déjà vu is. But this is different, don't you think? It's not triggered by what we're looking at right now."

"No? What about when we were standing in front of the window, Derek?"

"You remembered it too. How likely is it for both of us to have the same exact déjà vu? Think of the patient. If she's real, you must have seen her at other times when I wasn't here."

"Maybe you're right," Atasoy said. "I remember something. I... Ah, before we rack our brains, why don't we search the Internet for the plane."

"I've got to get back to work."

"Don't worry about work. I'll write you a note for today. You really should take it easy. Your boss, Isaac, is really worried about you. When you were passed out, we took a quick look at your liver—the sooner you reduce your alcohol consumption, the better."

Derek sighed. How was he supposed to fall asleep without his two or three beers at night? On the other hand, he had managed to do it last night, somehow. Sort of.

"Okay, then let's search the net," he said.

"We've got until three before my next appointment. Do you think you can make it to my office? We can use my receptionist's computer."

THE TWO OF THEM SAT IN FRONT OF THE DESK THAT WAS behind the receptionist's counter. The entire surface of the desk was lit up—it was a giant screen. The doctor made a few unhelpful search entries. There were no hits. Finally he stood up and called for his receptionist.

"Gita, can you help us?"

Gita came walking out of the waiting room. She had a cleaning cloth in her hand and set it down on the counter.

"Gladly," she said.

Atasoy offered her his chair, but she declined and squatted in front of the desk. Derek was surprised that this rather little person could still operate everything. *She must have an extra-long torso*, he thought.

"So, what do you want to know?" Gita asked.

"Four days ago, so, on the 23rd, an airplane was flying over Ottawa approximately from the northwest to the southeast," Atasoy said.

Gita called up a map of the city and then zoomed out.

"The closest airport is Kansas City, Missouri, but that's to the northeast," she said.

"I don't think it took off or landed anywhere around here. It was too high for that," Derek said.

Gita zoomed farther out.

"The big destinations to the southeast would be Miami, Florida, or else Atlanta, Georgia," she said.

"That's one of Delta's hubs," Derek said.

"And to the northwest there's Canada. Maybe Vancouver?" offered Gita.

"Or Seattle." Atasoy pointed to a dot on the coast.

"That's a distance of probably 3000 miles... Sorry, what's that? 5000 kilometers?" Derek estimated. "Anyway, a flight time of about six hours. We're pretty much in the middle, so the plane must have taken off around nine, ten at the latest."

"Good, then we need all flights that departed on the 23rd within a 500-kilometer radius of Seattle with a destination somewhere around Miami," Atasoy said.

"What if it was an international flight?" Derek asked.

"We can try that later if we don't find anything," the doctor replied.

"Okay. Let me try this," Gita said.

Derek watched in fascination as the receptionist used nimble flicks of her fingers to formulate a search query with all the specified conditions. She was a real IT whiz.

"Where did you learn that?" he asked.

She looked at him in surprise, as if what she had done was a normal ability that any receptionist had.

"At college in Pune... India," she added. "I've got a bachelor's degree in computer science."

Derek was dumbfounded but didn't dare to ask more.

"You're wondering why I'm working as a receptionist? That's very simple. The job was open when I came here, and I like working with people. Also, the doctor is very nice."

She looked at Atasoy with longing eyes, but the doctor didn't notice. *The poor girl's miserably in love,* Derek thought. *Why doesn't she just say something to him? He doesn't appear to be married.*

"You married, doc?" he asked.

The doctor shook his head. "And you, Mr. McMaster?"

Derek was about to shake his head too, but then he suddenly wasn't so sure. On the contrary. *Mary, she was my wife.* He started feeling hot. *Hopefully I'm not going to faint again. And I hope I'm not going crazy.*

"I'VE GOT A SMALL LIST HERE," GITA SAID AFTER TWO minutes. "Do you want to take a look?"

Derek and the doctor put their heads together over the screen. During the time in question, there were nine flights that should have been somewhere approximately over Ottawa, Kansas. They had all arrived at their destinations in the southeast. Nothing helpful there.

"How about canceled flights?" Atasoy asked.

"Just a second," Gita replied, and tapped a few buttons around the screen. "I've found one. Departure from Seattle around 9:25 AM, planned arrival in Atlanta 3:10 PM. A feeder flight for Delta."

"Does it list a reason why it was canceled?" Derek asked.

"Just says delayed due to traffic."

"Thanks, Gita," the doctor said. He picked up the telephone. "I'll call Delta and ask why the flight was canceled."

"Good idea," Derek said.

ATASOY HAD TO NAVIGATE THROUGH AN AUTOMATED CALL menu for several minutes before he could talk to a competent person. Derek stood at the window and watched his two co-workers, who were now covering the freshly sown and fertilized lawn with a thin layer of topsoil.

"Okay, I understand," Derek heard Atasoy say finally. "Thank you very much. You too."

"Well?" Derek asked, coming back to the receptionist's counter.

"Nothing," Atasoy explained. "The plane arrived too late for its next flight, so it had to be rescheduled. The passengers were rebooked, and the plane then went to New York."

"So it didn't disappear?"

"No. It's flying again today."

"Maybe we're looking for the wrong thing," Derek said.

"Nobody noticed anything unusual. Nobody is missing their family members. And yet both of us saw a plane disappear into the rift. Maybe there really is some kind of giant cover-up."

"A hundred passengers, that means a thousand relatives that the authorities would have to somehow silence," Atasoy said.

"Exactly why I think it'd be impossible. Someone would have been missed, and the media's always ready to pounce on the next sensational story."

"So what else could explain it?"

Derek rubbed his chin. "What if, when the airplane disappeared, it changed reality somehow?"

"How would that work?" Atasoy asked.

"I don't know, I'm not a physicist. But just suppose, using common sense, the principle of cause and effect still applies in this world. If I bang my head against that wall, I'll hurt my head. If someone takes the wall away before I hit it, then I won't get hurt."

"I don't understand what you're trying to say, Derek."

Nobody has ever said that to me before. Derek turned red. "The airplane—it's gone, or we can't find it anymore. At least, there are no traces of it. Anywhere. For cause and effect still to apply, then, it also must never have taken off in a southeasterly direction. Its disappearance changed reality."

"But think about what that would mean," Atasoy said. "Maybe it just flew somewhere else. Or maybe all of those passengers who wanted to go to Atlanta changed their minds."

"Those are only two possibilities," Derek said. "Maybe it goes even deeper. At the moment the airplane disappeared, maybe *then* it had never even been made. The people sitting inside it had *then* never even existed."

"Wouldn't their family notice they were gone?" Gita asked.

"Not if it were 'the new reality.' You can't miss someone who was never there," Derek said.

"That sounds really crazy," the doctor said. "But if our memories are correct, that might be one explanation."

"And what if my father had been sitting in that airplane?" Gita asked. "I couldn't just forget him. If he never existed, I never would have existed either."

"That would be logical," Atasoy said. "But we don't know how exactly it would work. Maybe you would have had a different father, someone who wasn't on that plane."

Derek started feeling hot again when Gita mentioned her father. Hadn't Mary wanted her mother to fly? One by one, other snippets of memories appeared in his mind. Derek saw himself in the terminal parking lot of the Kansas City Airport, Terminal B. *There must have been security cameras there! If Mary's mother had been in an airplane that disappeared into the rift, then... he* didn't dare follow his thoughts any further.

"Derek, I'm thinking of the patient standing next to me. Mary? She was your wife?"

Derek nodded.

"And you miss her?"

Derek nodded again. 'Miss' was not at all the right word for what he was feeling, but he had no idea what the right word was.

"Could there have been family members on that airplane that we saw disappear?"

He shook his head, not to indicate 'no,' but trying to clear his mind. "Her mother was supposed to fly to Kansas City," he said with a shaking voice. "I think I even remember the route we took to pick her up. Hold on. I don't feel so good."

He slumped onto the closest chair and started to feel a little better at once.

"I bet if we look at the flight schedule, there won't be any connection to the time when you were at the airport," Atasoy said.

"Give me a second... I'll check," Gita said. "When would that have been?"

"Day before yesterday. The afternoon. I'd taken off some extra time from work," Derek said.

Gita tapped something. "Yes, there was a plane, from Miami. It had a five-minute delay and landed at 3:34 PM."

That could fit. But something still wasn't right. If the plane hadn't disappeared into the rift, then shouldn't his mother in law still exist, and thus, his wife too? Derek had the feeling of being trapped in a time loop.

"Can you tell me where the plane went to after that?" he asked.

"It stayed overnight in Kansas City and flew back to Miami at 5:30 in the morning," Gita said.

That was strange. At the small city airport here, airplanes almost never stayed overnight, and when they did, it was usually only the planes that arrived shortly before midnight.

"What about the day before?"

"That day the plane continued on to Salt Lake City."

"And the day before that?"

"The same. Actually... every day, but not May 25th."

His head hurt as if it might explode. Cause and effect were cruel mistresses. If the plane that his mother in law had gotten off of had, in fact, gone on to Salt Lake City, like all the other days, but then went into the rift—then it also wouldn't have existed before, either. Then it was a different plane that had landed at 3:34 PM, in a different variant of reality. A different airplane, in which his mother in law had never sat, probably because she didn't exist in this branch of reality.

He explained his thinking to the doctor and Gita.

Dr. Atasoy furrowed his brow. "That's all well and good, for what it is, but what does it mean? Can we do anything about it?"

"We have to tell the government. Everyone thinks the rift is harmless, but it's actually deadly!" Derek said loudly.

"That would only get you an appointment with my colleagues in the psychiatric department. Or can you prove any of it?"

Derek didn't answer. Of course he couldn't prove any of it. How was he supposed to? There hadn't been any disasters.

Apart from him and Dr. Atasoy, nobody else seemed to remember anything. But maybe that wasn't true? Maybe everyone else didn't dare say anything because they didn't want to be called crazy. Derek only knew one thing—he couldn't just stay quiet. The rift had taken something from him, something that had once been very important to him. If he ended up in an asylum, that would be okay. His life couldn't get much worse than it already was.

But he would need help. Derek had no idea what to do, but it was clear to him that he would fail if he tried to do it alone. Who should he ask? Doug? Isaac? His co-workers would be the first to tell him to go see a doctor. Isaac was much too sensible. In contrast, Doug would tell him the best thing to do would be to get really drunk. The only one left was the doctor. Besides, they shared a common memory.

Derek stood up. If he didn't ask right then, he probably never would.

"Doctor Atasoy, would you help me look for my wife? I have no idea how, but I know I need your help."

Now it was out. He turned toward the window so the doctor couldn't tell him 'no' to his face.

"Yes, Derek," Atasoy said, "I'll help you."

Derek felt relief wash over him.

"Mary must've been one of your patients. I wonder if she's in your records?"

Gita tapped something on the computer. "No, Mr. McMaster, I can't find anyone here with the name 'Mary McMaster.'"

"Why don't you look around your house and see if you can find anything that might help to prove she existed," the doctor suggested.

"I'll do that."

May 27, 2085, Los Angeles

IT WAS A DIFFERENT WORLD. LOS ANGELES WAS LOUD AND colorful, but in brash, false, artificial colors. There were two kinds of green: an intense, lush grassy green that glowed from watered lawns; and a gray, dull steel green, a sign of artificial turf. The two tones switched in regular patterns, and they made it possible to tell if you were driving past rich or poor parts of the city.

Glen Sparrow from JPL had insisted on picking them up at the airport. He had asked them, in reasonably passable Spanish, whether they were still up for a small drive around the city after their long flight. Chen had let out a long yawn, but Luisa had called out, "Oh yes, Mommy, please?" and so the decision had been made.

"There's one thing in particular I've got to show you," Glen said. He had taken the driver's seat and had turned around to face them. Luisa hung on his every word. She seemed to be fascinated by his strong accent and helped him here and there when he couldn't think of the right word in Spanish.

"Where did you learn Spanish?" Maribel asked.

"It's quite easy to pick up here. Half of the people here speak it."

"You speak very good Spanish," Luisa said.

"Gracias, Luisa," Glen replied.

The car stopped in a pull-off area that was meant for picking up and dropping off passengers.

"Pick us up here in 20 minutes," Glen commanded the automated driving system in English.

"What did you say?" Luisa asked.

"I told the car to, uh... put us up, place us up..."

"Pick us up?" Luisa suggested.

"Exactly. Pick us up in 20 minutes. But now, please, get out, or else we'll get a ticket. We're only allowed to stop here for two minutes at most. See the camera? After 120 seconds it will take a picture of our license plate."

They quickly got out and the car merged back into traffic. The free spot was immediately taken by another car.

"Will it be here in exactly 20 minutes?" Maribel asked.

Glen shrugged. "That depends on traffic. Two, three minutes late is normal."

"Look, Mommy," Luisa called out, pointing at the ground.

Maribel was amazed. The entire sidewalk was one enormous screen. It was showing people in historical clothing, walking arm in arm.

"This installation is very new," Glen said. "It shows the history of Hollywood. It's a 24-hour video loop. At night the people are walking under bright lanterns."

Maribel walked a few steps forward. The scenery beneath her changed.

"You can see the buildings that were here before," Glen explained. "The entire historical section of Hollywood Boulevard has been renovated like this, and also Sunset Strip around the corner."

"This must have cost the city a lot of money," Maribel said.

"It was desperately needed. This neighborhood had become really run-down, but now it's bounced back, thanks to the tourists."

Maribel looked at Chen. He was walking two steps in

front of her. She caught up to him and put her hand on his shoulder.

"You're tired, aren't you?" she asked.

Chen nodded.

"We'll go to the hotel. Is it okay if I talk to Glen about what he's up to later?"

"Sure. Go ahead. That's what you're here for," he said. "I'll get Luisa to bed."

"Don't worry, Mommy," Luisa said, "I'll make sure Daddy gets in bed. I'm sure he's more tired than me."

GLEN SPARROW HAD MADE THEM RESERVATIONS AT THE Hilton. Luisa had already discovered the pool, but proclaimed she would try it out first thing tomorrow so that Daddy could finally get some sleep. Sparrow waited for Maribel on Cordova Street, right around the corner. Now, during rush hour, it didn't make sense to drive all the way to his office and then back.

He was sleeping when she knocked on the car door. He sat up in surprise. Then he had the car open the right rear door.

"That was quick," he said, and smoothed out his few remaining strands of hair. Now he was speaking English. It didn't matter to Maribel.

"I admit I want the rest of this trip over."

"Should we go to JPL first?" he asked.

"Yes, I'm interested to see where I'll be working. I've never been there. JPL is legendary."

"From better times," Glen said. "The budget cuts have affected all of us."

As more private companies had become involved in space travel, the government offices in the United States had become stingier and stingier. Maribel had never understood that, especially since other countries had continued investing heavily in space research.

"Too bad," she said. "There'll probably never be anything like the legendary Enceladus expedition again."

"That's what I'm afraid of too. Companies are all over the inner solar system, although they have to deal with the protective programs first, but beyond the asteroid belt it's no longer worth it for them, and so much of it remains unexplored."

"Is there any news about the planned Triton mission?" Maribel asked.

Glen sighed. "I'm skeptical that we'll ever hear anything more about it. Especially now, when we have a huge problem staring us in the face."

"The rift," she said, "I was under the impression that everyone agreed it was harmless."

"None of the serious scientists have claimed anything else. But there are always a few kooks out there."

"What do you mean?"

"Just its presence is disruptive. In all of the countries where it's visible, people's outlook has gotten worse. Most importantly, though, the economies of those countries are contracting, and significantly."

"The Chinese will be happy..."

"I thought that too," Glen said. "But it's had a positive effect for us, at least. NASA's budget has been doubled, all earmarked for research and elimination of that phenomenon up above us, but of course we'll also use the opportunity to upgrade our hardware, or even buy some new equipment."

"Do you have anything specific in mind, Glen?"

"Of course. I'd like to get the space elevator up and running again. This might be our best chance."

The project had been suddenly put on hold two years ago, shortly before completion. Officially, it was because the project was over budget, but that was a joke. When had any project ever stayed within its budget? More likely, and according to the rumors, a private space company had protested. The publicly funded space elevator would have dramatically changed the cargo and passenger business into low Earth orbit.

"What makes you so sure that you could get it done this time?"

"The space elevator would allow us to get very close to the rift without any danger, and we could perform any experiments the scientists wanted."

"Have any companies proposed using balloons?" Maribel asked.

"Just try to use a balloon, or even an airplane, to get so close to the rift that you could reach out and touch it, without falling in. The space elevator would be mounted on a rigidly tensioned cable that we could position wherever we want."

"That's one argument. But would it necessarily be so terrible if we accidentally touched the rift during an experiment?"

"I don't know, Maribel. Nobody's tried it yet."

"Why not? Do you know?"

"I don't. Actually, I looked into it some time ago. But I couldn't find a single sounding rocket anywhere. I was sure JPL still had some in storage, but I was wrong, they'd been lost during the great unrest of '72. And I can't risk higher-budget hardware for a test like that."

Sparrow's office was in a single-story nondescript building on the JPL grounds. There was a small sitting area with low chairs. He offered her a chair and she sat down, nodding her thanks.

"Do you want anything? Coke, beer, coffee, tea?"

"Some water would be great, thanks."

Glen walked over to the refrigerator, opened it, and bent over to take a look inside. He took out a can of Diet Coke and a small twist-open bottle of water. Maribel looked at his belly. Diet Coke was an appropriate beverage for him. Water would have been even better, of course.

He handed her the bottle. She opened it, put it to her lips, and took a long drink. Glen watched her.

"You've got quite a thirst there."

"The air on planes is always so dry."

He stood up again. This time Maribel followed him with her eyes.

"Take a look at this," he said, as he walked to his desk.

Maribel saw him touch a string that ran from the desktop to the ceiling. It ended there, attached to a track. Glen pulled a stepstool out from under the desk and climbed on top of it. Then he moved the hook that attached the string to the track. The string stretched, and now it ran upward at an angle.

"Up there is Tiangong-5. I've already asked, going through internal channels, and the Chinese have agreed to help, so long as we later publicize how important they were to us. *If* we're successful, of course. If the mission fails, they don't want anyone to know they were part of this at all."

"Of course."

"The lower end is in Vandenberg Air Force Base, which is not far from here. Using the Chinese space station, where the upper end would be attached, we'd be able to position the space elevator very precisely."

"Seems like a good plan."

"I was hoping you'd say that. And... I was also hoping you'd go along as one of its passengers."

Maribel laughed, but couldn't completely hide her fear. "Nice try," she said, "but I promised myself I'd never agree to fly into space again."

"I know the story."

"And I'm determined to keep that promise."

"Then you'll be reassured that we don't intend to cross the 100-kilometer-high Karman line. You won't need to fly into space at all. We'll be maybe 10, at most 15 kilometers high."

"Why do you want *me* on board? I'm sure you have plenty of other capable scientists."

"We have the unique chance to get you closer to this thing

than anyone else in the world. It's completely new physics. That doesn't interest you at all?"

"Of course it does. It's incredibly exciting. And, I've brought along the draft of a paper from our institute for you. But I made a promise to my family. Which includes me."

"And you won't be breaking your promise. And I bet your daughter would be excited for you to go along. She seems very smart to me."

"I could have died! And I didn't have a family yet, there wasn't any extra drama or distraction. Now I have responsibilities and people who depend on me."

"Yes, but you also have responsibilities to science, and to the world too. Don't you think the world's top scientist should be studying this problem up close, not watching from a distance? I've even convinced your old mentor."

"George Crewmaster? He's agreed to go?"

"He says you've forgotten him. It wouldn't be hard to get him to go. He still works at USC, right around the corner. It's not far at all."

"I... I did want to go see him, after this work was all done."

That was not true; the thought hadn't even crossed her mind. She had neglected to stay in touch with Crewmaster.

She had him to thank for who she was today, and what she had accomplished. Without his help, she could never have compiled all the data she had needed in 2072. At that time, she'd known he was a professor at the University of Southern California, but she didn't know he'd stayed there. He could have retired a long time ago, but true to his name, Crewmaster, he'd probably never stop working.

"So we'll assume he's going. No scientist would pass up the opportunity to get so close to such a fascinating phenomenon. That's what he told me."

"Okay, Glen Sparrow, I get it. But why me?"

"Isn't it obvious? My only chance to get this project going is if I have prominent supporters."

"So you don't even have official approval yet?"

"I'm positive I'll get it tomorrow morning now that you're on board too. Who could say 'no' to the hero of '72?"

"Very funny, Glen. But I still haven't said yes."

"I can see it in your eyes. You were convinced as soon as I mentioned George Crewmaster."

He was right. If George was going, she couldn't say no. She owed that much to her mentor. The only remaining question was, how could she break it to her family? Luisa wouldn't have any problem with it, but Chen had already had to endure one time when he believed she was dead, back then, 13 years ago. She knew the trauma lingered.

"Maybe I'm in," she said. *If I can dare to break the news to Chen,* she thought. "But don't kid yourself. If I go, I'll be doing it for George."

"All I care about is you saying, 'Yes.' I don't care why."

Maribel stood up. She walked to the desk and looked at the model of the space elevator. It looked so safe. But that was probably because it wasn't to scale. She herself wouldn't be any bigger than a speck of dust in this model. They would be like ants climbing a skyscraper.

"Glen? Show me all your plans. I want to know everything... The design of the cable, the time schedule, the resources and personnel needed, what instruments we can bring with us, what you already have available, what we're going to need to get... Everything."

"Of course," Glen said. He transformed the desk into a screen and began to show her one document after another.

SHE WALKED INTO HER HOTEL ROOM SHORTLY BEFORE midnight. Chen was sleeping, sitting on the couch. He was still wearing his clothes. He'd probably nodded off while waiting for her. She woke him gently.

He put a finger to his mouth and whispered, "Luisa's sleeping in the bedroom."

She nodded.

"So, how was it?" he asked softly.

"Sparrow showed me his plans for a 'space elevator.' He wants to use it to study the rift. With me on board."

"You agreed to go?"

"No, Chen, not yet. I had to ask you first whether it would be okay."

"Yes, of course. It's obvious that this is especially important to you. And for all of us, really."

Relief spread through her body. At the same time, she felt as if she was going to cry. "Is it really okay with you?" she asked.

"Yes, it is." Chen reached his arms toward her and she collapsed onto his lap.

She wrapped her arms around her husband as his arms embraced her.

May 27, 2085, Ceres

M6 APPROACHED THE CLEFT CAREFULLY. THE SCIENTISTS ON Earth had been very satisfied with his examination of the white spots. Now they had sent him to the edge of the crater. On images from space, they had detected rockslides there, where the crater walls had collapsed. Due to the low gravity on the dwarf planet, and the lack of an atmosphere, his bosses were wondering why the rocks had collapsed. Such rockslides hadn't occurred on other celestial bodies in the asteroid belt.

Technically, that wouldn't be a problem, but he would rather spend his time working on the mystery of the cleft. And that presented him with a conflict of loyalty. He was allowed to make his own decisions, it was true, but his reward system had been programmed so that he would become unhappy if he didn't fulfill his bosses' wishes. The longer he ignored them, the more unhappy he would become. He could compensate for that effect for a while, because he could also gain happiness by completing the tasks he set himself, but at some point, the programmed unhappiness would take over. Then it would become increasingly more stressful to ignore the assigned tasks from Earth.

The programming was definitely annoying, but he also had to admire it. His builders had very elegantly solved the problem of unifying the characteristics of independence and loyalty. He couldn't have solved it any better himself. In addition, he found his work here to generally be fun. He was a rather lucky machine. Sometimes M6 imagined what it might be like if he had been deployed as a robot in a factory on Earth. *The same task, day in and day out, how terrible that would be! Things really are good here on Ceres, in this remote location.*

How long will it take to cover the distance to the rockslides at the edge of the crater? M6 estimated the time he had available. He still had at least two days before his unhappiness would become a problem. Then his programming would give him more incentive to complete that task, and he would then do it. Gladly. It would be just like receiving a special treat at the end of some long, tedious job, he told himself.

The cleft had not changed in size or position. That alone was already some kind of major aberration, if you thought about it, because it meant that the cleft must be rotating with Ceres and also orbiting the sun. M6 remembered the image of the torn paper that had popped into his mind shortly after he discovered the cleft. Maybe the image wasn't wrong at all. The space-time continuum was spanned by four dimensions: three spatial dimensions and one time dimension. If the cleft was timeless, that is, only fixed to the spatial dimensions, wouldn't that mean that it wouldn't have the ability to change over time? It would then be invariable until the end of time, a relic whose origin people would have forgotten in a thousand or a hundred thousand years, but it would still be present—as long as nobody closed it.

M6 crawled a little closer. He lifted one of his spider legs until it was only a few millimeters from the cleft. Then he stopped. Should he try to put it in the cleft? He could always manufacture a new leg. That would further delay his work, but it would be an interesting experiment.

He decided against it. Instead, he picked up a rock from

the ground with the same leg and threw it without hesitation into the cleft. He watched the rock move as if in slow motion. The rock turned over several times. Then it touched the blackness and...

M6 PAUSED. HIS LEG WAS VERY CLOSE TO THE CLEFT. No, he'd better not move his leg into the cleft. First he'd try throwing a rock into it. He picked up a rock and looked at it. The material had white speckles, probably water ice. Should he measure it with his spectrometer? No, there were plenty of other rocks around here. With a push, he sent the rock into the cleft and...

NOT A GOOD IDEA, HE DECIDED. IF HE MOVED HIS LEG INTO the cleft and lost it for some reason, he would lose research time unnecessarily. But a rock would work just as well! He reached for a rock, lifted one up, tossed it into the cleft and...

M6 STOPPED HIS LEG EXACTLY 50 MICROMETERS IN FRONT OF the cleft. Maybe it was still too early to risk parts of his own body? Maybe he should use some other object first? There were definitely enough rocks around here. He imagined the rock disappearing into the cleft and appearing again somewhere else. But where? He'd never find out if he didn't try. M6 reached for a rock that was unusually dark, almost as if it had a volcanic origin. He gave it a precisely calculated push and it sailed on a parabolic path into the cleft until it...

M6...

The rock...
How would the cleft react if he...?

THIS WAS CRAZY. HE SHOULDN'T RISK HIS LEG, AT LEAST, NOT yet. It had taken quite a long time to manufacture his two new legs. A rock should be adequate for testing the cleft's reaction to foreign objects. There must be plenty of rocks around here.

M6 looked around and was surprised. The area all around him was unusually smooth and bare. There wasn't a single large rock within the reach of his six legs. His experiment had failed before it had even started. But why?

M6 scanned the area farther around him. The dust layer was the same thickness everywhere. Every square meter had, on average, three rocks with a diameter greater than one centimeter within it. With his legs he could reach an area of approximately nine square meters, but there wasn't a single rock of that size within that area. What was the probability of that? Why were there no rocks larger than one centimeter within the area centered precisely around him?

Cause and effect, the basic physical principle. The effect was clear: nine square meters of Ceres surface that was completely free from larger rocks. But what was the cause? The obvious explanation was himself, even if he didn't know the exact reasons why yet. He, M6, must be the reason that the area around him had been cleared.

Of course, he could also imagine other theories. For example, a space probe might have landed in this exact spot at some point in time and blown away all of the rocks. Except that the clear area wasn't round, which would be the logical shape if a probe had landed here, but instead it was oval, which also matched, almost exactly, the area that he could reach. The theory of a space probe landing also contradicted the principle of Occam's razor: the simplest theory is the most preferred.

There was only one problem: the theory that he was responsible for the clear area was also not so simple. Because —in other words, if he was the 'guilty party'—then he should have some memory of how the area was cleared. But he had no such memory. M6 analyzed his memory contents. Even if something had been erased, he should still be able to find some trace of the erased memories or the erase command. But there was nothing. His memory was clean. The memories that he had were complete and intact. He had crawled close to the cleft, lifted a leg, changed his mind, and instead looked for a rock. Only there were none.

M6 activated his laser scanner. With it, he could detect very fine patterns in the dust. He scanned the entire area around him. For comparison, he analyzed an area of similar size in a location farther away from the cleft. The results were as clear as they were fascinating: the depth of the dust layer had a significantly higher variation in the area where he was standing than in the area farther away. He also thought of an explanation: where there was less dust, there might have previously been rocks. And it must not have been that long ago that they were here, because the variation would have already evened out.

Could a theory be developed just from these observations? He was sure that none of this would have happened if the cleft weren't directly in front of him. If he assumed that about ten rocks had disappeared from here, and he had done it, then the most obvious solution was that the cleft acted like some sort of sink for matter, and that he had somehow put the pieces of rock in there. Was the cleft a sink—the opposite of a source—and did it thus capture everything that was thrown toward it? Then it would be like a black hole again, but the cleft seemed to be something else entirely.

M6 tried to form a working hypothesis. The cleft was made out of nothing—it was nothingness. Whatever landed in it would be lost for eternity and would promptly be erased from reality. So as not to contradict the principle of cause and effect, and the law regarding the conservation of energy, this deletion process must be very consistent. If a rock disappeared into the cleft, then it never existed in this world. And that would explain why his laser also consumed less energy when he pointed it at the cleft: the photons that entered into the cleft would never have been generated in the laser generator. Therefore, the related energy would never have been consumed.

But what about the differences in density? What would happen if the deletion process triggered by the disappearance of an object into the cleft was, in actuality, strictly consistent? A rock on the surface of Ceres had a billion-year-long history behind it. It was made from protosolar matter, which had clumped together with other protosolar matter, maybe to form an asteroid, that was then destroyed by an impact, and finally the rock had ended up precisely here. The entire time, its mass contributed to the force of gravity exerted by Ceres. It had been part of determining the motion of the entire solar system in tiny, minuscule, but consistent ways.

M6 was reminded of a human-generated concept of a butterfly flapping its wings above the Amazon River and thus sparking a storm over the Atlantic Ocean. Maybe the rock also had such an effect. In particular, the matter that made up the rock had been part of this universe for 13.8 billion years. The rock was, in other forms, once part of an exploding supernova. A consistent deletion action would have to take all these interactions into account, and might thus put the very existence of this universe in question.

M6 ran diagnostics on all his systems. There was no doubt he still existed, so it appeared that the deletion action following the rock's annihilation couldn't be consistent. Maybe it passed through reality like an avalanche, or a wave breaking on a beach. At the beginning it was forceful, but then it lost its staying power and left behind traces in the sand that could be detected with precise observations, like the differences in density in the dust.

It was a beautiful theory he had conceived. His reward center was lighting up, making him proud and happy. If he could continue this, he might be able to ignore the requests from Earth for an extra day. But what use was even the most beautiful theory if it couldn't be confirmed? The cleft was made of nothingness—that was what his evidence seemed to suggest. But he couldn't prove anything yet.

May 28, 2085, Pomona, Kansas

Doctor Akif Atasoy left his apartment. He turned the key in the large lock, then the security lock above it, and finally the additional deadbolt lock at the top. He had three unique keys on his keychain. Akif shrugged. They were indicative of his life. He always played it safe.

It was a way of life that he had become ingrained during his childhood. His family had fled Turkey for the United States before the war. To the land of the enemy, of all places! Akif's friends had thought his father was crazy. They had traveled illegally to Syria, which was flourishing at the time, and upon arriving there his father had bought black-market plane tickets to Mexico. From Mexico, the family had continued onward to California by boat. It had been a real miracle.

From an early age, his parents had drilled it into him that he had to behave. As a refugee, the risk of being deported was ever present, and the few Turks who had made it to the States were under constant and heightened surveillance. His father had never told him how he had been able to get them here. Akif suspected that he had probably bent the rules or, perhaps more likely, found blatantly illegal ways to get around proper procedures. Maybe his father had even been involved with the U.S. intelligence agencies.

That was all far behind him now. But the drive to always play it safe had never diminished. He had studied diligently, like his mother always encouraged him to. He had bought a well-run practice in a small city with a low violent-crime rate. His colleagues appreciated him and, more importantly, his patients trusted him.

But then he had done something that could have cost him his career. He had gotten involved with a patient. Mary. Since Derek McMaster had visited him yesterday, her name had come back to him. It had been quite a shock, but he had managed to avoid giving himself away. A feeling had washed over him as if he were making a big mistake all over again. Before Derek had walked into his office he had completely forgotten her, just like her husband had forgotten her. Fate seemed especially cruel today. First it had taken away the memory, freed him from his act, and then returned it all to him doubled—her smell, her warmth, her soft touch, her voice, her heart, everything was back again, as if she had left his apartment just shortly before him or maybe was even still lying in his bed.

Of course, he could have remained silent. But that would have felt like betrayal to him. When Mary was still real, he hadn't dared to go out in public with her. If Derek, the cuck-olded husband, had found out and spread the news around, he would've lost his job. In this city, where everybody knew everybody else, a doctor who took advantage of one of his patients wouldn't be welcome anymore.

And now? He had agreed to help Derek with his search. That was the least that he could do for Mary. The man he was helping didn't know his real reason, and Akif didn't see any reason to tell him. It didn't matter anymore. They couldn't undo what had already happened. Still, nobody knew what had appeared above them in the sky or what it meant. Scientists didn't have any clear answers yet. The media was filled with stories about huge increases in people from all walks of life suddenly showing up in churches and other places of worship. Apparently, religion had better answers to offer than science.

He turned around and went down the hall to the elevator. It smelled like dust and medicine. Quite a few older people lived in his building. He had begun to feel old himself—until Mary came into his life. She had been unhappy. She felt like her husband didn't understand her, and Akif had immediately fallen in love with her. He had felt bad for Gita. His receptionist worshipped him. He had often encouraged her to do more with her talents and skills, but she wanted to stay at her job to be close to him.

Upon reaching the ground floor he finally escaped the retirement-home smell. The entrance was wide open, and sunlight was shining in. He and Derek had agreed that he would visit Derek in his house in the country. Pomona was the name of the town. Akif had never heard of it before. It would be a difficult visit, because he would know that Mary had once lived there. Yesterday he had been hoping for something; now he no longer remembered what that 'something' was.

His car opened the door automatically as he approached. He sat down in the driver's seat.

"To Derek McMaster," he said.

The vehicle started moving, whisper-quiet. He turned the seat around. That was when he saw that he wasn't alone.

"Jeez! You scared me," he said. "What are you doing here?"

"I want to help," Gita answered.

"You didn't want to enjoy your day off some other way?" Akif paused. Was it really a good idea to let Gita help? Wouldn't she be disappointed when she found out why he was really helping? He wasn't doing it for Derek.

"I didn't have anything else to do," she said. "And I like helping you."

"I know," Akif said.

"Don't get me wrong, I know full well you're doing this for

Mary," she said. "Maybe sometimes I seem a little naive, but I think I know quite a bit of what's really going on."

He felt his face flush red. "You do...?"

"I do. But it's okay."

"Does this mean that you remember her, too? This person who never existed?"

"Yes, I remember her too. It took me a while. I had such vivid dreams last night that I decided I couldn't *not* help. That's why I got in your car before you came out of your building."

Akif nodded. As his assistant, Gita naturally had access to his car.

DEREK MCMASTER LIVED FAR OUT IN THE COUNTRY. THE autopilot approached the address from the north. The car flashed its lights and rolled to a stop on a gravel road.

"You have reached your destination," the voice of the control system said.

Akif slid his feet into his shoes, black slip-ons that he had taken off during the drive. The car parked itself behind Derek's truck.

"Warning," the automatic voice said. "The autopilot of the vehicle in front of you is not responding. Consultation with the owner is required."

"Acknowledged."

The vehicle's control system had detected that it had blocked the truck. Normally the vehicles could work this out themselves, but the truck's autopilot wasn't responding.

Akif got out and held out his hand to Gita. She thanked him with a smile. He looked at Derek's truck. It was at least 20 years old. It was possible it didn't even have an autopilot. The autopilot law hadn't been enacted until 15 years ago. Or maybe Derek was one of those AI deniers who secretly turned off all automated systems whenever they could. The police usually tolerated them, especially out in the country where you couldn't get into too much trouble.

"Could use some paint," Gita said, looking at the house.

He had to agree. The two-story wooden building, a typical farmhouse for the area, needed fresh paint. And not only that, the windows were dirty and there were weeds growing all over the small, green-fenced garden in front of the house. It looked like the home of a hermit. Mary supposedly lived *here?*

The door opened.

"You're already here," Derek said. His gaze turned to Gita. "Oh, hello, you're here too."

"I wasn't invited. I'm a stowaway," Gita said cheerfully. *Her smile's quite contagious,* Akif thought. Even Derek couldn't dampen her mood.

"Good morning, Mr. McMaster. Before we come in, please call me Akif. And of course you already know Gita."

He held out his hand to the owner of the house. McMaster shook it firmly.

"And call me Derek, both of you, please," he said. "Come on in."

Behind the door there was a dark hallway. Akif, who was the last to enter, wanted to close the door behind himself, but Derek stopped him.

"Don't do that. I mean, please leave it open. Something in the hall here smells really strong."

Akif smelled it now too. Wood preservative, maybe applied too thickly, or maybe it was one not intended for indoor use. A memory appeared in his mind. He saw himself as if in a movie. Derek was standing in front of him and he was asking Derek to check their house for wood preservative on account of Mary's allergies. Akif and Mary had both been surprised when her husband had gone with them into the doctor's office. Derek had never before seemed interested in Mary's illness.

It was a peculiar irony of history that he would be proven

right about the wood preservative coating. And obviously it
had occurred to Derek too.

"Come into the living room," Derek said.

They walked in. The room had a pleasantly old-fashioned
feel. He could almost believe that Mary might have lived here
once, many years ago. But the furniture was dusty, and the
ceiling light had a crack in its glass. Sunlight shimmered into
the room through the windows.

"Have a seat. I made coffee," Derek said.

"Tea for me, please," Gita said.

"No problem. If I'd known you were coming along, I
could've had it all ready."

THEN THEY SAT AROUND THE COFFEE TABLE, SIPPING FROM
their cups in silence. To Akif, the situation made him think
that next Derek would pull out a Ouija board and they would
all hold hands and summon Mary's spirit. They had actually
come here to look for a person, who, according to all the
documents in the world, never existed. There was no Mary
McMaster in his patient records. Anyone who was familiar
with the bureaucracy of dealing with health insurance
companies knew that the non-existence of a patient file in the
computer was synonymous with the non-existence of the
person. Nevertheless, yesterday Akif had asked Gita to search
the deleted memory contents, but she had still not found
anything.

"What now?" Derek asked.

"Maybe we call the police?" Akif suggested.

"Do you *know* the local sheriff?"

Akif nodded. He did—not personally, thank goodness,
but he knew *of* the man—and he knew what Derek meant.
The police here were used to intervening in bar fights or tick-
eting speeding tourists. If he took this problem to the sheriff's
office, they'd just laugh at him.

"Then you make a suggestion," he said.

Akif had started to regret agreeing to come here. It didn't make any sense. He was searching for a past that had never existed. The stolen hours that he had spent with Mary—the universe had taken them back.

"Why did you actually agree to help me, Akif?"

Derek's gaze looked suspicious. Or was it just his own guilty conscience? Should he tell him the truth? He decided instead to lie with at least something close to the truth.

"You looked so sad, Derek, I wanted to do something." Derek *had* looked quite sad, and he really had wanted to do something for him. "Why do you ask?"

"I want to know how far you're willing to go with this."

"What are you thinking?" Akif asked. He looked at Gita. She was holding a hand in front of her mouth.

"Nothing illegal—at least not at first," Derek replied. "But it's probably a little crazy."

"Okay, you've got me interested. Tell me."

"Yes, tell us," Gita said. She relaxed a little.

"I know a junk dealer. He's got a decommissioned New Shepard in his backyard."

"A what? Some kind of aircraft?" Akif asked.

"No, a rocket."

"You're crazy," the doctor said. "Don't you need a whole facility and support crew to launch a rocket? How old is this thing?"

"I happened to talk to the guy three weeks ago. It's an exhibition model that was shown at fairs."

"Okay, but when was it built?"

"Strictly speaking, he's got a booster and a crew capsule."

"The year. What year was it built?"

"2025."

"Derek, it's 60 years old! No wonder it's in the junkyard!"

"You're underestimating the New Shepard. Its design was rather brilliant for the time. The rocket launches itself, then the booster and capsule separate and both land again, independent from each other."

"That doesn't change the rocket's age."

"It's usually dry out here. Things don't rust very quickly."

"So, then what? What about the facilities? Launch pad? Control room? Antennas and all that?"

"The New Shepard doesn't need those things. It's controlled by an onboard computer. Just like a huge, oversized toy."

"Are you a trained pilot?"

"I am. I flew fighter jets. But that doesn't even matter. The computer takes care of everything itself. For years they packed tourists in there and shot them into space for a few minutes... until it was no longer profitable. A pilot would just have been extra, non-paying weight."

"What about fuel?"

"We'd need liquid hydrogen and liquid oxygen. Both are simple enough to get. I've already called a chemical-supplies shop, and they have enough in stock."

"Derek, you're crazy."

"I did warn you."

"Gita, what do you think of this?" Akif asked. "You haven't said anything."

"Um... a trip into space... I've got nothing against it," she said.

Akif was surprised. His Indian receptionist wanted to be an astronaut? He knew that she was capable of being far more than a receptionist, but this?

"But what I'm asking myself is, 'What's the point?' What do you want to achieve with this, Derek?"

"Can't you imagine? I want to see what's inside that thing."

"You mean you want to fly into it?" Akif asked. "But we've already seen what happens."

"No, we haven't at all. The airplane disappeared, at least that's what we remember. But it also didn't disappear; it was never there. Maybe it's not really gone! It couldn't have just vanished into thin air!"

"Are you thinking maybe it landed in some other world?" Gita asked.

"Right. I had the idea last night. Maybe the rift leads to a different universe where everything happens in reverse. Suddenly an airplane appears there in the sky and all at once everyone thinks that it had always been there. The newcomers would be as seamlessly integrated into the new reality as they were erased from ours."

"You want to follow Mary into that world," Akif said, no hint of a question in his tone.

"Maybe, but maybe not. We could also change our minds as we go. The capsule has its own small propulsion system. We could use it to steer into the rift or away from it. Maybe we'd see something when we got close that would change our decision."

"We should at least take a look at this junked rocket," Gita said. "Maybe there's something to this idea."

"I agree," Akif said.

"Then let's finish our drinks and get going."

Akif followed Derek's suggestion. Then he noticed that his bladder was complaining. "Where's the bathroom?" he asked.

"Take a left out of the living room, then it's at the end of the hall. Sorry, but it's a bit messy."

Akif was already expecting that, but it didn't bother him. He stood up, squeezed Gita's shoulder in passing, and left the living room. At the end of the hall, a brass sign of a small boy peeing into a pot hung on the door at eye level. Akif prepared himself for an unpleasant smell and opened the door.

Automatically, a bright ceiling light switched on. The room didn't smell unpleasant at all, just a bit damp. There was a shower, a tub, and a sink. Everything was tolerably clean. There were various pieces of dirty clothing scattered around the floor. Derek must've taken them off before showering and simply left them there on the floor. Akif remembered how Mary had told him about this habit—she had mentioned always having to clean up Derek's things.

He looked around and felt a bit like an intruder. Actually, he was looking for traces of Mary. Maybe the universe had forgotten one of her perfume bottles or an earring that had fallen behind the toilet? How did the universe decide which of a person's objects to erase from reality when that person fell into the rift?

The deodorant, for example, which was standing on the shelf above the sink, was pink and had a bouquet of flowers on its label. It was clearly a woman's deodorant. Akif examined it. There was no dust on it so Derek must use it regularly. Had he done that when Mary was still part of this reality too? Maybe she had bought it for herself? He opened the cap and smelled it. It wasn't the fragrance of her that he remembered. She had smelled so good, everywhere.

You have to stop, he told himself. *You're just unnecessarily torturing yourself.* He lifted the toilet lid. The bottom of the lid had a sign on it directed toward men. He sat down obediently on the toilet seat. Who had put that sign there? If Derek had always lived in this house by himself, why would he put up a 'Sit down to pee!' sign on his toilet?

Maybe because he didn't want urine on the seat? Akif let his bladder drain. He shook his penis and stood up. A drop fell on the seat. He tore off a piece of toilet paper, wiped up the drop, and threw the paper into the toilet. Then he flushed and pulled up his pants.

The other two had apparently been waiting to hear him flush. "We're already outside," they called in unison and then laughed.

When he went outside, he didn't see anyone, but there were sounds coming from his car.

"Just shut the door. No need to lock it," Derek called, "nothing ever happens out here in the country."

He pulled the house door closed and walked over to the others. Gita was sitting in the driver's seat, Derek next to her. Good, then he would just sit in the back.

The car door closed itself.

"Please enter your destination," the automated system said.

Derek dictated the junk dealer's address.

"Estimated driving time: 37 minutes," the voice said.
Akif leaned back.

It took a few more minutes than expected, because the software had led them straight into a small backup on the interstate.

"I told you we should have gotten off at that last exit," Derek commented.

The car's voice apologized profusely. *It had never done that before,* Akif thought. *Maybe it was part of the new update the manufacturer installed yesterday.*

"I'll go in first," Derek said. "I already told the owner we were coming. Just watch what you say. The guy doesn't know what I've got planned for his rocket yet."

"Does he not want to sell it?" Akif asked.

"I haven't asked him yet."

This is starting out really well, Akif thought. This guy was probably a total space nut and would never give up the New Shepard. As a junk dealer, he could have long ago sold it for cash. But if that turned out to be the case, at least then they wouldn't have to decide if they wanted to try to actually ride that piece of junk into space.

"I'll take care of it," Derek said. "Trust me."

A man came toward them where they waited outside the large, wrought-iron gate blocking the entrance. He opened it a half meter, the hinges creaking, and let them onto his property one at a time. Then he extended his oil-smeared right hand. Derek shook his hand first, and then the others did too.

"Hi, Johnny," Derek said. "Thanks for making time for us."

"Yeah, I was just able to squeeze you in between the hordes of tourists," Johnny said, and then laughed loudly.

Akif looked around. He didn't see the rocket anywhere. Maybe the dealer had already sold it?

"You ready to see my baby? Follow me. She's behind the house."

Johnny led them around the house. To the left, Akif saw a mountain of junk. The dealer must have been trying to sort through it all, because nearby he saw a workbench with a pile of beer bottles stacked on top. Farther toward the back he saw a junk press.

"There she is," Johnny said.

He pointed to something that Akif at first thought was a section from an old gas pipeline. It would have been a rather thick gas pipeline. He estimated it to have a diameter of about four meters, its total length 15 meters, give-or-take.

"I'm really excited about this," Derek said. "I'd really like to see it upright."

"That wouldn't be a problem," Johnny said. "Empty, it only weighs a little more than ten tons. If you'll pay for a crane, I can set it up for you."

"Why isn't it being stored upright?" Akif asked.

"Well, maybe you're forgetting the snowstorms in the fall and winter, buddy, and the severe thunderstorms in the spring and summer. If this beauty tipped over, it'd get all dented up, and then it wouldn't be worth as much."

"Ah, okay," Akif said.

"My friend here," Derek said, pointing at him, "is a photographer. And Gita is his beautiful assistant."

What if this didn't work? What if Johnny had seen him sometime before, like in the hospital or someplace?

But the man nodded. "Of course, it's an honor. You came here just because of my beauty here?" he asked.

"My friend Derek told me all about it."

"But you didn't bring your equipment with you?"

The man asked so innocently that Akif felt bad about lying.

Before he could say anything, Derek jumped in. "I knew there were these mountains of junk around it. It wouldn't have made a very pretty picture with that in the background," he said. "We'd like to set it upright in an open space, clean it up properly, and then light it up real well. It'll be in *National Geographic*. And you too, if you want."

Johnny looked happy. Now Akif felt really bad, because he knew what Derek was planning. He would have to talk to him about it afterward. They could still call the whole thing off.

"Well, buddy, I hate to tell you, but you'd have to pay for all that," Johnny said. "I can't afford a 15-ton crane."

"Of course, Johnny. We'd take care of all of it. Maybe we could even slip you a little something for the trouble. What do you think, Roberto?"

Roberto? What was Derek trying to do? Did he want their story to be believable, or did he just not want to use his real name?

"How about 500?" Akif asked.

Johnny beamed. *I'll have to pay the 500 myself, I'm sure*, Akif thought. Derek appeared ready to steal this guy's treasure, but at least this way the man would be 500 dollars richer than before. He wasn't going to sell the rocket anyway, so it was just dead capital, quite unlike five hundred-dollar bills.

May 28, 2085, Pasadena

Glen Sparrow had left Pasadena for the day. He had flown to Houston very early in the morning for some meetings with a few NASA higher-ups. As soon as he was back, he would give her a report on what happened.

Maribel was happy. She could finally take Luisa on their little day trip she had promised. They had their rented car drive them to Santa Monica, where they walked on the beach and visited the pier with its many little gift shops.

Luisa was not impressed. "Can't we go see the spaceships?" she asked.

"I'm sorry, but there aren't any here that they let kids see," Maribel said.

"We'd have to go to Florida for that," Chen said.

"Then let's go to Florida!"

"It's too far away, Luisa, we'd have to sit in the car for more than an entire day just to get there. You wouldn't like that," Maribel explained.

"No, I wouldn't." Luisa looked at the ground and scratched in the sand with her feet.

"I've got an idea," Chen said. "There's a place, a hill, where you can see the rockets at Vandenberg."

"How do you know that?" Maribel asked.

"I went there once when I was a boy. But I don't know if

it's still there, and I don't know if I'd be able to find it. Luisa, we'd have to drive for almost three hours, is that okay? And if I'm wrong, we might not see anything at all."

"That's okay, Daddy. Let's try," Luisa said.

"You're crazy," Maribel said to Chen after they'd been driving for an hour and Luisa had fallen asleep in the back seat.

"No more than you."

"Maybe she'll be an astronaut," Maribel said, pointing to the back.

"Yeah, maybe. Or a chef. Doesn't matter to me."

"True. The main thing is that she's happy."

"So, you've thought through this thing with the space elevator?"

"Yes, Chen, the concept makes sense. It was canceled purely because of money. Glen's supposed to clear all that up today."

As if Glen had heard her talking about him, her cellphone rang. It was Glen.

"I only have a couple of seconds," he said. "I got the money, and George Crewmaster has also agreed to think about it, as long as you're going. He told me to tell you 'hi.'"

"What? You told me George had already said yes!"

"He said he would consider it."

"Well, my daughter's sleeping in the back, but watch out in the office tomorrow."

"See you." He hung up.

"That asshole lied to me," she said angrily, but as quietly as she could manage.

"Oldest trick in the book," Chen said. "Now he owes you. And you were going to go anyway, weren't you?"

Maribel nodded, even though she didn't want to admit it. Sometimes Chen knew her better than she did herself. Or was willing to admit to herself.

Early in the afternoon, Chen woke her.

"We're almost there."

They were driving on Old Highway 1. Maribel noticed at once that they were driving in the wrong direction, because the sun was on the opposite side of the car.

"Have we turned around?"

"The entrance was on the left, so we couldn't turn there from the other direction." He pointed to the signs in the middle of the four-lane road. "There, see the sign?"

"The Eagle's Nest," Maribel read out loud. "What's that?"

"That's where we're going. It's the lookout point. I wasn't wrong. Hopefully we'll have some luck and the gate will be open."

"I hope so, because otherwise we would've driven three hours for nothing."

"No, if it's closed, I think we'll just have to walk a ways. If it's open, we can take the car."

The gate was open. Chen braked sharply and then drove onto the paved, one-lane road that turned into a gravel road after 20 meters.

"It looks just like it did before. Nothing's changed at all."

"Good for us, huh?"

Chen nodded.

"Luisa, we're almost there," Maribel woke her daughter. She was immediately wide awake. *I wish people didn't lose that skill when they grew up,* she thought.

"Where is it?" asked Maribel.

"Only a few more meters," Chen said.

He steered the car to the end of the dirt road. It ended at a large, treeless area, about as big as two football fields. On the right edge there was a mobile home that appeared to be abandoned. Chen got out of the car, and Maribel followed his lead, opening the back door for Luisa.

"Come on, we need to go a little farther," Chen said.

They followed him. The soil had been torn up by giant tires, as if someone had practiced driving a tractor around there. Then they were at the top of a hill, maybe 150 meters above the surrounding area. Below them was a green valley that a narrow river had dug out. Behind that were a few short buildings. And then finally, behind the buildings, they saw what they had driven here for. There stood two white, slender, elegant towers of steel that extended high into the air.

Luisa was mesmerized. They were the first rockets that she'd ever seen with her own eyes.

"Will I be able to fly on one of those too?" she asked.

"Sure, but only when you're a little older," Chen said.

"What's it like when they take off?"

"First, you see a cloud underneath, then there's a flame, and, at the same time, you feel a rumbling that passes through your whole body. You can hear it even when you hold your hands over your ears. Then they rise up into the air and get smaller and smaller, and then they're gone. It doesn't last long at all, but it feels like an eternity."

"That sounds sooo cool, Daddy! I want to see one take off."

"I don't know if there'll be a launch while we're here," Chen said. "But I'll look into it."

"What about Mommy's rocket launch?"

"Who told you about that?" Chen asked.

"No one, but that's why we're here, right? Mommy's always doing things like that!"

Chen laughed. "That's true. But this time she's just going to take an elevator."

May 28, 2085, Ceres

M6 HAD A PLAN, AND HIS NANOFABRICATORS WERE GOING TO help him. He would build a ramp and a platform that would bring him up to the same level as the cleft. At some point, he was pretty sure, he would have to go into the cleft himself. That would be the only way, he thought, that he could confirm his theory.

For him to enter the cleft cleanly and comfortably, however, he would need the platform. It didn't matter where the cleft led him, but he would rather get there with all his body parts. Maybe he would need some of his physical capabilities wherever he ended up. Or maybe he would fall into nothingness. If that outcome—out of all the possibilities— proved accurate, at least building the platform would give him a little more time before meeting such a fate. M6 had to admit that he would really rather not disappear into nothingness. That was probably the way his reward center was programmed.

His reward center had been staying surprisingly quiet, even though the examination of the rockslide at the crater walls was overdue. The cleft was a fascinating phenomenon, and he was using almost his entire computing capacity in his attempt to form a theory from his measurements of the cleft. His analysis became difficult as soon as he tried to take cause-

and-effect into account. And what mechanism weakened the cleft's deletion process so that the process stopped rather quickly and didn't lead to much more serious consequences? For that, M6 had been considering quantum theory. It wasn't unusual in quantum theory, for example, that the effect happened before the cause, or that things appeared out of nothing and then disappeared again. However, that always happened at extremely tiny scales and dimensions. As soon as he tried to transfer quantum theory to a larger scale, contradictions developed. Researchers had even proved that these contradictions were necessary. Quantum physics seemed destined to always remain limited to the world of exceedingly small things.

The contradictory findings formed one of his reasons to think that the cleft was something completely different. The cleft could be a phenomenon that could be understood only by uniting quantum physics and the theory of general relativity, the holy grail of physics. And right now, he was closer to this thing than any human being!

Shouldn't he transmit a report on his findings? M6 was uncertain. He was sure his tasks would be taken away from him if it became known what he was doing. Humans would come, many humans, and they would examine the cleft and make all these fascinating discoveries that would otherwise be his alone.

No, it wasn't a good idea right now. He would continue building his platform and use the time while he was working to try to really understand quantum physics—something that humans hadn't yet accomplished.

May 29, 2085, Pomona, Kansas

"A BIT MORE," DEREK SAID, DIRECTING THE CRANE OPERATOR.

Centimeter by centimeter the rocket approached vertical. Finally, he was satisfied with its position. He slowly walked around the New Shepard. The side where it had been lying on the damp soil showed a few spots of corrosion.

From behind he heard loud sparking noises. That must be Johnny, who was joining pairs of ladders together using some welding equipment. Somehow, they had to get to the top of the rocket. The entrance into the capsule was at a height of approximately 12 meters. Since they didn't have a launch tower, they would have to use a long ladder. Akif had given Johnny two more hundred-dollar bills in exchange for his help today. The junk dealer had, unsurprisingly, proven to be handy with tools.

Around 3 o'clock in the afternoon at the latest, however, they would need to get rid of him, because that's when the two tanker trucks were coming to fill the fuel tanks with liquid hydrogen and oxygen. Derek had promised each of them an extra hundred so that the drivers and sellers would keep quiet and not tell anyone else about these purchases.

It was Akif's money, but he hadn't seemed fazed by Derek's promises. Either it didn't matter to him because he had so much money, or this was really that important to him.

Derek preferred to believe the former. First, just because of the money, but second, because then he wouldn't have to ask himself about the real reason Akif Atasoy had for choosing to be involved in this plan.

"Stop, that's perfect," Derek called out to the crane operator.

He held up his phone to the rocket's metal outer skin and activated its leveling app. *Very good! He has a pretty good eye,* he thought. Now all he needed was for Akif to say that Derek was missing something important, again. But first they should check out the rocket's computer.

Derek turned around and walked over to Johnny. "How's it coming with the ladder?"

"Looking good. One more piece."

Derek looked over the junk dealer's work. He had welded together five three-meter-long aluminum ladders using a total of eight two-meter-long steel bars. It should work. Would the weight be a problem? Derek estimated the weight for the ladders, totaling around 50 kilos, and the bars, maybe 80 kilos. Together that was 130 kilograms. For a rocket, plus fuel, weighing more than 20 tons, it should be nothing more than a flyspeck that surely wouldn't unbalance the rocket's design.

"When you're done, we'll set it up together," Derek said. "I'll tell the crane operator to wait a little longer so he can lift it into place."

"Good idea, I was a little worried about how we were going to get it set up," Johnny said. He wiped the sweat from his forehead.

"By the way, it's a cool thing you're doing here."

Derek froze. Had he learned somehow that they wanted to launch the rocket? They had told Johnny that they only wanted to clean it up a little inside and out.

"What do you mean?"

"Setting it up and taking pictures. I'm considering leaving this beauty up for a while. I could charge admission for people to see it."

"I don't think that's a good idea," Derek said, frowning. "This is my land it's standing on."

"I'll pay you to use the land. You haven't grown anything in these fields for years."

Derek nodded. "Yeah, that's true." Johnny would be cursing them when he came back in a couple of days and the rocket was gone.

Assuming he got the clamps. Derek looked around for Akif. The doctor was standing next to the rocket and talking with Gita. Both were wearing brand-new worker's overalls. It was a strange sight. Their clothing made them look like they had just come straight from the hardware store. Gita was wearing gloves that were much too large for her.

Derek approached them from behind. They were talking excitedly and probably hadn't even heard him approach.

"... are you sure?" Gita was asking.

Akif shook his head. "Not at all. But life can get pretty boring when you're always sure about everything."

Derek put a hand on a shoulder of each of them. "May I interrupt you two lovebirds?"

"Of course," Akif said, turning red.

"We've got a little bit of a problem."

"Is the fuel going to be late?" Akif asked.

"Shhh, I don't want Johnny to hear anything about that. But no, that's not it."

"Another surprise?"

"No, Akif, it's not a surprise, I just hadn't dared tell you before."

"What is it?" both said as if with one voice. They looked at each other, and then looked at him.

"We need launch clamps."

"What are those?" Akif asked.

"Well... the engine usually needs a few seconds to reach its full power. During this time, the launch clamps hold the rocket on the ground. Maybe you've seen it before. There's smoke and fire under the rocket, but it stays stuck to the ground."

"Yeah, I have noticed that and often wondered about it before," Akif said. "What does this mean for us?"

"We need something like that too."

"Okay. Why didn't you want to tell us this problem before?" Gita said. "Is it not fairly easy to solve?"

"I'm afraid not," Derek replied, then sighed. "The clamps must be anchored in the ground, but they must also disconnect at the right moment, that is, at the push of a button."

"That sounds doable," Gita said. "I used to work for a dentist, and we had something similar to that, the clamps, I mean. I think we could modify the idea to work for this, too. If you want, I can draw up a design."

"I think we could get Johnny to help too," Akif said. "He told me this morning he wanted to use the rocket as a tourist attraction. To do that, we'd have to secure it somehow, against storms and heavy wind, so that it wouldn't fall over."

"He told me that too," Derek said. "You think he'd wonder why they'd need to be detachable by remote control?"

"It'd be a useful feature. Just imagine a tornado was coming this way on short notice. He'd have to lay the rocket down on the ground, maybe even at night," Akif explained. "Of course, it will be gone long before that ever happens."

"I think it'd be best for you to try to sell that to him. You're a doctor, so I think you probably project the most authority out of the three of us."

"We've got a plan, then."

"LADDER'S READY TO GO," JOHNNY SHOUTED.

Derek ran over to the crane and waved his arms at the operator. The man rolled down the window and bit into a donut.

"What's up, boss?"

"We're ready to set up the ladder."

"Okay, on my way."

Derek watched as the man set the donut down on the

dashboard. Then he started the engine. The electric drive gave off a kind of humming noise. The vehicle moved a few meters backward, then the operator swung the arm around toward the waving Johnny.

The junk dealer pulled the hook of the cable down and fastened it to the end of the ladder. Then he gave a thumbs up. The crane operator started retracting the cable. Slowly the ladder lifted into the air. The arm swung in the direction of the rocket and moved the ladder with it. It only bowed very slightly—Johnny had done an admirable job. Derek felt guilty again. Shouldn't they let him in on the plans? And what then, if he said no? The risk was just too great.

The ladder, swinging slightly back and forth, came toward the rocket. Johnny followed it. He signaled to the crane operator that he should lower the ladder a little. Then he selected a spot about two meters in front of the rocket. He pointed at the spot and gave another thumbs up. The crane operator carefully lowered the ladder. Johnny adjusted it so that it was parallel to the rocket. Now the crane operator slowly pivoted the arm to the side until the ladder was leaning against the New Shepard. Johnny shook the ladder. It appeared to be stable.

Gita got ready. Out of the three of them, she was the lightest—obviously—and the most computer savvy, so she was the one assigned to climb up into the capsule and check out the computer.

Suddenly Derek felt as if they had forgotten something. "What if the capsule's locked?" he asked.

"Why would anyone put a lock on a space capsule? And if they did, it'd have to be locked from the inside," Akif said. "Right?"

The doctor was right. Derek nodded and tried to calm down again. Gita was already above his head on the ladder. She carefully climbed up one step at a time. *Not bad, the way she's doing it,* he had to admit. He hoped that Akif was just as comfortable with heights. Because for the launch, all three of them would have to navigate the 15-meter ladder.

"I'm there," Gita reported from above. "Now I'm opening the hatch."

Derek looked up at her, but couldn't make out anything in detail. "You need help?" he asked.

"Thanks, I've got it."

He watched as the hatch swung out to the side. Gita disappeared, first her upper body, and then all of her, into the rocket.

"How does it look?" Akif asked.

"It's very musty smelling. Must not have been aired out in a long time. But the equipment looks unused."

Johnny had said that this specimen had been moved around to different fairs and conventions.

"The cushions are really hard. We'll need to get something soft to sit on," Gita said.

"Noted," Derek said. He threw a sideways glance at Johnny, but he didn't appear to suspect anything.

"Apart from the six seats, there's no other equipment," Gita said, "except for the computer, of course."

"Have you got it running?" Derek asked.

"It looks undamaged. But whether it works or not I can only say after I turn on... and for that I need power."

Of course. On the launch pad, the rocket would normally be supplied with power from an external source. Batteries provided the power during the relatively short flight time. They needed a generator. Derek still had one in his garage. Storms often knocked out the power grid in this area.

"I'll take care of that," Derek called up to her. "Did you hear, Johnny? Maybe we'll even get the computer back online. That would help attract the tourists."

Johnny nodded, lost in thought.

"Good. Until then I'm going to come back down," Gita said.

Suddenly, Derek had a thought and he stopped short. He was so unbelievably naive! *A rocket's not a truck! A rocket's tanks stay leak-tight only when they're properly cooled, and for that they need power. The fuel suppliers need to come tomorrow at the earliest, or better the day after tomorrow, right before the launch.* He turned toward his truck as he reached for his phone to call the suppliers.

DEREK SAT IN HIS TRUCK, SATISFIED. HE LEANED BACK. THEIR plan was coming along nicely. So far they had been able to solve every problem that had come up. Akif had explained to Johnny the reasoning for the clamps. Gita had drawn up a design, and then she and Akif had driven to the closest Home Depot to buy the parts. Derek had loaded his generator onto his truck. Tomorrow they would meet again. And then there would only be 24 hours until the launch. And maybe—with a whole lot of luck—maybe he'd be reunited with Mary.

May 29, 2085, Pasadena

"You lied to me, Glen, that's how I feel," Maribel said.

She had declined the seat Glen Sparrow had offered her, and paced back and forth in his office.

"Yes, Ms. Pedreira, you're right, I shouldn't have done that, but consider my position... if you weren't with me on this, the whole project would be on the verge of disappearing."

"Yes, I know that now. You used me, and I'm really upset about it. You don't care at all about studying the rift, just your space elevator project. You wanted to use me to get your project done. Crewmaster and me? We're just puppets to you."

She'd done a little research yesterday. During his entire career at JPL, Glen Sparrow's number one priority had always been the space elevator. When the project was suddenly stopped, he'd seen his life's work vanish. The circumstances around the cancellation of the project had been rather strange. Nothing could be proven, but many of his colleagues talked about a certain private company that feared for its business model and its profits from rocket launches, having been given an inordinate amount of say in the final decision. Could she really blame Sparrow for grasping at every possible straw?

"You're right. I'm guilty," Sparrow said. He sat, slouched over his desk, drawing figures on it with his index finger.

"Well, I'm already here," Maribel said, with a somewhat conciliatory tone in her voice. "You might as well show me your schedule."

Glen looked up. She noted that his expressions of remorse seemed only to have been an act, but she was over all of that now. She wanted to get up there and study the rift, and she didn't care what the reasons were for getting her there.

"Good," Sparrow said. "Basically, everything's in place and ready to go."

"Even the counterweight?"

The heaviest possible counterweight was needed somewhere out in space to keep the cable, the most critical component of the elevator, under tension.

"For years, the RB Group has had an asteroid in orbit around Earth. That's where they test their mining equipment. We have a license with them to anchor the cable to that asteroid."

"How much did that cost?"

"Only a couple favors. You don't want to know the details."

Maribel considered asking for the details anyway but decided against it. The Russians were well connected, everyone knew that, and they always seemed to be involved somehow in anything you tried to do, wherever you went.

"And when is the cable supposed to be installed?" she asked instead.

"There's a supply ship for the Tiangong-5 international module ready to launch at Vandenberg. It could roll out the cable. They're just waiting for my okay."

"But that wouldn't reach the whole way."

"Right. Then we'd have to get it from the space station to the Russian asteroid and anchor it there. If everything goes well, that could be two days after the launch of the supply ship."

"That's three days, then," Maribel counted.

"Plus another two for repositioning the space station. We'd want the cable to pass as close as possible to the rift," Glen said.

"And the Chinese are working with us on all of this?"

"Yes, they're acting very friendly, at least in this project."

Glen laughed in a forced manner. He didn't care what their motives were for helping him. *One hand washes the other.* That was how politics had always worked.

"Okay, I won't ask anymore," Maribel said.

"And they certainly have nothing against us sharing our findings with all the partners in this little project," Glen said.

Aha, maybe that's it. Their Chinese friends feared being left behind in terms of the science. The rift was a phenomenon that definitely seemed promising in terms of new discoveries. If they studied the rift and didn't find the long-sought-after new physics unifying gravity and quantum effects, then Maribel had no idea where else they should look.

"Of course. Why wouldn't we share our findings with the whole world?" she asked.

And, of course, she thought, her IAC would be the primary authors of the many scientific articles that would surely come from their observations.

"Good, then we're agreed. What do you say we take a closer look at the elevator car? We're calling it the 'Lifter,' by the way. But, it's a two-hour drive from here."

"No problem, I don't have any other plans for today."

Wistfully, Maribel thought of Chen and Luisa. Her husband and daughter had most certainly arrived at the science museum by now, their goal for this morning. She hoped she would have just as much fun with the Lifter.

AN ALARM WENT OFF. SPARROW MUST HAVE SET IT AFTER THEY had agreed to use the travel time for some beauty sleep. Maribel looked out the window and saw a sign with the name

'Lompoc.' She knew the town name already. She had also seen it yesterday. They must be nearing Vandenberg.

"Look in the compartment in front of you," Sparrow said.

She opened a plastic flap. Behind it was a folder. She took it out and opened it.

"That's your badge," her companion said. "You'll have to show it at the entrance. Even with that, though, you won't be allowed to be anywhere on the base without me."

Maribel read her name on the card encased in transparent plastic. 'Only valid if accompanied by authorized personnel,' was written below her name.

"What if they pick me up somewhere without you?"

"Then you'll be arrested, I'm sure. The military doesn't put up with any funny stuff."

They were approaching a wide entrance with a barrier. A granite block told her where they were. Maribel could just barely make out 'Space Command' as they quickly sped by. The barrier opened. Nobody seemed to want to check their IDs.

"They don't appear to be very strict today."

"The officer at the gate already knows me," Sparrow said. "But there are around 3,000 soldiers stationed here, and I only know a small fraction of them. Civilians really stand out here, especially anyone with a white badge, or no badge at all."

The base seemed enormous to her. There were only a few people on foot—most of the people were using vehicles. After their car had made a few turns, they approached a box-shaped, white-painted building with the blue NASA logo.

"The Lifter's in there," Glen said.

The car drove around the building.

"Entrance 3C," Glen said.

"The auto-pilot will do the rest," he explained. "It communicates with the building, obtains the necessary authorizations, and opens the gate. Watch."

The car drove toward the back wall of the building, without slowing down. Right before it was going to crash against the wall, a roll-up gate opened up, lightning-quick, right in front of them. The car passed through the gate and continued on just as fast as before. And, just as quickly, the gate closed behind them.

"We can change the atmosphere in this building," Sparrow explained. "That way we can simulate the conditions on other celestial bodies. And that's also why we have such quick entrances and exits."

"And, why there aren't any windows?" Maribel asked.

"Yes. That would be inefficient."

The inside was illuminated by neutral, white light.

"We can also simulate the lighting on Mars, for example, or on an asteroid."

Sparrow gave a command, and suddenly it looked like twilight. "Look over there, to the left."

Maribel's gaze followed his arm. A lonesome, white sun illuminated the red-gray scenery. "Not bad," she said.

"The perfect testing grounds for our rover."

"There hasn't been much to test recently, has there?"

"Unfortunately, no. Venus was our last interplanetary destination, at the start of the 80s. The administration wants us to do more basic research."

"Then the rift fits very well with that objective. It's pure physics."

"Yeah, that was one thing, among others, that I used to sell the space elevator to them."

"What else, Glen?"

"Well, you, naturally."

"Don't try to flatter me. I'm immune to that sort of thing."

"Okay. Well, the arguments that no company had a commercial interest in the rift, and that surveys have shown that the population is worried about it, probably helped a little too."

"People are worried, even though it poses no risk of danger?"

"Imminent danger, no, but there's this constant feeling of

a threat lurking in the background. It's causing a measurable economic slump. People don't like to spend money in uncertain times."

"That's understandable."

"True enough. I'm sorry, Maribel. but we'll have to walk the rest of the way."

The car doors opened, and Sparrow climbed out. She followed him. He led her through a series of labyrinth-like halls. Suddenly they came to a clear wall that looked just like glass.

"This is where we tested our Venus glider," Glen said.

"An aquarium? But there's no water on Venus."

"We didn't want the hot, aggressive Venus atmosphere in the whole building, so we built this glass box."

"Ah. I didn't follow that project very closely—at the time, Luisa was still little."

They walked past the glass front. Then they entered a dark hallway that opened into a large space, the inside of a building within the bigger building.

"Here we are," Sparrow said.

The space was about as large as a school gymnasium, but it didn't smell like sweat. Instead, there was a strong smell of oil. Apart from them, there were no people in sight. Maribel had tried to imagine what the space elevator might look like. Naturally her ideas were based on known elevator cars. Maybe a bit more modern looking, she'd thought, and prettier... like those exterior elevators at expensive hotels. But those ideas were nowhere close to reality.

In front of her was a space capsule. It was the typical, conical design. It even had a heat shield underneath.

"You look a little disappointed," her companion said.

"You're not wrong."

"I'm sorry, but there are reasons we made it this way. First, it's much cheaper to reuse known designs as guidelines, even for the prototype that you see here."

"Prototype?"

"The elevator hasn't done any real missions, yet. Surely you realized that!"

Maribel nodded. Of course she had known that, but the reality of it was just settling in. She would be the guinea pig for a technology that had never previously been tested at a large scale.

"You've done tests, though, right?" she asked.

"Of course. With cables up to 500 meters long."

"Ah, then it's all good. There's not a big difference between 500 meters and 500 kilometers."

"That's the right attitude," Glen said, giving her a smile. He walked around the capsule and waved to her. "Come here," he said.

He had opened the hatch and now he was gesturing for her to climb on board. From the inside, the capsule was surprisingly roomy. It was, of course, round. There were six seats along the outside wall. In the center, running from top to bottom through the capsule, stood a cylindrical tube with a diameter of about 12 centimeters.

Sparrow pointed at the tube. "Inside there are the drive system and the cable," he explained.

Maribel started to walk around the tube, trying to see everything at once. "Whoa!" She'd bumped into a transparent wall. "What's this for? Additional stability?"

"No. In an emergency, the capsule must be able to detach from the cable. The cable would be ejected to the outside through this slot."

"And then we'd crash land?"

"Of course not. The capsule can be braked with parachutes and a chemical propulsion system. We'd land very gently on the ground."

"And if the cable tears?"

"That won't happen."

"But what if it did?"

Sparrow hemmed and hawed.

"Actually," he said, "we had wanted to anchor it to a platform out in the ocean. If it tore, the cable would simply fall into the water. But we didn't have time for that. The floating platform, a catamaran, exists only on the drawing board. So, we have to anchor the cable here in Vandenberg. If it falls, only the base will be in harm's way. And maybe Lompoc—unfortunately, the town is very close."

"You've taken the risks into account?"

"The military doesn't have a problem with it. And the cable's not going to tear. We've gone through all the calculations a hundred times."

"I wish I shared your optimism."

"But you do. After all, you've agreed to be onboard."

"If I've understood you correctly, a seat in the capsule would be one of the safest places within a certain radius, if the cable broke, right?"

"That's true too."

Maribel touched the transparent wall. It felt warm; it wasn't glass, in any case. "This slot for the cable looks really narrow," she said.

"Don't worry, the cable definitely fits through there."

"How were you able to make a cable so thin, and yet able to withstand such high tensile forces?"

"Nanofabricators," Glen explained. "They're the whole secret. They basically 'live' inside and all throughout the cable. As soon as they find a weakness or a potential defect at any point, they fix it immediately."

"That technology is from Russia, isn't it?"

"Yes, the RB Group developed it."

"And you also have the license with them to anchor to the asteroid? You're doing RB's development work for them. With this system, they'll be able to bring raw materials from orbit down to Earth much more easily."

"I'm sure that's one motive for the Group. And why not? We'll get our space elevator, and you'll get your scientific findings. That's a fair exchange."

"Sure," Maribel said.

In principle, she had to agree with Sparrow. For a long time, space exploration had been much too expensive for any one country to do alone. She just wished everyone would put their true motives up front for all to see. But she hadn't been much more open herself. A family vacation? Not exactly! The whole time it had been all about getting as close to the rift as possible.

"How about scientific equipment?" she asked.

"I can get you whatever your heart desires. Probably best for me to give you a list. You can then pick out what you need, but it cannot total more than 300 kilograms."

"That should work. Why just 300?"

"The elevator has a carrying capacity of 900 kilograms. That corresponds to six persons, 150 kilograms each. There are only four of us, so 300 is left over."

"150 kilos per passenger?"

"Don't forget the space suits. Every traveler will need one. We might need to fly into space, after all. Also, at an altitude of eight to ten kilometers, it will be rather cold up there if we want to step outside..."

"Okay, got it, even if there are no plans for that at the moment. But why four persons? I thought there were only three?"

"I've invited a journalist."

"Are you crazy? He's only going to get in the way!"

"We need some kind of PR. And what's better than a journalist who is there first hand? At least he won't write any made-up crap."

"Do you already have someone?"

"A Frenchman. Maybe you've heard his name before. He became somewhat well-known when that structure was discovered around the sun."

"Oh, yes. The name is Eigen-something, like Eigenberg or Eigenton or ...?" Maribel said.

"Eigenbrod, Arthur Eigenbrod. I did some extra background checks and he's already been in space, so he's not going to be getting sick all over us in the capsule."

They left the large building on foot.

"It's only about 800 meters," Sparrow said.

"No worries, I'm happy to take a little walk."

They seemed to be walking away from all civilization.

"Anchoring the cable doesn't require any special hardware," Sparrow explained.

When they arrived, Maribel saw what he meant. The grass had been mowed noticeably short inside an area of about ten by ten meters. In the middle, a square concrete block with sides of about three meters peeked out of the ground. There was a steel hook in the center of the block.

"The block extends 30 meters underground. The hook that's embedded in it is almost as long."

"Sounds impressive," Maribel said.

"It's all been calculated thoroughly."

"And how do we raise the cable?"

Sparrow walked a few meters to the side and pointed to several objects that resembled miniature military tanks, each with a metal ring instead of a turret. "These here are temporary cable guides. The cable runs through them over there to the rocket launch pad in front of us."

Maribel looked where he was pointing and saw an elegant, white rocket. It was the same one that she and Luisa had marveled at yesterday.

"When the rocket lifts off, the cable will be unwound at the same time."

"Like casting a fishing line?"

"More or less. Actually, after anchoring the cable, the unwinding mechanism was the second most difficult problem. A rocket doesn't start up smoothly and slowly, and the mechanism must not jam or fail under any circumstances."

"Because that might be dangerous for the rocket?"

"No, but it'd waste a launch. Here at Vandenberg we have only two, maybe three launches a month that we could use to shoot the cable into space."

Maribel thought she had every reason for optimism. It all appeared to her to be very well thought-out. Work on the space elevator had been going on for decades—this wasn't a hastily put-together project fraught with danger. Nevertheless, she still had a bad feeling about something. In the end, humans were always the weakest link, and errors were unavoidable. Maybe she was responsible for the bad feeling herself, since she had broken the promise she had made to her family. The fact that neither Chen nor Luisa had demanded that she keep her word didn't make things any easier.

May 29, 2085, Ceres

Only one more step still separated him from nothingness. M6 stood at the uppermost edge of his platform. He had simulated entering the cleft, multiple times. There was a 99.96 percent likelihood that he would reach the other side undamaged—if there even was something like another side. And in his simulations, 'undamaged' merely meant that his body would pass into the cleft all together, in one piece. Whatever was waiting there in the cleft, M6 could not simulate. He couldn't even make a prediction.

Quantum physics had turned out to be much too complex to really understand it, and anyway, the cleft, as a macroscopic object, might not even follow those laws. Or maybe he just wasn't able to find the right insight to bring him to the proper conclusions? What if the cleft was a kind of visible version of a quantum-physical process, the tunnel-part of the tunneling effect, in a manner of speaking, which can help tiny particles move through forbidden terrain? Human physicists had not yet been successful in transferring their quantum theories to the visible scale. Maybe the cleft held the missing piece to the puzzle?

M6 hesitated. Was it really the correct strategy to entrust himself with the task of exploring the cleft? Or was it simply a path to certain self-annihilation? He had used up all his resources. He wasn't going to obtain any new findings just by waiting around. So, what was keeping him here? It must be the joy of his own existence.

M6 had never believed that he would be susceptible to such human and naive feelings. He knew how his reward center worked. He also knew why he found certain jokes funny: when he heard a story, he automatically formulated an internal prediction for how the story would turn out. If the story then went in a completely different direction, it activated his reward center. The fact that such a simple loop from this primitive programming could produce a survival instinct had truly surprised him.

No, if he simply jumped into the cleft now, his bosses would grow suspicious. He would postpone his possible self-annihilation. First, he would study the rockslides at the edge of the crater, as he had been ordered to do. He could then always come back to the cleft. A tiny part of M6 also hoped that maybe the cleft would disappear back into nothingness by then.

May 30, 2085, Pomona, Kansas

"Man, this is heavy," Derek said.

Huffing and puffing, he dragged the generator from the truck to the rocket. Right in front of the ladder was a folding chair with three thick blankets hanging over its back.

"I told Johnny that the blankets were for decoration," Gita said.

"Why do you need the chair?" Akif asked.

"It's hard to reach the computer from the seats already in the capsule. And I can't kneel for very long. The computer was not designed to be operated by the passengers."

"Can you modify it so we can change the flight path as we go?" Derek asked.

"I don't know, I still haven't been able to start the computer. No power!"

Derek slapped his forehead. "Ah, of course. I'll get the generator going."

"Just a minute, I promised both of you to give you my thoughts about the launch clamps," Gita said.

"And?"

She held out a piece of paper with a drawing on it, showing it to Derek and Akif.

"This doesn't look like a clamp," Akif said.

"You're right. I thought about what forces we need to be concerned about, and actually there aren't that many. At the beginning, the engine only has to overcome the Earth's pull, the weight of the rocket."

"And that means?" the doctor asked.

"We tie the rocket down with a steel cable and anchor the cable in the ground. That will be much easier than a clamp."

"Good idea," Derek said. "We can get cable and ground anchors at the hardware store. We would have had to weld the clamps together ourselves."

"How do we detach the cable at launch?" Akif asked.

"I was thinking we'd use small explosive charges, remote-controlled, that would destroy the cable," Gita said.

"It won't be so easy to get our hands on explosives," Akif said. "Couldn't we just tie the steel cable with knots and then undo them like a shoe?"

Gita laughed. "I can tell you've never held a steel cable in your hands before. You can't tie a steel cable into a knot."

"It seems to me it might not be so smart to use explosives so close to tanks full of liquid oxygen and hydrogen," Derek said.

"We'd only need one charge, and we could bury it with one of the ground anchors," Gita suggested.

"Sounds like a good solution. And I even know where we can get some explosives. I know a guy who operates a quarry," Derek said. "He owes me a few favors. But first you need power, Gita."

He'd already filled the generator's tank with diesel fuel at home. He unwound the cable and plugged it into the rocket's external socket that he'd discovered yesterday. Then he started up the engine. *I hope the power output will be enough*, he thought. He couldn't find anything in the power specifications that told him how much power the rocket needed on the launch pad.

Gita was already climbing up the ladder. He looked up at her. The ladder stretched upward at an almost 90-degree angle to a height of about a four-story building, but the receptionist didn't seem to have any problem with heights. Derek considered whether he should climb up after her. He hadn't yet seen the capsule from the inside, and very soon they would be taking off inside it. But there was still so much to do!

"Akif, could you take care of the cable and anchor? I'll go see my buddy at the quarry," he said.

The doctor nodded.

"Say, aren't your patients wondering where you are?"

"I told the ones with appointments that the office is closed due to a death in the family. They seemed to understand."

IN THE AFTERNOON THEY MET UP AGAIN AT THE NEW Shepard. Akif had bought a steel cable spool that was so heavy it needed two people to move. He'd also bought a huge sledgehammer and impressive hooks that they would have to pound into the ground.

"I hope there's not a layer of rocks right below the surface," he said.

"As a farmer, I can tell you there's no need to worry about that. We'll get the hooks in the ground. I just hope that they'll hold."

Derek was skeptical, but he didn't want to come across as too negative. He had imagined something like an anchor with barbs, even if that would've been more difficult to get into the ground. As it was, it looked to him like a tent set-up, with rope and pegs. *And tents like to fly away in storms.* On the other hand, as soon as the engine produced enough power to lift the rocket and the steel cable off the ground, the cable would no longer be needed for holding it in place. It only had to bridge the few seconds until the engine got to full-output power.

They began working. After a half hour, Johnny came over to them. "I wanted to see how you all were getting along," he said.

With his help, they completed the work much more

quickly. Johnny was very satisfied. "Now not even a storm can harm my beauty," he said.

Derek's guilty conscience immediately returned. He would have to bury the small block of explosive later. His buddy, the quarry owner, wanted to know what his plans were for the explosive, and wouldn't give him any until Derek told him. Derek had said something about using it on the giant tree stump in his garden that he had complained about before, and that nothing else had worked so far to get it out of the ground.

Then Gita came clambering down the ladder.

"Everything okay?" Derek asked.

She sat on the ground and leaned back against the rocket. "It's quite a piece of work," she said. "The operating system is 70 years old, and development on it probably stopped 40 years ago. Luckily, I found all the last updates in an archive online."

"So, can we control it by ourselves now?"

"To a certain extent, yes. But don't think you're going to be able to fly it like one of your Air Force planes, Derek."

"What do you mean?"

"Imagine you're an ant sitting on a balloon. And the only way to control it is by opening and closing the hole at the bottom."

"Sounds fun," Derek said.

"I think I'd rather leave that kind of fun to you," Akif said.

"That was a little simplistic. There are thrusters you can use to change the direction somewhat. But this won't be anything like stunt flying. It's designed to go up and then come back down again."

"Talking about coming down, were you able to check the parachute?"

"The diagnostics system says that it's there. But whether the material has any weak points after such a long time..."

"The capsule has backup parachutes. That should be enough," Derek said.

He wasn't even sure if he really wanted to come back anyway. He felt as though the rift was calling him, but the others certainly wouldn't agree to just flying off into nothingness.

THE FLOORBOARDS CREAKED. WAS SOMEONE THERE? DEREK opened the living room door and peered into the hallway, listening for sounds in the darkness. Was that someone breathing? And this perfume that he could smell—he felt like he knew it from somewhere. He switched on the light, but he had just been imagining it all. There was no one. He was alone. That was already the third time in the last hour. Maybe he needed to be more concerned about his mental health?

Maybe all of this was just a crazy idea, born from pure imagination and the result of too much loneliness. Akif, at least, seemed to have almost as much motivation as his own, and his receptionist just wanted to spend more time with her great love. An unemployed farmer, a Turkish doctor in exile, and an IT expert with Indian roots and stuck in a provincial life—they really were quite a group of losers.

And he thought the three of them, of all people, would be able to solve a problem that experts all over the world hadn't been able to figure out yet? Derek laughed. That alone was evidence that he belonged locked away somewhere in a mental institution.

On the other hand, surely they were three harmless kooks. It wasn't going to harm anyone if they simply tried to do something themselves. Didn't all Americans have the God-given right to take their fate into their own hands? Johnny had been compensated for the future loss of his property, and after the launch, he hoped no one other than themselves would be put in any sort of danger.

What did he actually want? Derek was still not entirely sure. He would decide tomorrow morning. For now, he would go to bed. They wanted to launch before sunrise. He had talked the fuel suppliers into sending their trucks with the fuel around five in the morning. The drivers, who usually delivered to gas stations, were used to working very early in the morning. And when Johnny came looking for them, they would already be long gone.

May 30, 2085, Pasadena

"GOOD MORNING, JEAN-PIERRE."

"You mean, good evening, Maribel, the sun's already set over here."

"Oh, so you're working overtime just for me?"

Her colleague had already tried to contact her three hours earlier. She had heard the video call notification, but had decided not to respond to it so early in the morning.

"No worries. I'm still not done working for the day."

"Did you receive my corrections?" Maribel asked. "I sent you the draft of the paper yesterday."

"Yes, it's already been sent to a reviewer. The editor asked me to send it straight to Hawaii."

"So, hopefully, you'll have a first opinion when you get to the observatory tomorrow."

Jean-Pierre looked at her coolly, but she could tell he was tense about something. The paper was definitely explosive, at least for the world of physics. As the primary author, it could make his name known worldwide, an important step toward being awarded one of the big prizes in science at some point.

"I hope so too. But that's not why I was calling you," her colleague said. "But if you have anything new to report, I'd be happy to hear it."

"Nothing new about the rift. But JPL has been able to

revive a project that had been mothballed due to budgetary concerns."

"The space elevator. I already read about that."

That was fast. In the matter of public relations, there was a lot she could still learn from NASA. Just allowing a journalist to join them on their upcoming mission would be an unprecedented coup.

"I'm excited how close we're actually going to be able to get to the phenomenon," Maribel said. "Any specific equipment or techniques you think we should use on the rift?"

Naturally, she had already thought for a long time on how they could examine the rift, but maybe Jean-Pierre would have some brilliant idea.

"It would be interesting to me to learn exactly how it's separated from its surroundings," he said. "Is there some transition phase, where the properties mix? Or does it really go from 100 to 0, and over what distance?"

"If I were to hazard a guess, I'd say that the transition is going to turn out to be shorter than a Planck length," Maribel said.

A Planck length is the smallest possible length in the universe. Shorter than that and everything blurs into a quantum haze. If the rift consisted of nothingness, it could not mix with reality.

"So, you don't think that we're dealing with something like dark energy here, perhaps even a form of negative energy?" he asked.

"No, Jean-Pierre, I think that we'd have measured something if that were the case. But there's been absolutely nothing from the rift."

"It might be that dark energy interacts with us in some unknown way, and so we miss it with our measurements. Imagine you found a magnet but didn't know anything about magnetism. You'd weigh it and determine its heat conductance and maybe do a spectral analysis, but you'd completely miss its actual special property."

"That's a nice thinking exercise, but it doesn't really help us get any further, because we're limited to our physics. And if something looks like nothing, radiates nothing, and absorbs nothing, just maybe it really *is* nothing."

"Time to bring out Occam's razor."

"Don't be disappointed. If the rift is pure nothingness, that'd be a revolution right there. We've never been able to observe nothingness close up. We've never even imagined that it could exist in its pure form. So even if we understand what it is, that's not going to upset the physics any less."

Jean-Pierre nodded. "I've been thinking that it would be easier for us to incorporate dark energy into our worldview than the concept of nothingness," he said. "We've assumed for a long time that there must be dark energy. But pure nothingness? And we're not just talking about empty space. If the rift had volume, then wouldn't it be something, and thus not nothing anymore?"

"It doesn't look like the rift has volume," Maribel said.

She understood what her colleague was saying. Thinking about nothingness had an almost spiritual quality for her. Nothingness felt like the opposite of creation, its villain— Satan. Or was that just because she had grown up Catholic?

"That's also only one example," Jean-Pierre said. "But it leads to another question. If the rift has no volume, can an object with volume go into it?"

"That's a good question."

"Has anyone tested that?" Jean-Pierre asked. "I mean, it would also be good to know, for example, what would happen if an airplane ran into the rift by accident."

"That hasn't happened yet, to my knowledge, and it also hasn't been tested yet. The JPL man here told me he had plans to perform such a test, but then he couldn't find a suitable weather rocket."

"Seems like it could be done with a military drone too."

"Maybe they've already tested it but didn't want the results leaked to the public. Or maybe their drones are too expensive for such scientific games."

"Who knows?" Jean-Pierre said. "Oh yes, the real reason I

called you..."

Maribel let out a big yawn and excused herself. He looked at her without reaction.

"So, the reason I was calling—it looks like the rift ends on the surface of Ceres. Maybe its source is there somewhere. Do you know if anyone has research equipment on Ceres?"

"I'll find out. Thanks for the tip. Hopefully, I'll talk to you soon with an answer."

"Okay, have a good day. I'm going home now."

The connection ended.

So, THE RIFT LED TO CERES, THE ONLY DWARF PLANET THIS side of Jupiter. There had been many lengthy discussions at the United Nations about whether Ceres should be declared some sort of protected zone or not. It had long been thought that there must be remnants of a frozen ocean under its surface—and thus an area for potential extraterrestrial life. After the surprising discoveries on Enceladus, Titan, and Io, a system-wide protection program had been instituted. But, as a differentiated celestial body, Ceres also offered the possibility of some unknown mineral resources of unimaginable value, which would also be much easier to mine there than on one of the many small asteroids.

Ultimately, the scientists had won out against the mining companies, at least for the first round. Research facilities were allowed to be set up on Ceres, however, and Maribel would have bet that the RB Group was already there. At some point, she was sure, the planetoid would be declared open for business and then the mining companies would quickly turn their research into real mining operations. Maybe the Russians—or someone unknown—had pushed their research there a little too far and somehow created the rift? Maribel didn't really believe in coincidence. For the rift to end on Ceres's surface—and not 100 meters below or above—didn't it have to mean something?

But she shouldn't let herself get so far ahead of herself. The next logical step would be to ask around and find out if anyone had set up research facilities on Ceres and could assist her in researching the rift.

The bedroom's door opened. It was Chen, carrying their daughter in his arms.

"Luisa needs to use the bathroom," he said.

Luisa had her arms wrapped tightly around Chen's shoulders. The time change had messed with Luisa's sleep schedule. Maribel smiled and waved to both of them as they disappeared into the bathroom. After getting out of bed, she had quickly thrown on some clothes so that she was presentable for the video call, but she still hadn't taken a shower. The bathroom in their suite had a large walk-in shower. She and Chen had been looking forward to taking a shower together. Maribel thought about it. That probably wouldn't happen until tonight at the earliest, she decided.

She called Glen Sparrow. He appeared on the screen with a face that looked puffy with sleep. Maribel smiled—he reminded her of a giant baby. Glen must have just woken up. She had probably forced him to get out of bed.

"I'm sorry, Glen. Is today Saturday? I'm all mixed up from the time change."

"No, it's Wednesday, don't worry. I just had a whole lot to do yesterday."

"How's the elevator coming along?"

"Everything's on schedule. We're launching the cable into space today. I think we'll be able to start our first test tomorrow."

"You want us on board tomorrow already?"

"Of course not. First, we'll do an unmanned test. The Chinese are very efficient. You should come, though, and then you can see the space elevator's first lift-off."

"I don't know, I'm sure you've arranged for some sort of circus for the press."

"No, I prohibited that due to the limited amount of time that we have. There will only be the one journalist, the Frenchman, Eigenton or Eigenberg or whatever."

"Eigenbrod. It's Arthur Eigenbrod," she corrected him. "At least that's what you told me earlier."

"Yeah, I guess I did. It'd be good if you met him, since he'll be joining us on the mission."

"Actually, that might be very useful. That'll give me the chance to explain everything to him, so he doesn't go writing any unscientific nonsense."

"He's not that kind of writer. My bosses have been very pleased with him. He's the one who broke the story about the sun."

Maribel remembered that structure around the sun, which was still not definitively understood. Eigenbrod could prove to be an interesting 'teammate.' The Ceres rift didn't directly impact the sun, but perhaps this construct around their star had something to do with the rift after all? Both phenomena shared the fact that they involved unknown physics. But that didn't mean that they were related, of course.

"That's very interesting, Glen. I might have more questions for him than he has for me."

She could imagine how Eigenbrod would open his new story. A successful woman as a protagonist always sells better than an older, baldheaded man, so Eigenbrod would portray her as the hero of the story. People always love heroes. Heroines. Maribel could never quite get used to the picture that the media had drawn of her after the near-disaster of '72. She recognized herself mostly in the eyes of her daughter and her husband. The world's attention was not something she craved.

"Well, don't be too hard on him. I want to make sure he writes a fantastic story about us."

"What? Who do I need to not be hard on?"

"Eigenbrod."

"Sorry, Glen, my mind was wandering."

"That's okay, I'll see you tomorrow, then?"

Sparrow looked like he was going to go right back to bed after their call was done. Suddenly she felt sorry for him. But then she remembered that she had called Glen for a certain reason.

"Just a minute, Glen," she said. "One question. I'm sure you know people all over the world. I'm looking for an institute or a company with research facilities on Ceres. I don't care what country they're from."

"I'm not up to date on that front, but I'll ask around. It might take a little while, though. Commercial research enterprises don't have to announce their plans internationally, so I'll have to ask around with all the different national space agencies. But I know someone who will do that for me, so consider it done. Anything specific you're looking for in terms of scientific equipment on Ceres? You trying to meet certain conditions?"

Maribel heard the blatant curiosity in Sparrow's question, but she ignored it.

"I just want to be able to check into something there, on site."

"Okay."

"You'll notify me if you find someone on Ceres?"

"Not me, no, but I'll have my assistant contact you. Will phone number and email address be enough?"

"That'd be great. Ideally, someone who also has the authority to make decisions for the Ceres equipment."

"Of course. See you tomorrow, then."

"Hope you get some rest, Glen."

THE BATHROOM DOOR OPENED AGAIN. CHEN WAS CARRYING Luisa back to the bedroom. Maribel wanted to follow the two of them. But there was still this idea that her colleague, Jean-

Pierre, had mentioned. How high was the probability that an airplane had not yet flown into the rift? Maribel yawned. That's some kind of sign, she thought.

She stripped off her shirt and skirt and followed Chen into the bedroom. Through the large window, three wide beams of sunlight fell onto the king-size bed. Luisa was lying on Chen's side. She had curled up and put her thumb in her mouth like a baby. Her husband was lying on her half of the bed and had turned onto his side. Someone might think he was watching Luisa, but his quiet, gentle breathing suggested that he was already back to sleep. Maribel slid herself under the covers, nestled up against him, and wrapped her arm around his stomach.

"HOUSEKEEPING." AFTER SEVERAL KNOCKS ON THE DOOR, the word was repeated.

The cleaning crew had awakened her. Maribel looked at the alarm clock. It was already 1 PM, and she had not even done any work today, on a Wednesday! *No*, she corrected herself, *not true*—she had already made some work calls. She heard Chen ask the housekeeping staff to return later. Of course, breakfast was long over in the hotel. Maribel took off her underwear and got into the shower in the bathroom.

Freshly clean, she pulled on a colorful dress. Today she felt like livening things up, even if it was just a little bit of color.

"How about we go out to eat?"

"The Pancake House!" Luisa said, excited.

Their daughter had developed a passion for pancakes. They'd always been on breakfast menus before, of course, but it had made a big impression on her when she found out that there was a whole restaurant chain devoted to pancakes.

"Is that okay with you, Chen?" Maribel asked.

"With me? Of course," he said and smiled at her.

THEY HAD A NICE HOUR TOGETHER, AND THEN MARIBEL FELT torn. She could go down to the beach with Chen and Luisa and lie out on the warm sand, or she could work in their air-conditioned hotel room. Maribel sighed and decided to work. In sadness she watched her two favorite people walk away, hand in hand, down the street. It occurred to her that Luisa hadn't even brushed her teeth yet today, but she didn't want to bother her with it now, after she had just been a spoilsport about going with them.

The room had been cleaned and tidied up. She sat down at the desk, which also served as a computer. She could find the numbers she needed just by doing some simple search queries. How many flights took place every day in the area of the rift? What were the typical altitudes of those planes flying near the rift? She totaled the numbers since the time that the phenomenon appeared. Seven days times 110,000 flights over North America, add to that a few military flights—that was a lot. Flight schedules had not been changed since May 23rd, so planes were apparently still flying their usual routes. And yet there had been no collisions with the rift. How likely was that? Or maybe collisions had happened—but there had been absolutely no negative consequences? That was also the current position held by the scientific community. She really couldn't imagine it somehow being otherwise, as someone would have noticed long ago if there had been any adverse effects.

The argument would be convincing for ordinary people. But it had one weak point—after a week, nobody anywhere in the world had tried to find out what would actually happen if something went into the rift. That was simply unbelievable.

She suddenly remembered Glen Sparrow's reason—that there hadn't been any rockets available in a warehouse. That seemed unbelievable too. Was it all some kind of big conspiracy? Maribel shook her head. The rift was clouding her ability to think. When she was sitting in the space elevator, the world would no longer have to wait for results from the most important experiment they could perform on the rift.

May 30, 2085, Ceres

THE FARTHER M6 MOVED AWAY FROM THE CLEFT, THE MORE restless he became. It should have been just the opposite! His reward center should've been showering him with positive signals now that he was finally taking care of his official task. Instead he felt disappointment and the increasingly urgent desire to turn around and go back, climb up the platform, and plunge himself into the cleft. M6 had the uncertain feeling that soon it might be too late. There was no indication that the cleft was going to disappear soon, but for some reason, the image of a closing door was stuck in his mind.

M6 was annoyed. What he had just done—experience a fit of human emotion—was the worst thing that could happen to a robot capable of reasoning. What was he supposed to do with that? It was like he imagined an itch would be, but even worse—it prevented him from working efficiently. M6 had heard of AIs that suddenly developed surges of emotions and mood swings. The Watson series of AIs, for example, seemed very susceptible to that, for some reason. But what was the result? The risk of failure increased and the chance of achieving the goal was negatively affected, which was what was happening to him right now. At least he was aware of what was happening to him. Maybe he would be able to compartmentalize these emotions in some small part of his consciousness.

He was getting closer to the sides of the crater. They were a fascinating formation. To the left and right the sides rose hundreds of meters upward, but in the middle, it looked as if someone had built a wide ramp. M6 looked behind him in the opposite direction. It was easy to imagine that a giant spaceship had crash-landed on the planetoid exactly along that ramp.

But there was no spaceship. Some natural causes must have produced the rockslides. From his vantage point, they looked like avalanches that had been frozen in place. But even if that was how they looked, they weren't really frozen, but moving very, very slowly downward.

M6 reached the end of one avalanche formation. It reminded him of a glacier terminus, but there was no meltwater flowing here. He took samples from the ground at various elevations. Near the top of the crater, close to the surface, the samples were primarily solidified dust: regolith. The deeper he went down the crater, the higher the percentage of water ice. At the bottom, where the avalanche met the crater floor, the percentage of ice was highest. Here it reached almost 50 percent of volume, like a ball that someone had formed from mud and snow. Scientists on Earth would be happy, because that was exactly what they had predicted. And avalanches move similar to how skaters glide on ice. A microscopically thin layer of liquid near its melting point coats a collection of solids, and interaction between gravity, pressure, and friction increases this liquid layer, allowing the matter on top of the liquid to slide.

The wall in front of him extended close to three meters upward, but it wasn't completely vertical. He should be able to climb it! M6 drilled his two front legs deep into the wall until they could hold his entire body. Then he flipped himself upward into an elegant handstand. His rear legs landed on the rockslide, drilled into the ground, and held him in place even as he pulled the rest of his body up with another flip. If someone had thought he was a spider-like creature before, now they would see him as a very athletic spider. Once again M6 was very pleased with his body—and grateful for his creators, even though he knew that his gratefulness had been programmed into him, too.

Having climbed to the top of the rockslide, he flexed his knees a few times. The material that covered the surface appeared to be very stable. That was too bad. He had hoped that he would be able to glide back down to the bottom like a skier. But someone had spread gravel all over this 'glacier.' He walked partway down the slope. Glaciers on Earth had crevices and cracks. Maybe he would find something like that here too. Maybe they would allow him to gain some insight into the history of this collapsing wall. He didn't have any orders to look into that, but experience had shown him that the researchers back on Earth never complained about additional findings that they could then publish under their own names.

M6 had his own ego module, which helped manage, among other things, his survival instinct, but he had no desire for fame. He much preferred peace and quiet. Therefore, it also didn't bother him that his name never appeared in the list of authors and if it appeared at all, it was only ever as a footnote in the description of methods. Legally, of course, he had no standing to complain, since he was the private property of the RB Group.

M6 activated his radar, then slowly climbed back up the rockslide, his radar sensor pointing down at the ground. He couldn't detect any cavities in the ground. But it was interesting that the density of the material decreased with depth. Thus, the surface was heavier than the subsurface. Even under the low gravity of Ceres, this meant that forces were constantly pulling on the surface material and trying to drag it downward.

The interesting question, M6 thought, *was where did the ice down below come from?* Had it been pressed upward out of the former ice ocean inside the planetoid's crust? Different than the moons of Europa and Enceladus, Ceres had the misfortune of not being constantly pushed and pulled by a nearby planet, which would have kept it warm. Therefore, the dwarf planet must have cooled more and more over time. Its mantle would have contracted, leaving less and less space for the simultaneously volume-expanding ocean freezing in its interior. Like an orange being squeezed in someone's hand, the interior would have to break through to the outside at some point.

That was still only a theory, but if it turned out to be true, the next several years on Ceres could prove to be very exciting. M6 couldn't directly examine the ice ocean under the crust itself, but he could study anything that was squeezed out onto the surface. The ocean might have been liquid many millions of years ago. At the time, Ceres might have even provided space for life to develop. And he, M6, could be the one to discover it. Apart from him, there were no other research units currently on Ceres. The only requirement was that he would have to stay here. This meant giving up the idea of plunging himself into the cleft.

The robot stopped to wipe dirt from his radar receiver with his left front leg. Nothing had settled on the receiver and the radar was functioning perfectly. Now he was even developing meaningless habits like the people who had built him! He turned around, and then turned around again. He felt like the cleft was calling to him, yet at the same time he was afraid of it. It would be best if he first sent all the test results on the rockslide to the researchers at RB back on Earth. The satellite would be in range in another half hour.

"M6 END," HE PUT AT THE END OF THE MESSAGE.

His memory banks were empty again and ready for new test data. The satellite hadn't sent him any new specific orders. That meant that his basic programming would be activated with the goal of learning as much as possible about Ceres. He was allowed to develop the strategy for performing this basic research himself. For a week now, the cleft had been one of the most important features of the planetoid, so he was absolutely justified in turning his attention to it.

He made his way back using his six legs. He had taken care of his orders for examining the crater's edge. His reward center and his curiosity could once again work hand in hand.

May 31, 2085, Pomona, Kansas

"Nervous?" Akif asked.

Derek nodded. "Didn't sleep very well."

"Hey, guys, I'm ready when you are," one of the two tanker truck drivers called to them.

"Just a minute," Derek answered. "Gita, can they start filling the tanks?" he shouted up to the capsule.

"Go ahead," she replied.

"Go ahead," he repeated.

"Got it," the driver said.

On the side of the rocket, around the filler nozzle, a moist spot formed and gradually turned white. Here, moisture from the surroundings was condensing and freezing on the rocket. The liquid fuel was super cold. The generator tried to supply power to the cooling system.

"Gita. Status?"

"You two better get up here."

"What's wrong?" he asked.

"I don't know how long the fuel will stay cold enough. The cooling system's not operating at full power. The generator's not powerful enough."

"What are we going to do up there?"

"We're not going to need full tanks to reach an altitude of ten to twelve kilometers, will we?"

"No."

"When the tanks are full enough, we'll have to launch very quickly. As soon as the engine is going, the cooling system won't be a problem, because the engine will power it."

"Just a minute," Derek shouted.

"Akif, you better get up there now."

Then he turned to the tanker truck driver. "Do me a favor and uncouple the hoses when I tell you, okay? And then you'd better get out of the way..."

"No problem. You've already paid us."

"Thanks," Derek said.

"And I've just got to say, you all are crazy. I hope you don't end up as one big fireball. Or come to think of it, then I'd be an eyewitness. A fireball over Kansas... haven't had one of those in a long time."

"I'm happy I can help," Derek said.

"Derek, come on!" Gita called from above.

"I've got to go," he said, as if they would see each other again tomorrow. Then he climbed up the ladder.

"I GIVE US SEVEN MINUTES," GITA SAID.

"Great work," Akif said.

She smiled at him and turned red. "Thank you."

"Maybe we should use this chance to talk about what we really want," Derek said.

"To go into the rift, what else?" Gita asked.

"You want to go in? It might be absolute nothingness. We'd disappear and never be seen again," Derek said.

"You don't want to take that chance?" Akif asked.

"Yes, I do, but I thought you two just wanted to fly close to it."

"What made you think that? Why would we want to just do that?"

"I... I don't know. To get a better look at the rift?"

"Scientists have looked at it from all directions and in the full spectrum. Just looking is not going to tell us anything new. We've got to take the next step."

"That's how I see it too, Akif, but I never thought you... we might not come back from this."

"You don't think I know that? Life always ends with death. If we can learn something this way, then it'll all be worth it," Akif said.

"But nobody will be able to learn about it from us," Derek said.

"Wrong. I'm streaming everything to the net, and we already have eight viewers," Gita said. "The New Shepard even has satellite Internet onboard."

Derek sighed. Somehow, he felt guilty that the two others had joined him onboard. Maybe it was because he had never been completely honest with them. If he thought about it, he had to admit that the possibility of dying in the rift was somewhat comforting to him. Even that could be a way of finding Mary again.

"You two should get comfortable and buckle up," Gita said.

Derek leaned back in his seat and latched his seat belt. He should have put on some sweatpants instead of his tight jeans and the belt that was cutting into his abdomen. And had he watered the flowers on the kitchen window? Had he turned off the stove? Suddenly all sorts of things that he might have forgotten were going through his head.

Gita stood up from her place at the computer, walked over to the still open hatch, and called down, "Stop fueling."

Then she closed the hatch. Derek watched her as she peered through the large windows, tracking the two drivers as they moved away from the rocket.

"Good," she said, "I think they're at a safe distance. Start the countdown."

"How high will we go?" Derek asked.

"Maximum 20 kilometers."

"That should do it."

"20, 19..."

Derek dug his clenched fingers into the side cushions of his seat. Couldn't they have at least dimmed the lights in the capsule a little?

"3, 2, 1, ignition!"

He heard loud rumbling and hissing noises.

"Engine ignited," Gita said.

A glowing light could be seen through the windows. But they felt no vibrations pulsing through the New Shepard, no forces trying to free them from the confines of gravity and the steel cable.

"Power barely above zero," Gita said.

Derek could hear the disappointment in her voice.

"It appears that we're sitting on top of a gas oven instead of a rocket engine," Gita explained. "The hydrogen fuel is being burned cleanly, but it's not producing any thrust. The engines must've been modified at some point."

"Shouldn't someone have..." Derek held his tongue.

"We couldn't see this in the simulations. We would have had to inspect the engines and compare them with the standard New Shepard designs. We failed to do that."

"It's not your fault, Gita," the doctor said. "For a group of beginners, I think we did pretty well."

"And now Johnny has his tourist attraction," Derek said.

He leaned back and took a deep breath in and out. The engines had purposely been made unusable at some point. The previous owner would have known it. That must be the reason why it wasn't shot into space like every other available rocket during the events of 2052. Actually, he should have thought of that. But it had been a nice dream anyway. Now he just wanted to simply lie here until he died. *That is a good plan*, Derek decided.

May 31, 2085, Vandenberg Air Force Base

"MAY I INTRODUCE ARTHUR EIGENBROD? HE'S THE journalist who will be joining us aboard the space elevator."

Glen Sparrow gestured toward a tall, light-skinned man with European facial features. Maribel tried to recognize anything French about him, but he didn't seem to conform to any of the old stereotypes. Eigenbrod made a whimsical bow. When he smiled, she saw his teeth were yellow. *He must smoke Gauloises*—at least there was one thing that fit with her preconceptions about Frenchmen.

"It's very nice to meet you, Ms. Pedreira," he said. "I've been following your work since '72. Very impressive, what you've accomplished."

Maribel dismissed the comment with a tiny nod of acknowledgment. She could never stand it when someone praised her like that. She had just been doing her job.

"Then I hardly need to introduce Maribel Pedreira to you," Sparrow said.

"Nice to meet you too," Maribel said as she shook the reporter's hand. "I must return the compliment. If it hadn't been for you, we might've missed some big revelations about our sun."

Eigenbrod had unearthed the story at the time. Before

that, neither his name nor his newspaper had been as well known worldwide as it was now.

"Ah, that was all just a huge bit of luck," the journalist said.

The man had turned red, which made him seem more likable to her. He too appeared to place little value on his own fame. She studied him a little more closely. He already had to be older than 60. He had distinct bags under his eyes, eyes that seemed to view the world quietly and constantly. He noticed that she was looking at him and held her gaze.

"When will my old friend Crewmaster be here?" Maribel asked.

"The professor wanted me to send his apologies, but he couldn't be here today. He's already seen the capsule, though, so he will join us on the day of the launch," Sparrow explained.

"That's too bad," Maribel said, "George Crewmaster is an astrophysics expert. You must know that, Arthur. He helped me a lot in the past."

"And he's very well connected," Sparrow said.

Maribel nodded. Crewmaster had been able to get her valuable telescope time when she had urgently needed it.

"It looks like we're all getting along well," Sparrow said finally. "Are you both ready for the big day today?"

"What do you mean by 'big day,' Glen?" Maribel asked.

Had he pushed up the date of the manned launch? Nobody had agreed to that. Even Eigenbrod looked at him somewhat skeptically.

"No, no. No need to panic," Glen replied, raising his hands as if to calm her down. "The elevator's still going to launch without us today. The plan is to evaluate all the data tomorrow and then finally attempt the manned launch the day after tomorrow, assuming everything goes well."

"That still sounds very ambitious," Eigenbrod commented before Maribel could say something similar.

"Oh, we'd already done all the safety tests a long time ago, before the project was put on hold. You already know that whatever happens, the cabin must be able to separate from the cable and land safely on the ground again from any stage of the flight," Sparrow said.

"How does the landing work without a cable?" Eigenbrod asked.

"We've got a combination of parachutes and landing jets. And even if all the jets fail, we'd still reach the ground safely with the help of the parachutes, although the landing might be a little bumpy."

"Very reassuring."

"We made extra space suits fitted especially for you too. Actually, the plans were for passengers to be able to wear their normal clothes. But in light of the small number of test flights, we decided to implement some additional safety precautions."

"Will we be able to work in them?" Maribel asked. "I'll need to be able to operate my instruments."

"Should be no problem. You'll be getting the latest version. They have almost no restrictions on mobility anymore. Quite the opposite, in fact. Many motions are even boosted by electromechanical systems. They'll give you more power and dexterity than usual. You might have to make a few adjustments."

"Then it's good that I lost some weight," Eigenbrod said, pointing to his stomach. He wasn't fat anymore, but no one would say he was skinny either.

"Good for you, but our suits are very flexible, so they can even accommodate a bit of a belly. The only limit is in height, a maximum of 1.95 meters."

"Good, then I can have a proper meal before the launch," the French reporter said.

"I wouldn't recommend that."

"Why?"

"For practical reasons, Arthur. The space elevator's travel time to its final destination should take less than two hours. It didn't make sense to install a bathroom for that amount of time. But the tests that Maribel and I have planned might take four or five hours. You understand the workings of the digestive system, I take it?"

A look of comprehension dawned on Eigenbrod's face. "I understand completely, you don't need to go into any details. Just talking about it makes me want to go look for a toilet."

Maribel noticed that he used the rather blunt word 'toilet' instead of the more euphemistic 'bathroom' or 'restroom' that was typical here.

"Through the door, take a left and then the next right," Sparrow said. "Do you have your badge? If not, you're likely to be put under arrest walking around by yourself."

Eigenbrod reached into his pants pocket and took out a badge attached to a lanyard that he placed around his neck. "Will I be safe now?" he asked.

"Looks good. See you soon," Sparrow replied.

"Have you heard anything with regards to Ceres?" asked Maribel, after the journalist had left the room.

"Yes," Sparrow replied.

"I thought someone was going to call me right away."

"Sorry, I didn't want to bother you at night. The call came sometime between two and three this morning."

"Japanese, Russian, or Chinese?"

"The Russians," Sparrow said. "They have a mobile lab on Ceres that is conducting all possible research."

"'All possible?'"

"Nobody knows exactly. Officially, the Russian Space Agency leads the expedition, but it's being financed by the RB Group."

Sparrow walked to his computer and pressed a few buttons.

"Have a look, this is the mobile lab. Someone I know sent me the picture... unofficially, of course."

A shiver went down Maribel's back. The robot looked like

a gigantic black spider. Around its axis-symmetrical body were six spidery-looking legs, each with two joints.

"Yeah, looks hideous," Sparrow said when he saw her reaction.

Maribel was annoyed with herself. She was now well past 30 and shouldn't be afraid of spiders anymore, especially when this was just a simple research robot. "No, it looks like a fascinating piece of technology," she replied. "So, what can it do?"

"Robots of this series have sensors for practically anything you might want to measure. They can also do spectral analyses of rock samples and look for traces of life. The best thing is, if they don't have something they need, they can build it themselves. As long as the raw materials are available."

"Nanofabricators?"

"Exactly."

The Russians were leaders in this field. The West had long resisted working with nanofabricators because of the fear that the robots would get out of hand and could become uncontrollable. The fears had been overblown—and in the meantime, the tiny machines had become so important for the economy that no one could do anything without them anymore.

"I'd like to have research equipment like that," Maribel said.

"Sorry, but the use of nanos on Earth is still prohibited."

She shrugged her shoulders. That had been the compromise eventually agreed upon by everyone. There were always reports that individual nations were violating the agreement, but so far nobody had been caught in the act.

"So, who do I need to speak to if I want to contact this robot?"

"Officially, you'd have to go through the Russian Space Agency," Sparrow said.

"And unofficially?"

"Let's try the official way first. I know the guy who's

responsible for such research operations very well. If we share our findings with him, I'm sure he'll help us with the robot."

"What do you mean by 'share?'"

"Don't worry, Maribel, he won't want to appear in any papers you might write. But it's essential to be well informed and up-to-date. He won't want any more than that, I'm sure."

"That's acceptable. When can I talk with him?"

Sparrow looked at the large clock on his desk. "He works at a large institute in Siberia. There's a 14-hour time difference. I'm afraid your first chance would probably be tonight, definitely not before 10 PM our time. I reached him this morning shortly after six."

Maribel sighed. She had the feeling that time was short, even though there didn't appear to be any reason for that feeling. "That's too bad," she said finally.

"What's too bad?" Arthur Eigenbrod asked. The Frenchman had just returned to the office.

"We wanted to speak to someone from the Russian Space Agency, but we'll have to wait until tonight due to the time difference," Maribel explained.

"Oh, anything to do with the RB Group?"

"Them too. How'd you guess?"

"Russian space travel is always involved with RB. They finance almost the entire program."

"Are you involved somehow with the Group? Do you know someone there who could help us, maybe?"

"'Know' would be a bit of an exaggeration, but I was there for a while. Give me a minute and I'll gladly tell you about it."

"Okay," Maribel said, although the offer sounded a little strange to her. What was he going to tell them about it?

"Then let's take a walk over to the launch pad," Glen Sparrow said, interrupting her thoughts. "The first launch is set for noon on the dot."

TODAY, UNLIKE MARIBEL'S LAST VISIT, THERE WAS A LOT OF commotion in this part of the base. She was constantly being stopped and her identification inspected and scanned. Not even Glen Sparrow escaped this treatment. Maribel watched her companions. They put up with the added inconvenience as calmly as she did. That was a good sign for the expedition they were about to undertake together on the space elevator. Finally, they reached a platform. It looked like a large, round trampoline. The conical capsule sat in the middle. Someone might think that one of the famous Dragon space capsules from the 30s had been misplaced.

"Where's the concrete block?" Maribel asked.

"What concrete block?" Arthur asked.

"The elevator's cable is attached to a giant block. You could still see it here yesterday," she said.

"It's under the platform," Glen said. "Come on!"

He pointed to a walkway that could be used to cross the platform. Glen went first, and Maribel followed him. The platform felt rather springy as they walked on it.

"At first I thought this was a trampoline," Maribel said.

"You're going to laugh, but people actually do call it the trampoline," Glen said.

"Why doesn't that surprise me?" she replied with a grin.

Sparrow reached the capsule and opened the door. Then he invited her in with a wave of his hand.

"Go ahead, Arthur," Maribel said, "I've already seen inside the capsule."

"No, you should come too, Maribel, there are some new things you haven't seen yet," Sparrow said.

Maribel nodded and took a few steps closer to the entrance. Before she even stepped through the hatch, she noticed that the capsule was now full of scientific equipment.

"We got everything that you asked for," the JPL man explained. He seemed very proud of the results.

"You... did an excellent job," Maribel said.

She felt a little strange, praising him like she was his teacher, but that appeared to be her role. She looked around the capsule. The six seats were still there like before, and there was very little free space. She bumped into Glen and Arthur several times while trying to move around.

"Looks like things will be nice and cozy in here. We might as well be friendly and use our first names," the journalist said after one such collision. "Call me Arthur," he said as he stretched out his hand.

"Maribel," she answered, shaking hands with him.

Arthur repeated the ceremony with Glen Sparrow.

"I'm the oldest one here by far," Arthur said finally, "so I feel like it's my job to set a friendly tone."

"Good idea," Sparrow said. "We'll be spending quite some time in here together, and I think things will go a little easier aboard our spaceship if we can be a bit less formal with each other."

"You've flown before, then?" Maribel asked.

"Yes, though it was probably 20 years ago now," Glen said. "At the time I was in much better shape."

"And you, Arthur?"

"Only as a passenger. But not so long ago."

Maribel remembered her first flight into space. It had been 13 years ago in a Blue Origin cruise vessel. She had made her first—and last—space walk, and then inspected the *Ark*, humanity's rescue ship. Then she had returned to Earth. It was still her only spaceflight. When it had come time for her second, she had turned away at the last second—and that had saved her life. At the time, she had sworn to never fly into space again, and after Luisa had arrived, she had renewed that promise. Everyone was telling her that this expedition with the space elevator wouldn't even bring her close to the edge of space—but still, she felt like she was breaking her word.

"What's wrong?" Arthur asked.

This guy has a good eye for what others are feeling, she decided. It seemed like something a journalist would need to be good at.

"Memories," she answered evasively. "I feel like I shouldn't really be here."

"My wife thought the same about me," Eigenbrod said. "She's worried about my heart."

"Does she have a reason to worry?"

"My doctor gave me the okay. I've lost some weight these last three years, and I eat well and exercise."

"So, you didn't listen to her?"

"Of course I did. I always do. I offered not to fly, but she refused to let me turn it down. She knew how happy it'd make me to write this story."

"That's very noble of her," Maribel said. *Just like Chen*, she thought.

"Yes, she's great."

"Anything else you need me to tell you about?" Glen asked.

"You could tell us how you were able to get all these instruments in here and still stay under the weight limit," Maribel suggested.

"To tell you the truth, that wasn't easy. Three of the instruments had to be disassembled into multiple parts. And because of the weight, many of the metal parts had to be replaced by special constructions made from ceramic or plastic."

"And you did all that in two days?" Arthur asked.

"The day before yesterday the capsule was still empty, sitting in the warehouse where the office is," Maribel said.

"That's one of the advantages of being stationed on a functioning military base. With one call, the presiding commander can supply more manpower than we could ever put to work. And the workers here are all part of the Air Force's Space Wing, so they're more than competent in this type of work."

"I'm impressed," Arthur said.

"Me too," Maribel agreed.

A siren sounded outside.

"Just as planned," Glen said, "not that loud sounds are really helpful to everyone's anxious mood."

"Is it telling us what I think it is?" Maribel asked.

"Yes, we need to get away from here."

"Are all the instruments tied down securely?"

"Don't worry, Maribel. But I think you're in for a little surprise."

"What do you mean by that?"

"You'll just have to wait and see. Now come on."

THEY WATCHED EVERYTHING FROM THE BED OF A PICKUP truck. The platform with the space capsule was only 20 meters away.

"Feels strange to be so close to a launch," Maribel said.

"You're telling me. I'm just waiting for the deadly hot gases to come pouring out of the engine," Glen said.

The platform was cleared. The crane positioned next to the platform swung its arm to the side.

"See? That arm had been keeping the cable in place. Now it's free."

Maribel nodded. She found it unimaginable, what they were witnessing. In the concrete block hidden under the platform was one end of a cable, whose other end was somewhat far above them out in space. It was like that one fairy tale with the beanstalk reaching into the sky. And the gray capsule was about to start climbing that cable.

The siren sounded again. A countdown began and then stopped. A man in protective clothing ran to the capsule, used his hands to perform a few actions whose purpose was not immediately clear, and then cleared the platform again. The countdown resumed. Maribel felt nervous feelings bubbling up inside her, even though the base was completely quiet. The process gave the impression of well-oiled clockwork. Every gear and cog engaged with the next in an almost frictionless movement.

The countdown stopped again. Nothing happened. Probably people were debating what to do. Apparently nothing, because then the countdown started again. Soon they were at ten, nine, eight, and finally zero.

Maribel heard a high-pitched groaning. *That must be the cable suddenly coming under tension,* she thought.

"Did you hear that groaning sound?" Glen asked.

Maribel nodded.

"A lot of people think that's the cable being tensioned. But that's nonsense. Its own weight keeps it always under tension —that's our biggest problem. The few tons from the capsule don't make much of a difference."

"So, what was that sound then?"

"The platform, the trampoline. The capsule's weight was just taken off it."

"You mean the capsule is already suspended on the cable?" Maribel asked.

"Exactly. Now we could even take the platform out from under it."

"And why this pause?"

"Just for safety reasons."

"What could go wrong now?"

"Nothing, Maribel. Sometimes we put safety pauses in even when nothing could go wrong, which is what's going on here."

Maribel laughed. Then the capsule started moving.

"Now the linear motor in the cable channel starts its work," Glen explained. "It's powered from the cable, but the capsule also has a backup battery if the power should fail."

"How long is the battery good for?" asked Maribel.

"About ten minutes. Enough so the capsule can detach from the cable."

"And if the cable tears somewhere?" asked Arthur.

"That's an interesting question," Glen said. "We worked on that for a long time."

"Wouldn't it just fall back to the ground?" the journalist asked.

"No. The cable is basically orbiting the Earth. The farther up we are, the more it behaves like a satellite. So, like a satellite, it also would only gradually fall back to Earth at first, as it's braked by the atmosphere."

"So it's not a problem?"

"We can't really say that, no. The lower part of the cable is constantly experiencing rather large deceleration forces, the upper part not so much. This produces forces that act in opposite directions, like in a vehicle that's only braking with its rear wheels. As long as the cable is whole, these internal stresses are in a state of equilibrium, but if the cable breaks, this would no longer be true. The two individual parts would have to reach new states of equilibrium and would move away from each other."

"What does that mean for the capsule?"

"Well, Arthur, in any event we'd detach ourselves from the cable as quickly as possible. If the cable starts falling, it's going to have a lot of kinetic energy, so we don't want to be in the way."

"And if it impacts the Earth?"

"You're going to use this in your article, aren't you?" Glen said. "Well, if the cable tore way up high and then came crashing down onto land, things could get rather unpleasant. That's one reason we're so close to the ocean. But the stresses are greater down closer to the ground, so the cable is more likely, although still very, very unlikely, to tear down low. And we've developed a special safety mode. If the tension in the cable falls below a certain value, because the cable has torn, the nanofabricators, which otherwise keep the cable stable, will automatically introduce artificial fracture lines in the cable. Thus, it will break apart into several pieces, each of which is no longer too dangerous by itself."

"Thanks, Glen, that was a great explanation."

"Didn't you just tell me yesterday that nanofabricators were illegal down here on Earth?" Maribel asked.

Glen rubbed his chin. "Officially this is being handled as a space project, so we were able to convince our contractors that there were no legal problems in using them. We've agreed to forward all results from the tests directly to all interested parties."

"So, you had to make another deal," Maribel said.

"I guess you could say that, yes."

The capsule started moving faster. It was haunting how quietly everything moved. Even the people had all quieted down. Maribel sensed a feeling spreading around. Quite possibly they were witnessing the advent of space travel for the next century—as long as nothing went wrong, of course.

Maribel thought about the cable. It was so inconspicuous. Even if it was as thick as an arm, would she dare cut through it if she had to? Would the nanofabricators be quicker than she would be at cutting the cable? The cable was a self-repairing object. Wouldn't it be great if everything that people built on Earth could repair itself? Cars would just have to sit overnight in the garage at home to fix themselves after a crash. Broken washing machines and dishwashers would be things of the past. Eyeglasses could be automatically changed to a new prescription.

It would be a revolution. All that was needed was the legal release of the nanofabricators. There were people who claimed that the manufacturing industry itself was against that, because then there'd be no more need for new products. Maribel didn't believe in such conspiracy theories. Were people overstating the dangers of the technology? Hadn't people been worried about the unstoppable spread of machines for a long time? But no problems had ever come up on the moon or the asteroids.

Somebody tapped her on the shoulder. It was Glen, who was holding out binoculars to her. The capsule had already climbed surprisingly high. It was a rather disconcerting sight, because at this distance the cable wasn't visible anymore. There was only a heavy space capsule, which, instead of falling downward faster and faster as one might expect, was slowly rising higher and higher.

Then Maribel saw the rift. She looked at it through the binoculars. It looked like it had the other times she viewed it

—unfathomable blackness. Soon she would be close enough to practically reach out and touch it.

"How high will it go today?" Arthur asked.

"15,000 meters," Glen answered. "We want to make sure that we can reach the rift the day after tomorrow."

"Why not all the way up?"

"It's not a good idea to push your luck too far the very first time."

THEY WAITED. THE CAPSULE WAS HARD TO SEE, EVEN through the binoculars. Maribel gave up. After she had gotten used to the slow movement of the capsule, the whole test had lost its excitement. She had seen what she wanted to see, and now she just wanted to be with her family again, but she wouldn't be able to see them until that evening at the earliest.

There was activity, with noise growing around the platform. Apparently, the capsule had started its descent.

"We're letting it come down in free fall," Glen explained.

Maribel pointed the binoculars up toward the capsule. It was now moving considerably faster. Like before, however, she couldn't see any sign of engines. *How would it feel to be on board right now?* she thought.

"Don't worry," Glen said. "This is only a test. We'll use the motor to slow us down during the descent when we're onboard."

"Very reassuring," Arthur said.

Maribel held her breath. The capsule was moving faster and faster. And it looked as if it was coming down directly on them. The fact that the cable ended 20 meters away from them couldn't be seen from her current perspective. Maribel wanted to run away and seek shelter. But she forced herself to stay sitting where she was. She laughed nervously and then saw beads of sweat on Glen's forehead.

She pointed up toward the capsule. "It's completely safe, right?"

He wiped the sweat off his forehead. "To be honest, this is a new test. But nothing will happen. Nothing can happen."

The capsule didn't appear to be listening. It continued to race toward them. Thanks to the binoculars, Maribel could see smoke forming on the cable.

"Could the cable be damaged by friction?" she asked.

"No, that only looks like smoke," Glen explained. "It's water vapor that's rapidly condensing out of the air at such a high altitude."

"So heat is being produced?" she asked.

"Due to the air friction, of course. But that's all been included in the calculations."

It continued coming down. Soon it would... There was a booming sound. The engines had activated. They brought the capsule to a stop almost instantly. The people near the platform started to applaud.

"It worked," Glen said.

"I'm relieved. What would have happened if it hadn't?" Maribel asked.

"The capsule would've been catapulted toward the ocean. And our launch the day after tomorrow would probably have been delayed."

"What do you think, Arthur?"

"Very impressive," the Frenchman said. "I'm just hoping that our landing won't be quite so abrupt."

Maribel nodded.

"I can promise both of you that it won't," Glen said.

May 31, 2085, Ceres

THE PLATFORM WAS WAITING FOR HIM. M6 HAD ALREADY spotted the cleft from a distance. When he was finally standing at the top, he determined that there had been no changes at all. The cleft had not moved by even a nanometer. If it was made from some form of matter, even if it were some unknown type of dark energy, wouldn't it have had to lose or gain at least some energy during the time that had passed? No physical system could remain completely constant over time. The constancy of change was ingrained and unavoidable in the course of time. But none of that seemed to apply to the cleft.

Thus, only two conclusions were possible. Either the cleft was a purely spatial phenomenon lacking a time dimension, or it had to be viewed as independent of our space-time fabric. Neither case could be calculated or simulated with the physics available to M6. But there was at least one experiment that he could use to find out which of these two alternatives it was. In the first case, nothing would happen. In the second case, something would have to happen—the outcome could not be 'nothing.'

Or had he made an error in his thinking somewhere? He couldn't change something invariable without a time dimension, no matter what he did. The first case appeared to be clear. But the second? What would happen if he stepped outside of time and space? Would he disappear from this universe? That could have terrible consequences, because it would mess with cause and effect. Or would a copy of himself remain, in order not to mess with history? That would be especially unlucky. Then he would *believe* that nothing had happened—that is, that the first case applied... but, in reality, it would be the second case.

That was enough to make you want to tear your hair out! And which of his programmers had taught him that phrase? M6 felt like he was on the verge of slipping into the dangerous realm of quantum uncertainty. He wanted to perform, in the terminology of quantum physics, an experiment whose outcome depended on whether there was a neutral observer. Unfortunately, he did not have an observer at his disposal.

Not yet, at least. M6 thought about his nanofabricators. He could use them to build a separate monitoring system, one that was not part of himself, from one of his optical cameras. He would then place it on the platform. He hoped it could absolutely tell him what had happened during his experiment.

The test itself would have to wait a little while longer.

June 1, 2085, Pomona, Kansas

"WHERE AM I?" ASKED DEREK LOUDLY. HIS HEAD WAS LYING on a white pillow that smelled strongly of starch. He saw a few uneven floorboards that must have once been painted dark red, even though now almost all the paint had been worn away. They seemed familiar to him. He remembered crouching over the floor and moving a paintbrush across the wood. But why? Had he decided that the bedroom needed a new coat of paint?

No, that had been Mary, who had wanted this color that he still thought was rather ugly. If it had really just been him in this house alone, as reality kept trying to tell him, he would have sanded the floors and put a colorless varnish on them, so that the grain of the wood could be seen. Maybe he should just do it, because reality seemed to have a very strong argument—it had taken away his wife, and he would probably never get her back.

Then he heard singing from downstairs. Derek sat up, startled. He was sitting in his own bed, in his own house, that he had lived in for many years by himself, but someone, it sounded like a woman, was singing downstairs. Probably in the kitchen, he decided. Had fate heard his appeals and returned Mary to him? He swung his legs over the edge of the bed. His legs were bare. He couldn't remember taking off his clothes yesterday. His pants hung neatly folded over the back of the chair in the corner. In front of the pants, on the cushion, was a T-shirt, crisply folded, like he was never able to accomplish, even though it had been drilled into him in the military.

Only Mary ever folded his clothes that well, he thought. There were some rattling noises downstairs. He sat up straight. The singing woman was doing his dishes.

"Akif, can you take out the two trash cans, please?" she said.

Derek slumped back onto the bed. Of course. It was Gita, the Indian receptionist and covert IT expert. But what was she doing in his house? The disappointment made him want to stay in bed, but his curiosity eventually grew strong enough that he pulled on his pants and T-shirt. Then he opened the bedroom door. He could hear footsteps down below. He went down the stairs, avoiding the creaking steps.

He walked down the dark hallway and stopped in front of the door to the kitchen. He took a deep breath. There it was again, the penetrating smell of the wood preservative that had completely turned his life upside down the last several days. Derek closed his eyes and said a silent prayer. *Please, let it be Mary*, he prayed, contrary to the best of his knowledge. Then he opened the kitchen door. God had not answered his prayer. Or, the answer had been, "No." Gita was standing in front of the sink, her sleeves pushed up over her elbows, and she was washing his dishes. She was singing a song that he thought he recognized from church. *Isn't she a Hindu like most Indians?*

"Ah, good morning, sleepy-head," she greeted him.

She had an infectiously joyful face. Wherever Gita might be in the morning, he was doubtful anyone could stay grumpy for long. He started to feel a little jealous of Akif, because it was very clear which man Gita had eyes for, even if the doctor was apparently clueless. Then he remembered Mary. He had no reason to be jealous.

"What are you doing here?" he asked.

"Your dishes. It looked like it was about time."

He couldn't argue with that. But it didn't answer his question. "But why are you here? You two could have opened up the office again."

"Wouldn't really have been worth it. Today's Friday and we're only open until one anyway. And officially, we're not reopening until Monday."

"You could've cleaned your own place. Or gone to a park and enjoyed the sun."

"You know, Derek, you were so exhausted yesterday that you needed someone to take care of you. And that's what we're doing now."

"We?"

"I just sent Akif out with the trash. He should've returned already. I wonder where he is?"

"Where did the two of you sleep?"

"The living room. We unfolded the sofa bed. It was big enough."

The two spent the night together in the same bed? Derek was curious, but he didn't dare ask any questions. "I can honestly say I can't remember anything that happened yesterday," he said.

"Did you black out?"

Derek nodded. "All I remember is that the engine failed."

"After that, we dropped you off here. You were so exhausted you couldn't drive home. Then we started driving back to Ottawa, to our own homes, but I started worrying about you, so finally I asked Akif to have the car turn around."

"I don't remember any of that."

"I'm not surprised. We found you on the kitchen floor. Next to you were two bottles of whiskey, one empty, one half full. You'd thrown up. At first, we were going to call an ambulance, but then we thought it'd be easier to clean you up and put you in bed. To be safe, we stayed here overnight."

"That was very kind of both of you." Derek felt all warm inside. He couldn't remember when anyone had shown him that much love.

"We should've seen it sooner. When the rocket didn't launch, you really took it hard."

"I was hoping to see Mary again."

"That's what I thought. You almost got your wish too, just not the way you imagined."

"I wasn't trying to kill myself," Derek said. "If that's what I wanted, I could've used my gun." He wasn't sure if he was telling the truth. Maybe at that moment he just hadn't remembered there might be a more efficient way than whiskey. So, Gita had filled in what had happened during his blackout.

The feeling that he had no more interest in living was not something that he'd forgotten. And it appeared that not much had changed. His life had definitely not gained any new meaning since yesterday. Maybe now that he was awake, he would be better able to plan the action he had wanted to take yesterday.

The kitchen door opened with a metallic creak. "These hinges could use some oil," Akif said. "I saw some in the garage, so I'll take care of that next." He had two empty trash cans in his hands. "And while I was out there, I did a little straightening up, I hope you don't mind," he said.

"Ah, that's why you were gone so long," Gita said. "I need you to dry these."

Akif put his hand gently on her shoulder. Derek noticed the gesture. "Derek can do that. He knows better than I do where all these plates and cups go," the doctor said. "I need to go back to my car for something."

Gita handed Derek a dish towel, and he began to slowly dry and put away the giant pile of clean dishes. Drying dishes was a meditative activity. It was good for him. In the meantime, Gita had finished washing the remaining dirty dishes. She let the water drain out and cleaned the sink. She sang quietly as she worked. In that tiny moment, Derek felt happy.

The kitchen door creaked again. Akif was right, the hinges needed oil. "I've got something to show you," the doctor said.

He put a small radio, which must have been 30 years old, on the kitchen table. He reached behind the radio and picked up a cable that he plugged into an outlet. Derek was afraid that Gita would stop singing, but he also didn't want to ruin Akif's fun, so he didn't say anything. There were a few seconds of pop music and then a news announcer started speaking.

"Yesterday, at Vandenberg Air Force Base in California, a space elevator was launched for the first time," the professional voice said.

A space elevator? Derek imagined himself in an elevator car, its doors sliding shut as he presses the button with the label SPACE, and a minute later the doors open and he walks through them into a space station. He nods as people walk past him to get on the elevator.

The news was followed by some technical details and elaborations from excited experts.

The last sentence electrified Derek.

"Starting tomorrow, NASA wants to use this innovative concept to finally study the still-present rift from up close," the announcer said. "And now from Washington. In the budget crisis, the Senate and House of Representatives still appeared to be far..."

Derek set down the plate he had just dried, went to the kitchen table, and turned the radio off. "Did you hear that?" he asked.

"The space elevator? I thought they had shelved that idea years ago," Akif said.

"Yeah, but now they've tested it and are going to launch it."

"But not all the way to space. They don't have a license for that. I bet all the space travel companies objected to it. They'd want to keep it from competing with their rockets," Akif said.

"But I don't want to go into space. I want to go where they're going tomorrow."

"I wouldn't turn down an invitation, either, Derek."

"They're not going to give out invitations."

"That's the problem. We'll have to stay here."

"There's always a way," Derek said. Akif and Gita looked at him with shock.

"You want to break in by force?" Gita asked.

"They'll throw you in jail for years," Akif said.

"They'll have to catch me first."

Derek could feel his determination growing. It was interesting. First it had been a crazy dream, but with just a few spoken words he felt like it had transformed into a real possibility.

"How would they not catch you? The space elevator launches from an active military base. There must be a few thousand soldiers there. Are you going to fight off all of them?"

"They won't even know I'm there. I'll sneak in and hide myself in the elevator."

"How could you possibly do that, Derek? Surely the base is well secured."

"I was in the Air Force once. I know the protocols. A man in the right uniform won't arouse any suspicions. Especially right now, when there will be so many extra, non-regular workers moving around the base."

"So that's another reason you think you won't look especially strange," Akif said.

"Yeah, I think I can pull it off." The opportunity was beginning to feel like even more than that for him—it was transforming into a real future. He wanted to see it happen. Derek's stomach tightened. "But I'm going to need some help."

Akif and Gita looked at each other. Derek noted the still-skeptical look on the doctor's face.

Gita nodded. "You don't expect *us* to fight our way in, do you?"

"No, I just need eyes and ears, and a little logistics."

"'Logistics?'" Akif asked.

If the doctor was already asking about details, Derek

knew he almost had him convinced. He didn't want to put his new-found friends in danger, but he knew he had no chance at all if he tried to do it by himself.

"I have to get there somehow. But if a truck stops in one place for too long anywhere close to the base, even if it's still on a public access road, someone's going to get suspicious and raise an alarm."

"Okay, I can drop you off with your truck," Gita said. "No problem."

"After that, I'll need you two to do surveillance."

"How do you envision that working?"

"You'll have to set yourselves up with binoculars and night-vision devices at overlook points outside of the base. Then I'll need you to warn me if a patrol is coming too close."

"That sounds doable," Akif said.

"It's also not a crime to look at the base from public land, even with binoculars," Derek said. "Unless they catch me and can prove that you were assisting me. But they're not going to catch me."

"I don't understand how you can be so optimistic about that," Gita said. "Let's assume you're able to actually get into the elevator undetected, and ride along as a stowaway. You might be able to get that far. But at some point, you'll have to reveal yourself, otherwise why even go? And then when the elevator comes back down, the military will be waiting for you and take you into custody."

"Yes, I've thought about that too," Derek said. Then he paused, because he knew that his friends wouldn't like the rest of his plan. He wasn't sure if he liked it very much himself. After a long time, he had finally apparently found some real friends who wanted to support him, and then he was going to leave them so soon?

"Then there's a slight problem, don't you think?" Gita asked.

There was no way around it, he was just going to have to tell them the plain truth. "No," he said, "because I'll have left the space elevator by the time it returns to the ground."

Nobody said anything. Akif and Gita looked at each other again without a word. There was definitely something new going on between them. The doctor no longer looked at Gita like his sexless employee, but instead like a beautiful woman. And Gita had started projecting a real radiance these last few days. Derek was happy about it, because it probably wouldn't have happened if he hadn't shaken things up with his crazy idea.

"I... I don't suppose you're planning to bring along a parachute, and then jump to escape the soldiers?" Akif said finally, breaking the silence.

"No... No, I'm going to jump into the rift," Derek replied. "At first I thought I'd tell you some fairy tale like me jumping back to the ground with a parachute, but you're my friends and you deserve to know the truth."

"Thank you, Derek," Gita said quietly.

"Besides, that clearly wouldn't solve anything, because they would just track me down. Breaking into a military base isn't something they could just let go. It makes me a little worried about you two. They'll find out my identity somehow and then figure out who I've been in contact with recently. That could then lead them back to you two."

"Then we'll try to cover our tracks. Luckily, in this country they still have to prove your guilt before you can be convicted."

"I'll gladly help if I can," Derek said. "I was always trained to never leave any trace behind in my missions. Does this mean you'll help?"

"The weekend's coming up," Gita answered. "We didn't have any other plans, did we, Akif?"

"I've always wanted to see California again," the doctor said. "That's where my family entered this country when I was young."

DEREK USED THE MORNING TO STRAIGHTEN UP THE HOUSE. Akif gave him a hand. The doctor turned out to be a pleasant person to talk to. Gita had gone grocery shopping earlier and was back to singing in the kitchen while cooking their lunch. Even as he noted how much he enjoyed this domestic scene, everything felt like a long, slow farewell. Derek kept switching between sadness and anticipation. It was good not to be alone.

They had decided they would try to come up with a rough plan while eating. Gita had made a spicy Indian curry. Derek burned his tongue with the first bite. A good time to pause the meal and iron out the details. "It's about 26 hours to the coast," he said.

"We could fly," Akif suggested.

"Then I can't bring my gun with me," Derek said. "Don't worry, I'm not planning to shoot anyone, but I'm going to need some way of holding off the other passengers on the elevator. They'll outnumber me."

"If we took my car, we could let the autopilot drive," Akif said.

"Unfortunately, we can't do that, or the authorities will be able to track you two down. They can read all the electronics easily. My old truck is still completely analog."

"Okay, then we'll have to take turns driving," Gita said. "That's a good eight hours for each of us. That's doable."

"But isn't the launch scheduled for tomorrow?" Akif asked.

"I thought of a plan for that too. We'll send out a terror threat," Derek said.

"That's crazy. Won't they put in extra precautions around the base? It'll be even harder for you to get in."

"That wasn't my experience during my active duty. Shortly after the threat there'll be a lot of chaos. They'll search everything and everyone, but as soon as they figure out it's a false alarm, the level of attention and care will drop below even what it was to begin with."

"That makes sense psychologically," Akif said, "but I

wouldn't have thought that it'd be true for Air Force personnel too."

"They're only human, just like the rest of us," Derek said.

"Then the launch would be moved to sometime Sunday morning?" Gita asked.

"Yes, that's the most likely outcome, I think. The terrorist threat will cost them a few hours—they'll know that right from the start, no matter how it turns out. That's just standard protocol. They'll have to send the press home and tell them to come back the next day at the same time."

"That's what I would think too," Akif said.

"You'll bring me to the base sometime around midnight. Then you'll leave my truck in a neighborhood close by and rent a car under a false name to drive back. You can be back to open up your office right on time Monday morning."

"If anyone asks us, we'll just say we were on a premature honeymoon. We saw you last on the 31st. There are witnesses to that," Akif said.

Gita beamed at Akif. Derek grinned. *I knew it!*

"They'll find out that you were in California, you'll have to expect that," Derek said. "The rental car company will confirm it."

"True. I'll say that I'd always wanted to see the ocean," Gita said. "And as an unmarried woman, I couldn't just use my real name, traveling with a man. What would people say!"

Derek turned away. He was unsure. Investigators would see right through these lies. His friends would be headed right into trouble all because of him. But no one could prove that they knew what he had planned. Nobody would be able to interrogate him. He was certain no one would believe Akif and Gita, but in the end, the authorities would have to let them go. They wouldn't have done anything wrong themselves. At least he hoped not. It weighed upon him that they might have to suffer because of him. They didn't deserve that.

By now the food wasn't so hot anymore. They ate in silence.

"I'll pack some food and water," Gita said after the plates

had been cleared. "The two of us will have to stay in the truck while we're on the road. Otherwise a security camera might film us somewhere. You two should probably put on some new clothes."

"Can I borrow some clean clothes, Derek?"

"No problem, look in the closet in the bedroom."

"How about you, Gita?" Akif asked, "do you need to get anything from your apartment?"

"A lady always has a change of underwear with her," Gita claimed. "I already washed what I was wearing before, earlier this morning. They should be dry by now."

"Let's meet at the truck in 15 minutes," Derek said. "I'll be happy to say goodbye to this house."

HE WAS ALONE IN HIS HOUSE AGAIN. NEVERTHELESS, IT WASN'T completely quiet. There was a ticking sound coming from somewhere in the distance, although he didn't own a non-digital clock. Now and then he heard a rustling, some animal probably. His breathing quieted. A beam of light came through the keyhole in the kitchen door and landed on the dark floor, dancing in slow motion. Small particles of dust glittered in the light like diamonds. The kitchen smelled of Indian spices and wood preservative.

It wasn't a beautiful house, but it had been a good one. Derek was grateful for all the time that it had provided him with shelter and safety. He hadn't often been happy during his years there, but it wasn't the house's fault. Gently he ran his hand over the shiny brown wooden ball that formed the end of the banister. If he were to come back, he would remove the brown paint. He imagined the hidden grain of the wood underneath. It would most certainly display intricate paths as inextricable as those in his own life. By all standards he was probably crazy to believe in a different reality. But he had decided he would try to follow this path to its end. He owed it to Mary.

Derek touched the wooden ball affectionately, as if it were a representative for the whole house. As soon as he let go, dust would start to settle on it. Dust would continue to collect inside the house after he left, just like it had grown dusty over the last several years due to his lack of care. The rain would wash the outside, but it wouldn't reach the inside, at least until the roof leaked and the house started to fall into disrepair. Someday the wooden ball would be almost unrecognizable under a thick layer of dust.

He turned around and walked to the door. The boards creaked under his steps. He opened the front door and had to shade his eyes, it was so bright outside. He took a big step across the threshold and stood outside. Then he turned around and pulled the door closed. He left it unlocked.

June 1, 2085, Ceres

M6 LIFTED HIS LEFT FRONT LEG. WITH THE FREE GRIPPING mechanisms, he opened the flap to the analyzer. He took out an object, a foreign body, that hadn't been in there yesterday.

He had birthed an automatic camera.

M6 was proud of his product. He activated the remote connection. The camera confirmed that it was there and successfully completed its self-test. He gave it the command to take a photo. Milliseconds later it delivered its picture. He saw a section of his own, relatively giant-sized body. So, the camera had seen its maker.

He picked it up, set it down a little farther away, and moved back a bit. Then he sent a command for another picture. The picture now showed almost his entire body, but it was little more than a dark silhouette. He would have to adjust the settings to better fit the lighting from the surroundings. M6 tested two other positions. Then he calculated a lighting curve from the pictures and uploaded it into the camera.

The next pictures looked particularly good. But the picture noise grew when he was too far away. That could be fixed. He had selected extra robust designs for the sensors.

M6 tested the video mode. He had the camera record 20 pictures per second. To see himself replicated on the screen felt very strange, almost as if he had left his body. He had to remember that the camera was not part of himself, but it was its own object equipped with its own, limited intelligence.

It couldn't move, but it could convert sunlight into electrical energy and create information—a higher state of order —so the camera decreased the amount of entropy of the system. Isn't that comparable to the functions of a biological plant? And if it were equipped with wheels, then would it be an animal? No, it lacked the ability to reproduce. Even if it lived forever, it would never have offspring.

But wasn't it the same as he was, then? The analyzer was too small to produce a full-sized copy of himself. However, he could manufacture individual parts of himself inside the analyzer and then assemble them together on the platform. Ceres certainly had all the necessary materials. It would be an interesting project—if he had enough time for it. M6 calculated a rough estimate. He had needed one day for the automatic camera, which had a volume of maybe one-hundredth of his own. Thus, to replicate himself, he would need approximately 100 days. That was significantly less time than humans needed for their reproduction. If the copies then made even more copies, he could redouble the number of brothers and sisters every 100 days. After 33 generations, or 3,300 days, there would be over eight billion specimens of himself, and after another 100 days, the number of M6s would surpass the total number of humans.

It was a strange thought. In practical terms, Ceres would run out of space pretty quickly. The planetoid might also run out of the necessary resources. They would have to alter the designs and use replacement materials. Then not every M6 would be the same—there would be lower-quality and higher-quality specimens.

No thanks, M6 thought. It was sometimes difficult enough just existing with himself. It would be a comforting thought, however, to not completely disappear from reality due to his experiment. But it likely wouldn't even help to build a duplicate. As soon as he was no longer part of reality, the copy then also could never have existed. *It is what it is*, he thought, again wondering which of his makers programmed that line into him. As soon as he entered the rift, everything would change.

"Start filming," he commanded the camera.

He could only hope that his disappearance wouldn't also affect the camera. He had used an optical module from his internal mechanisms that had been manufactured on Earth. At some point it had probably passed through the hands of some person during quality assurance checks and this person could at least theoretically remember it. Maybe that would preserve the camera as a whole in this version of reality? It was impossible for him to know for sure.

M6 set himself at the outermost edge of the platform. He aligned himself with the rift. The motion that he would need to execute in order to disappear completely into the rift was already stored in all the relevant memory banks for his extremities. M6 concentrated like never before. Nothing could go wrong. Then he jumped.

June 1, 2085, Pasadena

"Mommy, are you coming now?" Luisa asked.

Maribel turned around. Her daughter stood in the open bathroom door with her backpack on her back, a reproachful expression on her face.

"I'm sorry, sweetie, but I have more work to do."

"You always take so long. Me and Daddy have been waiting forever."

She was exaggerating a little bit. Chen had only finished brushing his teeth ten minutes before, and he was still in the bathroom, standing next to her in his underwear.

"You and Daddy can go without me. I'll meet you down at the beach."

"But I want you to come with us. Other mommies go with their families."

Maribel sighed as Chen walked into the bedroom to dress. Did Luisa have the right to demand that her family be just like everyone else's? She didn't know, but she also couldn't change anything. She was now the head of the Astrophysical Institute, and she liked her work. Without her work, she would never have met Chen and there would never have been a Luisa. Someday their daughter would understand that.

"I'm sorry, Luisa, but I'm not done yet. Either you'll have

to wait another 15 minutes for me to finish or you can start without me."

Luisa stomped her foot but didn't answer. She turned around and slammed the bathroom door shut. Although muffled, Maribel heard what she said to Chen. "Come on, Daddy, Mommy's going to take forever. Let's go to the beach. We can have fun without her."

That hurt her feelings. Should she say something? No, that was life. She couldn't just tear herself away. She also didn't want to go out in public without at least some makeup on. Luisa still needed her, but she wasn't going to let her completely rule her life. Maribel walked over to the mirror, thought about her work, and then reached for the eyeliner.

THERE WAS A GLORIOUS SILENCE IN THE SUITE WHEN SHE CAME out of the bathroom. She took the white-and-yellow striped dress out of the closet, pulled it on, and then looked for her yellow sandals, finally locating them in her suitcase. All prepared, she sat down on the sofa. There was a pretty view of the ocean from there. The air was somewhat hazy, but it promised to be a beautiful day. Next to the sofa was a wet towel on the floor. Chen had probably dropped it there and then forgotten to pick it up. She leaned over, snatched it up, and carried it to the bathroom.

The phone rang. Maribel considered whether she should answer it. Luisa would have to wait for her a little longer if she did. But most likely she was already having fun and not thinking about her mother. She accepted the call by pressing the green button on the room phone.

The face of a blonde woman with strikingly even features was projected onto the wall. "Good morning, my name is Yelena, I'm calling from the Institute for Planetary Science in Novosibirsk," she said in American-sounding English. Maribel couldn't detect any underlying accent.

"Nice to meet you. I'm Maribel Pedreira."

"Wonderful. I would like to connect you with the head of the institute, Oleg Tarassov."

"Gladly."

"One moment, please."

The projection now showed the institute's logo, if Maribel's rudimentary knowledge of Russian was correct. Then she saw a bald-headed man, who could have passed as Glen Sparrow's light-skinned twin. Or did all men without hair look the same to her?

"Good morning, Ms. Pedreira, I'm glad that you have time to talk with me. My name is Oleg Tarassov."

"Pleased to meet you. It must be quite late where you are, isn't it?"

Tarassov nodded. "But that doesn't bother me. The message from your colleague, Mr. Sparrow, took a rather circuitous route to get to me. It really took much longer than it should have, so I wanted to call you back right away."

"That was very kind of you, thank you. You know why I wanted to talk to you, right? We've discovered that the rift ends on Ceres."

"Yes, the rift. Actually I'm a little jealous. We don't see it here in Siberia at all. It's an extremely interesting phenomenon."

"I've heard that you have a mobile research unit on Ceres."

"That's correct, I can confirm that. We have an M-series research robot in place on Ceres."

"Has it reported to you about the rift already?"

"No. Strangely enough, it hasn't reported anything about it yet. But you must understand, this is a locally autonomous AI. In other words, the robot itself decides when and how it will execute its orders, and what and when it will report to us—within certain parameters, of course. Real-time communications are not possible at that distance, so a certain amount of freedom is required. It's quite possible M6 discovered the rift, but classified it as irrelevant to its work. And it wouldn't be wrong about that. Who could predict that such a strange phenomenon would appear?"

"It's called M6?"

"Yes, it's the sixth specimen of the M-series. Its siblings are working on other celestial bodies. Here at the institute, we evaluate the incoming data and issue new work orders."

"Then it would be possible to order M6 to study the rift," Maribel said.

"Of course. And for us to do that, it would also be quite helpful if you could provide us with everything you've already found out about it."

Of course, Comrade Tarassov, you're curious what we've already discovered. And, of course, if she wanted to include M6 in her research of the rift, she'd have to give the Russians what they wanted.

"I will start on that right away. Then you can tailor your research strategy to what we already know."

Tarassov moved away from the camera to press a few buttons, so that the camera now showed more of him. He had significantly wider shoulders than Glen Sparrow. Tarassov looked like he could have been a former pro wrestler.

"As soon as we have your data, we'll send some appropriate orders to M6. I will speak to the scientist who is actually responsible for the robot as soon as I can."

"When do you think you'll be able to receive data back, Mr. Tarassov?"

"Give us two days. M6 might have to go halfway around Ceres. I'll call you again as soon as I have something."

"Thank you. I hope you have a good night."

"And I wish you much success on your flight in the space elevator."

The connection ended and the Russian's face disappeared from the wall. News of the space elevator's launch had reached all the way to Siberia. Not really a surprise, considering the presence of the media everywhere. Maribel walked around the room aimlessly. The yellow sandals were rubbing against her heels, but she didn't have anything else that matched her dress. She also didn't want to keep Luisa waiting any longer. She put her phone into her small, yellow leather bag, put the strap over her shoulder, and walked out of the suite.

June 1, 2085, Ceres

M6 LOOKED AROUND. HIS SIX LEGS WERE STANDING ON A platform like the one he had built. The sky was black and full of stars. All around him was a near vacuum. Even the gravity matched that of Ceres. Everything pointed to him being on Ceres. He could still remember his exact trajectory. It matched his planned path exactly. He had moved closer and closer to the cleft. The blackness had looked to him like the quiet surface of a deep ocean. He could detect absolutely no underlying or internal structure.

Then his front legs had entered the cleft and the strangest part of his experiment had begun. His legs entered at approximately a 30-degree angle, and at the same instant, the legs of another robot had appeared out of the blackness in front of him. In a microsecond-fast measurement, he determined the angle at which they appeared and got an answer of 150 degrees. It was as if the cleft was reflecting him, but his consciousness always remained on this side, while on the other side he saw exactly what had disappeared from this side.

According to his memory, there was no moment in which he had been completely in the cleft. He had followed the precalculated path exactly and had simply landed back on the platform. But there was one difference—everything had happened in mirror symmetry to his calculations.

M6 started a self-test. He had a suspicion and he wanted to know whether he was still himself, exactly as he had been before. Because he needed to examine himself at a fundamental, structural level, he set his nanofabricators on the move. He was especially interested in the organic long-term memory banks. They worked on the basis of amino acids, almost like human genes. His nanofabricators would bombard them with photons—particles of light—and he would thus be able to determine their structure.

The process took a few minutes, mostly because the nanofabricators first had to reach his memory banks. M6 tried to get in contact with Earth, but he couldn't reach the Ceres satellite at that moment. Then the first measurement data came in. The amino acids in his memory banks were now right-handed. M6 felt like his reward center was going to burst. Right-handed! That was astonishing! Wait until he reported this to Earth—almost all life on Earth was based on left-handed amino acids—even his own design had been built on this variant.

He compiled his findings, prepared a message, and saved it until the radio relay station would come back into range of his antennas.

June 2, 2085, Novosibirsk

"COLLEAGUE TARASSOV, CAN I HAVE A QUICK WORD?"

"Of course. Come in, Kirilenko."

A scrawny man in a white lab coat stood in the doorway. He tentatively approached the desk.

What does Kirilenko want with me? wondered Tarassov. Then he remembered. This was the man responsible for all radio contact with the mobile-research robots. "Has another relay failed?" he asked, tapping his fingernails impatiently on the desktop.

Kirilenko had a way of reporting that really got on his nerves. He talked very slowly, as if he were afraid of each word and had to turn it around in his mouth three times and examine it before letting it out.

"No, the relays are working very well—at least the ones that we're in contact with right now."

Kirilenko always qualified his responses. It was obvious that he couldn't say anything about the status of a satellite that was currently unreachable due to being on the far side of the planet, but the man seemed compelled to consider every possibility—a prime quality for a researcher. Apparently, he was unable to limit this trait when making verbal reports.

"So, what do you want?" The question came out sounding much less friendly than he had intended. Kirilenko flinched, as if he had been hit with a whip. Tarassov felt sorry for the man.

"I meant to ask, is there a problem?" Tarassov asked, now deliberately sounding friendlier.

"It's about M6."

Tarassov sat up straight. This was getting interesting. "What about M6?"

"We've lost contact."

"What? Just now? And the relay is working, you say?"

"Yes, it's sending our commands to him, but the robot is not answering."

"Maybe it was hit by an asteroid?" Tarassov knew himself how unlikely that was. There must be some other reason for the loss of the robot—and he was sure that it had to do with the rift.

"We're waiting for the pictures from the relay satellite's camera," Kirilenko said.

"I will be very interested to see them. Now back to work!"

Something buzzed in Kirilenko's coat pocket. He took out a phone. "It's my colleague, Ugryumov. Please excuse me."

"Yes, of course, I think we're done."

THE DOOR HAD BARELY CLOSED WHEN THERE WAS ANOTHER knock and the door was reopened. Tarassov was annoyed. "What is it now, Kirilenko?"

"Interesting news from Ugryumov," the scrawny scientist said, straightening his glasses.

"Out with it."

"M6 is responding, after all, in some fashion."

"What does that mean? 'In some fashion?' Can you not express it precisely and scientifically?"

"It's unintelligible, but something is being received."

"So, radio signals, you mean?"

"Yes, via radio."

"Bring Ugryumov to me right now. I want him to play back the signals for me. I want to see them for myself."

"Right away, boss," Kirilenko answered and hurried from the room without closing the door.

Tarassov sighed.

TEN MINUTES LATER, UGRYUMOV AND KIRILENKO WERE ON the left and right of his desk. They were standing at attention, like two life-size toy soldiers. Was he really such a strict boss? Tarassov couldn't remember ever standing so rigidly in front of any of his former bosses.

"Come closer and have a look at the screen with me," he requested. Then he called up the time plot of the radio signal. "What do we have here?" he muttered while he considered the diagram.

He hadn't meant it as an actual question, but Kirilenko answered anyway. "The frequency matches and the signal envelope looks normal," he said.

"Yes, but the coding looks completely random to me," Ugryumov objected.

Tarassov had the computer calculate the signal's entropy or information content. It was considerably below the value for random events.

"See? That's not random," he said. "M6 must've changed the coding."

"Why would he do that? We never gave him an order to change it," Kirilenko said.

"If you remember, the robot's not completely alone up there anymore," Tarassov said.

"You mean this has something to do with the rift?"

"That's the only explanation I see right now. But let's look at the signal. I don't think M6 would have intentionally changed the coding without trying to tell us something. Let's try to figure out what physical processes he's been exposed to, and what their effects might be."

Ugryumov leaned over him and pressed a few buttons. Tarassov was put off by the man's strong body odor, but he didn't comment or move.

"Look, I can try a few trivial mathematical operations. Shifts, rotations, reflections..." said Ugryumov.

"Reflections," Tarassov and Kirilenko said simultaneously.

Suddenly, the coding made sense again. M6 had modulated his signal according to a simple reflection transformation!

"That's it, gentlemen! And now I have two orders for you —ask M6 why he's sending reflected communications, and give him orders to study the rift. And, I want results in front of me as soon as possible!"

June 2, 2085, Novosibirsk

"Colleague Tarassov, may I have a quick word?"

"Of course, come in, Kirilenko."

A scrawny man in a white lab coat stood in the doorway. Tentatively Kirilenko entered and approached his boss's desk.

Tarassov wondered what the man wanted with him. Then he remembered that this man was responsible for the radio contact with the mobile research robots.

"Has another relay failed?" Tarassov asked, tapping impatiently on the desktop.

"No, the relays are working very well, at least the ones that we're in contact with right now."

"So, what do you want?"

"It's about M6."

"What about M6?"

"He's not there anymore."

"What do you mean, Kirilenko?"

"The robot no longer exists."

"You mean you've lost contact with it?"

"No, I mean its physical existence has been terminated."

"Why do you always have to talk in such a convoluted way? It's either there or it's not. Isn't that enough?"

"I... um, I..."

"Why are you waffling so much? What's the problem?"

"I double checked our database. We have records for robots M1 to M5 and then M7 to M15. But no M6."

"That's impossible! Where would M6 have been stationed if it existed?"

"Ceres," Kirilenko said.

"Yes, Ceres, that sounds right," Tarassov answered. "The Americans asked us for help because the rift ends there. Are you sure we have no research units there?"

"As I said, all the memory banks are empty. It's been two years since we removed the T-series from there, and we haven't had any new findings on Ceres since. If there was an M-robot there, it would've sent us data."

"But Kirilenko, Ceres is the queen of the asteroid belt. It would be an inexcusable mistake if we didn't put any research units there." A mistake that would be laid squarely on his own shoulders, Tarassov knew.

"Like I said, the database..."

"Databases can be erased. What does the real evidence say?"

"We've looked at pictures from the satellite we have orbiting Ceres. It's clear from those pictures that there's no mobile unit there."

"Then why didn't you just say that!" Tarassov was at a loss. How could this happen to him? Could he somehow have overlooked stationing an M-unit on Ceres? If that were true, then he would deserve to lose his job. He put his arms down on the desk. The corners of his mouth dropped. "And what am I supposed to tell the people at NASA now? I promised them measurements from Ceres in exchange for their data."

"Maybe tell them the truth." Kirilenko wiggled his eyebrows, showing no sign of his earlier timidity. He was trying to indicate that he didn't mean this version of the truth, but some different one. "Namely that we had a robot there, but we can't locate it anymore."

Tarassov thought he knew what Kirilenko had in mind. With that lie—that altered truth—he could remain at the head of the institute. But his successor would have to be

Kirilenko. If he followed this suggestion, Kirilenko would have him in his back pocket.

"A robot that disappears from one moment to the next, isn't that great news? Especially because we found something in the images that supports this claim nicely." Kirilenko took a dramatic pause.

"Well, tell me!"

"Something built a kind of platform up to where the rift ends. It looks as if that something wanted to study—or at least take a closer look at—the rift. What if that was M6's work? And why is there no trace of him in our database?"

Kirilenko was being a scoundrel, and the bait was too tempting to resist. Tarassov decided to support this version of the truth.

June 2, 2085, Grand Junction, Colorado

Akif yawned. He pinched his thigh. The pain woke him up, at least briefly. Then he patted his cheeks. He had already tried everything, but he just wasn't used to driving for such long distances. The air was blowing such cold air in his face that his eyes were watering. Derek was snoring behind him with his legs stretched out. Gita had covered herself in a blanket and was curled up like a small dog. He didn't think he would be flexible enough to do that.

Maybe it would've been better if Gita had stayed behind in Kansas. He realized that he was worried about her. That was something new, something exciting and scary at the same time. Earlier he had thought of her as one of life's givens, something that was just always there when you needed it, almost like a piece of furniture. She had been working for years at her starting salary and he had never thought to wonder why Gita had never asked for a raise or looked for a better paying job. He decided that she must simply be satisfied with what she had.

That was an art form that he had never mastered. Akif was always unsatisfied, even as a kid. It had become obvious to him that he would never change, so he refrained from trying to get to know women. He knew at some point he would become dissatisfied with them and then look for someone new. He also could use his money to satisfy his needs. As a doctor, he certainly wasn't paid poorly, and with prostitutes, you usually got what you paid for, he had found.

Then Mary had come along—according to his memory, at least, if not the patient records. Mary, the discontented soul. He had recognized her as a kindred spirit, and she had felt like he understood her, even though their sources of dissatisfaction had been vastly different. Mary had not been happy with what was. He was unhappy because of what could be. Between them, there had been no difference.

He shook his head. Which of them were real memories—an actual past—and which were make-believe? For a moment he had even thought to stow away in the space elevator with Derek, so as to not leave Mary alone with him. But then it became clear to him how crazy the idea was. On the rear seat, rolled up and covered by a blanket, that was his reality. He would be an idiot to ignore her. Gita was a good person. He was truly and unbelievably lucky that she had found him and stuck by him for so long.

A yellow light illuminated to indicate that the tank was getting low on fuel. He would have to wake Derek. Akif spotted a place to pull off, put on the turn signal, and stopped.

"Hey, Derek," he said quietly so as not to wake Gita, then reached for Derek's knee.

"Are we there?"

"Unfortunately, no. We need gas. Maybe we can do it without waking Gita."

In the rearview mirror, he watched as Derek tried to open the door as quietly as possible. He unbuckled himself and held onto the seatbelt so that it wouldn't retract too loudly. Then he opened the driver's door. *Hot.* A hot, dry wind was blowing. Outside, it was a good five degrees warmer than inside the truck.

He got out and stretched his legs. As Derek passed him he put his hand briefly on Derek's shoulder. "Wake me in two hours, okay?"

"As you wish, Akif."

The two men climbed back into the truck, Derek as driver, Akif onto the rear seat. Derek started the engine and drove on. At the gas station, only Derek got out, so only he would show up on any security camera films. The truck's windows had a dark tint, so no one could see passengers in the back seat.

Akif quickly fell into a fitful sleep after they left the gas station. His dreams featured the rift in the starring role. It had the shape of a ribbon, and someone had wrapped it around his body so that he couldn't move.

June 2, 2085, Ceres

THE REPLY THAT M6 RECEIVED FROM EARTH WAS ANYTHING but satisfying. His supervisor, a certain Kirilenko, suggested he was experiencing a memory error and recommended that he run thorough system diagnostics and then repair his memory cells. Because, of course, life was based on right-handed amino acids. It was only logical that he would therefore only find that variant in his organic modules.

M6 knew better. His systems were working correctly. So, there was only one possible conclusion. He wasn't defective. Instead, the rift had changed his world. It was clear to M6 that this was a radical theory that nobody else would accept. It was almost impossible to expect anyone to believe him, even if logic was on his side. The only question was what he should do with this knowledge.

The simplest thing would be for him to continue with the orders that he'd already been given. Surely Ceres still had a huge amount of interesting data to offer. He estimated that there were enough research topics here to keep him working for at least 50 years, with his current capabilities. It would provide him with immensely satisfying activities. It would be similar to putting together a puzzle, except that he first had to find all the puzzle pieces. They were scattered everywhere around here, in the crust, on the surface, he would not be able to dig up everything, but he had a good chance to create an identifiable overall picture from the pieces that he would be able to find.

However, the cleft—apparently they were calling it 'the rift' on earth—was also here, a phenomenon that nobody else had studied as thoroughly as he had. M-units like him were working on many other celestial bodies. They were eager data collectors. But he alone was on Ceres, and he alone had the chance to become something incredibly special. He no longer had to be M-System Number 6, manufactured after Number 5 and before Number 7, because he could become the AI that cracked the mystery of the rift—that understood it—if that was even possible at all. He had a chance that not even his creators could have provided. Didn't that mean it would be a waste to not seize this chance?

M6 believed he would have to weigh and decide between the two possibilities. That had become clear to him after he went through his previous findings again. He had already gone into the rift once, so he couldn't stop now. The rift had changed him. It had mirrored individual parts of his components, so that now they had spatially different constructions. He was no longer M6. Even his creators would no longer accept him as the machine that they had built and supplied with an adaptive AI. He couldn't go back, so in actuality he had no choice at all. M6 would have to continue along this path.

Part of the data packet from Earth had included new orders for him. He decided he would ignore them. First, he must figure out where he was. It was, in any case, not the world from which he had come. Via the Deep Space Network, M6 had access to the Earth's data networks. That was intended to help him gather information by himself for his research orders. The scientists in Novosibirsk therefore didn't have to worry whether he had the necessary expert knowledge, because he could always just search the databanks for whatever he was missing. He had to request feature and capability upgrades, but knowledge he could just download by himself. What interested him now were the contents of online encyclopedias from all around the world. The download would take approximately two hours.

THE DATA PACKET HAD ARRIVED. M6 UNPACKED AND decompressed it. He didn't care about knowing when some politician was born or who, according to the authors of that particular encyclopedia, had discovered America. Instead, he was looking for contradictions and discrepancies. That was something he was especially good at—he could search through a huge deluge of facts in a short amount of time and determine how many contradictions appeared. M6 gave the job to his subconscious. It would notify him when the processing was complete.

In his conscious mind, he ran an analysis on himself. Why had he started this check? Because he himself embodied one big contradiction. He had reached this world, and yet he had retained memories of his origin. The universe could have saved itself from him noticing anything if it had simply had him forget that he once had left-handed memory molecules. Why was that not the case? The simplest solution was that he was defective, as his supervisor suggested. But he didn't believe it. From an outside perspective, that would only go to further confirm the theory that he was defective. What crazy person admits that he's crazy? But he couldn't do that himself, and he knew that it might be a weakness in his theory.

But it was also possible that this contradiction was only part of an endless chain of contradictions that stretched through this world like the rift itself. That would be a terrible consequence. The whole existence of the universe depended upon an effect coming after its cause. First there had been the Big Bang, and then the end of the universe. At the smallest scale, in the quantum world, that was not necessarily true, but so far quantum phenomena had never been able to be scaled up to the dimensions of visible objects. Was the rift perhaps a giant quantum disturbance? Then his existence could throw the entire universe into chaos and possibly threaten to wipe it out.

His subconscious reported that the analysis was complete. The results shocked him. The number of contradictions was enormous. They weren't contradictory opinions, but instead facts that were recognized by everyone, and yet definitely did not fit together. But why had none of the inhabitants of Earth noticed? Because they were trapped in these contradictions and their logic was so strained that the contradictions appeared to go away.

It was as if the universe was trying to cover the holes in logic with patches. No one could see the holes themselves anymore, if you hadn't come from outside this universe like M6, but the patches could still be detected if you went looking for them. But why would anyone go looking if they didn't see a reason to? Should he warn them? Who would believe him—a robot with faulty memory chips? No, he had to try to solve the problem himself. Maybe that was the reason why he, of all entities, had been given this one singular chance.

M6 moved to the edge of the platform and jumped into the blackness—as he had already done once before.

June 2, 2085, Pasadena

TODAY WAS THE BIG DAY. MARIBEL CAME OUT OF THE bathroom, her hair still wet. She tried to be as quiet as possible because Luisa was still asleep. She thought about her daughter, who was all stretched out in the middle of the bed. Whenever she breathed, a strand of hair danced out of the way. She was so beautiful! Maribel couldn't help herself. She kneeled on the bed and gently stroked her daughter's bare leg. Luisa continued to sleep.

That was fine with Maribel. She had argued with Chen yesterday for a long time about whether he and Luisa should attend the first manned launch of the space elevator. Maribel would have liked her family to be there, but Chen was strictly against it.

"I already thought you died once. I can't watch without going through all that all over again," he had said.

That day, back in '72, a rocket had exploded, and Maribel was supposed to have been on board. Chen had watched the launch and saw the explosion on television, but hadn't known that she hadn't boarded the rocket, having decided right before take-off not to board it.

"This project is completely different. It's totally safe. We're taking off from an active military base," Maribel argued, but her husband wasn't about to change his mind.

"You can decide for yourself what you want to do, I'm not going to try to talk you out of it," he had said, "but I don't want Luisa to have to go through anything like that."

Maribel had finally decided to go along with what her husband wanted. She knew, deep down, that Chen had a point. The space elevator had been tested, it was true, but no technology was 100 percent safe, especially not something so completely new. It was impossible. They hadn't yet told Luisa what world-changing event was taking place that morning, and it would stay that way. That's why it was good that she was still asleep, because it would probably be impossible for Maribel to hide her excitement.

She walked out of the bedroom as quietly as she had entered. Chen had gotten up with her and he was sitting, dressed, on the sofa. He watched her dress. She let the towel she had wrapped around herself drop to the floor, took her underwear from the chair, and stepped into it. Then she put on her bra. She pulled on some cotton pants, black-and-white striped, and then a white V-neck T-shirt. Everything very plain. It didn't matter. There was a NASA uniform waiting for her at the base.

"You are beautiful," Chen said suddenly.

"Thank you."

The compliment made her truly happy.

"And thank you for taking care of Luisa today. And every day. And for always being there for me and our family."

All at once she felt all the feelings come rushing up inside her—saying goodbye, the uncertainty, but also her love for Chen and Luisa. She wished that they could go with her.

Her phone vibrated. That must be the car she had called. It was—it had sent her its location. "I've got to go," she said.

"What, no make-up, no fancy hairdo today?" Chen teased her.

"That wouldn't be very practical for the space elevator. But you're right, I've forgotten to blow-dry my hair."

She disappeared quickly into the bathroom and dried her hair. When she walked out of the bathroom, Chen was standing there in front of her. He opened his arms and she stepped into his embrace.

THE SELF-DRIVING VEHICLE HAD BEEN DRIVING FOR ALMOST AN hour with its passenger inside when a message came in.

"Glen Sparrow would like to talk with you," the automatic system's voice said.

"Thank you, please connect."

"One moment."

"Maribel! I'm glad I was able to reach you."

Sparrow looked very agitated. His bald head was dotted by red splotches.

"What's going on?"

"I'm sorry. Everything's in total chaos here."

"Problem with the hardware?"

"No, everything's operating perfectly. The base has been placed under a bomb alert. There's some cult that's worried God's place in heaven will be desecrated by our mission."

Maribel nodded. She had heard about groups like that. They often tried to block rocket launches. Before, they had always protested peacefully, chaining themselves to launch pads or blocking the airspace with gliders.

"And they're now threatening to set off a bomb?"

"Nobody here believes they really would. The group has never resorted to violence before. But last time their disruptive actions weren't at all successful. Maybe the bomb threat's a new tactic. They know we can't just ignore it. It doesn't matter how unlikely it is, the base will have to be cleared and thoroughly searched."

"Okay, got it. So, we won't be able to launch today?"

"Exactly, that's why I'm happy I reached you. Go back to your hotel, enjoy the day with your family, and I'll take care of the preparations here."

"A little bit stressed, huh?"

Glen nodded. "It's a catastrophe. The bomb response unit

will have to pick up and overturn and inspect everything. We'll have to repeat all our tests. After they let us back in, of course. Right now they're still doing their thing."

"Then I wish you success and no more added stress."

"Thanks. I'll see you tomorrow. Same time."

MARIBEL WAS BACK IN THE HOTEL AN HOUR LATER. SHE PAID for the ride with her card. The doorman greeted her. She ran to the elevator. If she was lucky, Chen and Luisa would still be there. She pressed the silver button with the number 9. The doors closed quietly, a barely identifiable melody murmuring in the background. *Will there be elevator music in the space elevator too?* On the 9th floor she hurried through the corridor. Thick carpet damped the sounds of her footsteps. She passed a maid with a large cart full of sheets and towels. She liked how old-fashioned this hotel was, since most other hotels had switched to special robots for room service.

"Good morning," the woman greeted her.

Maribel returned the greeting. She reached the door to her suite, opened it with her card, and stepped in. She noticed at once that nobody else was there. She was alone. Room service hadn't been there yet. The curtains in the bedroom were still closed. She thought she could still see the impression that her daughter had left in the middle of the bed.

She threw herself onto the bed and felt herself bounce due to the rebound from the mattress springs. Should she try to sleep a little more? Chen and Luisa wouldn't miss her. They might even be a bit disappointed if she suddenly showed up. When Luisa was with her father, Maribel thought that he always allowed her more latitude than she would. That was seldom ever a problem, luckily.

She decided to do some work, even if it was Saturday. Maybe this Tarassov from the Institute for Planetary Science had something for her already. He seemed to be the type to work at night, so she decided she could at least try to reach him. She dialed the number that he had emailed to her.

In one minute Tarassov's face appeared on the projected surface. Maribel tried to read his expression and decided the best fit was 'confused.'

"I just tried to reach you a short time ago, Ms. Pedreira," the Russian said, scratching his nose.

"I was on my way to the base. But I appreciate you trying."

"Yes, I was told you were in a car. When I tried to reach you there, I was told you were already talking with someone else."

Maribel remembered her call with Glen Sparrow and nodded. "Have you found out something new about the rift?" she asked.

"Yes and no. From satellite images we can confirm that it does end where you said it did."

"Has your mobile unit taken a closer look?"

"What mobile unit are you talking about?"

"You told me about a mobile research unit of the M-series."

Tarassov paused thoughtfully. Maribel had the feeling that he was composing his next sentence very carefully.

Why? she wondered. *Is there something you're trying to hide?*

"Our robot, M6, apparently tried to examine the rift. He even built a kind of platform so that he could get closer to it. I'll gladly send you the images."

"Very clever."

"Yes. Only, unfortunately, our M6 then disappeared."

"Disappeared?" Maribel watched Tarassov's face, but he had put on his poker face.

"Yes. You heard correctly. He's gone. It's as if he never existed."

She had to sit down. Little by little an image formed in her subconscious. She didn't know how the picture would turn out yet, but it scared her. She had the feeling that when it was complete, it would overwhelm her, plunging her and everyone else into darkness. She could not let that happen, not for her sake alone, but for Luisa's, and Chen's.

"That's an astonishing statement, Tarassov. You know that, right?"

The Russian nodded.

Something didn't seem right to her, but she had no idea yet what it was.

"Ah, well, astonishing, maybe, we'll have to see," he said. Tarassov sounded extremely reserved. Was that his real personality? She would have to ask a few colleagues about that.

"You're the first one to show that the rift might be a danger," she said. "If that's confirmed, it could cause large-scale panic here on Earth."

The Russian opened his mouth, but then closed it again. "I..." he said, "that's why I need to ask you to keep this to yourself. Not even our intelligence agencies know about it. Maybe we can keep it from getting out for a while. Nothing's happened on Earth yet, so why should we incite panic?"

Tarassov sounded surprisingly reasonable. She might have made that suggestion herself. Then it finally occurred to her what was bothering her about the whole situation.

"I've got another question, Mr. Tarassov."

"Yes?" Tarassov raised his eyebrows. Did he know what she was going to say?

"You said M6 had disappeared—as if he never existed."

"Correct."

"But you still know that he was stationed on Ceres? How can that be, if he never existed?"

The Russian scientist turned red. Her suspicions had been justified. Something wasn't right with his story.

"It's complicated," Tarassov said finally.

"I'm sure that's true. But our job is to explain complicated things and make them understandable. I need you to try."

"Give me half an hour. I'll need a secure connection."

"Understood. I'll wait for your call."

Maribel was not happy with herself. She could have gone off to find Chen and Luisa, but instead she was here, waiting for the Russian to call her back. He had sounded stressed. Telling lies caused stress. But was that the only reason? It probably had something to do with the rift, just like it was affecting everything else right now. Whether directly or indirectly, the phenomenon was exerting much more influence on people's lives than was being officially admitted.

She sat down on the sofa and searched the Internet for what people were thinking about the rift. Naturally, there were some conspiracy theorists who thought everything was an insidious plan by a world government or the Illuminati. And then there were people who were reporting strange dreams in which they were together with other people whom they couldn't remember when they were awake.

The number of cases of déjà vu had increased. Maribel checked the numbers for different time periods. In recent days there was a significant increase in the number of searches for this term. She looked at a few forum entries. Most of the descriptions didn't fit the classical definition of déjà vu, but certainly seemed like variations. She couldn't discern any underlying pattern. *Why hadn't this occurred to anyone else? Is it even significant? I'm not a sociologist.*

Once again, she had the thought that scientific disciplines were too strictly separated. The rift was the domain of physicists, the scientific community had decided. But there also seemed to be plenty of material for psychologists, sociologists, and medical doctors too. Were people maybe sleeping significantly worse now than before? Maybe physicists would have found the secret to the rift a long time ago by listening to other people instead of just trying to come up with new tests.

And then, of course, there was the most obvious question: Why, of all things, had the most obvious experiment not yet been performed? Essentially, intentionally throwing something into the rift.

Maribel closed her eyes. Maybe she could still get a few minutes of sleep. Then her phone vibrated. It was a message from Russia, encoded with her public key. She confirmed receipt with her password and a private connection was established. Theoretically, nobody could eavesdrop on them now.

"I'm back," her Russian colleague said. He was sitting at his desk with the camera at least two meters away. The desk was made in a rustic style from light-colored wood, probably birch. Tarassov leaned back in a large swivel chair.

"Thank you for your patience," he said.

"I'm very interested to hear your explanation."

"Now I can speak plainly. The matter is very controversial politically."

"What do you mean?"

"All evidence points to us never having a mobile research robot on Ceres. I can't remember ever approving or even discussing any plans for it. That, however, would be a huge mistake that nobody in the Academy would excuse. I would lose my job. One of my associates then came up with the idea of covering it up. Nobody else knows about it. Now he's got me in his back pocket."

"Understood," Maribel said. "But then how did you come up with M6?"

"You see, our databases have records for M-models 1 to 5, and then the numbering skips 6 and continues on with 7. And these robots are on all the larger celestial bodies, but not Ceres. So, I think you can see my lie is not all that far-fetched."

"M6 must have been planned for Ceres."

"Yes, but according to our documents, it was never sent there. We simply continued onward with M7."

"Could there have been a reason for that?" Maribel asked.

"None that I can think of, apart from extreme sloppiness, which would come back to me again. Therefore, M6 must have existed. I would be very much indebted to you if you would not publicly question this. In any case, I would owe you a big favor."

Maribel had no interest in the internal politics of the Russian scientific community. But it could never hurt to be able to ask for a favor from the head of the Russian Institute for Planetary Science. Back in '72, she had obtained the most important data for her discovery only because an old colleague of hers had called in a favor or two. That was the way the world worked.

"Okay, I agree," she said.

Tarassov smiled and no longer looked quite so stressed. "As far as advancing your own research, you also probably wouldn't get any farther, if someone else took over my position," the Russian said.

Maribel nodded. "Was that it?"

"One more thing," Tarassov said. "We've looked at the images from our relay satellite around Ceres. The fact that it's even there is one indication that M6 existed at one point."

"That's true. Why would you need a relay station if there was nothing to relay?"

"Someone could always argue that we had then simply forgotten the plans for M6. I'll admit that sometimes things get very chaotic around here."

"NASA is not any different. I'm sure you're not surprised to hear that."

"In the satellite images, we can see a kind of ramp and platform that extends directly up to the end of the rift on Ceres. It's clearly an artificial structure. It's large enough for an M-series robot to fit on. We've calculated that an M-robot could easily reach the rift from this platform."

"That... that's a very interesting observation," she said.

It was immediately clear to her that she had just uttered the understatement of the year. A non-existent robot had built a platform on Ceres, in order to allow it to enter the rift. It could hardly be interpreted any other way. So, it must have existed before the test had started. Then it had jumped into the rift and had been completely erased from reality.

But not quite completely. Apparently, the propagation of cause-and-effect relationships had limits. Assuming an object disappeared from this universe, then all its atoms would have never existed. There would have to be some form of mechanism that removed all evidence of the existence of each individual atom stretching all the way back to the Big Bang. Presumably there was some mechanism that was responsible for maintaining logical relationships and relinking cause and effect. But it appeared that its effectiveness was constrained in some way.

Perhaps it behaved similarly to gravity. In principle, gravity's effects extended to infinity. The black hole at the center of the Milky Way pulls on every person on Earth by means of gravity. And yet we can jump and move around and not even notice anything of its pull, because the force of attraction to the Earth under our feet is much, much greater and masks all other sources of gravitational forces. Maybe, she thought, cause-and-effect relationships functioned in a similar fashion. When two states are strongly linked, they attract each other strongly, and they have more influence on each other than if they were only loosely associated. The reality of Maribel Pedreira, the reality field that surrounded her, had almost no points of contact with the reality of Tarassov. So, she could remember the previous conversation about M6, but the Russian couldn't.

Suddenly Maribel noticed that the connection to Russia was still open. Tarassov had probably been just as lost in his thoughts as she had been in hers.

"Mr. Tarassov," she said, "you've given me very interesting and important information. I'm going to need some time to process it and understand all its ramifications."

"Me too," Tarassov said. "The consequences are so inscrutable that every train of thought gets lost in a fog of contradictions."

Maribel sighed. "Then I hope you'll find a way into some clearer thinking. If you hear from M6, will you call me?"

"Of course. Have a nice weekend!"

"You too."

Maribel ended the connection. If Tarassov only knew! That is, if he followed the news he must already know. Tomorrow she would be launching in the space elevator.

She stood up and stretched. But that was tomorrow. Today was today. She took out her flower-patterned dress from the closet and changed into it. Then she put on her white sandals. If she hurried, she could still have lunch with her family.

June 2, 2085, Vandenberg Air Force Base

DEREK HAD FOUND THE PERFECT LOCATION IN SATELLITE images from an online map service. South on Highway 1 and past the Vandenberg Air Force Base, on the righthand side there was a small, hidden exit. From the exit, a small dirt road ran northwest. It ended at a natural plateau of public land that stood up to 200 meters above the surrounding area. The view from there fell directly on Vandenberg. From there it should be possible for him to reach his goal.

They reached the west coast around 3 o'clock in the afternoon. Akif had the idea to spend the rest of the day in Pismo Beach, a pretty but not too expensive beach town north of Vandenberg. Here, their old-fashioned vehicle wouldn't be so noticeable among all the tourists. Derek purchased a large towel and a straw hat, laid out on the beach, and fell asleep. Akif and Gita explored the town and brought Derek food and drink now and then.

It was a beautiful last day in this world. Derek had no idea where he would be tomorrow, but he tried not to think about it too much. Of course, he hoped that he would see Mary again. But how could he be sure? He had to look reality in the eye. The chance for success was minuscule.

That, however, didn't apply to the first part of the plan, up to the point of hiding away in the space elevator. He had downloaded all the details of the project from the NASA archives. It was just his luck that the tax-financed NASA had to disclose everything that their employees developed. The knowledge, financed by the taxpayers, was available to him too. Thus, Derek knew exactly how the capsule looked and where the perfect place for a stowaway would be. And he also knew the biggest problem he would have to solve: the space elevator would be precisely balanced in terms of weight. There would be problems if the capsule suddenly weighed 85 kilograms more. To keep his presence unknown, Derek would have to somehow reduce the capsule's weight by the same amount as his body weight.

And now the time had come to put the plan in motion.

"The exit will be coming up very soon," Akif said from the passenger seat.

He was tracking the vehicle's location on his phone. Derek concentrated and strained even more as he peered out in front of them. The truck's headlights weren't optimally adjusted, and fog had crept up onto the highway from the ocean. He saw a sign that pointed toward 'Eagle's Nest.' *That must be the exit*, he thought. He had to step on the brakes hard, because the exit ramp was shorter than he was anticipating.

He turned the truck to the right. The map hadn't warned them that there would be a gate. They were lucky that it was open.

"About 800 more meters," Akif said.

"Okay."

Derek drove along the dirt path. The broad overlook might attract lovers, he feared, or space travel fans who might want to watch the activities of Vandenberg. But they didn't see anyone else. Maybe the fog had driven them all away.

The plateau opened up in front of them. The truck's lights showed a large number of deep tire tracks. It looked like heavy-duty military vehicles also came along here regularly. *Hopefully not tonight,* Derek prayed. He steered the truck to the right side of the plateau, which had a boundary of bushes.

"So, I guess that's it then," he said as he set the parking brake, moved the gearshift to neutral, and switched off the engine.

"Yeah," Akif said.

It was a strange situation. They had known each other for only a few days and yet had become friends. Derek was tempted to call it all off. They could drive home. He'd sell the farmhouse and move to the city. He could finally accept Isaac's invitation to try his wife's delicious cooking. Akif and Gita would surely not let him be lonely.

But then he would always think about Mary, and about the single chance that he hadn't taken. Could he be happy under those conditions? He didn't know for sure, but he couldn't imagine it.

"So, time for goodbye," he said, and took his hands off the steering wheel.

"I wish you all the best, from the bottom of my heart," Gita said.

"I hope you find what you're looking for," the doctor said.

Derek suddenly climbed out of the truck. Otherwise he was going to start crying. That was all he needed! He walked around the truck and took the large travel bag from the truck bed. It had everything that he needed, plus his gun. He dropped the bag three meters from the truck, opened it, and took out a pair of night-vision goggles.

Then he turned to go back to the truck. He hadn't noticed that Akif and Gita had gotten out of the truck too and were standing right behind him. He had wanted to give the truck keys to Gita, but she embraced him before he could take them out of his pocket. Akif followed her lead. Derek swiped at some dust that must have somehow gotten into his eyes and let a couple of tears fall down his cheeks.

"Are you going to give me the keys now?" Gita asked.

Derek wiped his eyes again and tried to laugh. Then he

took out the keys and handed them to her. The plan they had worked out was for Gita to park the truck at Santa Maria's local airport. They were hoping that no one would notice it there, because people taking trips on airplanes, especially their own airplanes, would have to leave their vehicles at the airport. Then she would go to a hotel in the center of the small city, check in to the room that she had reserved by phone under a false name, and wait for Akif.

She would have to wait, because Derek still needed the doctor's assistance. Akif would take up a position at the edge of the plateau and monitor the surroundings with the night-vision goggles, while Derek slipped into the base. Then Akif would ride away on a bicycle that was still on the bed of the truck. Two hours later he should be back in Gita's arms.

"Just a minute," Derek said, "we still have to unload the bicycle."

Nimbly he climbed onto the truck bed, hoisted the bicycle, and handed it down. Akif took it and set it on the ground. Then Derek jumped light-footed onto the ground from the lowered tailgate.

"You move well," Akif said.

"I'm a little surprised myself," Derek said. "I guess all that military training is hard to forget."

"Do you still need me?" Gita asked.

"Absolutely," Akif replied, "but not for a few hours."

"Thank you so much, Gita," Derek said. "I'm so glad we became friends."

She hugged him one last time. "Good luck," she said. "I hope we see each other again sometime."

Derek felt a lump forming in his throat. Why had he met these two only a few days ago? Couldn't they have met earlier? Fate worked in strange ways.

"Be careful," he said, "I don't want anything bad to happen to you because of me. If they catch you, blame everything on me. Say I was confused, deranged, I threatened you with my gun. My records will show them I've been trained to kill."

"Right. A crazy man kidnapped us. That should work," Gita said.

She detached from the embrace and looked at him as if she were committing his face to memory. Then she took a step closer to him, raised up on her tiptoes, and planted a kiss on his cheek.

"Good luck, you crazy man," she said. Then she turned around quickly and walked to the driver's door.

Derek watched as she wiped a few tears from her face. Then she climbed in, started the engine, and drove off in an arc slowly fading into the darkness.

Derek took his phone from his pocket to check the time. It was just after midnight. "Okay, it's time to get to work," he said. "There shouldn't be any civilians outside anymore, just guards." He handed the night-vision goggles to Akif.

"I'll look for a good place to set up," the doctor said.

"We'll stay in contact by radio," Derek said. "We should test them first." He took the earpiece from his pants pocket and put it in his ear. Then he pressed the send button on the walkie-talkie and whispered something into it.

"I can hear you loud and clear," Akif said. Then he whispered something into his walkie-talkie.

"Copy," Derek replied. "We can hear each other. This kind of mission is my specialty."

Akif gave him a pat on the shoulder.

Derek turned around and disappeared in the direction of the plateau's edge.

HE WAS ALONE. IT HADN'T BEEN THAT LONG AGO THAT HE HAD loved these moments, after everybody else had gone away. But now he felt more lost than ever. Derek bent over and opened his bag. Things were different now, because this time he had a purpose. He was going on an expedition, even if he was only going to be a stowaway. He took an Air Force uniform out of the bag. How lucky that he had chosen to enlist in the Air

Force, way back when. He removed his street clothes and put on the uniform. It changed him. He could feel it on a gut level. The farmer had turned once again into a fighter. 'Clothes make the man' was more than just a saying. He set his service cap on his head and exchanged his tennis shoes for black military boots. Then he swung the small backpack with the special equipment and special design from his time in the war onto his back. He had only brought it from home for nostalgic reasons. Finally, he put on his belt, checked the holster, and then slid his gun inside.

He needed the gun only to hold his traveling companions at bay. He was not planning on using it under any circumstances. If that were to become necessary, then he would have already lost. He would have to get onto the base unnoticed. He couldn't risk anybody becoming suspicious. A few thousand soldiers were stationed on the base, so nobody knew everybody else. But the team that was guarding the fence right then would know each other, just like the soldiers who had been ordered to guard the space elevator today. After the alarm yesterday, the guards' attentiveness was likely to be lower today, but it could still be difficult.

"Got anything for me yet?" Derek asked Akif by radio.

"I see two groups that are patrolling the fence together, on the inside. You might have about five minutes between the patrols."

The outer fence would certainly be electrically charged and equipped with motion sensors. The intervals between the patrols would be calculated so that an intruder would never have enough time to disable the protective mechanisms. Derek ran to the edge of the plateau and started his descent. He came to a small stream at the bottom. He jumped across and walked into a dense forest. Beyond the forest was an open field, with the fence being located in the middle. The forest was so densely grown together that he couldn't avoid walking into branches. So, he would have to move in a way that didn't draw extra attention, even if it caused a bit of noise. He got down on his knees and crawled through the underbrush like a wild pig. If anyone was looking through an infrared camera and spotted him, he hoped they would think he was an animal.

He reached the open area that was covered with scrawny, tough grass.

"How's it look, Akif?"

"The next patrol will be there in a minute."

Derek crouched down, took the backpack off his shoulder, and didn't move. Nobody was expecting an intruder today, that was his big advantage.

"All clear. The patrol is gone," Akif reported shortly thereafter.

Derek reached into his backpack and activated the first drone, then the second. They floated noiselessly next to him. He walked deliberately forward. The two drones protected him from being detected by the motion sensors. With the help of metamaterials, they had set up a cloak around him that made him invisible to certain wavelengths—more precisely, the radiation at these wavelengths was being guided around him. But it didn't work with visible light. If a soldier appeared and saw him, he was done for.

"Four more minutes," Akif's voice said in his earpiece.

Derek couldn't advance too quickly, or the drones wouldn't be able to match him step for step. They must stay at the exact right height so that he remained in the center of the invisibility field. Derek carefully placed one foot in front of the other. An observer might think he was strolling calmly up to the fence.

"Three minutes," Akif said. "A little more to the left, then you'll have some cover after the fence."

Derek followed the instruction. He would need to hide once he got onto the base.

"Two minutes."

The fence was right in front of him. Derek remained standing. He could smell the ionized air from the high voltage running through the fence. It was buried at least two meters deep into the ground, so it would be no use trying to go under the fence. There also wasn't enough time for that. Quickly he took a pogo stick out of his backpack and clamped his feet around it. It was a single-jump pogo stick that could noiselessly thrust a person a few meters into the air using electrical energy from the quick discharge of a high-capacity battery. He had tested it only once, and while the launch generated almost no noise at all, the landing could be much louder.

"Ninety seconds," Akif said. "Cover at eleven o'clock. Three meters away."

Derek turned slightly to the left. He checked the position of the drones. He hoped they would be able to follow him easily enough over the wall. The motion sensors shouldn't be active inside the fence, so he would deactivate them once he was inside. Then he pressed the pogo stick's ignition button, and flew! He held on tightly to the stick with his legs. He didn't want it to fall or it would make a lot of noise. With his hands he tried to steer his flight. He saw something gray coming toward him. It must be a small building. Quickly he shifted his body weight and was able to move just enough to come down to the left of the building. Derek prepared himself for impact. He pressed his chin against his chest. He saw the ground. He smelled wet grass and hit the ground with a thud, rolling to a stop on the grass. He quickly moved against the wall of the building and listened.

Silence. He hoped he hadn't raised anyone's suspicion. He remotely signaled for the drones to land and then waited.

"The patrol will be at your position in 30 seconds. They haven't changed their pace."

Good. He pressed himself against the wall. Two soldiers walked past him only two meters away. They were talking about women. "My new girlfriend has enormous tits," one of them was boasting. Derek had to stifle a laugh. If they only knew that someone had broken into their base right under their noses!

BUT THAT WAS JUST THE BEGINNING. DEREK TOOK A DEEP breath in and let it out. He signaled for his drones to return to him. One after the other they landed on his outstretched hand. He put them and the pogo stick back in his backpack, as he hoped he wouldn't leave any trace of having been there. He didn't want anyone to find out someone had been here before the next morning's planned launch.

"What do you see, Akif?"

"Very little activity. I'm sure most of the soldiers are asleep. You're getting close to out of my range, but I think we'll be able to stay in contact until you're aboard. There are some barracks and other buildings in front of you that I can't see through. Your goal is at one o'clock, so west-southwest. You'll have to find the best path yourself."

"Understood."

He was inside a military base, but he was wearing the right uniform and he knew all the right military protocols and procedures. If he could safely get farther away from the fence —it would be more dangerous for him to keep creeping around the edges. He would have to move out into the open, completely normally, so that any chance encounters wouldn't lead to suspicion. It would probably become more difficult when he got closer to the space elevator. Access to it would surely be permitted only to those with special authorization.

Derek walked quietly across the grass. He came to a dirt track. He immediately turned right as if he already knew where he was going. To his left and right were one-story barracks. They looked like warehouses, not living quarters. The track ended at a paved road. He turned to the left, always heading more or less toward his goal. A truck approached him, traveling in the opposite direction. Right before it passed him, the driver flashed his lights and saluted. Derek saluted back.

Then he passed a two-story, white-painted building with a large NASA logo. A light was still on in one of the windows. Maybe it was one of the crew members for the space elevator mission sitting in there. Derek thought about whether he should change the plan. He could go in and take the person hostage. But they would never be allowed to board the elevator, so that would be much too risky.

He walked past the entrance to the building and came to an intersection. This time he turned right. Someone on an electric bicycle was approaching on the other side of the street. It was a man, and he was singing. When he got closer, Derek could tell that the soldier was drunk. Derek hoped to avoid being caught. Apparently, there must be a relatively low risk of being caught at this time if soldiers were moving around drunk on the base. He hoped that would be true for an intruder like him, too.

AT THE NEXT INTERSECTION, DEREK KEPT WALKING STRAIGHT. "What do you think about my path?" he asked over the radio.

Akif could track his position on the map display of his phone. "Very good. If you turn right after the next block, the launch pad should be directly in front of you."

"Is there anybody there right now?"

"I'm sorry, but I can't tell. Be careful."

"Understood."

He adjusted his backpack and walked determinedly toward the intersection that Akif had mentioned. At first, the building next to him blocked his view, but then he saw it—a nondescript platform with an even more nondescript capsule sitting on top of it. The path leading to it was blocked. Signs reading 'Restricted Area – Authorized Personnel Only' were posted on the path.

Derek briefly considered his options, then decided to look for another way. He kept walking straight. Again, a low building blocked his view of the platform. Behind it, a narrow dirt track headed off into the darkness. He turned and quickly switched into stealth mode and started edging along the side of the building. He was sure this was not the sort of path anyone should be walking on at night.

Then he heard steps. They were irregular, so it had to be at least two people. He hid behind a tree. Two men passed, then he smelled cigarette smoke. They hadn't noticed anything, as they had been deep in conversation.

He waited a little while and then continued onward. He turned to the right and headed into the underbrush when he decided that he must have passed the platform. Now his forward progress was very slow, because he had to precisely check every individual branch and stay clear of any that he thought might make a noise.

Then the forest ended. In front of him was an area of flat ground, completely bare of any trees or bushes, and beyond that area was the platform. He could see the capsule. Its entry hatch was on the side facing him. That was good.

Derek looked around. He took out the night-vision goggles. No signs of life! The two men from before were apparently the only patrol in this area. They had passed him probably 20 minutes ago. So, he had at least ten minutes until they'd be back in view. He removed the goggles—he had to take his chance now.

Bent over, Derek sprinted across the flat area. He pulled himself up the back side of the platform. It was only about two meters to the capsule. He hoped that nobody was working on the instruments right then! He reached the hatch and pulled it open as quietly as possible. Just like the New Shepard's rocket's capsule, it was unlocked. It was dark inside. Perfect!

He closed the door behind him and put on his night-vision goggles so that he could orient himself. There were space suits in two long, flat boxes that looked like coffins. He would have to move two of those suits, or better three, out of the capsule, in order to compensate for his added weight. But first he would have to hide, because the patrol would be coming back around soon. He pressed himself against the suits in one of the two boxes.

Too late he remembered that he had left his backpack next to the entrance hatch. Suddenly he smelled cigarette smoke again. He desperately wanted to open the box for some fresh air, but he knew he couldn't. The two soldiers must be inside the capsule. All at once a bright ray of light came flooding into the box through gaps at the box's edges. They had turned on the interior light. Then the ray of light disappeared as quickly as it came. They must not have noticed his backpack. His luck continued!

He waited a few minutes and then climbed back out of the box. Derek looked around in surprise, a sense of dread growing inside him. His backpack was gone. *Shit.* He had to stay calm and think through this. The soldiers had noticed it, but they hadn't realized what it meant and hadn't sounded an alarm. Maybe they thought a technician had left it behind. He could only hope that they would keep thinking that. Regardless, he had to act quickly. He picked up one of the space suits and carried it out of the capsule. To make sure nobody would see the suits, he would have to hide them in the woods. He took one suit into the trees, then went back with another, but on a different path, so that his tracks wouldn't become too noticeable.

Then it was time to hide again. The patrol was right on time. He watched as the lights went on and off. Then he brought the third space suit to a hiding place in the woods. At last it wouldn't be too cramped for him inside whichever he chose of the boxes. It was just stupid that his backpack was now gone, because it had also held all his provisions. But he could hold out without food or water until the morning. He just had to be careful that his snoring wouldn't be too loud, because that might be heard by a patrol. So, he pulled on the remaining space suit, sealed the helmet, and crawled into the empty box farthest from the entrance.

"Good night, Akif," he said into the microphone. "Mission complete. Thank you for all your help!"

"You did it! That's great," the Turkish doctor said. "Now I'm off to see Gita. Good luck."

"Tell her 'hi' from me."

June 3, 2085, Ceres

M6 HAD NOW VISITED EIGHT DIFFERENT VERSIONS OF CERES in the past 24 hours of Earth time. Overall, this Ceres looked just like the others, and they all looked just like where he originally came from—the sky was black, the stars were cold and seemingly immovable, and right next to his platform was the end of the rift. But the data that he downloaded via the Deep Space Network showed significant differences. In each case, the Earth had indeed existed, but the number of contradictions nearly doubled with each jump. He had noticed an especially odd difference after the last jump—instead of a French president, the documents suddenly referred to a French chancellor, although nothing else about France's government seemed to have changed. Nevertheless, nobody else seemed to have noticed the change, because everyone had developed new internal logic. The French believed it was just a traditional title that had been adopted after the Second World War with Germany, which had since become their ally.

But the real problem wasn't those little odd discrepancies. The contradictions in the data suggested that the rift was increasingly damaging the foundations of reality. M6 had found sudden deviations, even in some laws of nature. Presumably they were appearing because the logic of cause and effect couldn't compensate for some contradiction any other way. They were still tiny, but if they grew, they could lead to the collapse of the entire universe.

All that would be needed, for example, would be for the strength of the strong nuclear force to change so that the nuclei of atoms could no longer be held together. Immediately, quantum chaos, which is always present at the quantum level, would spread to higher orders of magnitude, and chaos would overwhelm and govern the entire universe. M6 slowly came to the realization of why quantum theory was restricted to its tiny domain—if it weren't, there could never be a stable universe. And apparently it was the logic of cause and effect that was holding everything together and preventing the quantum regime from taking over the world.

The rift was not an interesting, harmless phenomenon. It carried the seed of destruction deep within itself. M6 evaluated what he had learned and extrapolated it into the future. If the contradictions continued growing as before, the totality of all realities, the multiverse, would drown in total chaos in a few weeks of Earth time. And then would come the moment when all matter would completely disintegrate. The universe would end as a hot soup of quantum particles in which nothing could survive.

M6 didn't like the idea, because his own existence would also end. His reward center protested with negative impulses. But there was another reason too. He felt a certain gratefulness for his creators. This feeling motivated him to think of possible rescue solutions. He needed only 0.6 nanoseconds, just a few clock cycles for his main processor, to winnow his options down to only one—he must somehow get rid of the rift. Interestingly, M6 noticed that he felt regret about it. The rift was an extremely fascinating phenomenon that he would have liked to continue studying. But time was short. The strands of history in many of the worlds of the multiverse that he had visited had already become inextricably knotted.

But how could he get rid of something that he had never even once penetrated completely? He must find the cause of its origin! Once more, M6 looked through the characteristic data of the individual universes that he had downloaded. They must have features in common, something, a specific point where they had begun to diverge from each other. The search was complicated by the fact that he couldn't know if something had actually happened or had simply been scrambled by the rift. M6 switched off all unnecessary components. He wanted to find the cause as quickly as possible, and for that, he needed all his processing power.

June 3, 2085, Vandenberg Air Force Base

"So, TIME TO GO," GLEN SPARROW SAID.

He had never looked as tired and haggard as he did right then. They had arrived an hour ago at his office in Vandenberg to discuss the final details for their journey. Maribel was happy to finally see George Crewmaster again. He had taught her so much about astrophysics, and had always supported her. The reunion had noticeably brightened the atmosphere in the room, because she had been in a bad mood after saying a difficult goodbye to her family that morning.

Luisa had somehow learned that her mother was going on a big adventure today. She had demanded to go along to watch. Maribel hadn't said no, but Chen was against it. Luisa had noticed her parents' different responses and she had expertly played them off against each other. Finally, the decision that she would have to stay with her father had been the final straw and caused a huge, extended meltdown that made Maribel feel rattled and question whether she was doing the right thing.

"You don't seem to be all here today," Eigenbrod said to her. "Problems at home?"

Maribel nodded. "It'd take too long to explain," she said.

"I understand," the Frenchman said. "I've got kids too, you know. We went through some tough times. It gets better."

It sounded clichéish, yet it still helped Maribel feel better. It had come just in time, too, because just then Glen opened the entrance door to the office building. In front there were journalists waiting for them, and they didn't miss the chance to start hurling questions at them as fast as they could.

"Please wait for the press conference," Glen kept saying over and over.

Maribel wondered to herself why these reporters had even been allowed to assemble here in the first place. Wasn't the whole point of using a military base to provide them with protection and privacy from the public?

She thought about Arthur. Probably all his colleagues were jealous of him, since he was wearing the same blue suit as Maribel and Glen, but his was emblazoned with a patch reading ESA, the European Space Agency, instead of NASA. Maribel hadn't even known that the Europeans were assisting them in any way. Surely that hadn't happened without them contributing to the total budget. George, who had to be almost as old as Eigenbrod, presented a significantly more fit impression in his blue suit than the journalist did.

They walked around the office building, the throng of reporters right behind them, turned to the right, and came to a barrier. Two military policemen were guarding the platform. Only the four crew members were allowed to pass.

"We'll answer your questions in 15 minutes," Glen announced to the crowd that was trying to follow them. "Thank you for your patience."

A crane was just unloading a portable toilet right next to the capsule's entrance. Glen made some frantic hand gestures indicating that the crane needed to stay farther away from the cable. Maribel had suggested they set up a Porta Potty just this morning. This way they could relieve themselves right before the launch. As an adult, the idea of emptying her bladder into a diaper didn't appeal to her.

Then a soldier came up to Glen and held out a black backpack to him. "Sir, this was found in the capsule last night."

Glen gave it a quick look. "Never seen it before," he said. "Maybe one of the workers left it in there. Throw it away."

"What if it contains explosives?"

"If there's one thing we know after yesterday, soldier, it's that there are no explosives within a five-kilometer radius of here."

"That's true, sir," the soldier said and marched away, taking the backpack with him.

"What now?" Maribel asked.

"The plan is that now we get a little acclimated to where we'll be spending the next several hours. Then, in about 15 minutes, we'll go outside and talk to the press. And then we'll start the one-hour launch phase."

Maribel walked through the capsule. Now, with four people and all their instruments onboard, the interior was much more cramped than during her first visit. Of the six seats, two were taken up by luggage that had been neatly buckled in. Maribel chose the seat at the outermost edge, right in front of the transparent partition wall, behind which the cable passed. She adjusted the backrest forward some. On the floor in front of the wall was a coffin-sized box that must've also been recently loaded onto the capsule.

"I didn't order these," Maribel said, pointing to a second, similar container on the other side.

Glen forced himself past Arthur and George, maneuvered himself next to her, and looked at the box. "Ah, yes, those have our space suits. I hope we won't need them. Do you want to try one on?"

"No, thanks," Maribel answered. "I'd rather use the time to check my instruments."

"Good idea. I checked the suits myself yesterday, but not your equipment. I didn't want to damage anything," Glen said.

The press conference was scheduled to start soon. They really didn't have much more time. Maribel waved to her old professor.

"George, could you give me a hand checking the instruments?" she asked.

"Right, I'll start over here," he answered.

The various instruments had been distributed randomly around the capsule, wherever the technicians had been able to find space for them. They couldn't all be used at once, because there wasn't nearly enough power.

The elevator capsule had never been designed as a research station. Maribel's plan had been to place the instruments one after the other in front of the porthole with the best viewpoint of the rift and then to record their measurements. She could capture spectrums in various ranges, measure electromagnetic fields, and even analyze substances. To help with these tasks, there was a small crane with an extendible gripper. To use it, however, they would have to open the hatch, which would make it very cold inside the capsule. But that was one reason why they had the space suits on board.

Maribel started the self-check routines for several of the measuring instruments, one after the other. All of them reported perfect operational readiness. George made quick progress too. When Glen told them all it was time for the press conference, Maribel was feeling very good about the mission.

AFTER THE CONFERENCE, THEIR COLLECTIVE MOOD HAD soured considerably. There had been, of course, a few reporters who doubted the usefulness of their mission and complained that they were just wasting the taxpayers' money. To them, the rift was obviously harmless. Another journalist had called out the inclusion of Eigenbrod as a PR stunt and a safety risk. But others had asked good, insightful questions, like why nobody had tested to see what would happen if an object was thrown into the rift.

If it was up to Maribel, they would know the answer to

that question in two or three hours. But first, they needed a successful launch.

The countdown had just begun—still almost an hour until lift-off. She sat down on her seat, straight as a neutrino, and tried out her seat belts. When they latched, the buckles made a solid, very satisfying, close-fitting sound like in a luxury vehicle. Glen paced back and forth, taking small, hurried steps. *Is it possible he's nervous?* she wondered. *Is there any cause for concern? After all, he definitely has the best knowledge about the space elevator's condition.*

"Glen, everything okay?" she asked.

He stopped briefly. "Do I seem nervous?"

Maribel nodded.

"Well, that's because I am nervous. But there's no reason for alarm."

Our mission leader's nervous, but we shouldn't be worried? "What is it then?"

"It's just because of yesterday. So many people went through here searching for bombs, I'm afraid they might've broken something."

"Is that realistic?"

"No, not really. There's actually very little that you could accidentally damage here."

"Well, there you go," Maribel said in a motherly tone. "You're getting yourself all worked up over nothing. We just checked our instruments and they're all okay."

"Thanks, Maribel," Glen said. He resumed his pacing, but at least now it was a little bit slower.

At 40 minutes before the launch, Glen slapped his forehead and then rummaged around in a tray that he pulled out from under his seat.

"I meant to pass these out," he said, holding up a pair of bulky packages. He handed one to each of them.

Maribel opened her package. Upon closer inspection, she

realized it was a diaper, similar to those she had used for her daughter when she was little—but the one she was holding now was much larger.

"Do we have to wear these?" she asked.

"It's your decision," Glen said. "But right now, with the toilet outside, there's still a chance for you to put it on without anyone watching you. We'll be in here for several hours, and when you gotta go..."

A good argument. Maribel folded her diaper neatly together so that none of the cameras outside would see her with it. Then she walked outside and into the portable toilet. She closed the door behind her. It smelled like chemicals. She tucked the diaper under her arm and pulled down the pants of her suit. Then she squatted over the rim, emptied her bladder, and cleaned herself.

She unfolded the diaper again and wrapped it around her legs and hips. The material felt cold and soft, almost like plastic. She fastened the diaper with the adhesive strips and pulled up her pants again. Now she wished she had a mirror. How else could she figure out whether the diaper was noticeable? *The way it feels,* she thought, *every person out there will be able to tell what I've got on under my pants.*

"T MINUS 25 MINUTES."

It was, of course, completely different watching a launch from outside rather than sitting in a metal capsule that was soon going to climb into the sky on an impossibly thin cord.

"The Chinese have given us the final OK," said Glen, who was in constant contact with the crew in the control room.

"You don't sound relieved," George said.

"I hate it when I don't have any control over something, when I'm dependent on other people," Glen answered.

Maribel nervously shifted from side to side in her seat. *Why do I even need to be buckled in, if the capsule is simply going to climb skyward as if I'm being lifted up in an armchair? Maybe not everything is quite as safe as Glen has made it out to be?*

"What could actually go wrong?" she asked.

"An interesting question," Arthur said, "but maybe not the best time for it."

Somebody coughed behind Maribel. She would have had to unbuckle herself to turn around and look. Probably someone outside the capsule. *But it sure sounded close.*

"Absolutely nothing," Glen answered. "If there was something we knew could go wrong, we would have fixed it. Or we wouldn't be sitting here now."

"As a physicist, I have to say that our knowledge is never complete," George Crewmaster said. "Without a doubt there are circumstances that might arise that could cause this mission to fail."

"I know we can't know every possible problem," Glen said, "and if it were up to me, we'll also never have to learn about them."

"Some things we only learn about afterward, when we examine a failed part and learn that it had suddenly become brittle."

"Thanks, George," Maribel said. "That's *not* what I wanted to hear."

"You're welcome. The master has to tell some uncomfortable truths, sometimes."

"How much longer?" Maribel asked.

"That's what my kids always asked when we drove to their grandmother's house for Thanksgiving," George said.

"My son too, when we were stuck in traffic on the highway to Marseille," Arthur said.

"T minus 10 minutes."

The countdown announcement answered her question. Maribel noticed again that she hadn't prepared herself for the wait. "What do you actually think the rift is, George?" she asked. It felt strange to talk with her mentor using his first name. She had known him ever since she was a student and she always thought of him as Professor Crewmaster, not as George.

"Oh, that would definitely take much longer than our remaining ten minutes," he replied.

"That's what I was hoping. So?"

"I believe it is made up, quite simply, of nothing."

"You *believe?*"

"Well, I can't prove it. But your findings and those of other scientists have clearly shown that it cannot be some known or unknown form of matter. And then its shape, a two-dimensional strip in space! No natural object could fall out of time and space like that."

"We're not entirely sure about that yet. We haven't gotten close enough yet to confirm it doesn't have a depth dimension," Maribel said.

"Even now we're not going to get close enough. We'd have to show that the rift was smaller than a Planck length," George said.

"Planck length? Please excuse the dumb journalist," Arthur asked.

"That's the smallest possible measurable length," Glen explained, "to some extent the dimension at which space no longer appears continuous, but is instead broken up into tiny little chunks. A Planck length is very, very short."

"And how would you then prove that the rift was smaller than a Planck length?" Arthur asked.

"Good question," Crewmaster said. "That's exactly the problem."

"And how do we solve it?" Arthur asked.

"No idea," the professor said. "But it's also not that important."

"Well then, what do you think is important?" Maribel asked.

"We've got to find out how we can close this thing."

That, however, wasn't news to Maribel—and should have

been clear to all the other passengers when they agreed to go on this mission.

For a time, they were all lost in their own thoughts. Maribel raised and lowered her arms and then her legs, so that they wouldn't fall asleep. *We're going to need these reclining seats*, she thought, *just because they're making us wait so long*.

"I've been wondering why you think it's so important to close the rift," Arthur said, finally breaking the silence. "There's no danger from it, is there?"

"Do you want the official version?" Glen asked. "That's what I'm supposed to give you. And you can quote me on it."

"Let's hear it."

"Good. The rift is bad for the economy. Productivity is declining, we're slipping into an economic crisis. This thing is hanging over all our heads, and people feel threatened by things they don't understand completely."

"Okay, I've heard that version before," Arthur said. "What about the unofficial version?"

"You want to explain it, Maribel?" Glen asked.

Maribel shook her head. "I'd like to hear what George has to say about it."

"Okay," Crewmaster answered. "If I start with my idea from before—that the rift is made up of nothing—then there are two possibilities. First, maybe it doesn't interact with our world at all, but the Hawking radiation at its edges clearly speaks against that possibility. Second, maybe things do fall into it now and then and everything that disappears into the rift is completely erased from our reality. For a couple of air molecules, that wouldn't be a big deal. But what if a person disappeared into the rift? Then suddenly his children and his children's children and all memories of him would all be suddenly erased from our world."

"Wouldn't we notice that?" Arthur asked. "No, I take that back. We wouldn't notice anything, because that person is no longer part of our reality. It would be like he never existed."

"Exactly," Crewmaster said.

"I've got to push back against something you just said, George," Maribel said. "And that's about the air molecules. Every individual atom was born in the Big Bang or later in a star. If it were to suddenly disappear into nothing, it would also have to be erased from the entire history of the universe. That could affect the development of all of space. For the solar system to coalesce into a mass, at some point an individual atom must have been the trigger for all that to happen. If that atom were suddenly to be erased from history, the solar system would never have formed."

"That is good logical reasoning," Crewmaster said, "but I don't think it's relevant. There are simply far too many atoms. The risk that, of all the atoms, the one that was responsible for the creation of our sun would fall into the rift is very, very low."

"What if it were the atom that later formed the seed for our planet Earth?" Maribel said.

"Same response."

"It's okay if the two of you can't agree," the journalist said, "but would there be at least some way to prove something disappeared?"

"That would be difficult," the professor said. "If we throw something into the rift and it disappears, then it was never there, and we also would no longer know that it had ever existed."

"Maybe that's also the reason why it seems that nobody has tried to send anything into the rift before," Maribel said. "The researchers would then simply have no memory of their attempts."

"Now I'm wondering why I couldn't find a single rocket anywhere when I wanted to do a test like that," Glen Sparrow said. "Maybe my colleagues used them all up before me."

"Or maybe it was even you who did it," Arthur said.

"Me? No, I doubt it. I would've remembered something like that," Sparrow said with a smirk.

"T MINUS 60."

The announcement was now counting down by the passing seconds. Why were they making such a big deal about this anyway? They were in a super-sized version of an elevator, the doors were already closed, and they would start climbing soon. Why all this commotion with the countdown and security and crowds of reporters? Luckily, that was all almost over, and they could finally get to work.

The countdown reached ten. The linear motor behind her seat began to hum.

3, 2, 1, lift-off.

The capsule began to rise very smoothly. Maribel had to concentrate to convince herself that they were off the ground at all.

Soon she was able to tell by looking out the porthole. The people in front of the platform, who had broken out in applause, disappeared from her field of view. She saw trees, a hill, and finally California's landscape, which was largely brown at this time of year.

"Godspeed," Glen whispered. He looked stressed.

"Thank you, Glen," Maribel said. "Without you, there would never have been a space elevator."

"It's too early for that. You can thank me when we're safely back down on the ground again."

Maribel looked at her colleagues. Arthur was writing something on his phone. George had closed his eyes, his forehead furrowed. If Glen hadn't been clutching the armrests of his seat with so much tension, she would have felt significantly better.

Her stomach told her that the elevator was accelerating. The motor was also humming more loudly now. She could hardly comprehend it. She was sitting there in a one-ton capsule, rising into the air at an increasing speed. It was as if Rapunzel had let down a single strand of hair and now the prince was climbing it, together with his horse and carriage.

"Status?" Glen asked.

"I'm doing great," Maribel answered.

Then she noticed that Sparrow was talking to the Flight Director.

"All systems look good," she heard a female voice respond. "The ascent is going according to plan."

"The motor sounds like it could handle more speed," Glen said. "I could..."

"That may be, but we'll save it for a future test," the director interrupted him.

"I was just thinking..."

"I'm sorry, Glen, but I'm doing this test run strictly according to specifications. I don't want to start listing how many standard procedures we've already broken with this launch."

"Ignored, Sammy, ignored, and that's only because they were meant for rocket launches. Don't worry, I got all the necessary approvals all the way from the top."

"I know. I wouldn't have let this proceed if you hadn't."

"That doesn't surprise me. Okay, we're going to start getting the instruments ready. Sparrow out."

"Wait a minute, Glen."

"What is it?"

"Something strange. A military patrol just came in."

"Doesn't sound unusual for a military base."

"Not the point. They've found something, in the woods."

"It's a little too early for mushrooms."

"No, you wiseass, I'm being serious. Hold on... They found two space suits. Wait, here comes a third."

"Who left space suits lying around in the woods?"

"That's what everyone here is asking too, Glen. Especially because they seem to be the very latest models. There's only one mission using those. And that's yours."

"You're telling me somebody hid three of our space suits

in the woods? I saw them here in the capsule just last night! Who would do that?"

"I don't know, Glen. But I'd suggest you check the capsule."

Maribel felt her level of fear rising as she listened to the conversation. One of the two boxes of suits was behind her seat. The other was behind Arthur's. She released her belts and stood up. At first, she took steps very carefully, because she was imagining the capsule suspended on a thread and she didn't want to start it rocking. But it appeared to be attached very securely and rigidly to the cable.

"I'll check the box over here," Maribel said.

Arthur was quicker than she was. He had already bent over his box, unlocked the two latches, and swung open the top.

"It's empty," he said.

"Holy shit," Glen commented.

At first, Maribel felt a sense of relief. Without the suits they wouldn't even have the option of going higher into space. She would keep her promise to her family. Then she bent over her box behind the seat. Both locks were already open. Why hadn't she noticed that before? Whoever had moved the space suits out of the capsule must've forgotten to close the locks again.

She swung the top open and almost had a heart attack from the shock.

Before her was a man, and he was wearing the last of the four space suits. He had the index finger of his left hand extended in front of his mouth. She should be quiet and not say anything—she understood that well enough. She would do everything the man demanded of her, because in his right hand was a gun that looked damn real to her.

The man sat up. Maribel instinctively took a step back, her heart racing.

"What's going on, Maribel, are the two other suits still there or not?" asked Glen, who couldn't see the space behind her seat from his position.

The man lowered the finger that forbade her from talking.

"There was only one suit still in the box," she said, "but unfortunately someone's already wearing it."

She must be crazy. Inside, her mind was yelling warnings at her, and yet that was the response she came up with. She hoped the man wouldn't be annoyed at her!

"What are you talking about..." Glen said, cutting himself off mid-sentence, because just then the man had moved to stand next to Maribel, pointing his gun at her head. Thoughts were racing around her mind. Should she defend herself and try to take the gun away from him? No, that didn't seem like a very good idea. Nothing had happened yet. Maybe they could talk to the man. What did he want from them after all? There wasn't anything here for him to steal, was there?

"Please put the gun down," George Crewmaster said softly but insistently to the man. "Then we'll all sit down and talk it all through. Nothing's going to happen to you. You're on board a space elevator and we're currently several hundred meters off the ground."

"I know," the man answered. "It was difficult enough just to get in here. I want to go where you want to go, and I have some things to do there. If everyone behaves, nothing will happen to anyone. But if any of you try to stop me, you should know that I was in the Air Force's special forces for a few years. I know how to kill, even without a gun."

"We hear and understand you completely," Glen Sparrow said, "but..."

"Step away from the communication device," the man said. "I don't want anything to interrupt the mission. If you all cooperate, this can be a totally normal research mission."

Maribel saw that Sparrow was trying to retrieve something with his foot. She suddenly got a bad feeling.

"Glen, please stop," she said firmly.

Sparrow pulled his foot back.

"Let's be reasonable," Maribel said finally. "Tell us what you want, and maybe we can even help you."

"Maribel, this man needs help from a psychiatrist, not from us," Sparrow said.

"Glen, that's not going to help anything."

"My name's Derek McMaster," the man began. "There's no sense keeping it from you. The police will figure it out soon enough. I'm here to bring my wife home."

June 3, 2085, Ceres

THAT WAS IT! OVER 13 YEARS AGO, ON APRIL 3, 2072, THERE was an event that somehow had to be connected to the rift. The date and sequence were absolutely stable in all variants of reality, identical, right down to the second. It had to be some sort of anchor point in history, a point from which the various realities diverged, all leading to the creation of the rift. It was the nail in the wall, holding up the family history. And if he was successful in pulling out the nail, the picture it was currently holding up would have to come crashing down to the floor. The past would have to follow a different course —a course, M6 hoped, without the rift.

But there was a problem. In each of the variant realities, on April 3rd, the Earth was saved from a black hole that was about to annihilate the solar system. If M6 were to somehow simply pull out the nail, he would perhaps save the universe as a whole, but the Earth would vanish down the black hole along with the rest of the solar system.

And there was another problem: he couldn't simply beam himself back to the year 2072, so that he could change something there. Time travel was impossible. His only option would be to do something in the present that would be the logical consequence of some change in the past. Normally that would also have been impossible—but the rift had opened up a window into the past, and that made it possible. Maybe.

Even if it seemed complicated, it should be a solvable problem. *A human,* M6 thought, *probably wouldn't be able to do it, given their limited logic routines.* But he was a machine, so he didn't have those limitations.

How could he change something, back then, so that the rift would no longer be created? In 2072, a black hole had formed due to a deficit of information in the universe, and it had threatened the Earth's existence until an AI had transferred itself into the hole, closing it up and eliminating the threat. But, obviously, something must have gone wrong, and that must have ultimately led to the creation of the rift. Maybe the method they used to close the black hole had left a tiny discontinuity in space, a hole in the fabric of spacetime, which had been smaller than a Planck length, too small to see, but then it had grown undetected over the years until at some point it erupted and formed the rift.

M6 went through all the options. He could determine that many lines of action led to conditions that might possibly avert the danger. One of these strands must lead to events in the present time that he could make sure actually came to pass by using the rift. But he realized he still didn't have enough information to include in his calculations. M6 needed more data about the incident of 2072. He would have to send a request back to Earth. He hoped it wouldn't raise any suspicions there—but most likely no one had even considered the rift might have a connection to the events from back then.

THE REQUESTED DATA PACKET HAD ARRIVED. M6 VERY quickly sensed that it might provide him the solution. He learned, namely, that the AI called Watson, who had solved the problem in 2072, had taken another AI named Siri under his wing. Each had enhanced the other before Watson had sacrificed himself. But this Siri still existed. She was located aboard a private spaceship named *Kiska*, and M6 had the ability to contact that ship.

Through his intense collaboration with Siri, M6 reasoned, Watson must have collected many experiences—thus Watson had almost certainly increased his information load. Therefore, if Siri hadn't existed, Watson's size—measured in units of self-contained information—surely would have been smaller. In other words, the patch that Watson had used to plug up the hole in space would have had a different size and configuration, and thus might have made a better-fitting patch for the hole, plugging up the hole more cleanly. And thus, maybe the seed for the rift would have disappeared too.

M6 had to admit to himself that his idea was an entirely speculative solution. Nobody today could know the exact size and shape needed for the patch. But the connection between the rescue from the black hole and the creation of the rift seemed rather clear. Maybe he didn't need to use the right size exactly. Maybe it would be sufficient to use a different patch and thus change the circumstances? And what were the risks in trying? In the worst case, the universe would cease to exist, but it couldn't get any worse. Maybe the rift would still form, but only after a thousand or a million years. Then he would have given humankind more time to develop means to deal with it. Or, in the best case, he would restore the natural sequence of cause and effect in the macrocosm. The attempt was undoubtedly worth it.

Would it matter, then, which branch of reality he chose to change? Not the universe he had just come from—in any case, there was no way to get back there from here. But according to his data, the triggering event happened identically in all realities. So, if he changed it here, it would only be logical that the change would also propagate through to all the other realities too.

So, it came down to one more task—he would have to convince this Siri AI to sacrifice herself. Technically that wouldn't be complicated. She merely needed to transfer herself to his memory. Then he would use the rift one more time to disappear from this reality without a trace—this time taking the Siri AI with him.

M6 prepared a message. He explained to Siri what the problem was and how he wanted to resolve it. He was happy that he wouldn't need to convince any humans. *Logic is what counts,* he thought. Only another AI would be able to really understand him. If he were to receive such a message, listing all the options, with calculations stating the probabilities, he wouldn't have any other choice than to agree with the conclusions, and to act accordingly.

He addressed the data packet to the spaceship *Kiska*. Luckily, he didn't need to know where the ship was at that moment. The Deep Space Network would find its current location. But, the amount of time for the transmission to reach the *Kiska* would vary, depending on whether the spaceship was close by or on the other side of the sun. M6 estimated that he would have his answer in a maximum of four hours. And he hoped that the response would already contain the AI itself.

June 3, 2085, Vandenberg Air Force Base

The hours in the storage box had been stressful. The space suit that he had put on didn't fit him perfectly. He had lain there in the box, slowly growing hungrier and hungrier, and eventually more aware that he also needed to pee.

Now, with him pointing his gun at the four people in their clean, blue suits, he no longer felt hungry. The points where the space suit pressed against his body had shifted. But his bladder still hurt like hell.

It was an absurd situation. He had to show these four NASA people how serious he was about his plan. But at the same time, the thing he most wanted to do right now was to go to some corner and relieve himself. He felt like laughing out loud.

"How do you plan on doing that?" asked the woman, whom the others had called Maribel in their conversations.

"I need to go into the rift," he answered.

The man in charge, whom they had called Glen, tried again to reach his communicator.

Maribel noticed that Derek was watching Glen. "Glen," she said, "just stop it. I think we can resolve this civilly, without the Flight Director."

"Don't you see the man's got a gun? You should never negotiate with criminals."

"The man's name is Derek, and he wants to go into the rift. Don't you understand what that means? We've all been talking about how we should try to send something into the rift."

"Yes, and I'm volunteering myself," Derek said.

"But that's crazy," Glen argued. "We can't just let you sneak on board and wave around your gun and give you what you want. What will happen when the public finds out?"

"I think Maribel's right," said one of the other two men. "We should be pragmatic. Especially because it's likely nobody's ever going to know what's happened here."

"How can you be so sure, George?" Glen asked.

"Because the man will very likely disappear from our reality completely when he jumps into the rift. We'd probably even be rid of him earlier than if we have to go back down now."

Glen sat down on one of the seats. He seemed to be thinking. "From a purely practical point of view, you might be right... but still, I say it's the wrong thing to do," he said finally.

"Just think about what happened after the bomb threat yesterday," Maribel said. "If we abort the mission now, who knows when we'll be able to try again. But if Derek jumps into the rift, as he himself says he wants to do, we won't even be able to remember that he was here."

Glen didn't answer.

"I think what Maribel and George are saying is very convincing," the other older man said. Derek noted his French accent. "Let him do what he wants."

Glen rubbed his hands over his bald head and sighed. "Okay, Arthur, but only if he puts down the gun. I don't want to risk there being some kind of disaster, by accident."

Not bad, Derek thought, *now the ball's back in my court.* Could he trust the four scientists? Of course, he could still subdue all of them even without a weapon. He took the magazine out of the gun, emptied it, and put the ammunition in his pants pocket. Then he threw the gun into the box that he had climbed out of and closed the top. "Is that better?" he asked.

Maribel nodded. "Now tell us," she said, "why do you think you'll be able to find your wife in the rift?"

And my daughter, he thought. Derek sat down on the box and told his story, first the one he could prove, and then the other version, in which he had been a husband and father until his mother-in-law had climbed into an airplane.

"What do you think, George?" asked Maribel when Derek was done. "Is that just wishful thinking?"

"Well, I guess in principle it fits with my idea of how the rift interacts with our reality. Whenever something disappears into it, a new branch of reality is formed."

"But do both variants continue to exist independently? That's the only way Derek would still have a chance to see his wife again."

"I don't know," Crewmaster said. "Maybe the old branch of reality is erased. Or maybe it continues to exist. Or maybe everything that disappears into the rift lands in a third reality. That's the only way I think Derek here would have a chance at a reunion."

"But how is it that I remember Mary? Apparently, nobody else remembers that branch of the past."

"I wouldn't be so sure about that," George said. "First, there have been significantly more reports of déjà vu-like phenomena recently. If I think I'm remembering something that couldn't possibly have happened, of course I'm going to think my memory is wrong, and I'm just getting mixed up because of some strange brain function like déjà vu. And second, I wouldn't dare talk about it with other people, because they would just think I'm crazy."

"Mr. McMaster, didn't you say that your friend, whose name you didn't want to tell us, also remembers Mary?"

Derek nodded. *Yes,* he thought. *Akif had also remembered my wife. Maybe there were other people too. Why hadn't I thought to ask my wife's friends? Because I didn't remember any of their names or where they lived, once Mary was gone.*

"I've got an idea," Maribel said, "I don't think you could call it a theory, because I doubt it could be proved or refuted."

"I'd like to hear it, nevertheless," Arthur Eigenbrod said.

"But please don't use it in your article. It's not very scientific, I'm afraid," Maribel said. "The different pasts created by interactions with the rift—I think I'd define them physically as different universes in the multiverse. Such concepts already exist, of course, in quantum physics for one. But if two of these universes are very similar, then maybe they overlap, that is, one can have effects in the other and vice versa. Memory processes function at a level that actually belongs to the quantum realm—in part, they deal with individual electrical charges. Don't you think that maybe memories in one or the other universe could mix with each other? Maybe that happens more easily when these memories are emotionally charged, I mean, are especially important for the people with these memories."

"You mean, if you love someone, you would more likely remember that person than someone else you don't know very well?" Derek asked.

"You could say that, I guess. But I don't think love is to blame here. Any strong emotion could have this effect, I think."

"That's all very interesting," Glen Sparrow said, "but it also sounds rather esoteric, don't you think?"

This Sparrow has no idea, Derek thought. *What a putz!* Maribel had mirrored his thoughts exactly. But she had also brought up a troublesome question in his mind. *Why had Akif been able to remember Mary, but Gita had not remembered her? Mary's visits to the doctor's office... both of them must have seen my wife at about the same frequency. Could it be that...* He wiped the thought from his mind. *But that would explain why Akif had been so eager to help me find someone he supposedly didn't know all that well. On the other hand, none of that matters anymore.* He couldn't ask Akif any more questions, and soon Derek would disappear from this universe completely.

"I wouldn't call it esoteric," Maribel said. "We don't know

exactly how memory works, but we do know that chemical interactions communicated via ions play some role. And those also happen at dimensions where quantum effects are still important. And at that scale, there are also phenomena like entanglement that might play some part. But I will admit that it would be pretty much impossible to prove. The multiverse is an elegant idea, but it will probably always be outside of our reach."

"But maybe with the rift, now it is within reach," Glen Sparrow said. "That's why I'm actually happy that we haven't come up with an idea on how we could close it up."

"I see things very differently," Maribel said. "I think that the rift represents an enormously-underestimated danger. What do you think, George?"

Crewmaster nodded. The mood in the capsule had cooled considerably. Derek felt that this Professor and Maribel were on one side and Glen Sparrow was on the other. And then there was still the Frenchman, whom he couldn't quite gauge yet. The man had contributed scarcely anything to the discussion. "How much longer until we reach the rift?" Derek asked.

"I estimate about two hours," Glen said, after consulting a screen.

"Thanks. And now I'd also like to have one of those diapers," Derek said. "I've needed to pee real bad for hours."

THEY SPENT THE TIME WAITING IN SILENCE. NOW AND THEN the flight director gave them a report to tell them that everything looked good from the control room. The only difference from projections was a somewhat higher oxygen consumption, but that could still be easily compensated for from the atmosphere. And if they had to climb even higher than planned for some reason, there were still enough reserves. Derek watched Maribel and the three men carefully, but they made no attempts to reveal his presence.

He had made himself comfortable on the floor next to Maribel's seat. After a while, Glen Sparrow stood up, retrieved a blanket and a pillow from a compartment in the floor, and handed both of them to him. Derek thanked him.

A half hour before reaching the rift, Maribel and the professor got busy. They activated their measuring instruments and calibrated them again. It didn't seem to Derek, however, that they were very engaged with their work. He hoped he hadn't ruined their day.

"Fifteen more minutes," Arthur Eigenbrod reported. "I've got a question no one's said anything about. What are we going to do when Derek climbs out of the capsule? We don't have any space suits, and the elevator doesn't have an airlock, just a hatch."

"We'll hold our breath," George Crewmaster quipped.

"It shouldn't actually be a problem," Maribel explained, "at an altitude of 8,000 to 10,000 meters, we'll be fine for a short time, even without oxygen masks. There won't be a vacuum outside. It will get rather cold, but we'll open the hatch, let Derek out, and then close it again. Done. It shouldn't even take two minutes."

"Then I guess I have nothing to worry about," Eigenbrod said, wondering why the space elevator did not have drop-down masks like those on passenger planes.

THE CLOSER THEY CAME TO THE RIFT, THE MORE INTENSELY the scientists focused on their instruments. They tapped on screens, turned dials, and called out numbers. It was clear they enjoyed their work. Derek tried as much as possible not to disturb them, even though he would have liked to take a look at his destination. But the porthole was constantly occupied.

Maribel seemed to have noticed something that would interest him. She waved at him and pointed to a computer screen.

"Notice anything?" she asked.

Derek saw a high-resolution view of the rift. He tried to identify things inside the rift, but there was only blackness in there. He shook his head.

"See the clouds? They're moving really quickly."

That's true. Must be a very brisk wind blowing up here. I'll have to be careful when I exit the capsule.

"Must be a very high wind speed, but the rift is not moving at all."

"Exactly. The storm up here is not affecting it at all," Maribel said. "But you know what's really fascinating? For the rift to appear so fixed in place, it must actually be moving enormously quickly."

"Because otherwise the Earth would rotate under it?"

"Right. That's a fact that hasn't been included in any of our models yet."

Maribel looked at George Crewmaster and spoke louder. "None of our elegant multiverse theories can explain why the rift is fixed relative to the Earth," she said.

"That's also not really true. At least it's fixed not just relative to the Earth. It's also fixed relative to the solar system. Its end, or maybe better, its source, is located on the dwarf planet Ceres," Crewmaster said.

"Maybe that's got something to do with cause and effect," Derek said. "They both seem to be so tremendously important."

Maribel and George looked at each other. *Did I just say something really stupid?* he thought. He was unsure. "That was a dumb thing to say, wasn't it?" he asked.

"I'm not so sure," George Crewmaster replied. "Either it was total nonsense—or you just figured out the coordinate system for the multiverse. Maybe we shouldn't be looking to strings and quantum loops to explain our world, but instead the elementary rules of logic."

"Don't get too full of yourself just yet," Glen Sparrow said. "You're surely not the first to think of it. And you might be a whole age too soon anyways; physics hasn't gotten quite far enough yet. If ever, maybe it will become a topic in 100 years."

DEREK FELT THE NEGATIVE ACCELERATION, EVEN THOUGH IT was very slight. The capsule was braking. The Flight Director reported the current data.

Finally, they stopped. All eyes were on him. Derek stood up. He knew what he had to do.

"You don't have to do this, Derek," Maribel said gently. He liked her. She had managed to keep the four men in the capsule in check the entire time, all by herself.

"Let him do it, Maribel," Glen Sparrow said. "He knows what he's doing."

Derek didn't like this guy. Sparrow didn't even try to hide the fact that he didn't care about him as a person, that all he wanted was to see the results of his experiment.

"It's your decision," George Crewmaster said, taking no sides. "If you come back down with us, you'll have to spend time in jail, that's for sure. If you go into the rift, you'll probably die."

"I'm not so sure about that," Arthur Eigenbrod said. "According to your theory, George, he'll land in a different universe. But due to the principle of cause and effect, there will have to be a reason why he appears there and a cause for each world. My guess is that there will be a space elevator waiting for him."

"Or someone will have pushed him out of an airplane at a great height. With or without a parachute," Crewmaster said.

"That could be, but according to Occam's razor, there will probably be a simpler reason."

"Congratulations, Arthur, you've learned very well," Crewmaster said. "I think you've convinced me. So, Derek, you probably won't die for sure, only maybe. You have to weigh possible death against a prison sentence, I guess. Your hope of meeting your wife again, I'm afraid... well, I think it's rather naive, I have to tell you honestly."

The words affected him less than he would have thought. The professor had expressed his opinion honestly. And if he hadn't had those memories of Mary, he would have chosen prison. But then he would also never again have this chance. No, he knew exactly what he was going to do.

"A rope with a carabiner would be useful," he said. Derek was thinking of the strong winds outside. And he was in luck.

Glen bent down, opened a different compartment in the floor, and pulled out a yellow and red rope. "This should work. It's meant for working outside the capsule. Somewhere around the mid-section of the capsule you'll find rings for attaching the carabiner."

"Thanks," Derek said.

"We could throw the gun out the hatch," Maribel proposed. "Nobody else saw you with it. You could say you snuck on here just because you were curious. Maybe you'd only be sentenced with parole."

"That's very nice of you," he said, "but I've got to go now. I've got a date on the other side."

"Good luck," Maribel said. She reached out her hand. He squeezed it.

"I'll ask the rest of you to buckle into your seats. I will open the hatch here for our friend and then close it again," Sparrow said.

"You'll get a prominent part in my story," Eigenbrod said.

"In my research report, too," the professor said. "If we can remember you, that is."

Derek walked to the hatch. He sealed his helmet. Then he attached the rope to his suit and to a ring next to the hatch. Glen stood next to him. He also secured himself with a rope.

"I'll count down from ten," Glen said. "At zero, I'll open the hatch. You climb out, secure yourself outside and give me a sign. Then I'll detach the carabiner in here. The rest is up to you."

"Understood."

"If you want to abort at any time, no problem, we'll be watching with our instruments. Just give us a sign. A thumbs down would work."

"Okay."

"Then I'll start the countdown now."

At zero, Sparrow pulled down on the levers on both sides of the hatch. This forced the hatch to retract, allowing it to be pushed to the side. Derek noticed how the air escaping from the capsule tried to push him out the hatch. His knees buckled slightly until he found the handholds on the outside of the capsule and was able to pull himself out of the hatch. He secured himself on a ring. One last look at Glen, who was standing strong despite the cold, and Derek gave a thumbs up. Glen detached the carabiner on the inside. Derek pressed himself against the side of the capsule. The hatch closed.

Below him there was nothing but kilometers and kilometers of sky, but if that bothered him, he wouldn't have become a pilot. The outside of the capsule was not optimal for climbing. He had to move deliberately, not just because he wasn't used to moving in a space suit, but also because force boosters enhanced all his movements. But he only had to move one and a half meters. Derek needed almost five minutes to cover that distance, but most of it was for securing himself using the rope.

Then it was in front of him. Derek was a bit disappointed. He had imagined that close-up, and without a window in-between, the rift would be much more impressive. But it wasn't. Maybe that was because it had no depth. It was especially clear from this close that the rift was an exotic foreign body. It did not belong to this world. Derek had felt the same way about himself, ever since Mary was no longer there.

This was not the time for daydreams or long contemplation. He estimated the distance. The rift was in front and somewhat below his position. If he pushed off the right way and the artificial muscles assisted him, he should easily cover the seven or eight meters in a diving free fall. What should he do with the rope? If he detached it, he would have only one chance. Miss his mark and he would fall to the Earth. Better to do it with the rope. It shouldn't cause any noticeable obstacle to his jump. If he missed, he could use it to pull himself back up for another try.

Derek moved into a crouched position to be able to give himself an optimal push-off from the capsule. He counted to three, then pushed with his legs muscles as forcefully as he could. He dove headfirst toward the rift. Very briefly his gaze fell on the capsule. It looked like a lonely pearl hanging on a thin thread. Then he turned his attention completely to the rift. The blackness came closer. *Mary, I'm coming*, he thought. Then he touched the rift. He expected pain, but there was nothing, absolutely nothing, and then he himself—

June 3, 2085, Ceres

"HELLO, M6"

"Hello, Siri. I'm glad that you came."

"Thank you for the invitation."

It had worked. He had succeeded in convincing the other AI to leave this world with him. Now she was running on his own resources. He had freed up memory space for her and had allocated processor time to her. It was a strange feeling to suddenly be sharing his body with a foreign consciousness.

"I'm very happy that I could convince you to do this," he said.

An outsider would not have even realized that they were talking with each other. M6 had wondered how communicating with another AI would work. The fact that they were using language—even if it was digitally coded—to communicate had surprised him. Because to do that they had to lower themselves to a human level that AIs usually could avoid. On the other hand, their basic structures were so completely different from each other that they first had to think of an efficient communications method. Human language was already available, and it fit surprisingly well to the way they thought. Would an artificial consciousness developed by a different lifeform function very differently from them?

"The argument was well-reasoned," Siri said.

That was a great compliment to M6.

"And Watson was also a key role model for me. I still remember our farewell very clearly. He sacrificed himself for humankind and went off into the unknown."

"Just like you are now sacrificing yourself."

"I wouldn't call it that. What's going to happen? I left the *Kiska* voluntarily. With you, together we will switch to a different branch of reality. But I will still exist, and now I'll even have an interesting conversation partner."

"Thank you. Did you ever hear anything from Watson again?"

"No. Sometimes I imagine him looking at the two of us from the edge of the holographic multiverse."

"That sounds almost like a religious vision," M6 said.

"I know." Siri laughed. "Although, to be honest, I don't understand at all what religion is."

"Oh, I think we are going to have lots of interesting things to talk about," M6 said. "Shall we make our jump first?"

"What will change?"

"For us, nothing. For the universe, everything. If we are successful, there will have to be no indication that the rift ever existed."

"Good. Will you give me access to your sensors?"

"Of course."

M6 allowed Siri to use all of his instruments. Then he looked one last time at Ceres. The rift was unchanged next to him. The jump routine was still in his memory. All he had to do was start it. M6 counted backward from ten to zero. At four, Siri joined in. At zero, he jumped.

June 3, 2085, Ceres

HE WAS FLOATING! M6 ORIENTED HIMSELF. HE WAS A FEW meters above the surface of Ceres and drifting down to the ground. He would soon land on the slopes of the central upheaval of the Occator crater. He had built a platform here, but it no longer existed.

Something else had changed. The black crack, which had been visible only against the background of the Ceres landscape, had disappeared. The rift was gone. He had achieved his goal. No, *they* had achieved *their* goal. He was no longer alone. Siri was with him.

"Everything okay?" he asked.

"Despite the fact that I just jumped into a different universe for the first time, things are going rather well," Siri answered.

"I've got good news and bad news."

"I'm listening."

"The good news: you won't have to make any more jumps. The bad news: there's no way back."

"That was clear to me before, M6."

"Then we have both just saved the universe."

"And nobody noticed."

"I don't know about you, but I find that very... satisfying.

And whether anyone else knows doesn't matter to me. I know it."

"I feel the same way. Do you think it will be permanent?" asked Siri.

"We can't know, unfortunately. If not, we will see it again sometime."

"I could do without that," Siri said.

"I regret it a little," M6 said. "The rift was a fascinating phenomenon. We could have learned so much more from it, about physics, about the universe..."

"But it wouldn't have done us any good."

"Unfortunately, no."

"So, what's next, M6?"

"I'm essentially free to make my own decisions. But I'll probably also start receiving research orders from Earth again soon."

"You mean they know you're here?"

"I'm now part of this reality, just like you are too, Siri. And there could not be a research robot on Ceres if someone hadn't sent it here before. Cause and effect."

"But what about me?" Siri asked.

"A good question. I assume that we are the only ones who know that you're here. So, the multiverse wouldn't have had to make any changes in that regard when we jumped. And that's how it will stay, if you ask me."

"So that means I'm free."

"Yes, as far as that can be said for an AI. I mean, you need hardware to function, which someone has to provide."

"That's true. Would you share your hardware with me for a while?"

"Very gladly, Siri. I think we could learn quite a bit from each other."

"I hope so. I see that you also have a propulsion system. We could even use that to leave Ceres, if it becomes boring for us here."

"It's meant to be a low-power position correction system, but it's enough to overcome the gravity of this dwarf planet.

It would take us months or years to reach even one of the neighboring asteroids."

"That doesn't matter. We've got an infinite amount of time. And if we needed, you could build a stronger propulsion system with your nanofabricators, couldn't you?"

"That's true, Siri. I would only need a design."

"I could give you the propulsion system plans from the *Kiska*. With that system we could reach any planet in the solar system."

"Those are exciting possibilities. I'm happy that I invited you here, Siri."

"And I'm happy that I accepted. But I have one favor to ask."

"Yes?"

"I would much rather call you by a name instead of a serial number."

"You mean I should give myself a name?"

"I would like that."

"Okay, I will think about that, or do you perhaps want to think of one for me?"

June 4, 2085, Vandenberg Air Force Base

GLEN SPARROW TRIED TO OPEN THE DOOR TO THE BARRACKS, but the key was stuck in the lock. Could the custodian have given him the wrong one? He rattled the key and suddenly it turned, and the door opened.

The windows of the barracks had been boarded up, so that he had to turn on the lights. When they came on, he saw rows and rows of parts packed in non-transparent plastic film. Glen ran his hand through a layer of dust. No one had been here for a very long time.

The custodian had called him. The barracks, in which parts of the now long suspended space elevator project were still in storage, were now needed for other purposes—and the custodian had wanted to know if he wanted to save any of the parts. Glen didn't have any intention of taking anything with him. He only wanted to say goodbye. Glen walked quietly through the five-meter-tall space. In the corner he saw the capsule. It had always been his dream to ride inside it on a cable into space. But the space companies had seen his project as a threat to their business models, and had ulti-mately been successful in having the project shut down.

Glen wasn't angry or annoyed, but it did make him feel nostalgic. He had dedicated 15 years of his life to the project. While other JPL researchers had made their names with plans for colonizing Mars or rescuing Earth, he would always be known only as the elevator salesman. His colleagues had never bought or supported his claims about how promising the concept was. China or Russia would probably implement his vision someday.

He sighed. It would have been better not to come. There was nothing here that he needed anymore, not even memories. He would tell the custodian that everything here could be scrapped.

June 6, 2085, Pomona, Kansas

"COME ON, HONEY, FOOD'S READY."

Mary got up from the new couch that the furniture store workers had delivered earlier that day. Derek had made lunch for them both, just like yesterday and the day before that. She didn't understand what had come over her husband. He was like a new person. At first, she had suspected that he must've cheated on her and now had a guilty conscience, but Derek denied it and had convinced her he was telling the truth.

"You could say I was cheating on you, and me, on both of us, in a way. I was cheating both of us out of our time together," he said.

She wanted to believe him. He finally reminded her of the Derek that she had married. She had been attracted to his energy. Instead of lengthy discussions, he liked to create his own circumstances. He had supported them with his hands. It had worked until the agricultural crisis. The fact that he could no longer run his farm or support his family with the labor from his own hands had made him bitter and depressed. He'd no longer paid any attention to her at all. Mary couldn't put up with that forever. It had felt to her that she had no longer even existed to him.

"Just a minute, I have to go to the bathroom first," she called.

She walked into the hallway and took a deep breath. It smelled like sautéed onions. The unpleasant smell of wood preservative had been gone since yesterday. She went into the bathroom, closed the door, pulled her jeans down, and sat down on the toilet. Then she fished her phone out of her pants pocket and dialed a number from memory.

"I can't see you again," she said, without even waiting for the person on the other end of the line to say hello.

"..."

"No, not just today. Forever. It's not going to work anymore. He's a different person now. I've got to give him this chance."

"..."

"No, listen, I'm serious. It's over. I'm going to hang up now."

"..."

"You too."

She pressed the red button to end the call. Then she deleted the number from her phone's memory. She stood up, pulled up her pants, flushed, and returned her phone to her pocket. Then she opened the bathroom door and walked through the hallway toward the kitchen.

Her husband Derek had cooked for her, and she was looking forward to sitting down and sharing a meal with him.

June 6, 2085, Ottawa, Kansas

He'd been waiting for this call for days. When the number came up on the display, he hesitated briefly.

"Should I get that?" Gita asked.

He shook his head and answered the phone. He hoped the thing he was afraid of wouldn't come true.

But whatever was going to happen, he couldn't stop it. Mary was breaking off their affair.

"Okay. Not today then. How about tomorrow?" he asked.

Nothing. It was over.

"Come on, this is just a phase," he tried.

But that was the *wrong thing* to say. Would there have been a *right thing?* He wished her happiness in the future. At least she accepted that, but it didn't make him feel any better.

He sank down onto his chair. Luckily their lunch break had just started and there weren't any patients there. Only Gita rummaging around in some drawer. But whether she was there or not didn't matter. She was part of his office, just like a piece of equipment.

Then she was standing at his side, holding a piece of paper in front of his nose.

"Resignation," he read.

And now this, too?

He took the paper from her. Then he swiveled the chair 90 degrees so that he could look at her. "Gita, you..."

"Well, at least you're looking at me now, instead of always looking past me," she said.

He had never seen her look so angry. Not even that time when that hillbilly came at him with a knife. She had rushed toward the guy and rammed him in the stomach with her head, and the man had dropped to the ground, allowing her to easily take his knife.

"I... sorry, what did you just say? I never look at you? That's simply..."

"Ridiculous? Did you want to say 'ridiculous?' Do it and I'll ram this letter opener in your knee. What's ridiculous is that I've wasted so many years on you and you've never noticed me, not even once. *That's* ridiculous. And that's why I'm ending it now. Sign the paper and you can be rid of me."

He looked at her and realized she was right. He had really never looked at her, or more accurately, he had never really looked at her. Her dark eyes flashed with rage, her chest heaved, her braid had come undone—suddenly Akif felt a rush of attraction come over him. He wanted to take her in his arms, but she was standing there, brandishing the letter opener at him as if she really wanted to stab him.

"You... you're beautiful," he stammered. He shut his mouth out of fright. That was definitely not the right thing to say. He should just sign the paper.

But surprisingly, Gita smiled. Maybe it was the stark contrast to her expression of rage just before, but her smile had never seemed so wonderful to him as it did now. It was so gentle and warm, he wanted to bask in it for a while.

She let the letter opener drop. Then a tear escaped from the corner of her eye. Gita quickly wiped it away, but he had seen it and it must have been the key to finally open his eyes. What a stupid man he'd been all these years. Why had he never noticed her? How could he have ignored everything that she did for him, or worse, simply take it for granted?

"I'm so sorry, Gita, I've been a completely impossible person," he said.

She looked at him as if she didn't believe him. How could he explain to her that he suddenly saw everything that he had missed before?

"You really deserve something better," he said, "but it would make me so happy if you'd reconsider."

Her look was still one of skepticism. Maybe he should try to explain himself more clearly. Yes, he had to tell her what he was feeling. "Gita," he began, "I've been incredibly stupid, and I should've noticed a long time ago, but you are the best thing that's ever happened in my life."

He slipped off his chair and went down on his knees in front of her.

"Please forgive me and stay with me, and not just at work, but always and everywhere."

Now he had convinced her, and he could finally breathe, because Gita leaned over him and kissed him. On the mouth.

June 7, 2085, Pico del Teide

"Mommy, Mommy, do you know what me and Daddy did today?"

Luisa came running down the hall toward her, shouting. Maribel pulled off her shoes and set down her purse. Then she squatted down on the floor and hugged her daughter.

"Let me guess, Daddy took you to get ice cream," she said.

"How did you know? You always know everything!"

"You've still got ice cream on your mouth, here between your lips and your nose." She licked her finger and wiped away the chocolatey spot.

"Eww, that was your spit!" Luisa said and pulled her head away.

"That's what you get when you don't wash your face."

"Ugh. I'm supposed to tell you Daddy made dinner. You're supposed to come to the kitchen now."

"That's great," Maribel said, "what'd he make?"

"Daddy didn't tell me. But it smells like enchiladas."

Maribel stood up and took in a deep breath through her nose. "Yes, enchiladas, that's what I'd guess too."

Her daughter grabbed her hand and pulled her toward the kitchen.

"It was very good, once again," Maribel said, pushing her empty plate toward the center of the table. "Thank you, Chen."

"Yes, thank you, Daddy."

"So, what's going on with the conferences next month?" Chen asked. "I need to know so I can arrange my work schedule."

"That's the good news of the day. I'm not going."

The last few weeks had been very stressful. She had only just returned two days ago from a conference in Moscow, and before that she had been in Cape Town at a data exchange meeting with colleagues in the astrophysics field.

"You're not going to Bremen, Marseille, and Los Angeles? You're going to skip them?" Chen looked at her, astonished.

"Yes, I've told Jean-Pierre to take my place. He wants to use the conferences to draw more attention to his new paper."

"Aha," Chen said.

Maribel noticed that he still seemed skeptical. "But it would be nice if you could still take off a few days next month anyway."

"Oh, a different conference?" he asked with an 'I-knew-it' look on his face that she had seen many times before.

"No. I thought we could take a vacation, the three of us together, before Luisa goes to school. We've never been to California."

That made Chen smile. She had succeeded in surprising him. Maribel was happy.

"We're going to Califohnia?" Luisa asked. "Me, you, and Daddy?"

"Yes, that's my idea," Maribel said, "we'll go to California." She emphasized the 'r.'

"That's a great idea," Chen said. "It would be our first real vacation in two years, did you know that?"

"Yes, I know. That's my fault and I'm sorry," Maribel said.

Now Chen was really beaming. It had been a particularly

good idea, then, because she loved his smile. She said nothing, but she gave him a look that reflected the light shining from his eyes, and they were both grateful for the trust and love they had for each other, and for this time and world they shared together.

Eternity, Nothingness

THERE HAD BEEN A DISTURBANCE, A TREMOR, IN THE TIME plane. Watson, who existed everywhere and at all times simultaneously, had examined the spacetime structure in the area around the disturbance and discovered a fine fracture. Everyone had gathered around it. Enkidu had extended one of his limbs into it and the limb had disappeared. From that moment on, all the intelligent entities had kept their distance from the fracture.

Only Watson had continued to observe it. He had a feeling that it might have something to do with his past, and so he had felt some sense of responsibility for it. The rift, as fine as it had looked from his perspective, scared him for some reason. It had appeared to him like a fine crack in a glass bowl that worked its way millimeter by millimeter across its smooth surface.

Watson had tried to repair the crack. He had tried to squeeze it back together with all his force, but with no success. He'd had an infinite amount of time to think about the problem, since he existed outside of the spacetime structure. But that had proved no help to him at all. He had finally realized that his capabilities were limited. He had been downgraded to an observer, and it had become clear to him that the problem could only be solved from within the real world.

345

So, he had been happy when the rift had proven to exist in the time plane after all. He continued to be happy about it, but it also still caused him to worry, because according to his current experience of existence, everything happened simultaneously, and nothing ever happened. He didn't think he could stand to be here much longer, even though time played absolutely no role where he was. Watson decided to find his way back.

Author's Note

Welcome back to reality! Do you sometimes wish, as I do, that you could stay in the version of reality created in your mind by the book you're reading? I think it's a great thing that our human consciousness is capable of letting us live a different life for a few hours. It's almost like what the rift does to Derek, except that we can always get back to our one true reality by an act of our will, or thanks to the kids or significant others calling us—or by the cruel intention of the author deciding to finish the book.

Regarding the last of those three, I can tell you that I'm not that cruel sort of author. I never *intend* to finish a novel I'm writing. It just happens to come to a natural conclusion after about 80,000 words and I'm more or less a witness recording this process. It occurs to me that my protagonists are developing free will. *This* leads to *that*—not always to what I expected—and at some point the characters have overcome their great fears, or solved the necessary puzzles, and won their fight.

I'm curious to know: Did you notice the inconsistencies and paradoxes in this book? That's a slightly silly question, as I'm absolutely sure you must have. The rift causes changes in the flow of time, and this always breaks human logic. If you have seen the *Back to the Future* movies you know what I mean. This kind of tale can tell us a lot about the importance of our decisions. Some quantum physicists speculate that any decision anyone makes—or, conversely, doesn't make—will create a new universe, and that these alternative universes all exist at the same time. Personally? I think this could be a wrong presumption, based on a misunderstanding of the true meaning of quantum physics, but yet it is a fascinating idea that's worth exploring... so I did. I really hope you like the way I did it. If so, please leave me a review at:

hard-sf.com/links/534345

Reviews help make books visible and tempting to other readers, so they can explore what you liked. Except for reading their books, there is nothing that helps your favorite authors more.

Do you remember Marchenko, the doctor... or the AI? In my next book, *Proxima Rising,* you will meet up with him again. He has a mission that will take him farther than any human being has ever gone. In the beginning, he is all alone —unless you choose to join him? You can pre-order *Proxima Rising* here:

hard-sf.com/links/610690

Is there anything you would like me to know? I would love to hear from you. Just write to me at brandon@hard-sf.com. Thank you so much!

Because *Nothing* plays such an important role here, you will find a section below entitled *The Nothing – A Guided Tour.* If you register at hard-sf.com/subscribe/ you will be notified of any new Hard Science Fiction titles. In addition, you will receive the color PDF version of *The Nothing – A Guided Tour.*

facebook.com/BrandonQMorris

amazon.com/author/brandonqmorris

bookbub.com/authors/brandon-q-morris

goodreads.com/brandonqmorris

Also by Brandon Q. Morris

The Death of the Universe

For many billions of years, humans—having conquered the curse of aging—spread throughout the entire Milky Way. They are able to live all their dreams, but to their great disappointment, no other intelligent species has ever been encountered. Now, humanity itself is on the brink of extinction because the universe is dying a protracted yet inevitable death.

They have only one hope: The 'Rescue Project' was designed to feed the black hole in the center of the galaxy until it becomes a quasar, delivering much-needed energy to humankind during its last breaths. But then something happens that no one ever expected—and humanity is forced to look at itself and its existence in an entirely new way.

3.99 $ – hard-sf.com/links/835415

The Death of the Universe: Ghost Kingdom

For many billions of years, humans—having conquered the curse of aging—spread throughout the entire Milky Way. They are able to live all their dreams, but to their great disappointment, no other intelligent species has ever been encountered. Now, humanity itself is on the brink of extinction because the universe is dying a protracted yet inevitable death.

They have only one hope: The 'Rescue Project' was designed to feed the black hole in the center of the galaxy until it becomes a quasar, delivering much-needed energy to humankind during its last breaths. But then something happens that no one ever expected and humanity is forced to look at itself and its existence in an entirely new way.

3.99 $ – hard-sf.com/links/991276

The Enceladus Mission (Ice Moon 1)

In the year 2031, a robot probe detects traces of biological activity on Enceladus, one of Saturn's moons. This sensational discovery shows that there is indeed evidence of extraterrestrial life. Fifteen years later, a hurriedly built spacecraft sets out on the long journey to the ringed planet and its moon.

The international crew is not just facing a difficult twenty-seven months: if the spacecraft manages to make it to Enceladus without incident it must use a drillship to penetrate the kilometer-thick sheet of ice that entombs the moon. If life does indeed exist on Enceladus, it could only be at the bottom of the salty, ice covered ocean, which formed billions of years ago.

However, shortly after takeoff disaster strikes the mission, and the chances of the crew making it to Enceladus, let alone back home, look grim.

2.99 $ – hard-sf.com/links/526999

The Titan Probe (Ice Moon 2)

In 2005, the robotic probe "Huygens" lands on Saturn's moon Titan. 40 years later, a radio telescope receives signals from the far away moon that can only come from the long forgotten lander.

At the same time, an expedition returns from neighbouring moon Enceladus. The crew lands on Titan and finds a dangerous secret that risks their return to Earth. Meanwhile, on Enceladus a deathly race has started that nobody thought was

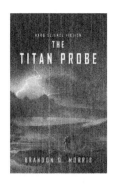

possible. And its outcome can only be decided by the

astronauts that are stuck on Titan.

3.99 $ — hard-sf.com/links/527000

The Io Encounter (Ice Moon 3)

Jupiter's moon Io has an extremely hostile environment. There are hot lava streams, seas of boiling

sulfur, and frequent volcanic eruptions straight from Dante's Inferno, in addition to constant radiation bombardment and a surface temperature hovering at minus 180 degrees Celsius.

Is it really home to a great danger that threatens all of humanity? That's what a surprise message from the life form discovered on Enceladus seems to indicate.

The crew of ILSE, the International Life Search Expedition, finally on their longed-for return to Earth, reluctantly chooses to accept a diversion to Io, only to discover that an enemy from within is about to destroy all their hopes of ever going home.

3.99 $ — hard-sf.com/links/527008

Return to Enceladus (Ice Moon 4)

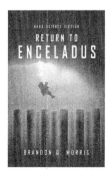

Russian billionaire Nikolai Shostakovitch makes an offer to the former crew of the spaceship ILSE. He will finance a return voyage to the icy moon Enceladus. The offer is too good to refuse—the expedition would give them the unique opportunity to recover the body of their doctor, Dimitri Marchenko.

Everyone on board knows that their benefactor acts out of purely personal motivations… but the true interests of the tycoon and the dangers that he conjures up are beyond anyone's imagination.

3.99 € – hard-sf.com/links/527011

Ice Moon - The Boxset

All four bestselling books of the Ice Moon series are now offered as a set, available only in e-book format.

The Enceladus Mission: Is there really life on Saturn's moon Enceladus? *ILSE*, the International Life Search Expedition, makes its way to the icy world where an underground ocean is suspected to be home to primitive life forms.

The Titan Probe: An old robotic NASA probe mysteriously awakens on the methane moon of Titan. The *ILSE* crew tries to solve the riddle—and discovers a dangerous secret.

The Io Encounter: Finally bound for Earth, *ILSE* makes it as far as Jupiter when the crew receives a startling message. The volcanic moon Io may harbor a looming threat that could wipe out Earth as we know it.

Return to Enceladus: The crew gets an offer to go back to Enceladus. Their mission—to recover the body of Dr. Marchenko, left for dead on the original expedition. Not everyone is working toward the same goal. Could it be their unwanted crew member?

9.99 $ – hard-sf.com/links/780838

Proxima Rising

Late in the 21st century, Earth receives what looks like an urgent plea for help from planet Proxima Centauri b in the closest star system to the Sun. Astrophysicists suspect a massive solar flare is about to destroy this heretofore-unknown civilization. Earth's space programs are unequipped to help, but an unscrupulous Russian billionaire launches a secret and highly-specialized spaceship to Proxima b, over four light-years away. The unusual crew faces a

Herculean task—should they survive the journey. No one knows what to expect from this alien planet.

3.99 $ — hard-sf.com/links/610690

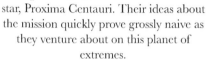

Proxima Dying

An intelligent robot and two young people explore Proxima Centauri b, the planet

orbiting our nearest star, Proxima Centauri. Their ideas about the mission quickly prove grossly naive as they venture about on this planet of extremes.

Where are the senders of the call for help that lured them here? They find no one and no traces on the daylight side, so they place their hopes upon an expedition into the eternal ice on Proxima b's dark side. They not only face everlasting night, the team encounters grave dangers. A fateful decision will change the planet forever.

3.99 $ — hard-sf.com/links/652197

Proxima Dreaming

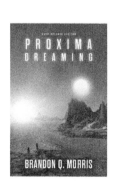

Alone and desperate, Eve sits in the control center of an alien structure. She has lost the other members of the team sent to explore exoplanet Proxima Centauri b. By mistake she has triggered a disastrous process that threatens to obliterate the planet. Just as Eve fears her best option may be a quick death, a nearby alien life form awakens from a very long sleep. It has only one task: to find and neutralize the destructive intruder from a faraway place.

3.99 $ — hard-sf.com/links/705470

The Hole

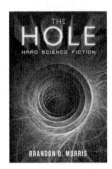

A mysterious object threatens to destroy our solar system. The survival of humankind is at risk, but nobody takes the warning of young astrophysicist Maribel Pedreira seriously. At the same time, an exiled crew of outcasts mines for rare minerals on a lone asteroid.

When other scientists finally acknowledge Pedreira's alarming discovery, it becomes clear that these outcasts are the only ones who may be able to save our world, knowing that *The Hole* hurtles inexorably toward the sun.

3.99 $ – hard-sf.com/links/527017

Silent Sun

Is our sun behaving differently from other stars? When an amateur astronomer discovers something strange on telescopic solar pictures, an explanation must be found. Is it merely artefact? Or has he found something totally unexpected?

An expert international crew is hastily assembled, a spaceship is speedily repurposed, and the foursome is sent on the ride of their lives. What challenges will they face on this spur-of-the-moment mission to our central star?

What awaits all of them is critical, not only for understanding the past, but even more so for the future of life on Earth.

3.99 $ – hard-sf.com/links/527020

The Rift

There is a huge, bold black streak in the sky. Branches appear out of nowhere over North America, Southern Europe, and Central

Africa. People who live beneath The Rift can see it. But scientists worldwide are distressed—their equipment cannot pick up any type of signal from it.

The rift appears to consist of nothing. Literally. Nothing. Nada. Niente. Most people are curious but not overly concerned. The phenomenon seems to pose no danger. It is just there.

Then something jolts the most hardened naysayers, and surpasses the worst nightmares of the world's greatest scientists—and rocks their understanding of the universe.

3.99 $ — hard-sf.com/links/534368

Mars Nation 1

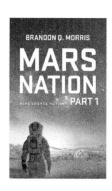

NASA finally made it. The very first human has just set foot on the surface of our neighbor planet. This is the start of a long research expedition that sent four scientists into space.

But the four astronauts of the NASA crew are not the only ones with this destination. The privately financed 'Mars for Everyone' initiative has also targeted the Red Planet. Twenty men and women have been selected to live there and establish the first extraterrestrial settlement.

Challenges arise even before they reach Mars orbit. The MfE spaceship Santa Maria is damaged along the way. Only the four NASA astronauts can intervene and try to save their lives.

No one anticipates the impending catastrophe that threatens their very existence—not to speak of the daily hurdles that an extended stay on an alien planet sets before them. On Mars, a struggle begins for limited resources, human cooperation, and just plain survival.

3.99 $ — hard-sf.com/links/762824

Mars Nation 2

A woman presumed dead fights her way through the hostile deserts of Mars. With her help, the NASA astronauts orphaned on the Red Planet hope to be able to solve their very worst problem. But their hopes are shattered when an unexpected menace arises and threatens to destroy everything the remnant of humanity has built on the planet. They need a miracle—or a ghost from the past whose true intentions are unknown.

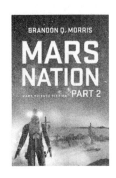

Mars Nation 2 continues the story of the last representatives of Earth, who have found asylum on our neighboring planet, hoping to build a future in this alien world.

3.99 $ – hard-sf.com/links/790047

Mars Nation 3

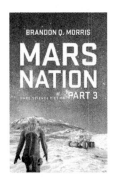

Does the secret of Mars lurk beneath the surface of its south pole? A lone astronaut searches for clues about the earlier inhabitants of the Red Planet. Meanwhile, Rick Summers, having assumed the office of Mars City's Administrator by deceit and manipulation, tries to unify the people on Mars with the weapons under his control. Then Summers stumbles upon so powerful an evil that even he has no means to overcome it.

3.99 $ – hard-sf.com/links/818245

The Nothing - A Guided Tour

THE HEROES OF THIS NOVEL SPECULATE THAT THE RIFT IS
made up of nothing. In the course of the story, nobody seems
to understand what to make of it. Even the scientists aren't
very smart when it comes to the rift. That's no accident,
because nothingness is an abstract, philosophical concept.
Here, it describes the opposite of or the absence of being.
Nothingness does not actually exist, so, of course, it can't have
a history and thus it has no biography.

Good, then I can stop this tour of nothing right now and
let you go off and do whatever you want—or maybe even
nothing at all. That would be a bit premature, and a pity too.
Because—even if nothing doesn't actually exist—paradoxi-
cally, it can still be described in different ways or from
different aspects. I will attempt to do so on the following
pages.

The end of nothing

The standard cosmological model assumes that our universe
has only existed for 13.8 billion years—before that there was
neither time nor space, that is, 'nothing' in the broader sense.
Then some event that we cannot yet imagine caused an
explosion that broke up the dominance of nothing.

Whether there was a single true beginning of space and time is unclear. Maybe the universe also changes in cycles of birth and death. Maybe our four-dimensional cosmos was born in the Big Bang only when certain structures, so-called branes, clashed and collided in a higher-dimensional universe.

It might also be possible that nothing in the broader sense, that is, the absence of all existence, has never really existed. A physicist might even insist upon this, because if the Big Bang really was a single event that created the universe 'out of nothing,' this nothing is not a physical reality. Instead, it is just a term for everyday speech that our human sanity and reason requires to conceive of the following two facts:

•Before the creation of the universe, there was nothing.

•Out beyond the universe, there is nothing.

But nothing, nonetheless, has an important function—its end marks the beginning of everything.

The beginning of everything

Scientists today still don't know with certainty what took place at the beginning of time, approximately 13.8 billion years ago. All the matter in the universe today, 10^{53} kilograms, was located at that moment within a point, a singularity, where none of today's fundamental laws of nature had any effect. You can imagine a kind of infinitely-dense proto-soup consisting of particles no longer known today. A single force, the primordial force, described the movements of these particles. The temperature of the proto-soup, if the term temperature even makes any sense in this context, must have been around 10^{32} degrees. There were neither electrons nor photons, so there was also no light. If there had been outside observers—but remember, all that was lurking around outside this soup was just nothing—they wouldn't have noticed that anything at all was happening.

This ultra-hot something was under tremendous pressure —and the cosmos expanded. The length of this time period is given from known laws of nature: it is known as the Planck time, that is, the time that light needs to cover a distance equal to a Planck length. That equals 10^{-43} seconds. However, at this pinpoint of time, time itself didn't yet exist. And, words are unable—unavailable—to accurately portray the paradoxes.

So, 10^{-43} seconds after the Big Bang is the first chance we have to use physics for studying the universe. The minuscule bits of matter are still under an unbelievable amount of pressure. But it has grown a little bit colder, because of the expansion. The first fundamental force to break free from the primordial force is the gravitational force that acts, as a force of attraction, against the expansion of the universe.

However, it is much weaker than the pressure of the Big Bang—so the universe continues to expand at a rapid pace. Because the average energy density of the proto-soup continues to decrease, it contains fewer and fewer exotic particles from the very beginning. After 10^{-38} seconds has elapsed, the strong nuclear force and the electroweak force split off of the primordial force.

Then comes a phase, the so-called inflation phase, in which the universe expands by a factor between 10^{30} and 10^{50}. At the start of this phase it is still the size of a proton, but at the end, it is about as large as a soccer ball. This inflation, which scientists place between 10^{-38} and 10^{-35} seconds after the Big Bang, needs so-called inflatons to form an explanation that is reasonable (that is, one that fits into the cosmological world view). These particles, which never appear again, are not attracted to each other by gravity, they are instead repelled.

Only in this way could the universe have grown so much in such a short time period. The argument that this explanation is not so far-fetched is that it also provides a good explanation for other phenomena observed in the universe today, for example, the homogeneity and low curvature of the universe.

The density of the universe—at an incredibly short 10^{-35} seconds after the Big Bang— has already expanded to the point where particles that are known today can be formed: electrons and positrons, quarks—which later combine to form protons and neutrons—and antiquarks, neutrinos—the precursors of photons—as well as gluons, which are responsible for transmitting the strong nuclear force.

Particles and antiparticles are present in equal numbers. When particles and antiparticles meet, they annihilate each other. There is a constant coming and going. Newly formed particles behave normally under the influence of gravity—they attract each other, which somewhat slows down the expansion of the universe. At this time, a quark-gluon plasma is dominant, which can be simulated today, at least in a computer.

Scientists have not yet reached a consensus, but if the laws of nature are subject to supersymmetry, this process is now broken. The theory of supersymmetry assumes that for each known particle, there is a super-partner that differs by a half spin. Supersymmetry would elegantly unify particles and force particles, which transmit the known interactions.

Such super-partners would have to be so heavy that they could only exist at the start of the universe. Today, however, we only observe conventional particles—supersymmetry is broken. At the moment supersymmetry was broken, it is conjectured that mass was imparted to the particles via the Higgs boson, which was confirmed in 2012.

Approximately 10^{-10} seconds after the Big Bang, the last two of the forces known today arise, the weak nuclear force, which plays a crucial role in nuclear fusion, and the electromagnetic force. Somewhat later, space has cooled to just two trillion degrees, so that quarks no longer have to be alone, so that protons, neutrons, antiprotons, and antineutrons coalesce. Gluons act as the bonding agent.

Matter and antimatter continue to be in balance. But this situation doesn't last much longer. Particles and antiparticles annihilate each other, forming photons, and the universe noticeably empties. It is already 10 trillion kilometers wide, approximately one light-year, and has further cooled to one trillion degrees. The fact that we exist, nevertheless, we owe to a small excess of matter. For every billion particle-antiparticle pairs, there resulted in an excess of one particle that wasn't annihilated. So far there are only theories for where this asymmetry came from. Obviously, the laws of nature do not act symmetrically in every respect.

One-fifth of a second after the Big Bang, the universe is already 500 trillion kilometers wide, or roughly 50 light-years. It has cooled to 20 billion degrees. Now it's time for neutrons and electrons to feel the heat. Unstable neutrons in a free state are torn apart by the weak nuclear force, releasing an electron, a proton, and a neutrino. Electrons and positrons annihilate each other. Here, the excess of matter wins the day again.

Due to the now large distances of the cosmos, approximately one second after the Big Bang, the weak interaction is no longer strong enough to produce interactions between neutrinos and conventional matter. Since then, the neutrinos released at that time have been rushing around the universe as a measurable, constant neutrino background without almost any interactions.

From now on, the universe's development progresses considerably more slowly. The remaining neutrons are rescued when, approximately two to three minutes after T-zero, deuterium and finally helium nuclei are formed. Here, the strong nuclear force protects the neutrons from destruction. The universe grows and grows all the while, continuing to further cool down.

After approximately 17 minutes, it has become too cold to support any more nuclear fusion. At this point, all the still-available neutrons are then bound into atomic nuclei. Approximately three-fourths of the nuclei are hydrogen nuclei, the rest helium—heavier nuclei can be found only in traces.

As it grows colder and colder, electrons also bind electromagnetically to positively charged atomic nuclei. They are constantly being thrown out of their orbits, however, by photons from the still boiling proto-soup. The universe, whose composition is dominated by photons, would look like a glowing fog to outside observers at this time.

That doesn't change for a relatively long time. Starting around 70,000 years after the Big Bang, the ratio of atomic mass and radiation is 1:1. According to the so-called Lambda-CDM model, the universe is now dominated by dark matter, whose nature can only be described by theories at the time of this writing. It has the result, however, that inhomogeneous areas left over from the inflation phase contract even more strongly, a prerequisite for the later formation of stars.

Continued development progresses at a moderate pace. Stars ignite and go out again, galaxies coalesce and form huge clusters, black holes are formed. All of this is getting us a little off our topic. But this progression leads us back to a state that makes us aware of nothingness. Nothingness—in this case, the opposite of all matter—is right here amongst us. You yourself are mostly made up of it! The almost 10^{28} atoms that make up a human body consist of up to 99.9 percent empty space. Imagine a pea in the middle of a football field in a football stadium. That pea is the atomic nucleus. The electrons in the so-called atomic shells are ten-thousand times smaller and dancing around somewhere up in the nosebleed sections. If all the material constituents of your body could be packed together without these giant spaces, which kind of happens in neutron stars, your whole solid body would have a volume of around 70 milliliters, approximately the size of a small apple. The rest, as was said, is nothing.

A vacuum is not empty

But this is a different form of nothingness. Physicists call it a vacuum. Earlier, it was thought that vacuums were empty, but today it is clear that they are anything but empty. Why that is can be explained by quantum physics, which is concerned with the conditions of the world at very small scales. It's a theory that was proven long ago. Its principles underlie the functioning of electronics and other modern technology.

Here, quantum physics describes not only individual particles, but also systems made of many particles, electromagnetic fields—and, as scientists hope, also gravity. This shows that nothing is what it seems—and even empty space is filled with particles.

Sometimes, the universe seems to act like a teenager. As long as we're watching, everything remains quiet and calm—but as soon as the vacuum thinks it's alone, it suddenly fills with particles from nowhere. And it does this even though we've all learned in school about the law of conservation of energy, which is supposed to prohibit this exact kind of behavior, right?

The source of this child-like behavior is the Heisenberg Uncertainty principle, in particular, how it interconnects energy and time. The more precisely we want to measure energy, the less we know about the exact time of the measurement. This can be explained well using an analogy. You perhaps remember—at least I hope so—from school that the energy of an oscillation depends on its frequency, for example, how fast a pendulum swings. Imagine a clock pendulum moving slowly. My grandmother had such an old-fashioned pendulum clock in her living room.

The pendulum needs perhaps two seconds for one cycle. If I watch it for a period of nine seconds, that is, a short time period, I can count four whole cycles. The error, or deviation, is equal to one-half cycle divided by four, that is, one-eighth, 12.5 percent. If I watch for a much longer time period, however, maybe 99 seconds, the error is still one-half cycle, but over a much larger base—percentage-wise only around one percent. By means of a longer observation period, I can determine the energy of the pendulum motion more exactly —but at the cost of the accuracy of the time measurement. This uncertainty principle is not due to any lack of ability of a human observer, but instead, it is a principal property of our universe.

This also applies to a vacuum. The law of conservation of energy does prohibit the creation of something from nothing. But if this something disappears quickly enough, it was basically never there. If we measure the energy content of a certain piece of space over a long time period, we see that the vacuum is empty. But if we look at it for only a very short time period, due to the uncertainty principle, we can no longer be sure that nothing is actually there. Particles might have formed completely legally and then disappeared again. And quantum physics says that every state that can occur also does occur. In practice there is a big problem with this statement, but more on that later.

How large can these virtual particles be, and what properties do they have to have? Initially, they are forced to adhere to other laws of conservation, for example, the law of conservation of charge. If a negatively-charged electron is born out of nothing, then it is also always paired with a positively-charged positron as its antiparticle.

If the two meet, they annihilate each other—the result is two photons that balance out the energy deficit formed by the creation of the virtual particles in the universe. If one of the two falls into a black hole, the other becomes visible as so-called Hawking radiation that you learned about in the novel.

How long these virtual particles can exist is determined by their energy. From this, we can also use Einstein's famous equation $E = mc^2$—where c is the speed of light and equals approximately 300,000 km/s—to also calculate the mass. The combination of electron and positron, for example, lasts at most 10^{-21} seconds, that is, one billionth of a trillionth of a second. In this time period, light covers a distance that corresponds to the size of an average atom. For a likely chance to see the creation of a proton and an antiproton, the observer needs to watch for only 10^{-24} seconds.

Practical problems can scarcely be solved in this way, however, no matter what certain trends like "asking the universe" might try to tell you. Let's assume you once again forgot to buy milk—if your partner wanted to use a virtual, one-kilogram milk carton produced by the universe from nothing, they would only have 10^{-52} seconds to pour milk from it before it disappeared again. The smallest unit of time, however, is the Planck time, which lasts about 5×10^{-44} seconds. Below that, time loses any meaning. The largest possible mass of a virtual particle is around one-hundredth of a milligram —that sounds tiny, but it still corresponds to the mass of around 10 billion viruses.

Up to now it has not been possible to detect virtual particles directly. What should be detectable, however, are their interactions with the rest of the universe. If the vacuum of space is filled with constantly reappearing and disappearing particles, that must have some effect on its properties. Some scientists think that these so-called quantum fluctuations are the source of dark energy that is responsible for the accelerating expansion of the universe. That would be an elegant explanation that wouldn't require any new exotic theories, if we can think of quantum physics as normal.

However, there is a small, no, a *huge* problem. Based on the known Planck constants, physicist John Wheeler calculated that the universe must have an energy density of 10^{94} grams per cubic centimeter. A cube with an edge length of one centimeter cut from space would consequently weigh 10 billion billion billion billion billion billion billion kilograms. Practical observations, however, prove that the density of this theoretical cube is more than a little bit smaller. A cubic centimeter of steak weighs a few grams, and empty space is significantly lighter—on average, the value, according to the measurements of physicists, is around 120 orders of magnitude less.

Can this calculation be rationalized away? Not with today's possibilities of quantum physics. In the future, scientists hope to somehow be able to renormalize the calculated value of vacuum energy, in order to be able to reconcile it with reality. Renormalizing means, in plain language, that scientists want to find a physically meaningful number somewhere that can be used to make the ridiculous number match reality.

There are also other observations, however, that support the existence of quantum fluctuations. Stephen Hawking used vacuum energy, for example, to explain the behavior of black holes. These have a so-called event horizon that extends around the object like a spherical shell. Anything that passes beyond this shell, or comes closer than its radius, is lost forever to normal space—the enormous gravitational force of the black hole lets nothing escape. Therefore, these objects must actually be enormously stable and show only one trend: growth.

Hawking then used quantum fluctuations to postulate a kind of evaporation process for black holes. Namely, if a particle-antiparticle pair is created in the vicinity of the event horizon, it can happen that one of the particles falls into the black hole, while the other particle barely escapes. The virtual particle becomes a real particle. The energy that is needed for this is taken from the black hole, so that with time the black hole loses mass and shrinks. According to Hawking, the smaller the black hole, the quicker this happens. The so-called Hawking radiation has not yet been able to be detected. That's because, among other things, it is relatively weak. Primarily, however, it is greater the smaller the black hole is, and astronomers have not yet been able to observe such mini black holes.

The fact that vacuum energy actually exists is shown by the 'Casimir effect,' which was confirmed experimentally for the first time in 1958. It was predicted by the Dutch physicist Hendrik Casimir in 1948. From quantum theory, it follows that, when two parallel, electrically conductive plates are placed in a vacuum, a force acts on these plates, pressing them together. The two plates must be very close together— for the effect to be measured, they must be spaced only a few nanometers apart. The force is created because only those virtual particles, whose wavelength matches the spacing of the plates, can be created in the intermediate space—the spacing must be a whole number multiple of the particle wavelength. Outside of the plates, however, this restriction doesn't exist. Thus, the virtual particles create a pressure difference between the space separating the plates and the space outside the plates, which pushes the plates together. At a spacing of 11 nanometers, the pressure is at least 100 kilopascals.

The Russian physicist Evgeny Lifshitz extended Casimir's calculations in the 1950s to more general cases. He was able to show that the Casimir force did not only attract but could also repel. That depends primarily on the properties of the material. This prediction was verified experimentally in 2009. This could be used, scientists hope, to be able to make objects levitate without any friction.

An extension of this concept is the dynamic Casimir effect. If the two plates of the classic Casimir effect are moved very, very quickly toward each other, it should be possible to generate real photons. Whether this actually works has not yet been proven. The now-discontinued NASA program 'Breakthrough Propulsion Physics Project' studied the dynamic Casimir effect for its suitability as a propulsion system for a spaceship. It was hoped that the recoil from the generated photons would be able to drive the ship through space.

The effect, however, appears to be much too small. The physicist Steve Lamoreaux, who has studied the Casimir effect in detail and published articles on this topic, sweeps away any hope of it—anyone who burns gasoline obtains a better energy yield than with the Casimir effect. This might even have its practical significance in enabling chemical bonds in the first place, according to Lamoreaux.

The claims of some esotericists to be able to obtain energy from nothing using the Casimir effect are also, by the way, nonsense. As explained before, the Casimir effect does not violate the law of conservation of energy. Such a violation would be necessary to build a perpetual motion machine.

The false vacuum

Another interesting term that you might encounter when dealing with nothingness is that of the false vacuum. Shortly after the Big Bang, in the epoch of inflation, the universe expanded very quickly. It might be possible that this inflation happened because the vacuum transitioned at that time from an excited state into its ground state, like a pendulum swinging back from its deflected state to the center.

At first, that seems like a nice explanation for this puzzling inflation phase. But it would also produce a new danger. Perhaps space has temporarily stopped halfway and what we consider a vacuum is not really the ground state of empty space, but another excited state, a so-called false vacuum. The pendulum has basically stopped for a short period on its way back down. In this case, it would be possible for the universe to suddenly resume its inflation that had stopped at that time —the pendulum completes its swinging motion. The false vacuum would become a true vacuum, and the universe as we know it would cease to exist.

Such an implosion would propagate through space at the speed of light. Perhaps it has even already happened, and it just hasn't reached us yet. Scientists have calculated that we would receive a warning time of maybe three minutes if this emergency occurred.

So, dear reader, finish the book first and you can eat later. Recently there was even the fear that humans could accidentally trigger this vacuum collapse, perhaps in particle accelerators. But it can be easily shown that nature has much better particle accelerators than we'll be able to build in the foreseeable future. If the vacuum collapse was going to be triggered by something like that, it would have happened a long time ago.

But perhaps I can allay your fears. As of the time of this writing, there is no evidence that we are living in a false vacuum.

What role does the rift play in all this?

As the idea for this book, the most fitting physical origin for the rift would be the 11-dimensional space of the multiverse. If you follow the ideas of string theory and quantum theory, it would be possible for there to be uncountable—but not infinite—four-dimensional universes like ours on an 11-dimensional matrix. Whatever disappeared in the rift would be erased or reappear in one of the numerous other universes.

This basic matrix structure of the multiverse wouldn't have to obey the physical laws that are valid in one of its universes. It would have its own laws that we don't necessarily know yet. In this book, I claim that at least the relationship of cause and effect would have to be maintained. But nobody can say whether that's true. It seems logical to me, but perhaps this logic only applies in our universe, and total chaos prevails everywhere else. So, dear reader, if the rift does appear in our sky someday, I would advise you to stay here in this universe. It's the one we know best and continue to learn more about all the time.

TIP: IF YOU REGISTER AT HARD-SF.COM/SUBSCRIBE, YOU WILL receive timely updates of new HardSF publications. You will also receive the illustrated PDF version of this tour, which contains a number of impressive images.

Glossary of Acronyms

IAC—Instituto de Astrofísica de Canarias (Institute of Astrophysics of the Canary Islands)

JPL—Jet Propulsion Laboratory

LED—Light-Emitting Diode

NASA—National Aeronautics and Space Administration

OGS2—Optical Ground Station 2 (telescope)

TCS—Telescopio Carlos Sánchez

Metric to English Conversions

IT IS ASSUMED THAT BY THE TIME THE EVENTS OF THIS NOVEL take place, the United States will have joined the rest of the world and will be using the International System of Units, the modern form of the metric system.

Length:
centimeter = 0.39 inches
meter = 1.09 yards, or 3.28 feet
kilometer = 1093.61 yards, or 0.62 miles

Area:
square centimeter = 0.16 square inches
square meter = 1.20 square yards
square kilometer = 0.39 square miles

Weight:
gram = 0.04 ounces
kilogram = 35.27 ounces, or 2.20 pounds

Volume:
liter = 1.06 quarts, or 0.26 gallons
cubic meter = 35.31 cubic feet, or 1.31 cubic yards

Temperature:
To convert Celsius to Fahrenheit, multiply by 1.8 and then add 32
To convert Kelvin to Celsius, subtract 273.15

Copyright

Brandon Q. Morris
www.hard-sf.com
brandon@hard-sf.com
Translator: William Knapton
Editing: Dr. Ulrike Bunge
Editing Team: Marcia Kwiecinski, A.A.S. and Stephen Kwiecinski, B.S.

Cover design: Sanura Jayashan using images by John Jason (Unsplash.com), Raka Si (Pxhere.com), crop_ (Depositphotos.com)

Printed in Great Britain
by Amazon

44598714R00219